Bridge To My Dreams

By: Daniel Speth

Chapter 1

Walking home this day, the sky seemed more brilliant than ever, smells stronger and sounds sharper. This was a day like no other. Through the neighborhoods, built in the mid-forties, majestic oak and maple trees stood as if guarding its inhabitants. Watching the leaves being moved slightly by nature's unseen force, one could hear the wind as a soft whisper in the ear, like a poem written just for this occasion. Joining in at Mother Nature's beckoning, birds sang their songs while moving from limb to limb and tree to tree. The Robin Red Breast, hopping along in neighbor's front yards, repeatedly cocking its head from side to side, trying to sense the presence of its next meal, or that of its young, is a common sight. They eat more than worms, but it is said a robin may eat up to fourteen feet of worms each day. Makes my stomach spasm just thinking about it.

I was walking home from work as I had many times in the past, but this time it was after saying my last goodbyes to my coworkers as I turned the last page on my exciting forty-year career as a corporate accountant. Not as exciting as many occupations, but there were tense moments, and some office romances spread about on the ever-active grapevine. I survived several downsizings and takeovers. The job was not on the same level as restarting a stalled heart as an EMT, a firefighter pulling a child out of a burning building, a police officer removing a criminal from the streets, or doctor providing the treatment you so desperately needed. Had my moments, but all is behind me now except for memories.

I surmise that putting that part of my life behind me may have decluttered my mind enough to shake out some cobwebs. Does preoccupation block out many of the minute details of our lives, and make it more difficult to stop and smell the roses, as the old saying goes? Walking home with numbers bouncing about my head, or concern over an out of balance account playing on my mind tends to do that. Now I will be able to go into the section of my cluttered mind full of accounting knowledge and experiences, sweep and straighten a bit, and box it up so there is more room for new experiences. It's like taking a breath of fresh air.

At first there were mixed feelings, but the closer the day of my retirement got, the more I knew I was ready for this change. Financially, my wife and I were set up well enough for my early retirement at the age of 62. I enjoyed the work, and was going to miss my coworkers, but was so ready for something else while my health was still good. I am an average looking bloke, 5' 8" tall, weigh 160, with gray hair and freckles. Still have all my teeth, and not the kind requiring an overnight soak to clean. Rather decent shape I would say. Visit the gym often. My hair used to be red, but that is a distant memory. Except for the occasional use of readers, I do not need glasses any more since my eye surgery. I take medication for high cholesterol and irregular heartbeat. Aren't medical advancements a wonder? People in their sixties were considered old in the bygone days, but not so much today. These days, high schoolers seem like babies to me. God willing, I hope to have many days ahead of me.

Two squirrels scurried across the street in front of me as I was walking. I smiled and made a clicking sound as if the animals would understand me and may even congratulate me on my successful career. They, however, ignored me and effortlessly climbed the tree on the other side of the road. "Well guys, I see how it's going to be," I hollered. "No extra treats for you tonight. Have to fend for yourselves." I laughed and continued along my way. Always wondered what it would be like to climb trees like a squirrel or fly like a bird without the fear of crashing to the earth into a heap of pain and regret. Watch your step Ethel, it's a doozy.

As I was nearly floating down the street in retirement bliss, enjoying God's nature and the blessings I was given, Mr. Friedlander came out on his porch and waved. A casual friend and neighbor of many years. A little older than I, much taller and heavier as well. I suppose he could be considered fluffy. Balding on the dome and didn't keep up well with wild nose and ear hairs. He is starting his own forest, I thought to myself as he spoke up. "Well Mr. Robert Johnson you seem rather chipper today," he commented in his usual proper but kind manner.

I walked up to his porch and shook the man's hand as I often do. Relationships are important to me. Trying to do my part to lessen loneliness in this world, including my own. The word neighbor doesn't seem to carry the same weight as it used to. People tend to keep to themselves. Shut-ins behind the endless fencing and hedges. Most people don't even know their neighbor's names. I try to wave at my next-door neighbors at least, but I fall short in the neighborliness factor like most. Some of my neighbors I hardly ever see.

With the coming of the scientific marvel of the cell phone, some feel it has brought people closer together, but I disagree. Texting or face booking has lessened the art of writing or talking. Personal time and physical contact are less, which is incredibly sad.

Noticing several wiry hairs waving at me from the man's left nostril, I wanted to wave back and tell Frank to get out his trimmer, but I did not want to appear rude. I'm sure he already knows unless he doesn't take advantage of his bathroom mirror. I worked close to home and chose to walk many days, so we would talk for a few minutes each time we saw each other. Nothing deep mind you. Just small talk about our families, the weather, and sports, including golf, my favorite.

After a few touchy conversations we had in the past, I avoid politics or religion. We have some strong opposing views, so we choose to not broach those subjects. I'm a Republican and he's a liberal Democrat, but I suppose everyone is entitled to their opinions. Doesn't mean we can't still be friends. Too much hate in the world already I would say.

For some odd reason, this man always calls me by my full name. I tried to get him to call me Bob. All my friends do, I would tell him. He is a bit of an odd bird but nice enough.

"Frank, it is so good to see you on such a fine day," I said with a smile, trying to match his proper tone. "This is my final walk home from work and am enjoying every moment of it. I am now among the retired. How about that, I made it."

He settled into his rocking chair and patted the one beside him, inviting me to sit for a spell. "So old man, what are your plans with all the newfound spare time?" the man asked as I settled into the other rocker. It was a standard wooden rocker, with a cloth cushion on it, which was great for my nonexistent butt. The arms were worn from use, but the chair was otherwise comfortable. It was a small porch with enough room for only two rockers, his and his wife's. The porch was concrete with peeling grey paint. The front right portion of his yard contained one of the largest oak trees on this stretch of road. His front yard and porch were almost always blanketed in the most glorious shade, which was fantastic in the heat of summer. I was however concerned about one of the limbs spanning over his roof. One of these days a severe storm was surely going to break the limb and take out a chunk of his house. We had discussed a few times, which led him to consider trimming the tree back a little, but he hated to mess with such a masterpiece. Even a masterpiece can have a destructive side. I never asked, but assumed he has good homeowners' insurance.

After his "old man" comment my grin grew, and I tilted my head, humored by the reference. "If I am not mistaken, Frank, you are older than me, and besides, I fully believe you are as old as you feel, and I feel fantastic." I gave it a second, watching the wheels turn behind those eyes of his. "At least I don't blow dust when I fart," I quickly threw in there with as much of a straight face as I could manage. The humor showed through his eyes as we both burst out laughing. He may have been a bit proper, but he had a great sense of humor. I really enjoy our talks.

"Okay, young man, so what are the plans? Lay it on me oh wise one. Are you going to invent the next amazing thing, or simply grow old gracefully like yours truly?"

"Could never be as graceful as you," I said with a smile, "but I don't plan on being bored that is for sure." Or let a forest grow in my nose or ears I thought.

I settled back in the rocker, held up my right hand and started ticking off the assorted items on my to do list. "First of all, I have a honey-do-list as long as my arm, starting with repainting several rooms and putting in a patio in the back yard." One finger in the air. I then added the second with a smile. "Definitely a lot more golf. I may even join a league." After thinking of some of our previous conversations, "You used to golf, didn't you? Perhaps you can join me. I would enjoy your company."

Frank put his hand out in front of him as if fending off an attack of an angry dog, or an extremely bright light, and his grin lessened. "My golfing days are over. Bad knees you know," he stated while starting to rub his right knee with his free hand for effect.

"Old man indeed," I chimed in with a bit of humor in my voice. "No excuse these days, Frank. Just go to the nearest drive through medical center and get them fixed." I then leaned more toward Frank because I thought this was important. "In all seriousness, Frank, you cannot stop moving when you retire. I don't plan on it. That's why I plan to continue my frequent trips to the gym. My goal is not to simply dry up and blow away." In a way Frank reminded me of someone else. "I watched my father-in-law simply stop doing much of anything after he retired. It was sad watching him go downhill after spending so much time in his recliner. He was a lovely man; God rest his soul."

"I'm sure I can still whip your butt young man," Frank stated with a grin, and a matter-of-fact countenance.

"Oh, I am sure you can, but you have to catch me first."

Frank grabbed a small rag he had draped over the right arm of his rocker and tossed it at me and laughed. "Young whipper snapper," he added in his best impression of the voice of Walter Brennan. He was an old movie star that played a very funny old man with a limp on "The Real McCoys". This actor's demeanor and voice were unique.

Since he said nothing further, I continued. "I used to like to draw and paint when I was younger, also like to get back into that. And one other thing I always wanted to do was attempt to write a book. It's my wish to stretch my artistic muscle."

Frank raised his eyebrows in interest. "What is your first book going to be about?"

I thought for a second. "My first may be about an old man with bad knees chasing criminals and title it, "The Detective That Can't."

Frank leaned forward in his seat. I thought he was going to get up at first. "Why you little shit," he said with a smile.

"I'm just saying. I could make you famous," I smiled back at him.

"Keep talking and I may become infamous. Just saying," he stated with an added devious laugh.

"You know, Frank, my dad would have liked you, he was a bullshit artist Democrat as well," and I meant it. He was a Democrat, but I must admit, he was somewhat open minded. My mother was a quiet person and a devout Catholic. Dad didn't go to church much, but she made sure my siblings and I were brought up with a strong belief in Christ. Bless her heart. Seldom a day goes by when I don't think of them. They loved each other to the end, even with a few bumps along the way. That day, six years ago now, when a young man decided to drink and drive, was the most horrible day of my life. The doctor assured me they probably died instantly which gave me the smallest bit of comfort, but at that moment I would take anything.

Frank smiled, knowing of my history with the parents, for it was part of our many discussions. "Come to think of it, Frank, if Dad was still alive you two would be about the same age, wouldn't you?"

I got up making him think perhaps I was getting ready to run for my life, but instead I smiled, took his hand and shook it because I had to go. We joke with each other often. "Sorry, Frank, but I must go. My wife is probably waiting. We are going out to dinner to celebrate. As always I enjoyed our conversation." On the way down the steps I added, "Frank, do you want me to pick up some Depends while I'm out?"

"You're pushing your luck mister," Frank said with a smile as he stood up and waved while I continued down the street, but not before patting his majestic tree, thinking it may give me good luck.

As I neared the corner of my street, which we lived on for nearly 30 years, suddenly I felt lightheaded and distracted. Didn't know by what. I was just walking home which was only perhaps another 100 yards. We only lived three houses down on the other side of the street. I stopped right before I blacked out. I don't remember anything. When the fog cleared from my head, I was standing in front of my house at 108 Arch Street, Jeffersonville, Indiana, staring at the front door, quietly cursing to myself. I don't remember the last 100 yards or even instructing my feet to start walking again. All I remembered was stopping and just blacking out. I was breathing hard but from what I do not know. This never happened before. I quickly looked around to see if anyone was watching, for I felt a little embarrassed.

After verifying no one was near-by, I shook my head as if shaking cobwebs loose and walked to the front door. Before walking in, knowing the door would be unlocked, for my wife's car was in the driveway, I was trying to decide if I should mention this to my wife. I didn't want to worry her. The first thing that came to mind was a mini stroke. I was 62 after all. Being a typical man, especially since I felt fine now, I decided to keep it to myself. The air strangely smelled like sea water. I was so puzzled as I entered the front door to my house.

Chapter 2

I quickly put on an all is right with the world grin before I walked through the house looking for my wife. She was a perceptive woman, so I had to put on my best face. "Honey, I'm home," I hollered. "Your ancient, retired fart is home." The saltwater smell was dissipating thankfully, for it was unnerving.

We first met through an introduction by this cute redhead, Kelly, who was a neighbor of my aunt and uncle. Kelly introduced both my best friend Rusty and me to Susan. Kelly had her eye on me, so she played matchmaker between Susan and my best friend. Kelly and I never went anywhere, but Susan and Rusty seemed to hit it off. I thought Susan was cute, with a great smile and a wonderful sense of humor. I couldn't help noticing, being I was a typical teenage boy, that she had some very enticing curves as well, but she was dating Rusty, so that was that.

I quickly learned what it felt like to be a third wheel. Rusty continued spending a fair amount of time with me, and even stranger, I was invited to many of Susan's family outings and dinners along with Rusty. I didn't complain because I loved being included, and I really liked Susan and her family, even Susan's pesky sister, but I always wondered wasn't three considered a crowd? Through fate or providence, sometimes the second wheel runs over a nail and gets replaced by a spare, or in this case the third wheel.

The time devoted to me instead of Susan eventually put a strain on their relationship. My analogy of a third wheel? Rusty didn't recognize the nail before running over it. It cut deep and deflated their relationship. She finally called it quits because she was beginning to feel like an afterthought, or perhaps she felt like the third wheel.

Life is full of twists, turns, and mystery. Because she and I had become good friends, thanks to Rusty, it was only a couple of days later that I invited her out on a date, and I wasn't about to invite any third wheel along. My relationship with Rusty went south quickly after that, but my life with Susan began on that day at the Country Jamboree on June 10, 1977. Our first date was great because we were already friends, and the chemistry was instant. Holding hands and locking lips passionately was electrifying. Thank you, Kelly, and Rusty. It was like I won the relationship lottery.

Forty years later the love of my life was in front of me after walking from the kitchen to the dining room where I was standing. "Hey," she said with a big smile. My love walked up to me and planted a juicy kiss on my lips. Even after forty years together her kisses still gave me the tingles. I am a lucky man. I grabbed her ample butt, pulled her close, and kissed her deeply. I love this woman.

My lovely wife of 38 years, Susan, completely gray haired now, clipped to the side to keep the hair out of her eyes, fluffy in her own right, but I didn't care. She is still the lovely woman I married so many years ago, mother of our two girls, and one hell of a grandma. We have four grandkids, and they love their Nana. They love me too, but sometimes I feel like I am an afterthought compared to Grandma of The Year. Our grandchildren range from 20, a boy, to the three girls between the ages of 18 and 11. Grandchildren are great. You can spoil them and hand them back. Isn't life great?

"Well, Honey, how does it feel to be retired?" She asked after we pried ourselves apart.

"It feels great," I said with a grin of satisfaction as I brushed a small lock of hair aside that had fallen across her beautiful eyes. "As I was walking home, I was wondering what I was going to do first. Perhaps I should take my lovely wife to bed for a little hayride," I said with a smile and a wink.

"Perhaps later my honey," Susan stated with a come and get it grin. "I am starved. I've been looking forward to a lovely steak dinner at Franks." A steakhouse we loved to visit. "We haven't gone in months. Absolutely love their baked potatoes."

"Ready when you are, Honey." I am so glad she didn't want to go out for fish. For some odd reason, the thought of seafood almost turned my stomach.

"You are insatiable, Honey, but I promise you will enjoy dessert," she said with raised eyebrows and a twinkle in her eyes.

It was nothing like the first few years of our marriage. Making love was not as frequent. The embers take a little more stoking these days to get the fire blazing, but there is still fire, nevertheless. We now go more for quality over quantity. Even without sex we are best friends, talk about many things, and enjoy each other's company even when we don't say a word.

She grabbed her monster purse, which I always felt was large enough to hide our youngest grandchild. A couple times I caught myself checking it. I opened the door for the young lady, always the gentleman like my mother taught me, fully expecting a giggle to sneak out of her purse.

We had a wonderful meal which we shared as is the usual. Don't eat as much as we used to, and they give you so much food these days. Filet Mignon, our favorite, so tender you can cut it with a fork. At the most only adding a touch of salt. We never add steak sauce. That is a sin, and besides if steak sauce is required, the steak should be given to the dog. At least that was my dad's feelings on the subject. We are both in agreement that the baked potato was to die for. We also enjoy their toasted and buttered hamburger buns. Thought it strange, but always tasty. After wrapping up our meal, my wife stacked the dishes, and even wiped the table, which was a carryover from her short stint as a waitress many years ago. She felt the waitress job was hard enough. After paying, along with a generous tip, we were anxious to get home for dessert. I opened the door for my wife and drove home slightly over the speed limit.

The after-dinner dessert was fantastic. Worth waiting for I would say. After exhausting ourselves in bed that night, Susan liked to wind down with a book, where I just enjoy falling asleep with a smile on my face.

"Goodnight, Honey," Susan said with a smile after we kissed once more. A lot can be read into facial expressions. Isn't there even studies on facial expressions and body language? Well, hers was easy to read.

"Oooby dooby doo," and other incoherent mush was all I could manage as my head buried deep in the pillow and my eyes closed for the night.

"I still got it," was all she said as my mind started fogging over.

I was soon sound asleep and sawing the logs in the forest of my dreams. Within minutes, after the end of one of the chapters where Juan the pool boy was glancing at the scantily clad sunbathing mistress of the house, Susan looked over at me and noticed my eyes were moving quickly under closed eyelids. She also saw my hands twitching as well, sort of like a dog does when he is seemingly running after a rabbit in his dreams.

"Well, Honey, you seem to be having an exciting dream," she whispered quietly not wishing to wake me. "Sleep well and goodnight" she again whispered. "I think I am going to join you," she stated with a yawn as she marked her place in the book, put it on her nightstand, and turned off the light. She kissed her man lightly on the cheek before rolling over and nestling her head into her own pile of pillows.

Chapter 3

The salty spray was hitting my face while standing next to the helmsman. "Haul to the wind!" I holler above the sound of the rising blow. The wind had changed direction, so we must adjust accordingly.

We left the port of Hampton Roads on August 08, 1800, under the command of Patrick Fletcher, and are now on our way to the West Indies. It had been over a month now. Our duty is to protect shipping lanes and America's interests.

After muster at 0545, on September 21, 1800, the watchmates were required to scrub and swab the decks. Our captain insists on keeping a tight ship. As one of the mates, I am responsible for the men, and made sure orders were followed.

The bell had rung. Six bells it now be. Time for breakfast. Nine sailors and I made our way down to the mess deck for some oatmeal and coffee. We were well fed, but with little variety. The life of a sea fairing man. Filling our stomachs and keeping us from the scurvy, or other possible maladies was important. There is nothing like eating on a rolling vessel. Worse than grandmother's rocker.

I downed the slop quickly and went back above deck to perform my morning inspection. All must be clean and in order. No room for sloppiness in my Navy. One of the headsail lines was loose I quickly noticed; I have eyes like a hawk. After walking up to the line, I noticed how sloppy the knot was. I yanked hard on the line until it worked itself loose. The heat rose within me, for this was unacceptable. "Men!" I shouted. Some turned but others continued their work. "Men!" I shouted once more. "I am not planning on shouting a third time, so pay me some mind!" They were all finally at attention and facing me, as they should be. "What son of a bitch was responsible for tying the jib lines?" They stood like statues and simply stared at me. I am second in command, so I must always make sure they respect command. "Speak up ladies. I can only kill you once." I kept my back stiff and looked around at my men anticipating a quick answer. The wind had been picking up steady like, so loose rigging is dangerous.

One of the sailors stepped forward. A young man no more than eighteen perhaps. A bean pole, scrawny jack tar. Seaman Steward if I recall. I make it a point to eventually become acquainted with all the men. "Sir, I do believe that would be Seaman Jackson," he stated while looking straight ahead with no expression.

"Where is Seaman Jackson now, young man?"

"He is off duty, down below, catching some sleep I suppose...sir!"

"Well Seaman, you go below and fetch young Jackson, and the rest of you GET BACK TO WORK!" No slackers on my shift. Hoping to earn my way to being a captain I will do my job.

They quickly done as they were told. A good crew even with a few expected mistakes now and again. Several of the men were checking lines so they would not be the next to be called on to face the first mate, Lieutenant Jonathan Boynes.

They considered me as fair but strict. Besides the cook I had the most years at sea. Slightly over six-foot tall, muscular, sky-blue eyes, with wavy black hair. The men respected me, not just because I could probably whip the lot of them, but because they knew I had their back.

I had been first mate on the USS Insurgent for near going on one year now since its capture from the French on February 9, 1799, by the USS Constellation. It is a fast ship originally named L'Insurgente. A beautiful 149 ft frigate with 26-18 pounders, 10-12 pounders, 4–36-pound howitzers, and a contingent of 340 officers and enlisted men. A force to contend with. Immensely proud of this ship I am.

While waiting on Seaman Jackson, I was thinking of our captain, who was a little green around the edges. My years total twenty-six, but I have been sailing for near thirteen years now. It be in my blood. My father before me was a whaler mate on the Volunteer from 1772-1797. He was Jermih Boynes, God rest his soul. Gone near a year now. I, his son, cut me eye teeth on the same whaler from 1787-1790, before I joined the Navy of these here United States. Took me near ten years to work my way up to first mate, but hard work paid off. Hope to get my own ship soon, got some coin in my pocket. Life is good.

A young sailor, after several minutes, ran up to the Lieutenant, and quickly snapped to attention. He was a bit rough around the edges. It appeared he did just awake. "Seaman Jackson, reporting as ordered sir," the young man shouted smartly as he was trained to do.

I held the loose end of the line out toward the young sailor. "I hear tell that tying the jib lines were your responsibility."

After seeing the line in the Lieutenant's hand, he swallowed hard before answering the man. "Yes sir! You are correct sir!"

"Well, why in the hell is it loose in my hand!"

"Don't know sir!"

I could tell the young man was starting to sweat, which is good, he needs to learn a lesson. "You don't know? Well, I am going to tell you why it is loose. I was able to pull it loose with little effort. Where in the hell did you learn to tie knots? At your momma's teat?"

"Sir, no sir! I learned it in the service."

"Appears you need a little more schooling young man. Do you know what a bowline is?"

"Sir, yes sir!" He continued answering sharply.

"Show me then," I stated as I tossed the loose end of the line to the young man and stood aside.

The man quickly wrapped the line around the beam to which it is to be attached, created a hole (loop) for the rabbit (loose end of rope) to go through, ran it around the tree (line from sail), back through the hole, and cinched it up tight.

The knot looked fine, but I went ahead and yanked on the line to test it. "Great job sailor. So why didn't you get it right the first time?"

"Don't know sir! Lazy I suppose!" The sweat was now pouring down the man's face.

"At least you're honest." I noticed some rope rolled up in one of the barrels nearby. Pointing to the barrel I said, "take the loose end of this rope, and tie and untie a bowline twenty times on this beam," pointing to the same beam the jib line was tied to. "When done, tie a clove hitch next and then roll the rope back up. I will be with the helmsman and watching your progress." I got up close to his face to make sure this sunk in. "Sloppy knots are dangerous sailor. Someone's life may depend on it someday. If this happens again, we may need to let the cat out of the bag." I knew I would never use such a harsh punishment for such an offense, but he didn't.

The young man swallowed hard as I backed away, went up the stairs to visit with the helmsman, and watched over the ship and the young man getting ready to practice the art of knots.

I stood next to the helmsman and watched the practice session. Understanding the sea, your ship, and tying knots was top of my list of necessities.

"Sir, it was a red sky this morn," the helmsman stated frankly, with a bit of nervousness in his voice. "You know, red sky in morning, sailors take warning."

"Keep ye head about yourself sailor. You be scrubbing the deck if you don't keep on an even keel. We never know what is coming. Just do your job." I know what it means, and many times a storm does follow, but the men must keep their minds on their tasks.

"Yes sir," he quickly responded, and faced forward. Better keep my mouth shut, the helmsman thought to himself.

The helmsmen kept to his task while I kept my eye on the rest of the ship, and the young man now beginning his first clove hitch. He seemed to be doing an excellent job, so maybe he learned the lesson.

While looking to the sky and gathering clouds, the wind did seem to pick up some. The helmsman may be right this time.

After the youth finished his knots and was dismissed by me to go back to his bunk, I pulled out a piece of beautiful scrimshaw given to me by my father. Normally I kept it among my things, but today I kept it out to examine. Always wished I were half the artist my father was. It was a beautifully carved whale's tooth depicting a stormy sea with my father's vessel, the Volunteer, cutting through the waves. The name of the vessel, my father's name, and the date of 28 March 1773 was circling the tooth like a fine lady's necklace. The loss of my father was still fresh while I rubbed my finger across his name carved deeply into the whale's tooth.

My mother died when I was young, only four years of age. There were few memories of her. I was raised in part by my grandmother. An extremely hard woman. Saw little of my father until I was able to join him on the Volunteer as a greenhorn sailor. Looked up to my father I did.

The man in the nest shouted over the rising wind, bringing my attention to the fast-approaching monstrous clouds to the southeast. Something any sensible sailor was afraid of.

"Men!" I shouted over the gusting winds. "Looks like we are in for a blow!" I again shouted while looking over my shoulder at the helmsman. I know he wishes to say something, but he dares not.

One of the other mates, Franklin, just came topside. "Franklin!" I shouted over the growing noise. "Wake the captain. Appears we're heading into a storm."

After several minutes, the captain and mate Franklin ran up to join me at the helm. "What's your orders Captain!"

"Thoughts Lieutenant?" Captain Fletcher asked. The captain looked at the approaching clouds and back at me.

"We could turn, drop most of our sail, and run before the wind in hopes of making it to a sheltered cover or inlet." I should have stopped there, for it felt that be our safest option, and we do have three hundred on board. "Much riskier, but doable I feel, since the storm appears a way off yet, use the wind and skirt the storm."

The captain's brow furrowed, and eyes squinted against the spray. "If there is a good chance, I am not one for running. We have our orders so now you have yours." Looking directly at me and the helmsman he stated his position clearly. "Head out to sea and make a run around her!"

I looked again at the approaching clouds and gathered my thoughts.

Quickly I began shouting orders. All crew were to be awoken and everything tied down. The young man was ordered down from the nest, our best steersman was put in charge of the helm, and most experienced men standing by the sails, for they may have to be lowered or raised quickly as situations change. Only his best was to remain on deck, and strapped in, for it was going to get rougher. The rest were ordered below deck and told to hang on.

The fate of the Insurgent was now in the hands of God and the brave men topside. I said a prayer and continued shouting orders into the rising wind as we continued southeast. Further from shore they sailed, for they needed more room to maneuver, because skirting the devil was difficult, and being close to shore could be disastrous.

The Insurgent did well for the first hour, for she was a solid and fast vessel. Waited as long as we dared, for full sail meant speed and better maneuverability. The storm however had a mind of its own, and predictability was not in the books. The storm was approaching fast, and seemingly started to wrap its dark arms around our fateful ship.

Most of the sails were now lowered, and the ship steered into the oncoming waves. More men were ordered below as a squall engulfed the Insurgent. Men below were furiously manning the pumps as rain thick enough to cut with a sword was slamming onto the deck with a sound like rocks blasted from a cannon. It was getting hard to breathe, and the remaining men on deck were being tossed around like empty sacks. Exposed skin was being nearly peeled by the stinging spray.

My arms are burning. It was taking two of us to steer the ship and keeping her cutting into the waves. It was getting like trying to steer a rock through the water. "Dearest God keep us safe amongst these waves of sorrow," I silently prayed as a near scream came from the captain who was strapped to the mast nearby. Looking at the captain, I could see he was desperately shouting and pointing to the port side. When I, Jonathan Boynes, proud son of Jermih Boynes, saw what was coming, my blood ran cold. A rogue wave higher than the ship itself was bearing down upon us. The helmsman saw it too. The two of us desperately tried to steer to the port with all our strength before the wave was upon us. We had little chance as it was, but if we were hit broadside by such a wave we would be swamped and rolled.

Fear was gripping the 300 souls on board the Insurgent, one of the fastest ships of the US Navy.

"God help us!" I screamed as we continued pulling with all we had, but it was too little, too late. The last thing I saw was a breaking beam smashing the captain's skull against the mast, and the ship rolling on its side, and the dark sea covering me in its cold grip.

Chapter 4

Susan was desperately shaking me, trying everything to wake me from this nightmare. "Honey! Wake up! Bob! Dammit wake up!" Susan screamed. In her forty years with me, she had never seen anything like what I was going through. She thought perhaps it was a seizure at first, but she finally realized it was a horrible nightmare. Could this be what they called a night terror, she wondered?

I felt as if I was dropping fast into a dark bottomless well. My lungs were burning from holding my breath. I must, or I will surely die. I could hear my Susan calling to me and reaching desperately, trying to pull me from its depths before I was forever lost. I could feel my body start to twitch as I was reaching the end of consciousness. Cold was gripping me, and pressure increasing on my lungs like a cranking vise. I was forced to release the stale air I was holding onto desperately, and finally opened my mouth to inevitability. One large pull, seeking the oxygen my body was screaming for, found nothing but churning brine. Oh my God, help me, was my last thought before bolting from my bed and dropping to the floor.

"Bob!" Susan cried out as she fell to her knees beside me.

I was on my side, on our hardwood floor, frantically hacking to clear my lungs. Water spilled to the floor from my mouth. Susan was beside me, crying and desperately smacking my back. My wife was horrified by what she was witnessing. After nearly a minute of this I was finally able to take a clean breath, and the fog of the dream was floating away like the dark waters that held me.

The air was sweet as I was filling my lungs with it, chasing away the fright that came with drowning. Tears were falling from my eyes, and confusion bounced around inside my head like in a pinball machine. "What the hell," were the first words I was able to rattle out from deep within me.

I was now sitting up, felt my wife sitting next to me, gently rubbing my back, reassuring me that I was okay. She, however, was just as confused as I was. Not only did I have a violent dream, hacked up water that had a slight smell of salt, but my body was soaked as if I sweated out one hell of a fever.

"Honey, what happened?" my wife quietly asked me as I placed my elbows on my knees and my head in my hands. I just shrugged, for I had no idea. An occasional hard cough was still sending pains through my chest. My face and arms stung, body ached severely, and my mind was filled with an overload of strange visions.

After several minutes, I lifted my head and blew out a cleansing breath. My breathing had slowed, and I was slowly able to calm myself. "Can dreams be in color?" I asked. "It was so real," I stated slowly and with conviction. Looking at my hands, I noticed they were calloused as if I had been shoveling dirt for days. I rubbed my hands together and noted the toughness of them, which only added to my confusion. Susan sat next to me, with her left arm around me. She didn't know what else to say, so she quietly comforted me with tears glistening in her eyes.

"Do you think you need to go to the doctor or hospital?" Susan asked. "You scared the hell out of me."

"No more than it scared me, believe me." I was feeling better by the minute even though my mind wasn't processing all that was going through my head very well. "I think I am feeling okay now. Just let me sit awhile longer, take a shower, and after that we can discuss this further." I wasn't prepared to talk about this yet because I was still processing. Of course, there was yesterday's blackout. Can't hardly ignore that little secret.

While I was taking a shower, Susan was stripping and making the bed. The sheets were wet and oddly stained with dirt or sand it appeared. Susan ran her fingers across the stains, squinting while puzzling over this strangeness.

"What are these?" I heard Susan inquire from the bedroom as I was toweling off.

"I really don't know what THESE are," I responded sarcastically. "I lost my Xray glasses Susan. Give me a moment to finish drying off and throw some clothing on."

The hot shower and clean clothes made me feel much better. I never waste time in the shower. I finish before the mirror has time to start fogging up.

The bed was already made, and dirty linens stuffed into our laundry baskets. We have three in our oversized bathroom, which I love. One basket for each, whites, colors, and darks. My wife is almost anal about the laundry. Don't mix them up, and run the whites through an extra rinse, so her sensitive skin doesn't itch. God forbid.

When I came out of the master bath, and back into the bedroom, all was straight as if nothing occurred. She takes great care of me. She was sitting on one end of the bed next to some items laid out on the new wedding ring quilt. She waved her right hand toward them to indicate those were the things I should have been able to see through the bathroom wall.

When I saw them up close, I was shocked, floored, and bamboozled. I knew exactly what they were, and there is no way they should be here in this reality, let alone our bedroom. "No way in hell!" I quickly blurted out. "Are they real?" I had to ask. They couldn't be.

"What do you mean are they real?" she questioned. The situation is already strange enough without my husband questioning my eyesight. "Do they look like holograms to you?"

I reached over and touched them to make sure this wasn't another dream, and perhaps I haven't woken up yet. "You don't understand," I almost pleaded after I picked up the last item and ran my fingers over the carved ridges on what is a whale's tooth. My legs were feeling a bit wobbly, so I sat down on the other end of the bed as I continued holding this wonderous object and glanced at the other items still on the bed.

"Naturally, I don't understand? This is very strange, and I also want you to know the bedding was not only wet but covered in dirt or sand. I think I will rinse them outside before I put them in the wash." She looked at me and then asked, "Are you okay, Honey? You look a bit peaked. I think we should call the doctor."

"Absolutely not!" I shouted, thinking maybe I was going nuts. "At least not yet. I'm not sure what I would tell him."

"You're scaring me, Honey. Help me to understand," she pleaded.

"It's my dream. I dreamed I was First Mate Jonathan Boynes. We were in a horrible storm and were hit broadside by a rogue wave. The Insurgent, our vessel, was swamped and rolled. I drowned. Sorry, Jonathan drowned," Bob quickly corrected himself, "and these items you discovered were in the man's pockets as he was tossed into the sea, and the fact there is sand in our bedding is even more alarming. You see," I added, "seawater is full of sand and salt."

Susan stared at me for a moment, trying to absorb what I just said. "That's impossible. Dreams aren't real, and you definitely can't bring back physical things from a dream." Susan grabbed her purse from the nightstand and fished out her cell phone. "I'm calling the doctor."

"And tell him what? I had a dream, and these things on our bed, which are real, passed through my anus? A gift that keeps on giving. I can't explain it, and not sure I ever could. Surely you don't want me in a padded room watching Teletubbies all day, do you?" I could see men in white coats dragging me down a hall.

"Maybe you had these things all along, and just don't remember. Maybe the thought of the carving sparked a dream somehow." Susan was running her hands through her hair and down her face as she often does when concerned.

"Honey, I would have remembered if I had gotten these items before last night. And how do we explain the sand. I guess I snuck out of bed after we made love and sprinkled sand on the sheets, or maybe I haven't bathed in weeks, and I sweated out two pounds of dirt during the night. I'm not ready to talk to anyone about this," I stated frankly because I was starting to get angry. But it wasn't her fault. "It's all still new to me. I need time, Honey. Let me look into this."

"Look into what?" Her voice raised. She was frustrated, but no more than I was.

"Just give me time. Perhaps a couple days. I can call around and perhaps visit some shops to see where these may have come from." I thought about it for a moment while my wife continued to play with her hair. "I'll make a deal with you. I am close to my next physical. I'll call the doctor to let him know I have been feeling a bit off, ask to have the physical moved up, and perhaps ask him to add some tests. Deal?"

She brought her hands down and took mine into hers. I think we were both shaking. "Thank you, Honey. It's a deal."

She glanced back at the mysterious items that seemed to have appeared out of nowhere. "You know, Honey, the coins are really old, and I suspect valuable."

I smiled, surprised by the switch in her attitude. "I know where you're coming from now," I snickered. "You see a cool shopping spree in your future."

"Don't be ridiculous. I was just thinking, while you're checking around, get them appraised."

"Uh huh?" I responded, giving her a wink.

Chapter 5

Later that afternoon, I spent time at the driving range smacking some little white balls around. Sometimes that is therapeutic, and I understood the golf balls. I needed to do something to take my mind off the previous night.

After dinner, and a movie on the television, we called it a night. My wife I am sure was concerned I was going to have another episode, but the night was uneventful, and I slept like a rock. She didn't sleep so well. The next day she admitted to watching me sleep and reading well into the night.

Saying the night was uneventful wasn't 100% the truth. The only dream I recalled, was of Jonathan's first time working on a ship. His father's whaler. A standard dream, but odd regardless. Deep down I knew this wasn't my dream. I had more dreams just like those for the next couple of nights.

On Sunday, I got up early, totally refreshed because my sleep was deep and restful. I went into the bathroom to take a long hot shower. After I closed the door, I caught myself turning the light on and off. Wasn't the electric light a wonder in these modern times? The many things we take for granted these days I dwelled upon for a moment while standing in the middle of our master bath. Wasn't long ago when indoor plumbing and electricity didn't exist. It would have been required to go out into the cold or heat to simply relieve myself. Dig a hole, or if you were fortunate, have your hole covered with an outhouse, with a wooden seat upon which you can even rest your bum. I could almost smell the wonderful aroma as I flushed our toilet several times. I was strangely fascinated by our own bathroom. The hot shower I next experienced was like heaven to me. It was if I was experiencing these things for the first time. I was finally able to snap out of it as I scrubbed my hair. That felt extremely weird.

There was plenty of time before I needed to wake Susan. We generally go to church at 9:30, but it was only about 7:00 AM. We were Southern Baptist and went to a midsized church across the river.

The hot water felt so good rolling down my back I broke into song. Not exactly sure where I heard it from.

Like a petrel she'll skim the blast.

While the spray sweeps her deck with snow,

As the waves, in their race, foam past.

Pack on every stitch she can bear.

Let her use, as she can, her wing.

Through the crests of the waves she'll tear,

While the blast through her taut shrouds sings. She's a clipper that none can match

At that sea, how she leapt and laughed.

Where's the boat that her heels can catch?

Then, "Here's to our peerless craft."

By this time, Susan had awoken, and was lying quietly in bed listening to the cheerful but strange ditty coming from the master bath.

I normally shave before my shower, but I felt like switching things up on this fine morn. So much time had passed as I was toweling off, I noticed the mirror had fogged up.

Walking up to the mirror, in the suit that God had given me, I grabbed a dry washcloth to clean off the mirror. I felt safer watching myself in the mirror as I shaved. No need to draw blood so early in the morning.

The mirror was oval and brightly lit by the four frosted bulbs above it. We had the bathroom installed within the last ten years, and all was still looking fresh and new.

As I raised the cloth, I was startled by what appeared to be an apparition hiding behind the fine mist coating the mirror. It moved as I moved, but even through the distortion it seemed different somehow. Hair darker and what appeared to be a beard. I don't have a beard. Just a five o'clock shadow. My hands shook as I stared at the face in the mirror. Don't be silly my man, just clean the mirror and get on with it.

After nearly a minute, like a child, I closed my eyes, hoping the boogey man would go away, and swiped at the mirror furiously, assuming it was just dirt I was seeing, and it would cling to the cloth. It can be washed after all. After I was sure I cleaned it thoroughly, and perhaps even took some of the finish off, if that was doable, I backed up a few steps.

What the hell am I afraid of? I'm 62 years old. I no longer believed in trolls living under bridges, the closet monster, or the boogey man under the bed. I didn't need to sleep with a night light on.

My heart was beating fast. I was being irrational. When I got up the courage to open my eyes I saw only me, looking at me in the mirror. I blew out a stress packed breath from my lungs. "You're being such a baby," I said to myself as I made faces in the mirror, attempting to cut the tension I felt.

After another moment, I rubbed my face hard with my hands, feeling like blood had flushed out of my skin into my rapidly beating heart. Stepping up to the mirror, oddly thinking a hand was going to reach out of the reflection from another world, I shakily grabbed my razor and the shaving cream, and began my standard shaving routine after pushing the other thoughts aside. While shaving, I still had roaming thoughts of a gnarly hand of death reaching for my throat, or perhaps one with knives for fingernails, like Freddy Kruger.

I was able to block most of the weird thoughts intruding on my brain as I wiped off the shaving cream residue, even some that found its way into my left nostril.

I quickly threw on my church clothes, spritzed on some English Leather that my wife liked so much, and opened the bathroom door. I was anxious to get out of there as I did a quick look over my shoulder, making sure nothing was following me.

My wife was sitting up in bed on her phone, probably reading her daily devotional. I gave her a quick peck on her cheek, hoping not to disturb her train of thought. Sometimes I purposely interrupt her reading of her love stories she likes so much, just to get a rise out of her.

"Honey, what were you singing in the shower?" she quietly asked while keeping her eyes on her phone.

After wrestling with the mirror and the ghoul peeking through the haze, I almost forgot. I had to think for a moment. "Oh, Honey, that was just an old song "Give Her a Gale and She'll Go", I answered nonchalantly as if I knew that song from childhood. After a second more thought, "I'm not sure where I heard it from, it just came to me while I was taking that lovely shower. We take so much for granted. You should have joined me," I followed. "We could have started the day off with a bang."

She looked up from her phone with a furrow in her brow. "What has gotten into you? I know I have a body of a goddess," she stated with an obvious sarcastic flare. "I'm just not sure steaming up the bathroom even more, right before church, would get us in the proper state of mind."

"As it says in Proverbs, Honey, "A loving doe, a graceful deer, may her breasts satisfy you always, may you ever be intoxicated with her love." I am just informing you that you intoxicate me," I added with a wink.

"Oh my God!" Susan exclaimed. "Sorry Lord", she quickly added. "Why don't you go back into the bathroom and take a cold shower, and when you come out read today's devotional while I get ready."

On the way to church I found myself apologizing to God for thinking mostly of boogeymen, sex in the shower, and the weird song I cannot seem to scrub from my brain. You know those times when you hear a song from your childhood, and you can't stop humming it. This is that on steroids.

Chapter 6

On Monday morning, before going to the gym, I discussed basics with my doctor over the phone. I also broached the subject of my blackout. This was never mentioned to my wife though. Didn't plan to unless they discovered something. The doctor ordered a complete blood workup and an MRI. He especially wanted to rule out a stroke.

I called my wife at work. She still worked, because she was younger than me, and she was able to add me to her insurance. "Okay, Honey," I said after she picked up her phone. "I talked to the doctor, and he is scheduling some tests for me."

"How soon can he see you? The sooner the better I think."

"They are taking blood on Tuesday, an MRI on Wednesday, and the follow up will be a week from today." I make good use of the calendar on my cell. Comes in very handy.

"An MRI? Why an MRI? What's he thinking could be wrong?"

"Please don't worry, Honey." My girl has the sweetest quality to her voice when she's concerned about things, especially me. One of the many things I love about this woman. "He's just covering the bases, and you know full well he isn't going to venture a guess over the phone. Anyway, I feel great. As a matter of fact, better than great. I'm a little sore yet, but I feel like I can conquer the world my sweetheart." I hope she doesn't think I am exaggerating on how I feel just to lessen her anxiety, but I am not, I feel fantastic.

"Okay, Bob, you have a great day. Oh, and by the way," she then whispered, "I'm a little sore myself, if you know what I mean. You were a beast last night," she giggled like a schoolgirl and hung up.

I had a little flush to my face as I hung up on my end.

I had the weekdays to myself since she worked. We had planned to get together for lunch on some days, but for now my plate was full.

I had some research to do on the items my wife discovered and some of my specific memories. I haven't gotten into this with my Susan yet, but in the same way my history is stored in my brain, so was Jonathan's. It was an awful lot for my subconscious to fabricate. I figure, either I am having medical or psychological issues, or somehow these are someone else's memories floating around in my head. They say we only partially use our grey matter anyway. Good thing, or my head would explode. I never believed in reincarnation, but I am rethinking that one. Why would it show up now? Or another thought crossed my mind. I was taken by aliens and experimented on. Did they do sexual things to me as well, directly after pouring a sailor's memory juice into my left ear?

After the gym, I spent all afternoon visiting antique and coin shops. I decided to tackle the antique shops first. I had an ornate wooden box I received as a gift from work. It was perfect for carrying the carving and coins. I wrapped the scrimshaw in a cloth and placed each coin carefully into individual coin carriers I purchased at the local Hobby Lobby after I left the gym. I emptied my gym bag, placed the box in it, and carried the bag over my shoulder with my hand tight around the strap. I felt like I was carrying the crown jewels.

I didn't have much luck in the four antique shops I visited, mostly filled with furniture, jewelry, and knickknacks. A couple of the places were a little musty smelling as well. It was a good thing I didn't have mold allergies, or I would be taking a couple puffs of an inhaler. I did see some scrimshaw, but nothing as elaborate as the one in my possession. They were expensive, especially if nearly as old as I expect mine to be. In my mind I had finally taken possession of the items. The shopkeepers were very intrigued by the piece I showed them. A couple offered about $50 for it, but I suspected it was worth a lot more. I was there to gather information however, not to sell.

There were a few coins in the antique shops, but I wasn't impressed enough to even take mine out of the box. The next stops would be the three-coin shops I had chosen to visit.

They were amazing. To a numismatic it would be like a small child in a candy shop. They were looking at me a little nervously. A man carrying a black gym bag over his shoulder. Could he be here to rob us, I am sure they were thinking. I tried to not make any sudden moves and kept my hands in my pockets as I looked over the display cases. I would take out my Uzi when the time was correct, I humored myself.

The day had flown, so I didn't really have time to browse, so at each store, after a quick glance, I went up to the counter and asked for their appraiser. The first two I showed my coins to were helpful to a point, but were more like a straight-faced poker player, keeping their good fortune close to the vest and off their faces. They were here to make money after all. They both told me what I had and offered me substantial money. Several thousand as a matter of fact. As before, I was here for information and not to sell. They even tried to dicker with me on the way out of the door, so I knew I had something special. I did buy a large book that specialized in American coins and bills. Perhaps that would help.

The third and last visit for the day was a much different and unexpected experience. The shop was old fashioned and amazing. A bell rang as I opened the heavy wooden door, announcing my entry. The air wasn't musty like the antique shops, nor was it antiseptic like a modern shop. It had the faint scent of flowers, which were strategically placed along the right wall in ornate niches, like what you may expect to contain things like a small statue of the Virgin Mary, or an ornate Catholic chalice. The walls were all made of dark walnut and the floor covered with highly polished hardwood. The ceiling was open, well over ten feet, with dark wooden beams and bowl-shaped lighting hanging by chains from the rafters. The glass was clear, exposing the fitting antique style Edison bulbs.

The display cases were wooden framed with thick glass. The cases were arranged only along the wall to the left as I entered. Four on the floor and four on the wall. To the right was one dark leather Chesterfield couch with Victorian style marble top tables on either end. In each corner of the room, on the same side, were matching Chesterfield leather chairs.

The coins and bills in the cases were very well organized and well-lit for easy browsing. It wasn't a large place, but it was designed for quality merchandise.

It was like I went back in time. I expected a woman of prestige, from the Victorian age, to come out at any moment, and offer me a spot of tea before her husband and I got down to business. I pictured the woman dressed in a flowing Marie Antoinette style dress, complete with bustle and corset, dark red with black trim.

I felt like I was in a trance, still at the front door, when a kindly voice interrupted my visit with the lovely lady. "May I help you, young man?" an elder gentleman called out in a softly spoken voice and New England accent.

When I snapped out of it, I noticed myself and the elderly man of perhaps eighty years old were the only two in the store. He was smiling at me from behind one of the display cases. I assumed the man might have been the owner. A small and thin man, almost gaunt with well-kept white hair, and black plastic framed glasses placed low upon his nose. He looked at me over the top of the frames, which I assumed were readers. He had on a tan jacket, unbuttoned to expose a white shirt with a dark brown tie, almost a match for the walnut walls. He fits the represented time and décor of the place.

"This place is amazing sir," I stated with a tone of glee, returning his warm smile.

"Designed and decorated by my wife of sixty years now," he proudly announced. "You don't plan on robbing me do you, young man?" he asked with humor, indicating the bag carried over my shoulder.

I nervously giggled as I quickly responded to his absurd, but understandable question. "Oh no sir. I am just using the bag to secure what I hope are priceless items I came to show you."

He was measuring me up for a moment when he said, "Because if you are, I am loaded for bear behind this counter," he stated flatly. The smile disappeared from his face as he stated his position, but the smile quickly reappeared when he finished sizing me up. "Show me what you have young man."

"Call me Bob," I first responded, for I preferred to be on a first name basis.

"My name is Jeremiah," the man said with a smile as he reached out and shook my hand. The man had one hell of a grip. Jeremiah also kept eye contact when we were talking. He was a man that was sure of himself, which I much preferred to a man with a limp, clammy grip that avoided eye contact. I felt he could be trusted.

Keeping my bag hanging from my shoulder, I unzipped it, pulled the wooden box out, and laid it carefully on the counter, not wanting to crack the glass. After removing my ten coins from the case I spread them out in front of the man. He scanned over them with just his readers at first. "Early Americana," he commented. "These are in excellent condition. Where did you come across these gems?"

"Handed down," I quickly lied. Not about to tell him the truth. He seemed to accept my explanation, but why wouldn't he?

He appeared to know his stuff, and he was thorough if nothing else. From behind the counter, he pulled a lighted, stand-alone magnifier, a large worn book of early American coins, a laptop, and a pair of clean jeweler's gloves. The laptop surprised me a bit, for most older people I knew weren't much for computers. The thought humored me some, for I was quickly slipping into the older people category myself, but I used computers a lot in my career.

After placing the items of his trade on the counter, and slipping the gloves on his boney hands, he began examining each coin under the magnifier after removing it from its holder, starting from left to right. He examined each coin carefully, looked them up on-line and in his books, while taking copious notes.

He went back to one particular coin several times, mumbling to himself. "Ummmm," he voiced quietly through his thin lips as he looked back and forth several times between his book and the coin. He spent about five minutes typing away on his computer with the finesse of a highly trained typist. He turned the coin over several times, seemingly examining each marking.

The man was starting to make me a little anxious. What was he looking at? I asked myself as I paced in front of the counter, which didn't interfere with the focus of the mature gentleman. After nearly ten minutes with just the one coin, the old man finished his notes, put the last of the coins back in their protective holder, and sat down in the chair he had placed behind the counter. He pulled the glasses off his face, placed them on the counter and sighed. He then rubbed his face with his hands just like my wife does. I knew that had to mean something.

"Wow," he stated quietly as he leaned forward on the counter with a smile on his face. He was not much of a poker player, I thought, as I smiled back at him, and breathed in anxiously.

By this time, another man came in, which he introduced as his grandson, and a couple customers. The owner picked up the ten coins I gave him, carefully handed them back to me, and motioned for me to follow him after instructing his grandson to help the other customers.

Carrying the gym bag even tighter now, with the precious cargo on board, I followed him into a small office at the back of the store, decorated in the same motif. It contained a tiny antique desk and two chairs. A small fridge was in the corner covered with a stack of books. An eclectic collection from Dickens and Twain to Stephen King. This must be his personal hideaway spot. I suspect he can't stand for too long, and when things got slow, he must come in here for a drink, rest and a casual read.

He waved at the chair across from his desk. "Have a seat Bob," he said as he settled into the other chair. He first pulled out a blank file folder, and after getting my full name, he wrote it neatly on the tab of the folder. "You have a fine collection Bob," he said in a soft voice as he arranged his notes in front of him.

My breath was starting to get caught in my throat in anticipation.

"Eight of your coins are fine examples of standard coins of the era. Exceptionally superb condition too." He pushed a single piece of paper toward me, which appeared to be a list of eight coins, descriptions, condition ratings, and their estimated retail value.

I couldn't help but smile as I scanned the list.

"As you can see, I estimate them to be worth in the range of about ten grand. Very nice indeed."

"Holy cow," was my only response as I looked from him to the list in my hand. I am so glad I came here, I thought to myself.

"If you want an offer from me," the man continued. "Since I am a retailer, I cannot offer full price. The best I could offer would be $6,000."

I didn't have a response for him at the moment. A stupid smile simply stayed plastered on my face. I wasn't expecting any of this, just hoping. "Jeremiah, what of the other two coins? I need a full picture, and some time to think before making any decisions," trying my best to reel my emotions back in.

"Yes of course," he responded. "I was saving the best for last," he added as he slipped another piece of paper across the desk towards me.

I about choked with glee as I examined the piece of paper with the last two items listed. I almost asked to borrow the man's readers, so I could be sure what I was seeing wasn't a figment of my imagination. I glanced back up at the man, and he seemed to read my mind.

"You are reading it correctly, Bob." He pointed his boney finger to the first on the list. "The first coin on the list is a duplicate of one of the first eight but is in nearly uncirculated condition. I expect it could bring as much as $10,000 on its own. I could offer you $6,000 for it." He then quickly moved his finger to the last on the list. "This last one however is in a different league."

I followed his finger and couldn't believe what he wrote. "Are you sure this is correct?" I asked Jeremiah.

"I would like to take some pictures, and do more research to be sure, but I am relatively certain you have a gem in your possession."

I glanced back at the paper where he wrote '1794 1c Liberty Cap, Large cent, Starred Reverse S-48, R5, PCGS graded 40.' It looked like Greek to me, but I understood the dollars and cents perfectly. I felt like I just swallowed a golf ball.

"In the right setting, I feel this coin alone could bring nearly $250,000. It's not only rare, but in extra fine condition." He removed his finger from the paper, and sat back in the chair, obviously enjoying the look on my face.

"Holy crap, Jeremiah. I'm afraid to leave the store with these coins without a police escort."

The smile he gave me reminded me of my dad when amused. "Like I said, I want to do further research, and reach out to other experts to get a better feel, and to make sure I am not missing anything. I would definitely lock these items up in a vault somewhere."

He wrote down my information on the inside of the folder, placed his notes in it, and filed his folder away in his small file cabinet next to the mini fridge. I asked for two of his cards. One I placed in my billfold, and the other in the box with the coins, the list he gave to me, and the carving.

"I will keep in touch," Jeremiah said as he gave me another hardy handshake. The man also had his grandson walk me to my car, which I almost wished was a Brinks truck.

My first stop, before going home to give my wife the good news, was at my bank, where I placed the wooden box into our personal lockbox. As soon as I left the bank, I was able to breathe easier.

I thought I was going to have to pick my wife's chin up off the floor when I commenced to tell her of our great luck. I informed her that more research was going to be done by Jeremiah and myself. I had more digging to do on the carving as well.

After dinner, I felt exhausted, and decided to go to bed early. I had a mixture of dreams, including one of Jonathan's, which didn't surprise me so much now. Overall, I slept well.

Chapter 7

The next day, after visiting the local vampire clinic for a quick stick and run, I was going to visit the local library, and then perform some major internet research. Would I find anything on the ships, Jonathan, or his father? Was this real, or made up by my own subconscious? Made up wouldn't explain away the items though.

Turns out I was able to find references to all three vessels, Insurgent, Constellation, and even the whaler Volunteer. Every detail of what I remember from my so-called dream was 100% accurate according to my sources at both the library and on-line.

Jonathan's father Jermih was listed as a second mate on board the Volunteer from March 1772 to August 1772. The Constellation did, in truth, capture the French vessel L'Insurgente on 9 February 1799, and the final piece in my mind was the fact the newly renamed Insurgent was lost in a storm around September 1800. There were over 300 souls on board, including a first mate by the name of Jonathan Boynes. I printed details from the internet and made copies of the library's reference material to show to my wife when she got home from work.

There was little doubt in my mind now. A supernatural event occurred a few nights previous. I may not be able to convince my wife, but I was convinced. That was not a dream. Somehow, I joined in more ways than mentally with First Mate Jonathan Boynes on the fateful day when the USS Insurgent went down with all men.

Even more unbelievable was what I brought back with me from over 200 years in the past after my wife seemingly saved my life. Saltwater was spewing forth from my lungs, clothing and bed soaked with the same, memories from a young man long since deceased, and some of his actual possessions which turned out to be unbelievably valuable.

The one question, besides why, I have yet to answer for myself was if Jonathan's actual spirit was attached to mine, or I just held onto his memories. I have a feeling it is more than memories. I can almost feel the young man walking along side of me, experiencing my life, evidenced by spiked interest in my surroundings especially in reference to modern contrivances. I'm not sure how my wife is going to handle such a revelation.

One last thing I needed to check off my list, was the completion of the medical testing, mainly for my wife's sake. I don't feel there is anything wrong with me.

After my wife came home, and we had dinner, I sat down with her, and went over what I had found so far. I insisted on waiting till the doctor was done with me, before revealing any of my thoughts on the matter. She listened with such fascination, and she agreed without argument to wait until the next week, after the doctor had time to review the results. I was to say the least a little surprised. Perhaps some of her own conclusions were being formed in her mind, one of which I hope didn't include my insanity.

Before we arrived at the doctor's office, I finally brought up the fact I had blacked out for a short period of time before that very unusual evening. She was upset with me that I kept such a thing to myself. "I am your wife," she said with fervor as she chastised me.

Susan insisted on coming along on this visit. The doctor performed some of his own tests, just to dot the I's and cross his T's. Got to pay his own rent I suppose.

"All your tests look fine, Bob," the doctor stated after reviewing all the test results on his laptop. "As a matter of fact, Susan," he added after turning his attention to my wife. "Your husband is in great shape." He passed several documents to me, showing the summary of the various tests. "The numbers from the blood work are substantially better than the last round, and they weren't that bad to start with. Your MRI is totally clear. Nothing unusual. I couldn't even find Waldo on any of the images," he added with a smile. "I don't have to see you again for six months unless something comes up you are concerned about. The great news is, if your numbers stay at these great levels I may consider cutting back on your medication."

I shook hands with the doctor and left after making my next appointment. I could tell Susan felt better after the visit.

After taking my wife out on a dinner date, we sat down at home, and went over everything, including my honest thoughts on the situation. Surprisingly, she listened carefully without interrupting me.

"I don't have any better explanation," she finally responded after my lengthy speech I had rehearsed all day in my head.

"Is that all?" I asked after her simple and surprising comment. I smiled. "I was thinking you may interrupt me, saying how insane my explanation was. I can say that I am a little surprised and pleased by your support of me on this. I could never explain why or how, obviously. It's just the only thing that makes sense to me so far. Is it something sinister? I don't feel it. The only two things I know for certain is that this event left me much better physically, and we have some very handsome trinkets. God gave me health and us wealth, I just don't know why.

My wife put her hand softly to my lips. "Please, Honey, don't be concerned, I will always have your back." She then smiled. "Now, Honey," she stated quietly and slowly, with a pause. "If you keep singing that odd song, I am going to have to buy a gun and learn how to use it." She then sat back in her chair and presented a very odd little smile, like she really meant it.

"Ha Ha," I responded with my own humor interjected into the situation. "I hope you're okay living with two men," I added.

I guess she never thought of it that way. After several moments, a little smirk flashed across her face. "There are some perks I'll just have to adjust to," she added simply, before she leaned over and gave me one of her patented kisses.

I wasn't sure how to take that, but what can I do?

Chapter 8

My wife and I settled into our new routine with our uninvited guest, once we accepted things for what they were, or at least what we thought they were.

I heard back from my new coin collecting friend Jeremiah. He was satisfied with his original appraisal and offered his help in any way he could. His original offer for nine of the ten coins still stood, but he had other ideas on how to market the jewel of my collection when I was ready to proceed. My preference was to wait for things to settle before making any decisions. Jeremiah understood.

My wife and I had a brief, and I do mean brief conversation regarding looking into buying a sailboat. "You are as bad as a man going through a midlife crisis, and buying an over-the-top new red Corvette," she stated flatly. "You need to inform your guest that this is our life and not his. We have a great chance here to insure our children's future, at least financially, and I don't want us to blow it on frills like a sailboat."

"I guess you told him," I laughed, and went back to typing away on my laptop. One thing I always wanted to do was write a book, and what happened to me gave me some great material.

Many things have happened since the dream, in addition to starting my book. Regarding my golf game? I had been looking forward to moving to the senior tees soon, since the older one gets, the shorter the tee shots, but now I am considering moving back to the blues. I never hit from the blues, even when much younger. Just never had the length off the tee to compete at that level. I seemed to have added at least fifteen yards to my tee shots. Both my friends and I are amazed.

My strength and stamina have improved noticeably. My younger brother and I trimmed back my friend Frank's tree, so it wouldn't damage his house during a storm. I was climbing ladders, using a chain saw, and tying knots in ropes like nobody's business.

I felt like a new man, or perhaps it is more accurate to say two men. My wife was enjoying my newfound vigor as well, or as she may say, her perks.

It is now obvious to me that his memories and valuables were not the only things I collected from my trip to the past. This gave a new meaning to God works in mysterious ways. I was not about to waste what I was given.

Six months had passed. I had my second visit with the doctor, and as promised he lowered my medication dosages. Most doctors I find are pretty straight laced, but mine was almost gushing over my progress. My numbers were to the moon good, he said. I simply shook my head and grinned. No sense in looking a gift horse in the mouth. Go with the flow.

I was up to chapter 25 on my first book, which is going to be a fictional/historical rendition of Jonathan's life on board the USS Insurgent. Adventure and death on the high seas. Also starting my autobiography, so when I was feeble, and my memory slipping, I would have a record of my life, even as unbelievable as it was going to appear. Now if I choose to publish it, only my family would know the truth behind the fiction.

Now, in celebration of my 25th chapter, good reason as any, I got a wild hair and wandered into a tattoo parlor. The stick in the mud accountant in me would not have done this in a million years, but I was writing about my alter-ego Jonathan, near captain of the high seas. I thought it wouldn't hurt to just look, and could leave at any time, until I saw it. A drawing of an old sailing ship that looked a lot like the USS Insurgent. I felt like something jumped inside of me. It was like being hit with a pile of nostalgia. "Hold your horse's young man," I whispered to myself or my alter-self, which still confuses me from time to time. "I don't think I can go through with this," I said, as I kept admiring the artwork.

"May I help you?" a voice came from behind, which gave me a start. I was hoping he didn't hear me mumbling to myself. Gray hair and mumbling to myself could send strange vibes, like nursing home escapee for one. He may doubt my ability to make such a decision on my own.

"She be one hell of a ship," I blurted out in my version of an old time New England accent. I cursed quietly as I turned around and smiled at the young man. The man was thin, yet muscular, well-tanned, with tattoos over nearly all his body, and even one of a bald eagle on his smooth scalp. The artistry was fantastic, if not a little overboard. He had earrings in his ears and nose. A walking billboard for poor parenting I was thinking. Lock up your little girls, I commented to myself.

"She sure is," he smiled at my choice as he lifted his pant leg, and revealed he had that very one on his left calf. "You interested sir?" he asked very politely. Maybe his parents didn't do so bad after all. Polite at least. Can't always trust first appearances, but in his case that would be tough.

I almost couldn't help it, for I was a little intrigued myself. It wasn't all Jonathan's doing, absolutely sure of it. I could easily add this to my bucket list and would make a neat entry in my autobiography. "The day I lost my mind, and had a sunken ship painted on my body."

I chose it, adding a few details to better represent my view of the Insurgent, and scheduled some chair time for later in the week. My wife is going to kill me, I thought as I left the parlor.

The day I showed it to her, seemingly sailing across my sore left shoulder blade, she didn't take it as bad as I thought she might. She did however give me a pat, square on my raw back, to get in a subtle point. She loves me so much, I thought at the time. The process wasn't the most enjoyable, but I took it like a man, and nearly started to cry as the ink was poked deep into my skin. I attempted to blame it on Jonathan, but she would have none of that. That night, when making love, my wife started singing, "Yo ho ho and a bottle of rum." We had a good laugh, and both accepted that it was what it was.

With youthful type energy to keep me going, I had already put in our patio, added a water feature, and rock garden to the back corner of our yard. My golf game had advanced to the point where I was shooting in the sub eighties. I had never been able to break eighty before. Helped one of my family to strip and install a new roof on their house. I was becoming a regular handyman. Surprising even myself, for I was far from being a mechanic, I even changed the starter on my eldest granddaughter's car. Google is amazing.

I was proud of my tattoo. For a while I thought regret would take over, but never did. The young version of the Painted Man did an excellent job. My grandchildren got a kick out of it because a couple of them already had tattoos of their own. I didn't mind taking off my shirt to show it, and my muscles that had started to present themselves. I was becoming what some people refer to as cut. The gym, along with all my other extracurricular activities were paying off.

After coming in the other day from cutting and trimming the yard in 90-degree heat, my wife was waiting for me with a glass of cold tea. "Aren't you tired, Honey," she asked with a little concern to her voice.

I was sweating but felt like I could cut the neighbor's yard next if it needed it. "I feel great, Honey. God is good all the time," I added as I took my first sip of the nectar that Susan had made for me.

"And all the time God is good," she followed immediately. Over the years this had turned into our mantra.

Chapter 9

I am wondering these days where our memories and spirits go after we kick the bucket. There are even debates among Christians. Are there bits and pieces floating around the cosmos with indexes to keep them together like a computer program? Is it like a spirit ball floating around? Is it a simple dot, the size of a molecule, unseen by the living? Are we aware or asleep until God calls us? None of us really know. It would be a great question to ask God when we finally meet eye to eye, or spirit to spirit. Naturally, there will be some deep thinkers who will want to know who really shot President Kennedy, or if Elvis is still alive. There are deep thinkers among us.

What happened in Jonathan's case? Did I have an out of body experience, and our dots, or spirit balls accidentally collided? I am of the belief however that most everything happens for a reason. Simply curious as to what the reason was.

While some are still trying to explain the universe, I was on a friend's roof laying tiles as if I've done it for years. I've heard it said that some people wonder how they got anything done before they retired. Many retirees are as busy as ever. Much of it is my choice, but I am busy. No grass growing under my feet.

"Did you hear about the fire at the Woolworths?" I asked Timothy while pulling and placing the next tile to be nailed into place. Timothy was the son of my friend Tony, whose house we were sitting upon at that moment. It was June, so the weather was rather good for roofing.

"No, I didn't, Bob," Tim said, seemingly annoyed by the interruption. This young man wasn't much for small talk, especially since he was working on a sloping roof. Hard ground could be very unforgiving.

He glanced at my work, and back at his, a little frustrated. "How do you get done so fast? Weren't you an accountant Bob? You work like you were a professional roofer, but you're my dad's age. He wouldn't dare get on a roof. His preference would be to lay in his recliner and flip channels," he giggled as he was clicking his imaginary remote.

I shrugged then laughed and refocused on the roof. My abilities are a gift, I told myself.

After placing the next tile, I seemingly froze into place, staring at the sharp angular edges of the roof. It wasn't until Timothy hollered at me that I snapped out of it. I didn't blackout like before, but rather spaced out. "Are you okay Bob?" Timothy asked with concern in his voice.

"I'm fine Timothy," I responded after several seconds as I looked over at the young man knowing something happened. "Jonathan, was that you?" I whispered. Didn't really expect an answer. We didn't really communicate as such. He was more of an observer was my experience. Occasionally he did seem to push his presence when something really caught his attention. Jonathan wasn't completely docile.

The two of us finished the roof and the cleanup in plenty of time for dinner. Cleaning up the mess was extremely important to me. I wanted to make sure we could find our tools later, and didn't want a paw, foot, or lawn mower to find a roofing nail in the grass.

Said my goodbyes to my friend and his son, and got a hearty thank you. Paying a professional roofer can run into some bucks, so I was happy to do it.

When I arrived home, my wife had already ordered dinner. She had a long day and so had I. It was going to be sweet and sour chicken and egg rolls delivered to our front door. I was starving.

When she saw me walk in the door, bringing the wonderful odor of sweat and dirt, she shooed me directly into the bathroom with a broom of all things. I guess she was trying to sweep the dirt under the rug, I quipped to myself. "You go straight into the bathroom, strip your clothes off, and drop them straight into the laundry basket, and make sure you sort them."

"Yes, Dear," I responded, laughing all the way to the master bath, staying one step ahead of the deadly bristles of the broom pointed at my back like a sawed-off shotgun. "Would you like to join me, Honey?" I asked in all seriousness.

"Just get in the shower," Susan insisted, "and I'll bring you some fresh clothes. We'll save the shenanigans for another night. I've got to wait for the delivery, and if you need another reason, I've got a headache, shingles, or some phobia they have yet to discover. Now get on with it."

"Yes, Dear," I stated again with disappointment. Shenanigans she says. Very serious business I say.

After disrobing and carefully separating my dirty clothes, avoiding the wrath of the sheriff, I jumped into the shower. She put my clean clothes on the pink vanity and went out to wait for the dinner delivery.

Just as I finished my shower, I heard my wife thanking the delivery man, and no sooner had I finished toweling off, I hear my wife say the magic words. "Dinner is on the table, Honey."

I was still in a playful mood, so I left the bathroom in my birthday suit and went directly to the dining room. Standing at the table, with hands on my hips I said, "the food smells wonderful, Honey."

My wife looked at me and shook her head. She then quietly walked into the kitchen and pulled the broom on me again, and I assumed it was loaded. I was almost defenseless. "Honey, what are you going to do with that stick? You know I have my own stick," I stated with a large smile.

"Yea, but mine is bigger," she giggled.

"But not near as much fun you must admit."

My wife then chased me into the bedroom with her broom extended as I ran for my very life. We were both laughing hysterically at that point.

I won this small altercation, and we were forced to microwave our cold Chinese food later that evening. The Chinese food tasted like victory to me. The mighty horde struck again.

Night was quiet and cool as we sunk into our own worlds.

Chapter 10

The USS Tad was making its third trip down the Hickory Switch, a tiny stream about a mile from my home in tiny Pickensville, Alabama. I carved her myself, with a little help from my Uncle Terry. School is out for the summer, so besides spending days fishing in the stream or the Tombigbee River, I like floatin my boat in the stream, pretending I'm a deliverin goods down the river to Mobile, Alabama, or I'm Tom Sawyer in my little rowboat. One of my favorite books is, "The Adventures of Tom Sawyer".

Before he left, my uncle helped me carve the boat out of a chunk of tree that done broke off when it was struck by lightnin. I thought it was touched by God, so would make a great boat. Proud of my boat I was. Painted it black with my name written in white onto the bow of the boat. I printed, "TAD" on the boat as neatly as I could, so there were no mistakin who it done belong to.

My home be on the Tombigbee River, which flows into the Mobile River. Never been to a big city before. I can only dream about what it would be like. My uncle always said Pickensville be so small he could almost throw a rock from one end of town to the other. We are poor black folk and never do much traveling, except for my Uncle Terry.

My uncle has a white friend named Frank, which you don't see much. Whites and blacks stay mostly to themselves. Three years ago, Frank's grandpa bought a gold claim in California. The California gold rush I heard about in school has been over with for some time, but there is still gold to be found if you are lucky and patient I been told. My uncle and Frank went out to help on the claim and maybe make their own fortune. There must be something there, or my uncle wouldn't travel a million miles away. He'd been gone for over a year, but he's supposed to come back today. I really miss him. We do get letters maybe once a month. Momma read his last letter to us which said he did well and is bringing something home to us. Can't wait to see him and hear about his adventure. The only real adventures happen somewhere else or in books.

Uncle Terry Tad Franklin is my momma's younger brother. Momma, named Francine, said he always got into trouble when he was young. I guess he grew up, but not according to Momma. He brought money into the house to make ends meet Momma would say. She was mad as a hornet when he left. I remember the big fight they had that day. Momma said we would have to tighten our belts. I didn't even have a belt, just a piece of rope to hold my pants up. I was used to not having much. "We just gotta make do," Momma would always say.

Now it was just me, Momma, Grandma Lincoln, and my little sister Mary, or Missy as my grandma always called her. My daddy left us when I was three, and Mary had just been born. Don't remember him, and Momma doesn't talk about him much.

We live in a small house built by my great grandad around 1880, at the end of Freedom Street. The name be a joke to us black folk. I counted them bunches of times. There are only eight streets in our town. Our house is rundown, like most in our neighborhood. Our area is called Blackeyville by the whites. The wooden walls have gaps in em, open to the outside. It be needin a new roof, which Uncle Terry was supposed to take care of before he left. Now we just keep buckets under the leaks. We have a working toilet, and a scarred up clawfoot tub my uncle scavenged from somewhere. To take baths we heat up our water on the stove and dump it in. It does drain though. We cook on a wood stove, which is also our heat on cold nights, which thanks Jesus isn't very often in Alabama. Our house only has two bedrooms. My uncle, sister, and I slept in one room on three small beds with creaky, rusty springs. My Momma has the better bed that both her and grandma sleep in. Momma works as a maid in the next town over, so she needs the bed to get a proper sleep. I don't mind. It's all I ever knew. Momma always said, "We are rich compared to some, so be thankful." Momma always tried to appear happy, but sometime things are still hard.

Sometimes I sleep on the floor when it's hot. I have to share with the critters though. A rat crawled across my leg one night. Gave me the biggest scare. I jumped back on my bed as quick as lightning. Thought he bit me, but it was just a scratch.

There's a hidden room below the floorboards, which has cooler air that seeps through the cracks. It has a dirt floor with creek rock for walls.

Grandpa knew there would be problems between whites and blacks sometimes, and he thought it best to have a "hidey hole" as he called it. I even saw some men walking through town one time in white sheets. Momma said they were bad men called the Klux Clan, or something like that. I later found out it was the KKK. They don't like anyone who ain't white.

Except for Uncle Frank, our last name is Lincoln, but we aren't related to the 16th president, Abraham Lincoln, being he's white and all. My mom insisted on naming me Tad, like my uncle's middle name, to honor the greatest president to us black folk that ever lived. She chose Tad, because it was one of his children's names, and she didn't want to be pretentious by naming me Abraham.

I am only ten, but I love using big words I find in books. Pretentious means to try to impress or look flashy. I have my own dictionary and try to learn a few new words every day. I found it outside the library one day in the trash. When I looked that word up, I saw another word, ostentatious, but I'm afraid if I used that word I may get beat up. I've learned to speak plain like around white folk though, or risk being called an uppity nigger.

I hate that word, but hear it often, even sometimes from other black folk. One day I called a white man obtuse, which means stupid or thickheaded. That was a big mistake. "Well, you a little uppity nigger ain't ya", he hollered. His white face turned really red, and he chased me down the street and into the woods. It was a good thing I was fast and good at hiding, or the man may have killed me.

I hear that they still string up black folk or hang em till they is dead. They be lots of trees around here, and the looks some white folks give me makes me think they might just string me up if I don't know my place as they says it sometime. Grandma called it the strange fruit, and she cries every time she talks about it. She once said her cousin Willie became strange fruit hanging from a cypress tree for looking at a white girl. "Lincoln may have freed us, but the white man still treats us like nigger slaves," Grandma would say when she was mad.

One day my whole family was hot enough to spit, my grandma's saying, when I came home covered in white paint. "What the hell done happen to you Tad?" my uncle asked, smiling at first. I'm sure I was a sight.

"Some white boys down on Beaker Street wondered what I would look like as a white boy." Cried a lot that day I sure did. "I tried to run, but one of them grabbed me up, and held me down while the other done poured whitewash all over me. It's even in my ears Momma."

Momma knelt next to me and started cleaning me down with an old cloth. She cried the whole time. "I'm sorry my little man, you got to see such evil in the world."

I got an extra bath that week.

As I watched the USS Tad bounce off a rock, thinking back to that time, I was thinking how someday I would like to be a doctor, and put all this bad behind me. If I became a doctor, I would get more respect, I thought. I read every book I could get my hands on and did well in school. I borrow books from the library in the next town. I ain't allowed inside, cause I'm black and can't be trusted whitey says, but the nice lady sneaks one or two books out the back door to me every week or so. Not all white folk are the same. Sometimes books are even tossed in the trash. I saved them. I can even name all the presidents, all the way up until today's, President Herbert Hoover, born in 1874, and elected in 1929.

This fine day be June 18, 1930. Grandma says, "we in a great depression, and most white folk struggling to live like we are." I'm not sure what a depression is, except a lot more people are poor. We poor already, so I can't tell the difference.

It's nearing dinner time, so I better be getting home. I learned to tell time by how high the sun is in the sky. If the sun is touching the rock up yonder, I be late, and Momma don't cotton with me being late. After gathering up my boat and fishing pole, which is nothing more than a long stick, a string with a hook, and rock on one end, I needed to get the two fish I had tied to the bank. I always take the fish home to eat unless they're too small. "It be your contribution to the household," Momma would always say. It's good when I can help out.

As I reached down into the stream to pull out the fish, I saw my reflection, but it wasn't me. I screamed and fell backwards onto the bank, with the stringer in my hand, and the fish flopping around on the ground. I got up quick like and grabbed my things, but I had to get another peek. "Had to be imagining what I saw."

I slowly peeked over the edge of the bank, but it still wasn't me staring back, it was two of not me. I couldn't help it; I screamed again and ran home as fast as my little legs would take me. I looked around to make sure they weren't following me. Maybe it was a ghost, or a witch nearby casting her spells. Grandma would say there were still witches around or old voodoo doctors. All I knew was that I was scared near to death.

When I got home, I nearly fell through the front door. Still breathing hard, now leaning against the door, holding it closed, Grandma came running into the front room. "What in tarnation gotten into you boy!" Grandma looked me over, making sure I wasn't hurt, but she could tell something was wrong, for I was still breathing hard, and "my eyes were near to popping out", Grandma asked. "Somebody chasing you?"

"I don't think so Grandma but could be I suppose."

"Well, you home now, so tell me what's the matter."

I swallowed hard, for Grandma was probably gonna think I was tetched in the head. "When I looked into the water, to look at myself, somebody else were a starin back at me. It were actual two somebodies."

"Now who would that be?" she asked with amusement.

I knew she wouldn't believe me, but I learned I must always tell the truth. "Two white men," I whispered, as if someone may be listening.

"Two white men?" she laughed. "Er you tetched boy?" See, I knew she thought I be tetched.

"No ma'am, I don't think so. I looked twice, and there they were, smiling back at me. I didn't see me at all, just two white men. One had a beard and long black hair, and the other was old with grey hair."

"They weren't just standing behind you?"

"No ma'am. I was the only one there all afternoon."

Grandma pulled the door open and checked outside. Nobody there except my momma walking down the street coming home from work.

"You safe youngin," she told me, after closing the door. "Nobody out there except your mom. You just imagined it."

I must be tetched, as Grandma said. "Please don't tell Momma, it be bad enough you think I'm tetched."

Momma walked in, with Missy right behind her. She must have been playing out back or at a neighbor's house. Grandma kept my secret, and we never talked about the two white men again.

Chapter 11

I cleaned the fish I done caught, so grandma could add some good old fried fish to our meal. Tonight, we were having beans, cornbread, and some greens. Momma also says, "you catch em, you clean em."

Just in time for dinner, my uncle walked in. Grandma already set him a place, for she seemed to know these things.

I ran up to him and gave him a hug, and Missy grabbed him around the legs. Even Momma seemed happy to see him. After a few tense moments, she finally smiled and hugged him around the neck. "Good to have you home brother," Momma said, with a tear rolling down her face. She couldn't be mad at him forever.

"Wash your hands young man," Grandma said flatly, followed by a swat on his backside with a towel. I think she was glad to see him too, even though she's good at hiding it.

"You gained a little weight Terry," Grandma said. Terry was wearing a large shirt that was tight. "They must feed you well out in California."

Terry looked down at his body and smiled, for he knew something we didn't. It wasn't fat that was filling him out at all. He removed the large shirt. There was the darndest contraption underneath. It was a heavy cloth bag wrapped tightly around his entire upper body, with holes for his arms and head to fit through.

Uncle Terry hooked his thumbs under the bag, near his shoulders, and lifted it over his head with a bit of a grunt. "Hold that for me Tad while I put my shirt back on." He handed it to me with a smile. He smiled because he knew what was about to happen. Always joking, my uncle. I nearly dropped the danged thing, for it was heavy. I had to put it on the floor. My uncle laughed as he put on the shirt and took the bag back from me. It looked a little like some of the vests I saw in books. I guess it could be a vest, but a thick and heavy one.

"What kinda clothing is that Terry," Grandma asked, while running her hand across the rough material. "Did you make this? I'm sure either you, or some blind man made this horrible vest."

It is a vest, I happily thought to myself. I knew it. I was rather proud.

"I'll tell you after we eat," Terry said with a frown after trashing his handiwork. "I am starving. I see you caught some fish Tad," he commented, after seeing the two small filets sitting on a plate in the middle of the worn wooden table. "Can't wait to take a bite. It sure is good to be home."

He walked to the bedroom and placed it on his bed, which let out a squeaky groan, like a whiney kid. The bed didn't like holding the bag either. After he came back to the table, we sat down, said grace to our God for our blessings, and as a complete family again, enjoyed a hot meal.

We cleaned up the table and dishes rather quick I'd say. We were anxious to see what Uncle Terry had brought home.

The four of us were sitting around the table, anxious as one could be, when my uncle brought the heavy vest in, and dropped it on the table with a loud bang. Don't break the table, I thought. It's the only one we have.

"What you got in there Uncle Terry?" Missy asked all excited like.

"Keep it quiet you all. This must be kept a secret. There be people around these parts that can't be trusted and would stop at nothin to get ahold of this." He leaned over and ran his hands over the vest like it were a soft kitten.

"I ain't gonna say nothin," I promised.

He looked at Momma and Grandma, and they nodded their heads. This must be big for him to swear us to secrecy. Kinda like the time he brought some corn home, that I found out he done stole from a farm. Grandma done took a switch to his backside, like he was a little one. "That be a stealin young man," Grandma hollered, as she started swinging that ole switch. We kept it a secret and ate the evidence. We were poor and hungry, and momma said admitting thievery to white folk could be dangerous, so we never talked about it after that night.

We kept staring at the bag, waiting on Uncle Terry to tell us this new secret. "We er rich," Terry whispered, with the biggest, most excited type of smile on his face. He rubbed his hand across the vest again. "This here be filled with gold, and a small bag of silver dollars, straight from the Philadelphia mint. The last year they made em. Frankie thought it great to sell some of the gold and buy some brand-new silver dollars for keepin."

"That heavy bag is full of gold?" Momma asked.

"Yes, gold. Honest to God, we are rich as a king gold." Uncle Terry was giggling like a little kid but keeping it quiet.

"Why are you keepin the silver dollars?" I asked. "Aren't dollars for buying food, clothing, or a new roof," I added, pointing at our leaky ceiling.

Grandma nodded her head at that one and added, "we are tired of moving and emptying buckets around this place."

"Keep your voice down," Uncle Terry responded. "We have more than enough gold for everything we need, maybe even buying a new house somewheres else," he whispered after leaning closer to us.

"This is big. Real big," I added as quietly as I could say it. I wanted to scream and dance around, but I dare not. "Maybe I can get a real fishing pole and tackle. Oh, and a belt to keep my pants up. A real leather one."

My uncle looked at me and smiled at my simple wants. The others started throwing their own lists of wants around. It started getting a little loud, and my uncle had to keep hushing us. This was so exciting.

We were all laughing and thanking God for our good luck, when a loud banging started at our door. We all got quiet quick like.

"Who is it?" Uncle Terry hollered through the door, after making sure the bar lock was in place. He then shewed us back into our bedroom, after handing the heavy vest to my Momma.

Missy started to cry, for it startled her, but I put my hand over her mouth, and pulled her into the bedroom.

The banging grew louder, as my uncle asked again, and louder as well. "Who is it!" He asked again.

"Your old friend Billy, from out on Beaker Street," came as a loud response, but we could hear whispers too. There were more folk than one out there.

"You ain't no friend of mine Billy Peters!" Uncle Terry answered angrily. He was bad news. I even knew it. I heard he was part of the KKK I saw that one day. "Now you go back home Billy, my family is havin dinner."

"My buddies and I heard tell that you and Frankie brought back some goodies. I just wanted to see for myself."

"Frankie has a big mouth", Uncle Terry whispered. He quickly stuck his head inside the bedroom. "Hidey Hole he whispered quietly to Momma," and went back to the front door.

"I don't know what you be referring to Billie, Franky's always telling stories." He had to stall, giving Momma time to hide us and the gold.

Momma and Grandma had already moved the one corner bed and lifted a plank, revealing steps down to the dark hidden room under the house. Momma threw the vest filled with gold down into the dark first and started pushing Missy and I to the stairs. Missy started crying again, and I was almost ready to start myself. "You and your sister hide down there and don't make a sound. Not a sound you hear me."

"Come with us Momma, I is scared," I said as I started resisting her push.

We then heard the window break in Momma's bedroom. It startled all of us. We didn't have one in our room. I always wish we had, but now I am thankful we don't.

Momma started pushing harder. "We ain't got time for this young man. Get down there and take care of your sister. They can't know you two, or the gold are down there." We climbed down the stairs into the near blackness, with only slight slivers of light sneaking through the floorboards. Momma and Grandma closed the opening and put the bed back into place. We were met with spider webs hanging from the floorboards, dust floating in the slivers of light, and a musty smell like the Miller's cellar. I got a face full of the sticky webs before I started brushing them away with my hands as we walked further into the room. It was tall enough for us to walk into without hitting our heads. I had been down here many times, so I knew the layout, but you never knew what might be crawling around in the dark, waiting for two little kids like us.

As a man was starting to climb through the broken window, Grandma Lincoln was already out of the small bedroom, armed with an iron skillet from the kitchen. She swung the skillet with all her might at the intruder and knocked him back through the window. It was such an impact she knocked the man out.

Tad's mom and uncle were bracing the front door as a couple of the men were ramming their shoulders into the wooden door. They weren't sure how long it would hold. Grandma had already picked up the frying pan she dropped and was ready for round two.

Our eyes were quickly adjusting to the darkness as the sounds were growing louder above us. Missy continued to blubber. "Missy you have to keep quiet, or the bad men are going to find us." I was proud of my little sister, because she understood and was able to quiet herself down.

"Are they going to get us Tad?" Missy quietly asked me, while holding tight to my arm. We were close after daddy left. I sort of helped raise her. She was depending on me, and I wasn't going to fail her.

"I'm gonna take care of you little sis, no matter what. God will help us." I knew what I had to do in case the men discovered our hidey hole. When grandpa was building the hidey hole, he planned an exit, but never finished. He had to stop and finish the house. He thought he would get back to finishing that part, but never did. Grandma said, "he had only two feet to go, but his lazy butt never got to it, and then he got sick." I could do two feet, I was thinking.

We moved over to the wall underneath Momma's bedroom, shuffling our feet on the dirt floor. Feeling along the wall I found what I was looking for. Some large but loose stones covering the entrance to the tunnel. It was hard, but I moved the stones to the side, scraping my knuckles. They were bleeding, I was sure. Like I remembered, when Uncle Terry showed me once, there was a rock tunnel behind it. My grandpa dug the tunnel into the dirt, but placed strong rock on the sides and top to keep it from caving in. My uncle said he did such an excellent job it should be there long after we are all dead and buried. I ran my hands along the inside of the dark tunnel and could feel the neatly stacked rocks on the sides and heavy slate rock along the top, smooth and strong. I couldn't see more than a couple feet inside. Last time, with my uncle, we explored it with a small torch. It goes back about fifty feet but stops at the end where my grandpa left some rock he was going to use when he finished. After he finished the roof, my uncle had plans to finish the tunnel too, but never did. Now was a great time. "We are going to dig our way out, Sissy," I assured my sister.

The first thing I had to do was pull the rocks out of the tunnel, and using a sharp rock try to dig out the last two feet, just big enough for the two of us to squeeze through and hide in the nearby woods. My heart was beating hard.

We heard the door break, and there were shouts and screams coming from above us. They kept shouting, "where's the gold you uppity niggers?" I could also here some squeaking in the darkness from mice and rats no doubt. I ain't got time to worry about them, but they still give me the shivers.

"Get out of my house!" Momma screamed. We heard what sounded like a slap and someone hitting the floor. It sounded like a fight going on, and stuff being thrown around. I was so afraid for my family, but I had to protect my sister, so I concentrated on that. I may be only ten, but I'm doin my part.

Luckily, there weren't a lot of rocks at the end of the tunnel, but I had to wade through a lot of spider webs as I pulled the rocks back into the room. I'm sure some spiders done crawled into my ears as I shook my head like a mangy dog. I was so afraid of the men above us though, so I kept on working anyhow, trying to ignore the critters and the dark. After clearing the rocks, I started digging fast, pushing the dirt behind me, spreading it out so the tunnel didn't fill up behind me. I was copying what I saw a groundhog do once. Scratch out some dirt and push it out of the way with his back feet. Seemed to work well for me, as I heard another crash up above, and Missy softly crying at the other end of the tunnel. "It'll be okay sis, I'm almost there," I kept reminding her.

The men had managed to tie up Terry, leaving him on the floor in the front room savagely beaten. While two of the men were holding the women,

Billie proceeded in tearing the house apart. There wasn't much to the house, so it wouldn't take long.

I could feel the tunnel closing in on me. I wasn't afraid of the dark, but this was different. I kept digging, but I felt like I was starting to suffocate. I kept scooping the dirt out of the wall in front of me as fast as I could and pushing it back, trying to ignore the spiders that were probably digging their way into my brain. Was the dirt above me gonna hold, or was I gonna be crushed trying to save me and my sister? I had to come out a couple times to get some air.

Billie came back out to the front room furious because he couldn't find the gold. The man, turns out is the head of the local chapter of the KKK, started slapping the women around, screaming, "where is the gold! Give it up and all this can be over with."

They don't dare tell because their children's lives would then be in jeopardy. They knew their children were hearing all this.

"If you don't tell me where it is I will kill your brother right where he lies," Billie stated angrily as he pulled a long knife out of a sheath hanging from his belt. He then turned and kicked the stove over, spilling the burning contents across the wooden floor and against the kindling stacked in the corner. They were in shock as the flame quickly caught on and went up the wall to the worn ceiling. The women knew the children were just beneath them, so they had to do something before they all burned to death.

Grandma broke away from the one man, picked up one of the burning logs, and jammed it into Billy's side, searing his flesh and catching his shirt on fire. Before Billie realized he was on fire, he turned on the older lady and jammed the knife up under her rib cage. With blood gushing down her side, she quickly dropped to the floor.

Francine screamed and went to the woman on the floor. The second man had already released her and went to Billy's aid, slapping furiously at the fire growing on Billy's shirt, burning his own hand in the process. Blood was flowing out of the grandma, across the floor, and dripping through the cracks. Knowing her mother-in-law was dead, she screamed at the men, "You killed her!"

The third man had already had enough of this and ran out the door. The fire was quickly spreading and smoke getting thick. The fire was now moving across the ceiling above their heads. The fire climbing up Billy's shirt was already put out, but the damage was done, and he was in great pain and confused. Watching the fire, coughing from the smoke, Billy realized he killed a woman, even if it was a black woman.

"Tad, I smell smoke and hear Momma screaming that grandma's dead," Missy shouted. She couldn't hold back any longer and started crying and screaming herself. The racket above was so loud they couldn't hear little Missy, but I could. About that time, I broke through the other end of the tunnel. "Thank you, Jesus!" I shouted, while carving out a hole just large enough for them to squeeze through. I could smell the smoke now and heard Missy's desperate cries, but I knew the best way to save my sister was to finish the tunnel and get her out before they all burned. My heart hurt for Momma, Grandma, and Uncle Terry. Even though only ten years old, I wanted to rush upstairs and help, but protecting my young sister was first.

About this time, Terry had gained consciousness, and was struggling to free himself from the rope. His eyes got huge as he saw the fire licking across the ceiling just over his head, and Grandma Lincoln lying on the floor in a puddle of blood. Francine lunged at the men with her fury unchecked, pinning them against the wall. The second man punched her in the face, knocking her back to the floor. The home built by great grandpa about fifty years ago was now nearly engulfed in the unforgiving flame. The two remaining men ran out of the house as Terry was pulling at his ropes and scooting toward his sister. He knew the ceiling was going to come down any second, so he had to get free and pull his sister out of the inferno. Through the fog in his mind, he just remembered the children trapped underneath the burning house. "The babies!" he started screaming as he finally pulled loose from his bindings, and drug his unconscious sister out of the front door.

The neighbors were outside, starting to move buckets of water to try and slow the fire, but it was too late. "Where were you when the men broke into our house!" Terry screamed, as a neighbor took over. "The babies! The babies! Still in the house!", he then shouted as he started running back into the house, but two of the neighbors tackled him. The house was fully engulfed now. They may have been too late to save the house and the children, but they weren't going to allow Terry to dive into the fire.

I quickly made my way back into the room from the tunnel. "Gotta get my sister out of here," I cried as the smoke was getting thicker, and I could see the flames through the openings in the floor. The heat was becoming unbearable. I grabbed my sister and pushed her into the tunnel ahead of me. She was crying, but I didn't have time to cry. I didn't have time to comfort her. We had to crawl to freedom.

She easily squeezed through the opening I made, which made me so happy. I was worried the tunnel might collapse. I felt the fresh air fill my lungs as I was part of the way out. "The gold," I just remembered. It's still back in the room. Should I go back and get it? Probably not a good idea, but it was so important to Uncle Terry.

"Come on Tad," Missy cried, grabbing my hands, while trying to help me the rest of the way out.

"The gold," I said as I pulled my hands back from my sister's. "I have to go back and get the gold." The decision was made, no matter how stupid it may have been.

"No Tad! "Don't leave me here," she cried.

"I'll be right back," I hollered down the tunnel as I crawled backwards into the room, now filled with smoke. She continued to cry for me, but I felt this was important. I held my breath and grabbed the heavy bag, which was illuminated by the fire above. The heat was bad, and the fire was now coming through the floorboards.

"Tad! Tad!" Missy kept hollering down the tunnel.

I heard a loud cracking and the roar of the fire as I crawled into the tunnel and reached back for the bag. The floor suddenly collapsed, and some of the rocks with it, trapping my arm and my leg, sending a sharp pain through them. The pain I felt was bad, and I couldn't move no matter how hard I tried. I started crying, I couldn't help it. "Mommy!" I cried out into the dark.

I kept pulling, but it was no use. The air was thick and hot. I felt like I was inside our stove. Am I going to burn to death? I couldn't feel my foot anymore and I was getting tired. Sweat was pouring into my eyes, causing them to burn. "Jesus help me," I started crying out in my weakening voice.

"Tad, let me help you," I heard Missy call in the dark. I thought maybe it was Jesus speaking, but it was my sister. My brave little sister crawled all the way back in the dark. She started pulling on my arm, but I knew it wasn't going to help. I never loved my little sister more than I did at that moment. I was really tired now, so before I went to sleep, I whispered to my sister. "Missy, you got to leave the tunnel before it collapses and go get help. I'm trapped honey." I never called her that before.

"I don't want to leave you here by yourself, Tad," Missy cried even louder.

She started coughing, so I knew I had to convince her before she died in here with me. "You have to go and get help; besides, you're blocking the only air I've got."

"Okay Tad," she sobbed as she started backing away.

But before she moved out of reach, I grabbed her hand. "I love you Missy," I said to her calmly, probably for the last time, and then released her hand.

"I love you too Tad," she quietly cried as she quickly crawled back out of the tunnel to freedom.

Somehow, I knew I wasn't going to make it, but I wasn't scared anymore. I reconciled my apparent fate in my mind. Another big word, I thought to myself and giggled in the closing darkness. I didn't feel alone as I closed my eyes. "We've got you little man," was the last thing I remembered hearing as all went black.

Chapter 12

I bolted up in bed, with tears in my eyes, and sorrow in my heart for Tad and his younger sister. Anger then joined my other extreme feelings. It felt like hot lava was being poured into my brain. The Bob I was familiar with has a reserved personality, but this dream awakened things in myself I didn't quite know how to deal with. I picked up my water glass from the nightstand and hurled it against the back wall with everything I had, screaming with fury as the water and shards of glass splattered across our previously quiet bedroom. Sobs started bubbling up from deep within like an extremely troubled child.

Susan had already awakened in a panic at the sudden racket. At first, she stared wide-eyed at me, in near shock, hoping this was simply a nightmare of her own concoction.

This was nothing like watching a sad and violent movie, feeling sorrow and anger for the main characters then turning it off and pushing it away like it never happened. This movie had no happy ending. Tad had died knowing his entire family was probably killed off, except maybe his sister. Worry was added to my mix of emotions. What was going to happen to Missy? She would be all alone. "My brave little sister," echoed through my brain.

Tad's entire life and death was shoved into my brain in one short evening, unasked for and unwanted.

With tears still welling up in my eyes, I started rubbing my leg to bring feeling back into it. Just a few moments ago I knew my left leg was trapped and I had lost all feeling in it. I could still feel the heat around me, and the smell of smoke still lingered in my nostrils.

Susan was finally alert and realized it wasn't her dream, but mine that woke her. She placed her hand on my back lightly. "Honey? Honey? What's wrong?" she asked.

My mind was clear on what just happened. "Another dream, Susan. Actually, a nightmare." I responded in fact, wiping away my tears with one hand, and rubbing my left leg with the other.

She thought about it for a second, after absorbing the condition I appeared to be in. "You mean another dream like the first one?" she asked, certainly frightened. I'm certain she didn't want this any more than I did. We just wanted to retire peacefully, but it appeared God had other plans for us.

"I am so sorry for the broken glass, and the obvious scare I gave you," I said, still looking into the darkness in front of me. I was calming down by this time, and the feeling was back in my leg.

In our now quiet and dark bedroom, at 5:00 AM, according to our dimly lit radio alarm clock on my nightstand, I slowly recounted the basic history of Tad and his family, all the way up until the young man died trying to recover Uncle Terry's gold. While telling the tale, I occasionally looked over at my wife's slightly illuminated face, obviously engrossed by each word, like children around a flickering campfire listening to ghost stories. She would occasionally let out a small sigh or groan, representing her own distaste for some of what happened.

I then cursed after I reached the end of the story. I turned quickly in our bed and switched on my bedside lamp. I started looking and feeling around our bed first and then around the room.

"What are you looking for, Honey?" Susan asked, still deeply worried over what was happening to her best friend and lover.

"The gold, Honey. The gold." I was now wondering if what happened in my first dream happened this time as well.

I swung my feet around, preparing to drop my feet into my waiting slippers, which was a great idea considering the shattered glass. I didn't have to go that far. There on the floor, leaning against the side of our bed, was the hand stitched bag or vest that Tad had risked and lost his life for. "Holy shit, Susan," I exclaimed, while reaching over and dragging the heavy bag up to the top of our bed.

"That's it?" my wife questioned.

"That is exactly it. Just as I visualized."

"All ours?" Susan quickly asked, thinking the same thing I was.

"No. Not ours this time. Tad felt this belonged to his family if there are any left." I can feel his concern. "Could there be any descendants?" I wondered.

"There could be, Honey, Susan added. "He died for this gold, so it made sense he wants it to go to his family. I predict there's more research in your future," she said, putting a finger on each side of her head like a professional mind reader.

"Oh great," I kicked back. "You're a regular Kreskin, Honey," I said with a laugh. My mood needed lightening, while my mind was back in control.

After thinking over things for a few moments, something interesting occurred to me. "Now, changing the subject somewhat, there is one odd coincidence, or maybe not a coincidence at all," I continued. "Today is June 19, 2017, I think. Tad died on June 18, 1930, 87 years ago. The Insurgent went down on September 21, 1800. The records estimated it went down sometime in September. If I remember correctly, I had the first dream on the night of September 21, of last year. The dates seem to be in sync. I don't know what that means, but it is interesting don't you think?"

"I guess a little," Susan responded flatly. "I'm most interested though in what you plan to do next."

"I think the first thing I need to do is clean up my mess. Glass shards in mine or your feet doesn't sound like a great start to our day."

"I'll help," she quickly volunteered as the two of us slipped into our house shoes. I went for the broom, dustpan, and mop, as Susan proceeded to pick up any large pieces of glass, while checking more closely around and under the bed to verify no other goodies mysteriously appeared out of thin air. She is if nothing else, thorough.

When I came back with the necessary tools, she took a closer look at my night clothes, and got a good whiff. "Your clothes are filthy, Honey, and is that smoke I smell"?

"Well, what do you expect?" I responded matter-of-factly, as if she knew better than to ask such a question. "Just like last time, the bed and I will need to be stripped, and bathing is in order."

Chapter 13

After breakfast, at the dining room table, with paper, pen, laptop, and the bag of gold in front of me, I got down to business. My wife had already gone to work, for it was Monday. Being an accountant at heart I hate loose ends. I so wanted to tie this one up with a nice, neat bow, but I knew it was too strange to get that far. I was going to try my best. Faith will have to fill in the blanks. I did have some experience on brain stowaways.

Putting pen to paper, I commenced writing down everything I could remember about Tad, his family, hometown, and details of his death. I could feel Tad's presence during all of this, for he wanted to help. My sailor companion, though truly outspoken now, was taking a backseat. I thank God my squatters were mostly simple observers because I couldn't function with three chiefs taking up residence in my rapidly shrinking brain.

I was still working on my first book, and this was turning out to be a gift that keeps on giving. If gift be the correct term, but if God gave this to me, there is no other way to see it.

After the first three pages I sighed and took a moment to talk to Tad, or myself, depending on how one looks at it. "Tad, I am so sorry for what you had to go through, and not just that last day." I could feel the tears welling up in my eyes again. Being white middle class and growing up not seeing what black people had to endure, there was no way I could really understand, except through this young man's eyes. "Tad, I promise to do everything I can to find your family and get Uncle Terry's gift to them." There wasn't much else I could say. I wiped the tears from my eyes and picked up the pen. "You were one brave little man," I said as I began to scribble away again.

I stopped for lunch after I completed and stacked thirty pages of neatly printed notes. I located a paper clip at our desk, and clipped the pages together, so they stayed in order. I chose to grab something out, because I wanted to go to the store and pick up some sealable plastic containers.

When I got back, I cleared everything off the dining room table, and covered it with a plastic tablecloth I had seen recently in the pantry. I suppose it was for a future birthday party, but I had a more urgent need for it.

After placing the mystery bag in the middle of the table, I retrieved a small scissors, brush, and the three plastic quart containers I just purchased, and put them on one end of the table.

Like a brain surgeon, I began operating on the bag of mystery. I didn't want to damage it, so after lifting one corner of the bag, I carefully cut the stitches away from about two inches of the seam. After moving one of the containers further to the center of the table, I carefully lifted the bag, making certain the opening was hovering over one of the three plastic containers.

Sweating over the procedure, it took me about ten minutes to empty the contents into the three containers. I didn't fill them up because gold is heavy. I marveled at the glitter of nuggets and dust covering the bottoms of the containers. I removed thirty silver dollars from the mixture, which I was pleased they were carefully wrapped in a soft cloth. They were wrapped in such a way they wouldn't touch the gold or the other coins. After I was sure there was no clinging gold dust on the wrapping or coins, I rewrapped them gently and placed them into a fourth container I already had.

After the bag was as empty as I could get it, I carefully cut all the stitches, and opened the bag up fully, to make sure I didn't miss anything. After sealing the containers and moving them aside, using the brush, I brushed every square inch of the insides onto the plastic cloth. I then rolled up the cloth, and into one of the containers shook out any dust that accumulated there. It took me ten minutes of careful inspection before I was sure enough to toss the cloth.

During the process I was afraid to breathe, for fear of blowing any dust onto the floor. Naturally, I shined a flashlight on the floor to be safe. I can see why people caught gold fever.

I got out our digital scales and weighed each container. Together they weighed 25.2 pounds. I knew there were 16 ounces in a pound, but for some odd reason gold is weighed in troy ounces. Google still comes in handy. For gold there are 14.58 troy ounces per pound. I just about choked when I started adding it up. That comes to 367 troy ounces, and at the current price of about $1,260 per ounce, that comes to $462,420. I about gagged on my spit when I saw the final calculation. "Tad you did good, but it still wasn't worth your life."

While I had the computer on, I went ahead and looked up the approximate value of a 1928 silver dollar minted in Philadelphia. I then raced to grab and empty my gym bag. Depending on the quality, they could be over $1,000 each. I was now staring at about a half million dollars' worth of stuff on our table. "The bank," I quickly barked out, as I put all three containers, and the silver dollars in my bag, zipped it up and ran out the door. I want to get to my lock box before the bank closed. To my relief, I had ten minutes to spare.

After my wife arrived home, we rehashed our day, but she quickly zoned in on what I had to say.

"Did you have any luck locating any of Tad's family?" Susan asked.

Do you think I am a miracle worker, I wanted to ask her? "No, Honey, I haven't gotten that far. When I realized what I had, I started to imagine criminals around every corner. I started to wish I had owned a gun and couldn't wait to get inside the bank. My gym bag felt like it weighed a hundred pounds."

Chapter 14

I didn't sleep well that evening. A lot of questions were playing in my head like a scratchy phonograph. Am I done with mind invaders? The next splendid video game, I'm sure. When I go to sleep each night, am I to imagine I am holding a laser cannon so I can fend off future invasions. The thought made me laugh, for I remember playing the old video game "TI Invader". How am I going to find Tad's family? They were a dirt-poor black family in the 1930s, in a small southern town to boot. I will do my best, but what if I fail? Are three people bouncing around in my head going to be too much? Time will tell I suppose.

My first errand of day two was a trip back to the bank to retrieve one example of the silver dollar. I still had some coin holders I purchased last time. Next stop was going to be with my friend Jeremiah, at the coin shop. I called him before the trip to the bank. I only wanted to deal with him, because he was straight forward and honest. We have talked a few times, including discussions about plans for the other coins. The carving of Jonathan's father I decided to keep. It was sentimental. I should have thought of Jeremiah yesterday, before I stored all the coins away, but I was too rattled, and I don't think I had the time.

He was happy to see me, and the new object I brought into his high-class establishment. The shop wasn't any less amazing my second visit.

After shaking hands, I handed him the new prize of my collection. I was honest up front. "I have a total of thirty of these little buggers," I told him. "Same quality and markings. They appear as if they are uncirculated."

He already had the tools of his trade on the counter, for he remembered last time I was here, and I didn't disappoint, based on the smile on his face as he started his process.

After removing the silver dollar from the plastic container, he examined it under the magnifier, carefully handling it with his gloved hands. "Well Bob, what you have here is a 1928 P Peace Dollar, in mint condition. They are scarce, especially in this condition." He placed it back in the container and handed it back. "You are either an exceptionally good collector, or one lucky son of a bitch. My initial estimate, at retail, is it could bring between $1,000 to $1,500. Now in a bidding war it could be higher. Here's a but for you. If you come out with all thirty at once, which I recommend against, the prices will drop some I am certain." He jotted the information down on a piece of paper and handed it to me.

After shaking hands with Jeremiah, the purveyor of great news, I said, "I'll be back," in my best impression of the "Terminator". He wrinkled his forehead, trying to rack his brain to remember where he heard that before. I left his shop a happy man. "Frank and your uncle were smart in buying these coins," I assured Tad.

The impression I got while heading back across the river, was that the coins belonged to me, or was that just wishful thinking. We were friends after all, roommates, brain-mates, or whatever mate there could be under this strange relationship.

I called my wife at work, and met her for lunch, reporting to her our continuing good news. After having a juicy burger and sharing fries with Susan, I ran by the bank to drop off the coin and drove home to continue my research.

I was going to tackle the low hanging fruit first. The internet I could do from home, and the next step would have to be a field trip. I wasn't looking forward to that eventuality. Trying to ask questions without the appearance of strangeness or intrusion was going to be difficult.

I was becoming better at this sleuthing stuff. "Elementary my dear Watson," I said with a smile and laugh while scanning the internet. I don't know if Sherlock said it, but I heard it somewhere. Tad had read several of Doyle's writings or was it me. I get mixed up sometime.

I spent the next two hours writing and rewriting the post I was planning for Facebook and Twitter. I wasn't planning on staying on Twitter, for I felt there was enough trash to be discovered on just the one platform, but for just this endeavor I wanted to improve my chances.

My butt rose and fell on the cushioned dining room chair during those two hours. A jumping jack came to mind as I stood for the fourth or perhaps fifth time. I got up to get a drink, got up to grab a snack, got up to blow my nose, but mostly got up to pace, going through what I was going to post in my head. More or less detail, the entire family tree that Tad or I could remember, or simply the names of the five family members alive on June 18, 1930. The town name and address were a given.

My mind began to drift. I was losing focus. "Get on with it," I chastised myself. "You're wasting time." Naturally, as a completely sane person would, I started talking back to myself. "Dammit," I said. "I'm retired and this happened 87 years ago. What's your hurry?" While saying this I was pacing and expressing myself with hand gestures, like I was convincing someone sitting on the other side of the table. I finally stopped, took stock of myself, and laughed as I sat down and started typing. "Padded walls and stylish straight jackets here I come," I stated with humor in my voice. At least I am able to laugh at myself. A person should never take themselves too seriously. As far as the rest of the world is concerned, we are no bigger than a speck on a gnat's ass, parked on single grain of sand on a beach in Senselessville, somewhere on this minor planet, floating in the endless void that only God could comprehend. Get over oneself is a good saying I would think.

Laughing about my weird sense of humor, I had made my decision, and was near finished as my wife walked in.

"How is the working world, Honey?" I asked in a comical tone, while retyping a misspelled word. I don't mean to rub in the fact I am retired...or maybe I do, in a loving sort of way. Who am I kidding? I earned it, and am older than Susan, but...I respect this lady to death for continuing to work. She doesn't have to.

"As well as expected," she flatly said with a slight sigh. "What's for dinner?" she then asked.

I was so engrossed in the task in front of me, didn't even think about food, what with my in between pacing, snacks, and drinks. "I am so sorry, Honey. My mind was occupied on the post I had been preparing."

"Well, how is it going my writer?" She said with a wink and a bit of a sparkle in her beautiful eyes.

"There were a lot of stops and starts, but I think I am near done."

"Order pizza," she suggested, to my relief, for I didn't feel like cooking, even though I did okay for an accountant. My French spécialité, artistically carved beurre d'arachide et gelée, with a side of croustilles. I missed my calling. I can plate one hell of a good-looking serving of peanut butter and jelly sandwiches, with a side of chips. Lightly salted and crinkled is my culinary preference, and I cut the sandwich in the cutest little triangles. A masterpiece if I say so myself. Sounded more appetizing in French.

"I'm right on it," I said with a slight giggle, as I switched back to the internet and loaded the Papa John's website. One of my favorite sites. I ordered a large pepperoni pizza, cinnamon bites, and a cold two liter of Pepsi. Our standard fare. It would take 45 minutes.

After sending the order, I looked up, and Susan had already left the room. With a shrug, I went back to writing my post.

After only a couple minutes I heard my wife clearing her throat. My face was buried in my computer. I hoped my honey wasn't coming down with something, but when I looked up, I noticed she was coming down with something alright. She must have been overheated, for she was standing in the doorway with nothing on but a smile. She is pulling a me, I thought with a tinge of pride.

What happened next, one could not have predicted. I would have jumped up and nearly carried my wife to our bed under normal circumstances. But, oh no! That is not what happened. Thinking back, the scene could be considered very comical, but my wife didn't take it that way.

A flush of red ran across my face, like I had just drunk an entire bottle of hot sauce, of the ghost pepper variety. My hands then involuntarily raised to cover my eyes, as an out of place embarrassed giggle crossed my trembling lips.

The realization of what just happened hit us both at the same time. Tad was seeing my wife's naked body from an innocent boy's point of view. I don't know if the lack of warning set this situation up, or if Tad was still adjusting to being a silent partner. Silent being the preferred status at this point.

My wife was embarrassed and left the room. At the same time, I lowered my head, and couldn't help but snicker a little. "Tad, you sure know how to ruin a lovely moment," was all I said as I removed my hands and sighed. "I'm sorry, Honey," I hollered from the dining room, but I knew better than to expect a response or to follow her. She needed some time alone with her thoughts, and I guess so did I. "Jonathan, I don't know if you can help, but can you talk to the young man?" Treating this as if they were sitting next to each other, watching the world through my eyes, like relaxing in two recliners before a big screen TV. I could hear them now. "Pass the popcorn Tad," Jonathan may be requesting. "Be quiet, this is the good part," he then may have added. "Couldn't you have just changed the channel?" I inquired.

We ended up eating in separate rooms, and at first, I thought I may have to curl up on the couch with an extra pillow for companionship that evening. Just the four of us, Larry, Moe, Curly, and Stuffy. It took a while for my wife to get over it. We didn't have sex for two months, and at first, understandably, she preferred the lights off.

We laugh about it now. I suppose they did figure out how to change the channel during intimate times. My memory is full of cartoons growing up. Tune to those. He was only ten.

Before I slept that night, I posted the following on social media.

***

Tad Lincoln-Pickensville, Alabama

I am urgently searching for the surviving family of Tad Michael Lincoln. Born February 10, 1920; Died June 18, 1930, in the town of Pickensville, Alabama. Mother-Francine Mary Lincoln, maiden name Franklin; Uncle-Terry Tad Franklin; Sister-Mary Louise Lincoln.

***

I waited two months, reposting the request several times. Nothing, Nada, No Luck Senor. I wasn't really expecting a response. What kind of faith was that?

In the meantime, Jeremiah purchased the lesser valued coins I had at the originally agreed upon price, and then helped me sell the 1794 1c Liberty Cap through networking, for a small finder's fee of course. He may be my new friend, but he is a businessman. All together I was able to add another $200,000 to our liquid investments. "God is good."

We celebrated with more than just steak and potato that evening. Tad must have been watching cartoons.

Chapter 15

In early October 2018, my wife and I scheduled a one-week field trip to Alabama. Still hadn't received any feedback from my posts, so this was the next obvious step. No idea what we would find if anything. "Pickensville, Alabama, here we come!" I shouted as we pulled out of the driveway. We are taking our Town & Country van, completely fueled, oil changed, and fluids checked. Seven long hours ahead of us, if we don't stop much, which isn't going to happen. At our ages, rest stops, and bathrooms are our friends.

We expected as much, based upon my research, but seeing it up close put a bow in it. Pickensville was a blip of a town, population around 600. "Hell, Susan, we have more people on one of our streets than they do in the whole town," I commented as I drove through town. There were some beautiful historic buildings there, and nice newer homes as well. Nowhere near what I remembered. The surrounding parks and the Pickensville campground seemed to be the biggest attractions. There was the Tom Bevill visitor center and museum, which is a replica of a plantation mansion. That was interesting and beautiful.

We were exhausted by dinner time. We chose to save the more exhaustive drive through town till tomorrow. It had been a long day. In the visitor center we found a pamphlet for the Bama Bed & Breakfast in Tuscaloosa. It was 43 miles away, but we had already discussed a bed and breakfast before we left home. We wanted to try something different. We were in luck, they had one room available. We grabbed a bite at a McDonalds we spotted on the way in, and then checked in for the week. Might as well enjoy our stay. The beds were soft, and atmosphere fantastic.

Breakfast was great, and we met some new friends around the table. The Benefields from Arkansas, and Stubblefields from Tennessee.

The Benefields, Brad and Sarah, were stopping for a couple of days on their way to Florida. A roundabout way to get there, but to each their own. They were both retired, so they were free to go with the wind. Brad wanted to try a little local fishing, and even invited me along. I declined, even though it sounded like fun.

The Stubblefields, George and Amanda, were here on business, at least the wife was. She was helping to install software at one of the local manufacturing companies. George was tagging along, and he took Brad up on the fishing. He was excited doing something during the day while his wife worked.

Our hosts, a wonderfully hospitable black couple in their late forties, William, and Mary Frederickson. My mind instantly went to the public research university by the same name.

When the conversation came around to our end of the table, Susan looked at me. I was quick because I was prepared for questions of why we were here. Susan and I talked about it on the way down.

"Well," I began, hoping they wouldn't call me on the details and dig too deep, "before I retired, one of the items on my retirement wish list was writing." I looked around the table, during a dramatic pause as if this was a prepared speech, and in a way it was. "I'm nearly done with my first. The life and death of the first mate on the fated USS Insurgent in the year 1800." Another minor pause, while their eyes lit up with obvious interest. Might as well start plugging my books now. I would hate to sweat over my manuscripts, just to leave them unread.

I then continued with the reason for our visit to such an out of the way place. At least as much as I am willing to tell them. "We are here now however, to do some research for my next tale of tragedy." I hope I wasn't being too theatrical. "I had been looking for another historical tragedy that would be considered more...how do I say, personal, or under the radar. Something not catastrophic like the sinking of a ship with 300 souls on board." Another shameless plug, I thought as I grinned and looked around the table again, watching their faces. "I was looking for something more local and centered on a single family. You know what I mean," almost pleading with the audience. I'm kind of good at this, I thought as I continued. "Like when a horribly senseless death happens to a child, played out against a backdrop of racial hatred and greed, like an incident in the small town of Pickensville, 87 years ago."

I looked at their faces, especially that of William and Mary, our hosts. I had them all intrigued. My wife was hanging on my every word as well. How nice, I was thinking. "On June 18, 1930," I continued, "a young black boy died in a fire while saving his younger sister. Rumor had it that their home was invaded by KKK members, a fire was started, and the two children were trapped in the basement."

Several of the guests sighed, and pain for the young man could be seen on their faces. "Wow, that's horrible," George Stubblefield said. "I like the sounds of both your books." He pulled a small piece of paper out of his pocket, tore it in half, and then pulled out a shiny purple ink pen with Practical Software LLC stenciled into it. Must be his wife's company. "Can we exchange information?" he asked. Can you call me when either of them is published? Maybe I could get you to sign them, and I can brag how I knew you when."

I could feel my head start to swell. "Sure thing," I quickly responded, feeling a little proud and embarrassed. Before we left the table, we all exchanged information. "Perhaps I need to get business cards," I quietly told my wife.

"What's the name of the boy and his family?" the Frederickson's asked before we left the BNB.

"Sorry, I should have mentioned that, for we can use all the help we can get with our research." I was still winging it, but this is a good start.

"The boy's name was Tad Michael Lincoln, born February 10, 1920, mother was Francine Mary Lincoln, uncle was Terry Tad Franklin, and little sister Mary Louise Lincoln." Mary took notes.

"The names don't ring a bell, but we've only lived here ten years," Mr. Frederickson added. "We can check around, especially with some old timers, to see what we can turn up. We do know a couple people in Pickensville. We'll get back with you."

I thanked them for the help in advance. We shook hands before stepping off their porch, which we couldn't wait to come back to, and spend some quiet time in the south, rocking away in their antique wooden rockers.

After we got into the van, my wife turned to me and smiled. "You did great, Honey," she reassured me.

That meant more to me than praise from all others, but rather than simply thank her in humility, I responded, “why thank ya, my honey suckle,” in a poor version of a southern accent.

“Stop talking and drive,” she instructed me as she started laughing. She knows me better than myself. Praise is welcomed yet tuned down to a more manageable morsel to swallow.

After arriving back in the town, we first drove around the area looking for some spark of familiarity to rise to the surface. This was 87 years ago, however. Progress had nearly scrubbed the area clear of the past and replaced it with a clean façade. Memories faded or replaced by the new was all we seemed to find. The Freedom Street remained, but nothing was the same. Sadness bubbled from within.

Susan and I chose to walk the center of town to get a better feel for the place. Downtown, especially for someplace so small, I expected to be the heartbeat of the town. I was going to attempt to take its pulse. We walked the streets, went into local barbershops and stores looking for anyone with the look of wisdom, or old if you prefer, that may have some memory of the long past.

One elderly gentleman, selling papers on the corner by the courthouse, probably to supplement his meager fixed income, caught my attention. My wife had gone to the car to read and rest awhile. “My feet are killing me,” she said.

I first bought a paper because I wanted to read it later. Tucking the paper under my left arm, I offered the man my hand to hopefully start up a conversation.

He took my hand happily and gave me the biggest smile. I am guessing most people just grab the paper, toss him some money, and walk away. I’ve learned, especially after the past year, that most people enjoy the human touch, a smile, thank you, or at least a how do you do. There are a lot of lonely people in the world, and they aren’t wearing a sign, “please show me some love”. It should be assumed.

“My name is Bob Johnson,” I said, returning his smile as we were shaking hands. “Would you have some time for a few questions?” I asked, hoping against hope, for my feet were getting a little sore too.

"Sure thing, young man. My name is William Peters, Billy to my friends."

The name instantly sent a kind of shock through my psyche. I pulled back my hand and the smile left my face. I couldn't help it. I don't think it was me, but Tad. He heard that name the night of his death, and somehow, he knew he was the cause of everything. Had to be a coincidence, I tried to convince myself and Tad as well. The man was not that old. The Billy of Tad's nightmares would have to be over 100 years old.

I could see the confusion in the man's eyes at my reaction. I had to get a handle on this quick, or my conversation with this man would be over.

"I am sorry Billy. Your name threw me a little. I know of a Billy Peters that came up in my research of an incident that happened in this very town 87 years ago."

The man had already backed up and sat on his little seat, now with a serious look on his face. The smile had left him as well, but he didn't appear angry, just curious, I guess.

"I grew up in this town. My father before me, and his father as well." Billy sighed, and his shoulders sagged noticeably. "I'm a guessing you be referring to my grandfather." He had to get up and service two customers that passed by asking for the paper. He then sat back down and smiled at me again. A slight smile, but a smile, nevertheless. "Go ahead and ask your questions. I am familiar with the incident you probably be referring to."

I was sweating now. Extremely uncomfortable, and the man could tell. "It's okay, Bob. Ask your questions." The man had gotten up and put a hand on my shoulder to reassure me. I was a bit shocked, but strangely comforted. "I already knew that my grandfather was a son of a bitch back then. Thank the Lord," he exclaimed in all honesty, pointing to the sky, before sitting down, recognizing who is in control, "he changed his life around after that day, and lost his life a few years later, fighting against the KKK."

"I'm sorry," was all I could say.

"Don't be," he quickly responded. "He walks with the Lord now. I'm sure it be a tad bit cooler than it is here," he said with a little laugh as he wiped his brow with a cloth he pulled out of his pocket, before standing again to pass out three more papers. He stays busy.

After letting out a breath of relief that this wouldn't turn into an altercation, I continued. "Assuming you are referring to the fire that claimed the life of Tad Lincoln, and according to the papers his grandmother as well?"

He nodded his head but added, "his grandma didn't die in the fire, she was stabbed by Billy Sr. It were all covered up like, and my good ole grandpa started the fire too. "

"I suspected as much," I added, so we were on the same page.

"I don't know how you know all this, but please continue."

Several more people passed by, requesting papers, and some even shook the man's hand as well, and seem to be good friends, or at least loyal customers.

He appeared to be a very nice God-fearing man. Someone I could call friend.

"Sorry, he said," after the customers cleared out, and he took his seat again.

"I want to write about the life of Tad Lincoln, his horrible death, and the way things appeared to be back then."

"You be a writer then?" The man asked.

"Trying my best to tell things as they were, but most important is to try and locate his family."

"They left the area after that. Sold their small lot, burnt house and all, after burying their kin. Can't say as I blame em," he said while shaking his head. "You know, old Grandma Lincoln was a tough old gal, ashamed she had to die so horrible like. According to grandad, she was trying to fight them off with a frying pan. She even knocked one of the guys out cold." Even though a sad event, it gave him a slight pause to find a little humor in something so horrible.

"Do you know where they went?" I asked with a bit of hope.

"No idea, Bob. We tried to find them, but after the way they were treated, and the tragedy covered up the way it was, they vanished. This was a dark time in our history, but God has this young man," he added with a sure smile.

"God is good all the time," I added.

"After the fire, my grandpa hit rock bottom. He became a drunk. It was about six months later he wandered into church and went forward, giving his life to Christ. It changed him and our family."

"You mentioned he was shot?" I asked.

"Yes. He started to battle evil in this here town, starting with his own chapter of the KKK. He turned, and hoped he could turn some of them, which he did. Until one day, someone shot him on his own porch."

"Damn," I simply cursed.

"Starting with my grandpa's fight, the KKK was cleaned out of this town, and to my knowledge never came back."

"Again, I am sorry, but he made a difference in the end. You should be proud."

He nodded his head, and before I left to go back to my wife, we exchanged information to keep in touch. "One favor young man," he asked. "If you locate the family, please let me know. I would like to meet them and attempt to reconcile for my grandpa's sake."

I left with an intake of fresh air regarding my view of humanity. It is never too late. I rushed back to my wife. Boy did I have an exceptional story to tell her.

After my unexpected visit with the man, and catching my wife up, it was near 2 PM, so we decided to head to the local library.

We went directly to the small information desk of the Pickens County Cooperative Library in Carrollton, Alabama. Sitting behind the clean counter was an older woman of at least seventy years old. Gray hair pulled up in a bun, warm smile, and wrinkles of wisdom etched into her face. She wore a long flowery dress, nearly to her ankles, with plain black leather shoes. My impression of her apparel and demeanor, was that she was of the Pentecostal persuasion.

I asked her about searching through any local papers around the year 1930. I gave her a brief of what I was looking for to help her lead us down the correct path. She was extremely helpful. She showed us how to access them through one of their computers, and suggested we search the Pickens County Herald and West Albanian.

Rather than searching by topic I went straight to the date of June 19, 1930 – June 25, 1930. As I expected, on June 19, the day after the fire, there was a small story on page two about the fire on Freedom Street.

We both read it. Twice as a matter of fact. I printed it out and read it a third time. "They did it, Honey," I said with quiet anger. "Whitey and their fake news. Even back then, money and power hid the truth." The tiny article read.

***

TRAGEDY ON FREEDOM STREET

On the evening of June 18, a fire started at #5 Freedom Street, fully destroying the property, and taking the lives of two members of the household, Molly Lincoln, age 55, and Tad Lincoln, age 10. The fire started due to a malfunctioning wood stove. Arson not suspected.

***

Even I didn't know the entire truth, only what was held in a tiny ten-year old's mind and what Billy told me. The truth was buried deep, along with two innocent people. More than ever, I wanted to learn the entire truth of what happened that day and publish it for all to read. Even I wasn't naive enough to believe it would amount to a hill of beans. Kingdoms wouldn't fall, guilty go to prison, the earth shake on its axis, or justice served. In the end, only God's justice is what counts.

At this very moment, it mattered most to young Tad and me. I spent the next two hours scouring that paper and others available to me during the weeks following the fire. I found a couple more articles, but they were basically the same, whitewashed and tied together in a nice, neat bow.

While I was doing this, Susan was picking the brain of our friendly librarian. She directed my wife to a genealogy and history service offered by this specific library.

She was smiling when I walked up to join her. "How's it going, Honey?" Susan asked as I touched her shoulder.

"I didn't find anything different, and believe me, I tried." I pulled up a chair and sat beside her. "What about you? What are you working on?" I leaned in and tried to make out what was on the screen in front of her.

"The military records of the one and only Terry Tad Lincoln," she said matter-of-factly.

"What?" I answered in disbelief. My interest was sparked.

"It doesn't appear he ever had children."

"What of the others?" I interrupted.

"Woah," she quickly fired back. "Hold your horses, Mr. Impatient," she said rather annoyed as she turned her head and gave me that look. You know that look right? The shut up and listen look?

"Sorry, Honey," I responded, while lowering my head to the alpha. "I was a little excited." I snickered a little while almost waiting for her to offer her hand for me to lick in a subservient dog kind of action.

She glanced back at the screen and continued. "I am choosing to follow each connection to its finish. I don't plan on jumping all over the place like someone I know."

I almost thought of whimpering and leaning my head against her shoulder like a loving pet, but I didn't. I got some humor out of the picture.

"Like I was saying," Susan said in a slow and cadenced manner. "He never had children. He joined the Air Force in August of 1942, after the United States entered the war. He died in battle, while flying a P51 Mustang, on October 12, 1944. His group was known as the "Red Tails", or better even, "The Tuskegee Airmen".

My wife stopped talking and looked over at me. I was shocked and excited at the same time. "Are you kidding me?" I looked up at the ceiling with pride as if it was a revelation about my own family member. "Tad? Your Uncle Terry served and died a hero, as part of one of the most famous groups of World War II." I started crying. I couldn't help it.

I thought maybe we were getting a little loud as the librarian started toward us. I was wiping my eyes, fully prepared to apologize profusely or grovel if I must, to avoid getting the boot.

"Appears you are having luck in your search," she stated with no sign of annoyance, which I was tickled with.

"We absolutely are," my wife said, "and you have been a great help," she said with a small wave at the stack of printouts she had already pulled from the records.

I was tickled as well as I wiped my eyes once more.

"I'm so sorry to do this in the middle of your search," she said while pointing at the fine gold watch on her wrist. "I've got to close up for the day. I've got a dinner invite to my daughter's."

"I apologize ma'am," I said, noticing it was 6:10 according to the clock on the wall. I recalled when coming in the door that they closed at six. "It wouldn't have upset us if you stopped us before six. We were just engrossed in the materials. I was wondering why my stomach was singing "Yankee Doodle Dandy" for the last half hour." I took the kind lady's hand gently and thanked her for her kindness and assistance in this deepening project.

My wife had already gathered up all our papers and started pushing me out the door. We were walking toward the car as we observed the lady smiling and locking the double glass doors behind us.

We left with a smile on our faces. "We're making some progress," I said. "It appears our trip is paying off."

"They open at nine tomorrow," Susan responded. "Do you want to be there first thing, and do more digging?"

"Well yea!" I fist bumped my wife, and we headed toward our fine dining destination. The one with the yellow arches.

After returning to the BNB, we joined one of our hosts, Mary Frederickson, and the Stubblefields, George and Amanda, on the porch. The other couple had already left to continue their trip to the Sunshine State. Mary offered us coffee and tea, which we gladly accepted. I preferred tea. Never was much on coffee.

After playing a round-robin of talking about our day, like families used to do at the dinner table, I decided to check my post on Facebook and Twitter. While pulling my I-Phone out of my pocket, I felt a touch of sadness about the dying tradition of the entire family sitting down for the evening meal and discussion. People have gotten much too busy for their own good. It's a small wonder families are starting to grow apart.

First going to Facebook, I saw there were 25 notifications. No surprise there. Haven't cleared it for two days. My eye quickly caught one notification, however. Not unlike a beacon in the storm. "Rose Thompson commented on your post," is what it said. "Honey, I got a nibble," I said as I excitedly clicked on the link.

Chapter 16

It read, "Dear Mr. Johnson, my name is Rose Thompson. I stumbled across your post the other day. I have a great grandmother by the name of Mary Louise Carpenter, but her maiden name was Lincoln, and she was born in Pickensville, Alabama. Must be the same, and she had a brother that died young."

I stopped at that point and looked over at my wife, with a look of surprise on my face. I swallowed hard as a lump formed in my throat. "She's alive?" I asked the air around me, as if that possibility never occurred to me. I looked back at the response again, to continue.

"I can't imagine what the urgency could be. My mind went wild. I don't wish to say more on Facebook. If you feel safe in providing either your cell number or e-mail, please do so. I will be checking daily. Looking forward to talking to you."

I quickly responded with both, anxious to hear back from her. "Susan, Missy's great granddaughter responded to my post. I guess that would make her Tad's great grandniece." I smiled and raised my hand in praise, like I was in a revival.

Susan and the others were smiling too, happy for me, and my obvious glee over the crack in the case of Tad Michael Lincoln.

Before going to bed that evening, after showering, I updated my notes, and attempted to write some more on my first book. Didn't get very far. Susan finally told me to join her in bed when she noticed I was nodding. "I'm just deep in thought, Honey," was my excuse. It wouldn't do the book much justice if I chose to write in a half-conscious state. I shut everything down, placed the computer and notes in my computer bag, and put it on my nightstand. After leaning in to give my wife a kiss, I squeezed under the sheets after giving my wife a loving squeeze and was out in a matter of minutes. Susan was always jealous as to how fast I could go to sleep. "At a drop of a hat," she would often say.

We were up bright and early the next day, ready for more excitement. Joined the Stubblefields and a new couple, the Rubins, for breakfast. Mary made some fluffy waffles, along with the other mouth-watering delicacies. I couldn't give her enough praise for her cooking skills. "Can we pack you up and take you home with us?" I asked before stuffing another bite of waffle into my mouth. "Your cooking is fantastic. Naturally, if your husband doesn't mind, maybe he can loan you out for a few months." Everyone around the table agreed with me on her culinary skills.

"We'll be as big as a house," Susan stated with a grin.

"Very true, but we'll be a happy house," I said with a smile while rubbing my belly.

A great breakfast, mixed with great friends is always a fabulous way to start a day. The Stubblefields asked us to join them later in the evening for a rousing game of Canasta. Agreements were made and bets laid down before saying our goodbyes, and off we went toward our visit with our friendly librarian.

"God is good all the time," I nearly sang as I put the van in gear and pulled out of the parking spot under the flowering magnolia. If it weren't so hot in the Summer I wouldn't mind living in the south.

"And all the time God is good," Susan responded in her sweet soprano voice.

"Honey, why do cows wear bells?" I asked after a few minutes, while pulling into the library parking lot.

"I haven't a clue," Susan responded with a sigh, while grabbing their notebooks, knowingly humoring her husband.

"Because their horns don't work," I said with a smile. I looked over, and Susan was rolling her eyes instead of laughing. "What? I thought it was hilarious, and so did Tad. George told me that one." I chortled and smacked the steering wheel. "What a card."

"Don't quit your day job, Honey," my unfunny honey said to me as she opened her door.

I could be a poet and comedian, I thought. Who am I kidding?

While I had only one foot out of the door, my cell phone rang. I started digging into my pocket. "Damned thing is stuck," I fussed, while desperately positioning the phone to release itself. I think it has a mind of its own. I hated those cases that hooked to your belt, so I chose to stuff my phone in my pockets.

"Why don't you stand up," Susan recommended.

Once I stood up, the danged thing came right out. "Oh, wise one," I commented to my wife as I pressed the mini phone receiver on my screen.

"Your level of common sense amazes me some days," my wife mumbled.

"I heard that," I fired back, prior to answering the phone.

"Hello. Hello," I spoke loudly into the magic plastic box. I heard nothing at first. It took a few seconds. I was sure I missed the call.

"Hello," I then heard from the other end. Sounded like a young lady's voice. "Is this Robert Johnson?" the soft voice inquired.

"Yes, it is. Is this Rose?" I quickly asked, with a touch of excitement.

"Yes sir," she said with a sweet voice and great southern accent.

"My wife and I are so happy you called." For some reason, the voice on the other end made my heart race. I wasn't sure how this was going to go. My tone or sounding like a lunatic might scare the young lady off. Honesty and kindly tones, I reminded myself.

"To be honest, Mr. Johnson, I almost didn't call." There was a pause and a sigh on the other end. "The world can be a scary place sometimes Mr. Johnson and being overly trusting can lead to trouble."

This young lady is very intelligent. A little like young Tad. "Rose, I understand completely. One must be careful. It is true, there is a lot of darkness in this world, but I am finding more and more there is light as well," I said, while remembering my conversation with Billy. "I realized that just yesterday after meeting an old soul selling papers on a street corner."

There was quiet on the other end as she was absorbing what I said. I tend to ramble at times, but I always feel if I am being honest and kind, I won't get far off base.

"Rose, I want to assure you that this is extremely important to me and your family. This may even bring some closure, especially to Mary."

"My grandmother is 97 years old. She still has all her faculties but is feeble. I don't wish to cause her any harm." She paused, and I could hear the trepidation in her voice. "I am her caretaker, Bob. I am responsible for her well-being. Is this truly that important? I love my grandma dearly, and don't want her upset."

"I understand more than you know. Can my wife and I meet you somewhere to just talk, because there is at least a financial issue I must talk to your family about. I made a promise, and I am determined to keep it."

She was silent for several moments, but I knew she was still there. I could hear her breathing. "Where do you live by the way?" She finally asked.

"We live in Southern Indiana, but we are currently visiting Pickensville, Alabama, doing research. We just found out yesterday about your Great Uncle Terry's military history. You should be immensely proud of him."

"We are. Immensely proud. Some of our family, including Grandma, have been to a couple of the Tuskegee celebrations. Uncle Terry received several medals and even a Bronze Star, one of 14. She has them and cherishes each one." I could hear the pride in her voice.

"The more research I perform, the more I feel like part of your family." Intimately part of your family I wanted to say but dared not. "So, Rose, can we meet?"

"I think that would be fine. I'm starting to be intrigued," Rose said, putting my mind at ease. "Do you like Italian?" She then asked.

"My wife and I love Italian."

"Fantastic. Early dinner? Let's say 4:00? And it will be my treat."

My excitement was rising, but I didn't want her to pay our way. "You don't have to do that Rose. We would prefer to pay for yours."

"Won't hear of it. My family is from the south, so you don't want to hurt my feelings do ya?" Rose said with a bit of a humorous tone, and accentuated southern drawl.

I think I am really going to like this young lady. "The furthest thing from my mind. So where are we going to share this Italian fare?"

"The Via Emilia in Mobile, Alabama. I just love their eggplant dishes. It is over three hours south from Pickensville, which I hope you don't mind. I can have my neighbor come over for a brief time, until my husband gets home."

"That would be fine, Rose," watching my wife for any signals of disapproval. There were none. She was as excited as I was.

"Fabulous. I will make a reservation for three under my name in case you arrive early."

"Thank you so much Rose for agreeing to meet," I said as we both hung up.

My wife and I were both smiling as we locked the car and went into the library for a brief period of research. We realized leaving as early as 11:30 would be best. "Being late would be bad form," I said to Susan as I gave her butt a little pinch.

Chapter 17

Not much was accomplished at the library that cool morning, except two shushes from our friendly Pentecostal. Up front of our minds, or at least mine, was the upcoming dinner with Rose. We kept talking like teenagers, unconcerned with our surroundings, much to the chagrin of our fellow occupants of this building of knowledge.

After leaving the library, near 11:00 AM, I stopped at the Shell station down the street, filled up our jalopy, grabbed each of us a Dasani and a packet of cinnamon rolls to share, and got on the road.

We started on highway 14 and switched to Interstate 59 after a bit. I don't mind highways and backroads myself, but my honey prefers to just get where we're headed. It's interstates for her, but I prefer a little scenery and intimacy with the countryside. Reminds me of a Jason Aldean song.

"Just a bunch of square cornfields and wheat farms

Man, it all looks the same

Miles and miles of back roads and highways

Connecting little towns with funny names

Who'd want to live down there in the middle of nowhere?"

"They've never drove through Indiana

Met the man who plowed that earth

Planted that seed, busted his ass for you and me

Or caught a harvest moon in Kansas

They'd understand why God made

Those fly over states."

Since being struck in the brain by other points of view, I tend to think about details in this life God gave me a lot more.

The GPS took us straight to our destination with an hour to spare. What a marvel the GPS, a cell phone, an even larger marvel, it is connected to a piece of metal floating high above our heads, but sometimes I miss using a map, marking it up along the way and scribbling little notes next to some points of interest we may have stumbled upon. If done right, it could be a bit of family history, handed down like an heirloom, showing where your ancestors traveled through the rough countryside of this these here United States of America, home of the brave and the free.

With time to kill, we drove down to take a quick peak at the Gulf of Mexico. I was still writing about my friend Jonathan Boynes, so breathing in the salt air and watching the splashing waves was exhilarating.

We arrived at the Via Emilia ten minutes early, went to our table, and ordered some sweet southern tea. While waiting for our host, we perused the menu.

At exactly 4:00 PM, a lovely young lady approached our table. In her mid-twenties, tall and sleek like a gazelle, glowing golden-brown skin that would look fantastic on an artist's canvas. She almost glided through the room, like she wasn't even touching the ground. My initial thoughts were of a dancer, ballerina to be more specific. Long dark hair, pulled back into one large ponytail that was draped across her right shoulder. She approached our table with a warm smile and a confident but not arrogant air about herself. Tight faded blue jeans, red high heel pumps, and a white form fitting sleeveless top. She was a beauty.

I instantly stood, as a gentleman should. "Rose Thompson?" I inquired, concentrating on her eyes so I wouldn't appear crude by scanning her figure. I might be 63, but I wasn't dead yet.

"Yes," she simply responded while nodding her head slightly. I pulled the chair out for the young lady and sat back down next to Susan after Rose was seated. Susan was observing my body language with a bit of humor, or perhaps jealousy.

"Rose, this is Susan, my beautiful wife of nearly forty years now." I figured I had better throw that in there after nearly ogling the young lady. Like I said, 63 but not dead. We shook hands and settled in for a hopefully enjoyable meal.

"Rose, I have to say, you are a gorgeous young lady," Susan commented. It was a good thing I didn't say it, for it may have seemed a little creepy coming from me.

"Why thank you, Mrs. Johnson," she said in her warm southern accent. "That is so very nice of you."

"Susan please. Call me Susan."

"Please Rose, call me Bob as well," I added. This isn't a business meeting. Hope it is a dinner with a future friend.

She nodded. "Then Susan and Bob it is."

I turned to Susan and smiled, before I turned back to Rose. "Rose, can you tell me why cows wear bells?"

Susan sighed and rolled her eyes. "Oh, my goodness," Susan mumbled before turning back to Rose and probably passed her a secret girls only message. "Men are such babies."

Rose smiled big, with an almost imperceptible nod toward Susan, indicating that she received my wife's message loud and clear.

"I have no idea Bob, why do cows wear bells?"

"Because their horns don't work." I was just as pleased that I remembered the joke as I was hearing the young lady laugh pleasingly.

"You are such a hoot," my wife added with a little sarcasm.

We were all laughing as the waiter came back to our table. The ice was broke, now time to experience the recommended cuisine. We saw the prices and felt a little uncomfortable having someone else pay for our meal. This was not Frank's Steakhouse. We went with the flow. Didn't want to insult our host.

My wife and I ordered the Eggplant Emilia to share. Followed by the Banana's Foster. Rose ordered the Bolognese Lasagna and asked that half be put in a box ahead of time. She was planning to take it home to her husband, who turned out is a Urologist.

While biting down on a perfectly cooked piece of eggplant, I couldn't help but watch Rose, but not in a weird way. What was she thinking of us? Two white people from 600 miles away inquiring about her small family, originally from a speck on the map, Pickensville, Alabama. It would sound weird to me.

Halfway through the meal, fantastic food for sure, the time for small talk was over.

"Mr. Johnson...Sorry, Bob. I am very intrigued by what you have told me so far, which is little. So, what actually brings you northern folk to mingle with us southerners?" She was playing the southern bell part very well. I was imagining my wife and I on a veranda of an exceptionally fine plantation home as I only saw on TV until recently at the Tom Bevill visitor center.

The need to step softly was important. It was my hope to tell as much as possible to dear Missy Lincoln if we have a chance to meet. I also had to keep in mind the old man I met the previous day, selling papers on the corner.

I wiped out the last of the eggplant and took a sip of the extremely good, iced tea. "How much did your family tell you of that day of the fire?" I asked Rose, after wiping my mouth off with a fine linen napkin. Hell, for the price of the food I expected nothing less.

"It has been retold many times over the years," Rose said, while shifting in her chair and sitting up straighter. The real conversation is on. "My grandmother even detailed the event in her diary she started right after the death of her brother, and it was rewritten into her autobiography, with more detail as given her by her mother and uncle Terry, before he left for the war. They both felt she should know what really happened that day. Within the family it was no secret, but it was kept there." She stopped and took another sip of her tea.

"Autobiography? That is fantastic," I said with a little selfish excitement. "We should all write one of those for our generations to come. I know truly little of the lives of my grandparents."

Rose agreed. "My daddy is writing one now. I insisted." She is an extraordinarily strong woman I am realizing, a lot like Grandma Lincoln was in Tad's memories. "The day they got the news of Uncle Terry, they were devastated. We keep a small section of grandma's room as a sort of memorial to him, with a proud display of his medals and information on the Tuskegee Airmen. She dusts it down at least once a week. I said I would do it, but she won't hear of it."

"You have a very strong and determined family, Rose." A smile broke out on my face, and I could feel it within. "I can see it in you. You are a lot like Grandma Lincoln, Mary's grandmother." I could see her smiling, yet stern demeanor in my mind as if it were just yesterday.

"Now how could you know that?" Rose asked, with a wrinkle on her brow, interrupting her near perfect skin.

"I know a lot more than you could imagine. For example, did anyone tell you that Grandma Lincoln chased the men around with a frying pan, and even managed to knock one of them cold? She was a fighter to the end."

"That I didn't know," she responded first with a smile, and then followed with a look of confusion on her face. "Who are you really?"

Don't push it, I thought. I glanced over at my wife, seeing that she was deep into my words as well, showing trust in her eyes. Trust in her husband. I so love that woman.

I then turned back to Rose, who was waiting patiently for a reasonable answer to the particularly good question. Who am I really? "I am a simple retired accountant Rose, husband to the love of my life, father and grandfather of six, with a simple plan of growing old with my wife and working on my meager bucket list." I briefly glanced and smiled at my wife. "As I am finding out, our plans don't necessarily coincide with God's." I was smiling at Rose, thinking back to my first dream of Jonathan and the Insurgent and then Tad. I was sitting in front of his very niece. Great or Great-Great, something like that. The world is full of mystery. One just had to be open to it.

"I then became a collector of sorts," I continued, noticing that I still had a captured audience. "A collector of stories and dreams, and writer of the same," I added. "And still a mystery to me, a collector of some valuable objects tied to the same." The object and my promise were the spark for my voyage Jonathan might say. The evolving story and my writings were just wonderful, unexpected gifts.

"Are these objects related to the financial issue you mentioned over the phone?" Very observant Rose. Mind like a vise.

"Yes. As a matter of fact. I can only assume you are aware that there was a mystery bag of gold in the room with your Uncle Tad and Grandmother when the fire started, which I am certain was never recovered."

Rose's countenance changed a little, to one of anger, at the mention of the gold. Her mouth twisted a little and furrows creeped across her brow. "That damned gold was the source of all this crap to begin with. After the fire, white men converged on the house like a pack of wolves. They cared little about the bodies of Grandma or Uncle Tad. All they wanted was that damned gold," she nearly shouted, turning some heads of the other diners. Tears started rolling down the young lady's cheeks as she recounted the story. "Uncle Terry and Grandma Francine had to fight with the white vultures to keep them from simply tossing their bodies aside like so much trash," Rose started sobbing. My wife moved close to her and put her arm around her, which gave her some comfort. "They never did find the bag of gold. Good riddance I say."

Rose stopped and took another sip of tea with shaking hands. I felt she may drop the glass. Susan held her tight. I don't want to upset her, which apparently, I already had. Tears started to well up in my eyes which I wiped repeatedly with my napkin. Rose noticed my obvious pain as well, as we smiled at each other, followed by a nervous little giggle.

"Sorry you two," Rose apologized, while attempting to dry her own tears. My wife wasn't fairing much better. She has always been an emotional woman, which is one of many things I love about her. "This is a dark and obviously painful part of our family's history."

I simply nodded and wiped my eyes again.

"Bob, please assure me that this isn't all about some story you want to write. A book. An author's fame and fortune. I am learning to like you two. Please tell me it isn't all about that."

She looked at me square in the eyes, hoping not to be disappointed on top of everything else. "The story is not why I am here Rose. If one does develop, it will only be with your family's blessing. The reason I am here is a promise I made to Tad. The promise to return to your family what is rightfully yours."

A look of intrigue returned to Rose's face. "Tad died 87 years ago Bob," she simply stated.

"In my way of thinking, a promise to the living or dead is just as binding."

She nodded her understanding of my comment, which eliminated the need to explain further. "That thing that belongs to your family is the bag and all of its contents, which had recently come into my possession."

Her eyes got as big as saucers. "How is that possible, Bob?" she asked. "That place was scoured by the white devils. My uncle even looked as well. It was as if it melted back into the earth." She looked from me to Susan and apologized after her reference to the white devils. "I'm sorry you guys. I don't mean to imply." I could tell she was searching for the correct words. "I'm not a racist person, but I hate those people and what that damned gold did to all of us."

"Rose, the gold is just a thing. The evil released into this world is what showed up on the doorstep that day. According to the Good Book, "For all have sinned and fall short of the glory of God." All of us are children of God, Rose, loved by him."

"Bob, I understand. It's just so hard to forgive such horrors."

"We all struggle with forgiveness toward our enemies. Forgiveness is most important for our own well-being, not just to help the other person. Holding to hate will eat us up from the inside out." I think it's time to bring Billy into the discussion. "Let me tell you a remarkable story of repentance."

"I'm sure you know of Billy Peters."

"OH YES," Rose quickly chimed in, with an ugly frown on her face. She definitely knows of this man.

"This man was the head of the KKK back in the day. Your Uncle Terry hated this man's guts. Him and a couple of his buddies showed up to the house on June 18, 1930. They heard about their good fortune and wanted to see for themselves if the rumor was true. They wanted in the house, and they weren't taking no for an answer. Even according to his own grandson, this man was a son of a bitch and about as racist as they come. Rose, Billy was the one who started the fire and killed your Grandma Lincoln."

"I know all about it, Bob, get to your point." I could tell the talk was starting to wear on her. Time to wrap things up.

"This man, after that day, was never the same. He hit rock bottom. What he done ate the man up inside."

"So what," Rose stated angrily. "He deserved it."

"Perhaps," I responded. "A brief time later, Billy Peters, head of the KKK, full of hate and a murderer, gave his life to Christ."

Rose continued listening, but I felt as if she preferred, he would have been burned at the stake and suffered a horrible death.

"This new man of Christ was instrumental in starting a movement to chase the KKK out of the area. These were his own people no longer. He had a different calling. He tried desperately to locate your family, but your kin had vanished. He was willing to do anything he could to make things right. His search didn't last long however, and he wasn't there when the last remnants of this group were chased out of the area. He was shot down on his own porch, in front of his family."

"This is all news to me. You know an awful lot about this subject." She wiped her eyes once more.

"There is one more thing," I continued. "I met an old man the other day in Pickensville, selling papers on the street corner. God has great timing. I believe he puts us where we need to be. It turns out that this man is the great grandson of the very same Billy Peters. His name is Billy as well, and I have yet to meet a nicer man. He was honest and up front. I've got his information, and I think he would like to meet your family as well. My gut tells me that a meeting with the family will be good for all of us."

We finally sat back and relaxed. The waiter had already cleared the table and left the ticket, which Rose quickly snatched up. She reminded me of a lizard snapping its sticky tongue out to snatch the unsuspecting bug from the branch. She was almost as quick. "I suppose you really meant it when you said, your treat." I laughed, as I wiped my brow of sweat, because during the story telling I started to get a little warm.

"I didn't know what to expect when I came here," Rose spoke as she handed the waiter the ticket and her credit card. "This was a whole lot more than I expected. I'm almost exhausted."

She smiled and then laughed, which put Susan and me at ease. At least I didn't cause catastrophic damage.

After the waiter came back with her check, which she promptly filled out, signed, and laid on the table with his pen, she stood up and grabbed her purse. A tiny thing compared to my wife's. "Walk me to my car?" Rose requested. We followed the young lady to her nearly new red BMW 3 Series car.

"Nice car Rose," I complemented her. Red was one of my favorite colors. "We drive a grocery getter," I laughed, pointing to our older, dark blue, Town & Country.

"Oh, this old thing," she laughed. There wasn't a snobby bone in her body. I could tell. Now if she showed up in an Aston Martin or a Rolls, I would have questioned my judgement.

"I have your number, and you did say you were going to be in town for another four days, so I will contact you as soon as I can. I must discuss this with the family and hopefully set up a time and place to meet."

Instead of shaking hands we hugged. I opened the car door for her, and we watched her drive away.

"What a nice lady," Susan commented, "and nice looking too, don't you think?"

"Never noticed," I quickly responded with a smile on my face. I am so fast, I thought, as we walked to our grocery getter and drove back to the BNB for another relaxing night on the veranda.

By the time we had breakfast the following morning, Rose had already called and set the plans for the following day. We were invited to dinner at their home, and so was Billy Peters. We were excited, and our excitement bled over to our roommates and hosts of the BNB.

After breakfast, we drove into Pickensville, and I paid Billy a visit on his street corner. I felt better if I paid him a personal visit rather than call. The man was incredibly happy, but naturally nervous about the invite. He had someone in mind to watch the stand for him. We invited him to ride with us, which he quickly agreed.

We were much too excited to do anything as mundane as research, so we bought a little fishing tackle and went to one of Tad's favorite places to fish, the Hickory Switch. While fishing, I could visualize the mighty USS Tad floating down the stream in front of us, just as it had many years ago. I was feeling a little morose thinking about his past and the future he was never allowed to experience. His first love, walking his sister down the aisle, getting married, having children, and watching them grow. I knew he wanted to become a doctor. Would he had made it under the environment back then? The poor young man never had a chance to find out. A tear rolled down my cheek as I thought of tomorrow. "You get to see your sister again young Tad," I whispered quietly to myself as I got my first bite. "God is good all the time."

"And all the time God is good," Susan followed. She overheard my comment to Tad, but never butted in. She felt it was a private conversation between two good friends.

We caught three panfish and two redeye bass between the two of us. They were large enough, so we took them back to the BNB, and I cleaned and offered them to our hosts for their great hospitality. Something they don't normally do. They deep fried them and offered a bite to all the guests. I asked for the recipe before I turned in that night. I might even put the recipe in one or two of my books. We shall see.

We slept like the dead that night. Full of great food and delightful stories among friends.

Chapter 18

Around the breakfast table, the following morning, we shared more stories, and welcomed the new houseguests, Jack, and Jillian Toupin. No relation to the tumblers in the nursery rhyme, but I am sure they hear a lot of comments, if not a few raised eyebrows. This breakfast has been very lucrative as well. I've already promised two dozen signed copies of my future books. I may have to pay the Fredericksons a commission.

We hung out around the place till lunch, playing Canasta with the Stubblefields, splitting one game each.

After leaving, I picked up one of our new friends, Billy Peters, which seems a little odd still, saying we were friends with the grandson of Grandma's murderer. The three of us grabbed a light lunch before heading south to the port city of Mobile and our anticipated visit with Mary Lincoln.

Getting closer to our destination, I was getting extremely nervous while watching the traffic, so I was forced to do it, to the annoyance of my wife. Somedays you just do what you must to survive. "So, Billy, what do cars eat on their toast?" I asked.

The man had been silent the last several miles. He was feeling it too, so as chauffeur it was my job to cheer him up.

He thought about it for a moment, for it is almost as much fun busting up a joke as it is telling it, but he didn't know. "Okay my friend, what do cars eat on their toast?"

"Traffic Jam," I responded. I crack me up sometimes. Both of my passengers laughed, so my job was done as we turned on the Johnson's street, or actually it was a boulevard.

I quickly realized why they called it a boulevard. "Very fancy," I commented, looking at the upscale, well-manicured properties. "No cookie cutter homes here." Not mansions by any stretch, but posh was a word that came to mind. "Tad? Your family have done very well for themselves."

We arrived at our destination. I pulled into a sweeping circular cobblestone drive, leading to a Mediterranean style home, like what you may find in a Spanish Villa. Across the front of the home was antique Victorian style cast iron fencing. Upon closer inspection I knew my assumption was correct. The fencing was the real thing and not fake antique wrought iron like us mere mortals may use. Whomever did this was an expert. It may not match exactly with Mediterranean, but we are in America and mix and match is our mantra.

In front of the entry portico was a cast iron gate of identical style, held by two stucco columns, adorned with roman style sculptures of scantily clad women. If I thought my wife wouldn't be mad, I would pick up a statue just like it. It would look gaudy on our front porch, but I could build a shrine to it.

The exterior features a red terra cotta roof, and stucco walls with some stone features painted a tan or light butterscotch. Windows were encased within some fine metal work. The front entrance was an intricately carved wooden door surrounded with fine metal work and glass.

The yard contained well-groomed hedges, and some of what looked like baby palm trees, and in the back, towering over the house, were two fine specimens of moss included Southern Magnolia trees still partially in bloom. "I would love to see these trees in the Spring," I commented as we got out of the van and headed to the front door. There were several other nice cars here, so I wondered how many people were in the house.

I could see Billy was getting anxious. "I'm nervous," he said as he slowed his pace.

Will I need to hold this man's hand? I was wondering. "It will be fine, Billy," I assured him. We had already told him how sweet Rose was. "I will take the front," I said with a smile. "The first hit will be mine if they come at us with weapons."

That made him laugh, which made us all feel better.

Looking at their ornate doorbell, I was prepared to hear an old southern tune like "Oh Susannah" or "Dixieland". Before I had the chance to find out, which was a slight disappointment, Rose was already at the door with a warm welcome to their home.

Just inside the front door, was an entryway with Red Verona Marble on the floor and lofty ceilings, with reflections of sunlight dancing along the walls and floors. “This is some place you have Rose, and I haven’t gotten past the front door. Now if you say this old thing again, I’ll begin questioning your eyesight.”

She laughed before we hugged like old friends. She hugged my wife as well before she turned to the old man standing partially behind me. He was probably waiting for the knife to come out. I almost thought of playfully standing between them like a referee, but I thought that might appear a bit crass. “Rose, I would like to introduce you to Billy Peters, and Billy, this would be Rose Thompson.” She offered her hand, which he happily took softly into his.

“I am so very pleased to meet you, Mrs. Thompson.,” Billy said very pleasantly with a slight bow. I thought he was going to kiss her hand and call her Madame. How very French I thought. But this man is definitely not French.

“Please call me Rose,” she insisted.

I patted the man on the back as we followed Rose into the house.

She led us down the hall to a large family room. A sunroom, bright and welcoming, with retractable shades. Standing in the entry to the room was Rose’s husband, Paul the Urologist. Rose had married a white gentleman, which would have been taboo back in the 30s.

Rose then led us around the room full of people. Tad’s family. I felt a tide of pride and something else rising within me, while meeting each member of the family. A strong feeling of being overwhelmed was washing through my brain, like the wave that swamped the Insurgent. Brian, Rose’s brother, CPA in a national firm, shook my hand warmly, which I returned with a nervous smile. Tad’s good-looking great grandnephew, I thought, trying to keep the lineage straight in my brain. It was a way for me to stay focused, for I felt myself slipping. Frankie Carpenter, Rose’s father, head of surgery at the local hospital, George Carpenter, her grandfather, retired general practitioner.

Hold yourself together Bob. You are not in control, I reminded the ten-year-old jumping around inside my head. Can’t take him anywhere, I tried to humor myself. My old psychological nemesis is now joining the party. I could feel an anxiety attack coming over the hill, like an army being outflanked, was what was rising to greet me with its stifling embrace. The old familiar flush was climbing up one side of my body. My legs were weakening. Baby steps I had to remind myself. Move forward Bob, don't fall and embarrass yourself, I was almost screaming inside my head. Gloria Carpenter Robinson, her aunt, tenured professor at the Strayer University.

Professionals all, I thought, trying my best to keep it together. Sweat was starting to bead on my forehead. There's only one more person to meet. Dear Missy. I was still standing in front of Rose's sister, holding on to her hand with my now cold and shaking hand. My legs also joined in on the party and started to tremble. I was now looking through a fog, and sounds were jumbled within my ears. "Dad?" I heard Rose call out, or was it, Gloria? Gloria tightened her grip on my hand and placed her other hand under my elbow. I was in trouble. It was obvious to all around me. Several people helped me to a chair. "Bob, are you okay?" Susan asked, with obvious concern. I've had many anxiety attacks in the past, but nothing like this. This was a new level of fun. I am on anxiety medication, to keep this critter at bay. Hadn't had an attack in over three years.

A flock of doctors were honking around me. I knew what this was, and I suspect, so did my Susan. My head was back in the chair, eyes closed, breathing deeply, arms and legs flayed out, muscles totally relaxed. It was the best way to help it pass. My legs were shaking like I was just pulled out of an icy lake after a near drowning. "Thanks a lot Tad," I was mumbling to myself. The blame was placed squarely on his shoulders if he had any. By the time I neared the end of the meet and greet line, I almost felt like Tad was going to jump out of my chest. "Surprise," he would have shouted. But not so much like a stripper popping out of an oversized birthday cake, closer to the creature jumping out of John Hurt's stomach in the movie Alien. There would have been some fainting, and it would not have done me much good either. They would have been cleaning muck off the walls for weeks.

Someone was checking my pulse, and a cool cloth was placed on my forehead. Susan was holding my hand to reassure me. A regular three ring circus. "Call 911," someone hollered, which I promptly nixed by pulling my hand away and raising it to get attention. "Anxiety attack," I mumbled between my cleansing breaths. "It's an anxiety attack," I repeated a little louder and clearer this time. "I'll be okay," I tried to reassure them. My legs had stop shaking and my eyes were clearing, but I closed them again to continue my relaxation techniques. "I'll be fine and dandy, just give me a minute," I stated even clearer after a nice refreshing breath.

"Bob's probably right," Susan added. "He's had them before. Not this bad though. He's been on Paroxetine for years."

"Honey," I said quietly, while rolling my head to the side toward my rock, my Susan. "Honey," I now whispered quietly, forcing her to place her ear close to my mouth, for I didn't want anyone else to hear. "It's all Tad's fault," I whispered softly, like I was blaming my little sister. I giggled a little. "I thought I was going to need an exorcist. I felt like Tad was going to reach up and crawl right out of my mouth." My wife pulled back after hearing what I said. I was smiling big now. "Should I tell a joke now?" I added loud enough for all to hear. "Everyone is so serious," I said with a laugh. My symptoms had subsided. "I have no plans for an encore," I said after sitting straight in my chair, and thanking everyone for their concern.

"You gave us such a fright young man," came a quiet and sweet voice from the overstuffed armchair across from me. Sitting no more than six feet away was a feeble, yet regal woman. Dressed in a comfortable, yet sharp, having special guests over type of blue dress. She nearly glowed in my eyes. The matriarch of this beautiful family.

My Missy. It was in her eyes. I could see the young girl playing with her one doll, watching her older brother with pride when he first launched the USS Tad. Pride when he talked about being a doctor when he grew up. Pride from watching her big brother reading all those books, and love while he read many of them to her in the shade of a tree on a sizzling summer afternoon. Love for him selflessly taking on the role of man of the house while Uncle Terry was away. They would say prayers together at night before bed, and sometimes her big brother would allow her to squeeze into his tiny squeaky bed when she became "afeared of the dark," she would have said so many years ago. She may have been feeble, but her eyes were clear and sparkled with love for her big brother and family. This was the brave little girl he was forced to say goodbye to in the dark, 87 years ago.

Tears were flowing freely from my eyes as I looked fondly on this girl of six, if only in my mind. She was still six for Tad, time for him had only moved forward a little over a year. The mystery of God and his time was unfolding before me. I was just along for the ride.

The entire family was deathly silent, observing this exchange between myself, a stranger, and the love of this family, Mary Louise Lincoln Carpenter. She is what held this family together after Terry and her mom were gone, gently pushing for Tad's dreams to be realized in her own family. Tad's pride and love were bubbling up inside of me, showing as glistening tears upon my face.

"Missy," I merely choked out in a near sob as a fact and not a question.

"Young man, I haven't been called Missy since my momma done died." She looked at me, still with concern. "You sure you be okay?" She asked sweetly. "I done figured a white man done died on my floor. We ain't got a big enough carpet to sweep you under," she said with a straight face, and then followed by a belly laugh, familiar to Tad.

"I always loved that laugh," I commented, forgetting myself. Didn't want them to now think I may have suffered a stroke or something.

"Who are you, young man?" Missy asked. "And how you be knowing I used to be called Missy?"

"This is Mr. Robert Johnson, Grandma," Rose interjected. "You know, Bob? I told you about Bob a couple nights ago."

"I know perfectly well what you told me young lady," she stated sharply. "I love you dear," she quickly followed. "My body may be weak, but my mind is as sharp as a tack. No dust growing there," she said with a warm smile.

She turned back to me. "What I mean Bob, is who are you really?" She reached and took my right hand in her feeble and cold hands. A spark jumped between us. Very strange I thought at the time. "I just met you, but you seem very familiar to me somehow." She was too full of wisdom and vinegar to be shy. While holding my hand, she stared deep into my eyes as if staring down into my soul.

It made me a slight bit uncomfortable, but I went with it, not wanting to insult this fine lady. Didn't really know how to answer her question, so I went into story telling mode.

"Tad used to sit on the bank of the Hickory Switch," I started, "fishing for pan fish or redeye bass, hoping to catch something good for dinner. Sometimes he would float his hand carved boat, the famous USS Tad down the very same stream." She was smiling. Those were wonderful days back then, I was thinking.

"On many a day, Missy, you would sit next to him, holding the hand of your big brother you were so proud of. Tad was not only your big brother and protector, but he was also a great fisherman, shipbuilder, book reader and future doctor. Tad would dig books out of the library's trash and borrow some occasionally from the kind librarian. She would have to sneak them out the back, because black people weren't allowed in the library. When fishing, he would even let you hold his fishing pole sometimes. You caught your first fish sitting alongside young Tad. You would always get really excited, screech, and let loose one of your belly laughs when Tad caught a big one. You were his best buddy, Missy." I stopped for a moment, when I saw tears flowing down her cheeks and detected a little shaking of her feeble hands. My heart went out to both of them as I recounted their story, while wiping furiously at my own tears. I'm a grown man, I thought. Don't start blubbering. Oh, what the hell. Big boys cry too.

Rose handed both of us some tissue. You could hear a pin drop in that room. Except for Rose's kind gesture, nobody moved a muscle because they were hearing some of their family history like never before.

"Your brother was proud of that wooden boat that your Uncle Terry helped him carve. Tad even imagined his mighty vessel floating all the way to Mobile. Your momma was flipping mad that day Terry left on his yearlong adventure, but deep down I think Tad knew it was his way of really helping the family out, more than one nickel and dime at a time."

I had to stop for a moment, not only to wipe my eyes again, but to ask for a drink of water. My mouth was as dry as the Sahara. Rose quickly ran to the kitchen to grab both myself and her grandmother a glass of ice water. Both of us took more than a sip. Our hands were noticeably shaking. My wife took both of our glasses and set them aside. This is the first time I noticed the large stone fireplace to our side. I almost felt like the president giving his fireside chat. It was a glorious piece of work.

I continued. "I don't know if you remember, but your brother spent a little more time with you after Terry left. He needed to fill Terry's shoes as the man of the family. He collected and sold stuff to help with the finances and fished more often to help with the food. He was a fine young man and would have grown to a fine adult if he had gotten the chance." I couldn't help myself but to glance around to locate Billy Peters, who was but a shadow in the corner, surely feeling more and more out of place. If I could have, I would have put my arm around this man, to assure him that all will be fine.

"That day, Tad ran home in a hurry from his latest fishing expedition. He was scared out of his wits." I let out a small laugh at the recollection. "Your grandma knew something was wrong when he slammed the door and leaned against it to keep out whoever he knew had to be following him. He admitted it to her but told nobody else. Grandma agreed to keep it a secret. Tad didn't want people thinking he done went crazy. Instead of his reflection that day, he saw two white men staring back at him, but after looking around, there was no one there. He figured he had to be tetched in the head."

"I forgot that" Missy chimed in. "I never told Tad I done overheard him. I saw him run into the house, and I done snuck a listen through the walls. So many things happened that day. Terrible things."

"It wasn't all terrible," I tried to remind her. "Your Uncle came home that day, and you were all so happy to see him. Your grandma even called the man fat. But he wasn't fat, he was hiding a secret, wasn't he?"

"He sure was," she replied. Most of that day was literally burned into her memory. "That's when he done drug out that bag of gold. He had hid it under his shirt. It was really heavy too. Tad said so."

I turned to my wife. "Honey, can you do me a favor and bring in my briefcase?" She did as I asked and returned promptly. I set the briefcase on my lap, opened it, and pulled out the now empty vest that I had roughly stitched back together. I unfolded it slowly and laid it on the floor, looking about the same as it may have 87 years ago, except it was now empty.

"Rose told me you had this thing, but that was hard to believe, but here it is," Missy exclaimed. "It was so long ago, and my memory ain't the best, but this thing reminds me of it. And the contents?"

"When I saw what was in here," pointing to the mystery object on the marble floor, "I high tailed it to our bank and locked it all up. It is very substantial."

"How substantial son?" George, Rose's grandpa asked. They were all huddling close now that I laid out the vest before them.

"Well. It was mostly gold, with some old silver dollars. Thirty to be exact." I know Tad wanted me to have the coins, but I still felt this was their inheritance and not mine. This was their decision to make. "I took the coins to an appraiser and weighed the gold." I paused. "I feel it is close to half a million."

A gasp rolled through the captured crowd. I could sense the wheels turning.

"Can we get back to the mystery package later?" I requested. "I've got much more to tell our dear Missy." I turned from the crowd and focused back on her. They nodded in agreement and went silent once more.

"That horrible day, when Billy Peters and his partners arrived at your door, you, your brother, and the gold were hidden under the house in the "Hidey Hole" your grandpa built."

"The Hidey Hole," Missy mumbled. "I remember Momma calling it that."

"As your grandma said several times. "Your lazy ass grandpa never finished it. Ain't much count without an escape." He left the escape tunnel finished except for the last two feet. Your uncle never finished it either. It was up to your brother to protect you by digging his way out."

"Tad was told to take care of his little sister, and he was determined to do just that. The two of you had to brave the spiders and rats in that damp and dark place. After the fights and screaming started, followed by the fire, you were one scared little girl."

I could see the recollection of that day coming back to her, as tears continued to fall. I hope this isn't too much for her, but Tad insisted she was a brave person and he had to get this out. "Missy, do we need to stop for a little?" I asked for myself. The last thing I wanted to do was overwhelm her.

"No. No," she insisted, while shaking her head. "I loved Tad so much," she said, while wiping another tear away.

"Bob, you really need to stop," George now insisted. "You're upsetting Mom. Besides, how do you know so much? It's almost as if you were there."

"Shut your trap, George," she quickly jumped on her son, nearly coming out of the chair. The feeble form can be a little deceptive, I thought. "I want to hear the man out. Don't make me send you out for a willow switch. I ain't so old I can't still whip your ass."

Several snickers went around the room. "Go Grandma," one of the younger men from the back cheered. I know who wears the pants in this bunch. She is one tough lady. Reminds me a little of my own grandma, who lived to be 99. I could feel Tad cheering on his little sister. I was surprised someone hadn't questioned me already. By the look in Missy's eyes, I am certain she felt her brother's presence, which is why she had let me ramble on.

George stepped back and simply shrugged, humor appeared on his face after realizing his momma was fine.

"Tad kept you as calm as he could, not wanting the bad men to know the two of you were right below their feet. After the fire started, Tad had nearly cleared the last two feet of this dark escape tunnel. Dirt was falling in the young man's hair, as the fear of a cave in was worrying him, and he felt like spiders were crawling all over him, but he was determined to save his little sister, his Missy, his best friend."

"I was his best friend," Missy agreed. She was nearly sobbing, and I wasn't far behind her. Like Tad, I was determined to get through this. You could cut the tension in the room with a knife. I could hear sniffling all around me. The entire family was feeling it.

"Yes, Honey, you were and still are his best friend." She sucked in a sharp breath and giggled at that realization, even with her face wet with tears. Somehow, I think she knows her Tad was with me.

"Smoke was starting to seep into your hiding place, and the heat was becoming unbearable when Tad broke through and pushed you to safety through that dark little tunnel starting to fill with smoke. Young Tad had kept his promise to protect his little sister."

"He now felt he had to go back for the gold. That could be your family's future. A way out of this life. It was important to his Uncle Terry, so it became important to him. He would only take a moment after all, he thought. He made it back into the tunnel, but as he reached for the bag, the house collapsed, trapping him and the gold on the other side. He couldn't move."

"You begged your brother not to go back in. When you knew he was in trouble, brave little Missy went back into the dark and smokey tunnel to save her big brother that day. He knew his fate, even at ten years old. Tad was upset with you, but very proud. He pleaded for you to leave, for you were in grave danger. "Missy," he said, "you got to leave the tunnel before it collapses and go get help. I'll need a grownup to get me out of here. I'm trapped honey, he said."

"I begged him not to leave me. Don't go back I told him," Missy cried. "My stubborn big brother."

She seemed shocked at the words coming out of my mouth, but she could feel his presence as well. I grabbed both of her hands with mine. "Before you finally left the tunnel that day, Missy, you shared something incredibly special with your brother. Jesus was there with the two of you, and his love surrounded you as you professed your deep love for each other and said your final goodbyes."

Both peace and exhaustion washed over me. I moved over to this regal lady's chair, knelt, and we embraced and simply cried. Many could feel Uncle Tad's presence, as a shiver went through the room. There wasn't a dry eye in the room.

Chapter 19

After several minutes of completing my taxing story, Susan tapped me on the shoulder. She hated to interrupt. "Bob, Billy's gone." I looked over where he was sitting earlier, and sure enough he was not there. "Oh Billy," I said sadly. I quickly stood and asked if anyone saw Billy leave. They had not. "I am so stupid." I said loudly. I was so engrossed with Missy, her family, and my anxiety attack, I never thought of how these stories would have affected him. The grandson of the man who started it. "I am so very stupid," I repeated. I could have done this so differently. I quickly faced the group and tried to explain. "Billy, my friend, came here to make peace with your family, and tell you what happened with his grandpa. He was so desperate to reconcile things for his ancestor, which he would have done himself if he could have." I lowered my head. "And what did I do? I subjected the poor man to details of that very day, and all emotions that went with it. I am so stupid," I said a third time, while looking up at the ceiling. "I've got to find him," I decided.

"Can we help?" several of them asked.

I thought for a second on their offer. There was a tap on my shoulder, which I ignored. Had to finish my thought. Didn't want to mess this up too. "Only a few of you," I finally responded. "The picture in my mind of the whole group running out into the street, may just send him a mixed signal."

I turned around, after the second tap on my shoulder. My patient, lovely wife, was standing there with her arms folded in front of her. There are times when she was needed to keep me in line. "Sorry, Honey," I said, fidgeting, anxious to get the search started. This was important. Her smile and facial expression were familiar to me. It was her comedic "You dummy. Did you leave your common sense at home?" look.

"Oh, wise one," she started with. Oh great, I thought. That locks it. I've done something stupid or forgot something important. That's what 40 years together does for you. "Honey, you could have simply called the man's cell, before you gathered the posse," she commented with a sort of sick smile. My face started to flush, and I'm sure I shrunk two inches in front of our new friends. "Orrrrr," she rolled out on her tongue for effect, while turning her head, "you could have simply looked through the back window."

Out back of their fancy Mediterranean style home there was a swimming pool. Why would I be surprised? Bobbing up and down in said pool, was a gray-haired old man, shooting water basketball with some young black youth. "Hey guys!" I shouted with some fake excitement. "My wife found Billy," I stated with a nervous smile.

"White people," Frankie Carpenter interjected, followed by a belly laugh not unlike Grandma's.

Rose, our hostess, led red faced me and the rest of the group out to the pool. Three young men and one old wrinkled white man were playing two on two in the pool. Billy was sporting the paper man's version of the farmer's tan. Rose introduced Susan and me to two more grandchildren and one neighborhood friend splashing around in the inviting pool. They simply waved, and continued with the game, passing the ball to the old man. "Everyone," Rose added, glancing back at the posse, and then gesturing to the gray head bobbing in the water and laughing his fool head off. "This is the infamous missing Billy Peters."

I glanced at Rose. "Okay Rose, just rub more salt into my wound." She smiled hugely after her one liner.

George then chimed in. He must fancy himself a budding comedian too. "Paul," George hollered with his fake straight face pasted on. "After they're done swimming, make sure you add two caps full of whitey remover to the water. I'm sure some rubbed off in the pool."

"George, you do know I'm white," Paul responded with a grin.

"Me too," hollered the neighborhood friend, not wanting to be overlooked, as if he could be.

"You guys have been cured though. Your whiteness doesn't rub off anymore." George added with all the seriousness he could muster and then busted out laughing. The rest of the group joined in.

"Hardy, Har, Har," responded Paul.

“That’s a good one,” added Billy, after passing the ball to his partner, who then made the winning shot.

“I hope you fine folks don’t mind”, Billy said. “These young men challenged me, and I had no choice but to defend the honor of old people everywhere. Lurch here loaned me some trunks,” pointing to the extremely tall, square jawed youth, who was Billy’s partner.

“The name is Logan, Mr. Stonehenge,” he added with a friendly laugh. “You’re pretty good for a mature gentleman.”

All of them got out of the pool and were drying off, when Billy noticed Mary standing in the doorway, enjoying the camaraderie.

I went to Billy to apologize for my shortsightedness. “Billy, I am so sorry to have put you through what I did.” He put his hand up to stop me right where I was.

“It’s okay Bob. You scared the crap out of me when I thought you were going down for the count though. After it started getting a little intense for me, I went outside for some air, where I met these fine young gentlemen. Besides, what was being said inside that house was none of my business. I’m a big boy and know when to skip.”

I was happy all went well. I grabbed the man’s hand and shook it vigorously, then hugged him around the shoulders. I got a little wet but didn’t care.

“If you’ll excuse me Bob, I would like to change.” He quickly ducked into the nice pool house/changing rooms. He appeared to be on a mission.

We all moved outside, around the large in-ground pool, finding our own places in the pool chairs scattered about. There were several tables with large umbrellas, providing luxurious shade, surrounded by standard outdoor chairs. They spared no expense here either. All the chairs and loungers were cushioned. Some with tiny built-in pillows, and a few had their own built in foldable canopies.

Missy found her a place beside my wife, around one of the shaded tables. Rose’s Aunt Gloria came out of the house with a tray full of glasses of lemonade and tea. I was parched again, so that was a welcomed sight. Rose was seeing to Missy's comfort and made sure there were places available at the same table for the guests.

The atmosphere was great, complete with laughter, as if the earlier intensities had merely floated away into the stratosphere. Life was too short as it was.

Billy came scuffling out of the pool house, still tucking his shirt, looking incredibly nervous. He came up to me and whispered, "it's time I speak up, before I lose my nerve."

Do I look like the master of ceremonies? I questioned myself. I hadn't quite made it to our table and a drink of lemonade.

After grabbing my glass of lemonade, which was actual glass, I stood tall, facing the group, focusing on Missy, and tapped the glass with my fingernails. "May I have your attention please," I announced, like I was ready to give a best man speech. I put my arm around Billy. "My wife, Billy and I would like to thank all of you for the warm welcome you gave us. None of us knew what to expect. I think all three of us were as nervous as a vampire in an Italian restaurant." I heard a few giggles. Some got it. My wife instantly put her head on the table. "I can see my wife is a fan," I added. "It got intense in the house, and I'm sure Billy wasn't sure if he was going to be accepted or not. Billy is a genuinely nice man, and I was so happy when you met him with open arms."

"When I met Rose the other day, she turned out to be the sweetest thing, so if she was an example of what the rest of the family was like, we were good. Frankie, you should be proud of your daughter."

"I am very," he responded with a huge smile.

"I have met many new friends today, and I am hoping we can still keep in touch, and I am praying my book will do this family justice. If I fail in that endeavor, I will willingly come back to Mobile to pick out my own willow switch, so Missy can beat my ass."

The laughter was instantaneous. I love it. Felt like home to me with friends and family.

"Billy, or Mr. Stonehenge, would like to say a few words also, if he may." I turned to the man and grabbed his shoulders. "It'll be okay," I whispered.

"As Mr. Johnson said, I didn't know what to expect either," Billy stated after a deep breath. "Before my grandpa was killed, he gave his life to the Lord." Several in the group raised their hands and said their hallelujahs. Billy smiled. "Like many of us sinners, he had lost his way, but he found it after that horrible day. His new path affected all his family and the town. My grandpa was instrumental in helping to remove the scourge from the area that was the KKK. The one thing he wanted to do more than anything else however, was to make recompense with your family for his evil deed." The man wiped his forehead and took a drink before continuing. "Before his death he was unable to locate your family. My father took up the torch without any luck. It was as if you had vanished, and many years passed."

"My father died of cancer about ten year ago. It was now up to me to keep the hope alive. It had been 87 years now, and I had given up. All I could do was pray your family was well." Billy looked around at the lovely family, and how well they appeared to have done. It made him smile. His prayers were answered, he thought.

"I was feeling a little low one day, thinking about my father and his father before him, knowing there was unfinished business. God sure does work in mysterious ways. Like an angel out of the blue, this man beside me showed up, bought a paper, and started asking about your very family. I was shocked but didn't want to get my hopes up." He breathed deeply.

"And here I am today, standing in front of you fine people, asking for your forgiveness." You could see tears starting to well up in this tough man's eyes.

I was instantly startled when a chair scooted away from the table, Missy shot to her feet, and threw her hands in the air like she was praising the Lord, and giving us a great big halleluiah, but I don't think that was her intention. "Oh, hell no!" she shouted. This woman's got energy when she needs it. Everyone turned to her. "Oh, to the double hell no!" She shouted again. I thought I was listening to Madea on one of Tyler Perry's movies. She must be a fan.

She toddled around the table toward the two of us. I admit, I was getting a little concerned. "I ain't got no more tears left you two," she said, after she stood in front of us. "No more sad stories please. If y'all need a reason to cry, I'll have you cut a bunch of switches and beat all your asses," she said, while waving her hands across the entire group. She was an equal opportunity ass whipper. A roar erupted, and the same man again said, "Go Grandma!"

The matriarch of this family, large and in charge Mary Louise Lincoln Carpenter grabbed Billy up in the warmest hug. "I forgive your grandpa Billy. I forgave him years ago. That was none of your fault, and I'm sure he would be proud of the man you became," she said loud enough for all to hear. Like in an old fashion revival, halleluiah and amen, the entire family came forward and surrounded us with a heartfelt group hug. I don't know about everyone else, but I felt the love of Jesus in this here place.

We shared a fabulous southern meal, sat around, talked and shared jokes. I was in my element. More jokes to share.

Missy was getting tired, and she was starting to say her goodnights. When she approached Billy, he pulled a small, wrapped package out of his front pocket that his family had since 1944. Billy was so pleased to present her with a gift his father collected during the war. I was standing near him being nosy, as was Rose. She unwrapped the gift carefully and opened the box.

"A penny?" she questioned, looking back up at Billy.

"Oh no," he disagreed. "Not just any penny. It's a very rare and valuable 1944-S Steel Wheat Lincoln Penny. I don't know its current value, but guess it is more than $100,000, so I would lock this in a safe."

"I could be wrong about this," I interrupted. "Your price could be extremely low. My coin appraiser could tell me for sure if you want me to find out."

Without any hesitation, she handed the box back to Billy. "I'm sorry, but I can't accept this. One could never put a price on forgiveness. I can't take it," she insisted.

"I made a solemn promise to father to give this to your family."

"You have met your promise young man. You gave it to us, and I gave it back. Look around you Billy. We have all that we need, and I am rich in so many other ways. Please keep it."

Billy rolled the box over in his hand and looked from the insistent old lady to me. He was at a loss. I shrugged but said nothing. He had waited much of his life for this very moment. Not quite what he expected.

He then grabbed my hand and placed the box in it. "Can you please show this to your appraiser and get back to me?"

"There must be several fine appraisers in Mobile or Tuscaloosa," I insisted, as I started to hand it back. I don't want to be responsible for it.

Billy pushed the box into my hand and folded my fingers over it. "Bob, I trust you to take care of this for me. Perhaps miss stubbornness will change her mind," Billy said, looking at Missy with humor on his face.

Missy smiled, kissed the man on the cheek, and whispered, "Don't count on it." She gave my wife and I a parting hug and walked quietly toward her bedroom.

"She is set in her ways, and yes she is very stubborn," Rose added with a giggle.

I pushed the box into my pocket as Rose walked the three of us to the van. We said our goodbyes to our fabulous hostess. Before driving away, Rose came to my window. "We will be in contact Bob. There is still the issue of the contents of Terry's old vest to consider. Our family could never thank you enough for what you have done for us and Billy. You are a fine man." She leaned in, gave me a kiss on the cheek and waved goodbye as she walked back to the house.

It was a long ride back in silence. A long roller coaster of a day led to exhaustion. Billy was sawing logs within ten minutes of leaving the house. We dropped Billy off at about 11:00 and made it back to the BNB by midnight. It took our last ounce of strength to strip and climb into the softest bed ever. At least for tonight.

The next day, we slept in and got some breakfast on the run. We rented a sailboat for just the two of us, much to the delight of Jonathan, I am sure. Sailed several miles of the Tombigbee River, shared a steak dinner later and arrived back at home base before 7:00. My wife packed our things before bed, for we were heading home after breakfast.

Another spectacular morning greeted us, as well as the others around the breakfast table. We said our goodbyes, promised to keep in touch, which I intended to do, and drove north to our home in Indiana. I was going to miss the place, but there was nothing like home. I started to sing, and my wife even joined in. “Oh, the moonlight’s fair tonight along the Wabash. From the fields there comes the breath of new mown hay. Through the sycamores the candle lights are gleaming, on the banks of the Wabash, far away.”

On the way home, I called my coin friend, Jeremiah, and described the coin to him. He promised to get back to me, but not before calling me “one lucky SOB,” again. Must be his favorite phrase. We made it home in time to lock the coin up. We so needed some vacation from our vacation. My recliner and keyboard were calling me, for I had tons to write about. “Sorry Jonathan, I think Tad’s story may be the best seller,” I said while stretching out on my Lazy boy. “The story is going to have to wait,” I soon said, while closing my eyes and grabbing a powernap.

Chapter 20

My wife went back to work on Monday, I paid Jeremiah a visit with the coin so he could confirm the grade, and as expected, he called me a lucky S.O.B. again. I was starting to get offended because I had a great mom. I had done some of my own research, so when he told me the coin could bring as much as a million, I wasn't as shocked as the last two times. But one million? Are you kidding me? Who in the hell would pay that much for a penny? More money than sense was my thinking.

After locking the coin back up, I immediately called Billy to give him the news.

"Holy tarnation," Billy nearly screamed in my ear. "That will be $1.00 he then said," sort of muffled. "Sorry Bob," Billy said after removing his hand from the phone. "Customer," he added. "I never guessed the old coin would be worth that much."

"Yea Billy, it be worth a pretty penny."

"You is some cutup ain't ya?" Billy laughed.

"So, Billy, what do you want to do now?"

"Maybe ifin we talk to em again, and tell em its worth, they may change their minds."

"I can call Rose tonight and have her get back with me. Anyway, they haven't decided yet on the other items."

"You mean the gold?"

"Exactly," I responded simply. "Billy, what do you want to do if Missy sticks to her guns on this?"

"What am I going to do with a million bucks Bob? I'm an old man and choose to live a simple life."

"Family?" I asked.

"No sir. I were married once, but we didn't have kids. She passed the same year as my pops."

"I'm sorry Billy."

"So am I. She was a sweet gal."

"How about give it to charity, or your church?"

"I have complete faith in the Lord, but no connection to a church. Some of them preachers and priests are crooks and pedofeelers."

I couldn't help but laugh at his southern drawl and pronunciation skills. "You mean pedophiles Billy."

"That's what I said. Those sickos that likes youngins."

"That is a rather general accusation, Billy, but I understand, so what do you want to do if Missy refuses? Wouldn't you at least like to stop having to sell papers?"

"Er you kiddin me. I love selling papers. Gets me outa the house, and I get to talk to people, some of which er my friends."

"Want to help your friends out then?"

"Hold on, Bob," Billy said as several customers must have come by. After he came back on the line he said, "you be my friend, right? You keep it. Do with it what you wish. Besides, ifin for some reason I need a little coin you can just send it to me."

I was wanting for words for a moment or two. "No Billy," I said after letting it process some. "My wife and I are in great shape Billy; we don't need the money."

"That be my final decision, Robert. If they won't take it, you keep it for your family." Before I could get another word in. "Gotta go young man," he said and then he hung up.

"You hung up on me, you old shit," was all I could say as I set the receiver down.

"Holy crap," I said, before going back in my contacts and dialed up Rose. "Rose of Alabam," I was saying when she picked up the phone.

"Hello," she said in her sweet southern tongue.

"Rose? Is this my sweet southern Rose?"

"Bob? This must be Bob. I would recognize that Yankee accent anywhere."

"Your one and only," I responded.

"Bob, it is so nice to hear from you. I've been meaning to call."

"That's great," I said. "Maybe we can compare notes."

"You first then. How's your lovely family?" Rose asked.

"They are great, and yours? Oh, and I have to know, has your Missy had to whip any butts lately?"

"No, Bob," she said, followed by a hardy laugh. "We have all been perfect little girls and boys. So, what's up Bob?"

"Are you sitting down?" I asked.

"Yes sir. You wouldn't know, but I am sitting outside, around the pool, with a cool glass of lemonade. Are you jealous?"

"One hundred percent jealous," I responded. Our visit to that area was wonderful. "The reason I called was to discuss the coin. I had a discussion with my coin dealer and then Billy. The coin it turns out is unbelievably valuable. According to Jeremiah, it could bring up to a million."

"Wow! That is a whole lot. Who would pay that much for such a small object?"

"My question exactly. Money must be burning through these people's pockets. So Rose," I said with a pause. "Billy was hoping, if you knew how much it may be worth, your family would change their minds and accept his gift."

She at first let off a little giggle. Wasn't anything funny about a cool million. "We discussed it several times among ourselves, and we are still adamant, we want Billy to keep it."

"You are a stubborn lot, I would have to say. Billy fits in the group too. He won't take it back. He even hung up on me. Can you believe that? If your family won't accept it, he insists I keep it. My wife and I don't need the money, Rose."

"Sorry for your bad luck, Bob." She started to laugh. "Just take your wife out for an expensive dinner and an ice cream cone," she said as she continued to giggle over my sad story.

"Are you really serious? God is truly good is all I can really say."

"All the time, as your wife may say."

"Wow. Wow. Wow. Okay Rose, about the bag's contents. The gold nuggets and silver dollars, shall I sell it and send you the money, or would your family prefer the original contents?"

She started laughing even more. "I'm sorry, I can't help it," she chortled.

"What's so funny?" I asked. "I wasn't telling a joke," I insisted. She continued to laugh with the phone away from her mouth. It then dawned on me as to why she may be laughing. "No Rose. Don't say it." I didn't ask for or deserve this.

"Sorry Bob. We all are so deeply sorry for the catastrophe that is now falling down upon your head." She said it with substantial sarcasm. "It is not as bad as it could be though," she added with a laugh. "We only wish for you to send us $200,000 to increase our children's college funds, and you keep the rest. It is yours to have and to hold."

"Oh my God," was all I said before going silent.

Rose waited several seconds. She must have thought I had fainted. "Are you okay, Bob?"

"Yes," I whimpered.

"Well Bob, I must go now. I hear Grandma calling me. Give my love to Susan."

"Rose," I spoke quietly into the now dead line. "She hung up on me. Why is everyone hanging up on me?" I sat quietly in my recliner, staring at the receiver in my hand, not sure what to do next.

After everything sunk in, I called Jeremiah to get the ball rolling on the coins, the 1928 P Peace Silver Dollars and the 1944 S Steel Lincoln penny. Jeremiah calls me lucky, but I'm not so sure. I still feel God's hand in this. I don't believe so much in fate or luck.

When Susan got home, and I filled her in, her first question was the top one on my mind as well. "What are we going to do with all this money?"

"Sell the coins first. I've already called Jeremiah. Send a check to Rose. Finally, convert the gold to cash, get with our investment counselor, and invest responsibly. After that, no clue, besides changing our wills."

Chapter 21

The next few months were rather adventuresome. Not on the same level as the time Susan and I spent in the South, or the two power dreams, but close.

Jeremiah and I sold the coins, the silver dollars at least. We decided it best to take the penny to auction. There were periodic, large-scale auctions, where invites go out across the globe. It was extremely exciting. Jeremiah and I attended. The place was packed. There were many people in the back of the room on phones. I was told they were in contact with customers who either chose to or couldn't physically attend. One bidder was as far away as Japan.

This event was so cool. Some fantastic coins and paper were up for auction.

I was starting to get the bug again. I collected as a youth and had a decent Lincoln Head Wheat penny collection. Stamps was another area I dabbled in.

Jeremiah bid on a few coins, but the prices quickly went over his predetermined limit. He was a collector, but not a stupid one. If it didn't make good business sense, he quickly declined.

Cards were being raised and lowered all over the room, money flowed freely, accompanied by shouts from the floor, and many times, incoherent rambling from the auctioneer. Did this person warm up like a singer before the curtain was raised on the first act? Most items went fast, but others ended up in a bidding war.

Jeremiah and I sat through over an hour of back and forth before my item came up, but I wasn't bored. The process was nearly mesmerizing.

A picture of what was now my coin was brought up on the bright screen at the front of the room. They showed the front and back of this coin. Our 16th president beautifully represented on the left side of the screen and the wheat adorned backside on the right. It was not wasted on me that the coin was adorned with President Lincoln, and what brought me here today was born out of the adventure that started with Tad Michael Lincoln.

"Next up for bid, ladies and gentlemen, is a mighty fine example of the exceedingly rare 1944 S Steel Lincoln Wheat Penny. This could be the gem of anyone's collection. So don't be shy. If you snooze you lose," he added.

"I think I like this man," I said to Jeremiah, but I don't think he heard me. He was focused. He had a small stake here, alongside the auction house. Without his help I wouldn't have gotten as far as I have. His expertise was valuable.

"Let's start the bidding at $100,000," he added before winding up his mouth, like a mechanical monkey. "Let the party begin," I said, but I still don't think Jeremiah was listening.

It started slowly but ended up in a firestorm. I could almost feel the heat, not unlike a forest fire racing across the tops of evergreens, threatening the smoke jumpers running into the mountain stream for protection. In a matter of moments, it jumped from the $100,000 starting point to $800,000. A bidding war was on between a well-dressed businessman, lady in a flowing white dress, and a mystery bidder on the phone.

After the $800,000 mark, it slowed to a crawl, but the auctioneer knew his stuff. The $800,000 would have been fine by me, but the auctioneer wasn't having it. There was a reason I liked him besides his friendly banter. "Don't give up guys," he chimed in, looking intently at each participant. I even wondered if he could see through the phone. "This prize is for bragging rights," he added. He could smell the blood in the water, as he glanced at the man in the suit. "You going to let this young lady out bid you?" The auctioneer was trying to give him a little push. This man wasn't a referee. He was an instigator. She held the high ground, but the auctioneer could tell the businessman wasn't done here, and one of the people in the back was in a heated discussion with the mystery bidder.

"$850,000," was shouted from the phone banks. The mystery bidder started the ball rolling on the new round of bloodletting. I glanced at Jeremiah. He was smiling like the Cheshire Cat. It was contagious. "$900,000," followed shortly by the woman in white, not willing to be outdone. The businessman was stoic, like a leopard waiting to pounce.

"$910,000," came quickly from the back. Was that someone else? I wondered. Who cares! I'm enjoying the hell out of this.

The bidding rose quickly in snatches of $10K at a time. $960K, $970K, and on it went until it got up to $1,100K. Jeremiah was jumping up and down in his seat by this time. It stalled for a moment until I heard a perceptible "F%*$& this," come out of the mouth of Mr. Stoic, followed by a resounding "One million, three hundred thousand, zero dollars and zero cents," exploding out of his mouth, with clarity of expression, to get the point across that he wasn't messing around.

The room went silent. A death stare rose from the woman's eyes and when I glanced back at the man on the phone, there was nothing happening there either. "You da man!" shouted the auctioneer, quickly embarrassed by his outburst. "You the person I meant to say. Sorry ma'am," he then added. He stood quiet for a few ticks of the clock, but he must have figured this man let the air out of this one.

"Okay ladies and gentlemen," he said, while raising his hands to make sure he had everyone's attention. "The last bid was $1,300,000. If there aren't any more bids, I'm about to start the countdown. Go big or go home." He first lowered his hands, and then raised his right hand and one finger, shouted "$1,300,000 going once." He and all the workers carefully watched the room. "$1,300,000 going twice," he shouted, raising his second finger. "Last call ladies and gentlemen." Silence continued across the room. No takers. "Sold," he shouted, lowering his hand like someone flagging at the finish line. I was almost finished and was ready for a drink. If I drank. "Raise your card a little higher sir," he instructed. "Sold to number 86 for the meager price of $1,300,000," he added before turning to Jeremiah and me, with a slight bow, recognizing our good luck.

I turned to Jeremiah and grabbed him up in a hug, which he eagerly returned. We both smiled and I almost cried. "God is not just good, he is grrrrreat!"

After we paid the fees, sent a check to Rose, and sold the gold at a great price, we invested another $1,380,000. I'm certain God doesn't want me to hoard the bounty. Now it's time to make decisions.

Chapter 22

My wife decided to retire early. We could afford it, and she didn't want to be left out of the fun of retirement. The first thing she did was plant a beautiful flower garden bordering the patio. The garden was breathtaking. My wife did a fantastic job.

Not wanting to leave Tad out, or show preference to Jonathan, I paid Mr. Painted Man a visit. I carefully drew a rendition of the USS Tad, along with some lapping waves and had my tattoo artist place it painfully just above my right shoulder blade. I decided to not only write about my visitors, but also have something of their lives painted on my body. Susan thought I was nuts. She may be right.

Susan and I discussed our finances at length. We decided it would be too easy to just give to various charities, not saying that would be wrong. My wife especially wanted to do more.

On Sundays after church, we enjoyed lunch out with some church friends, followed by a drive and unannounced visit with a family member, picked at random. Life had become an adventure, so we decided to spread it around. "Surprise," we may say. "What's for dinner?" We were kidding but would never turn down a great meal.

On one of our drives, we stumbled across a soup kitchen in the downtown area. It had been there for some time, tucked out of the way; we just hadn't paid much attention. We ignored it when we were so busy being busy. The place was in rather decent shape, but Susan and I wondered how availability of more services would be received.

We investigated things and realized there were several places like it in the area. I had no idea. Some were just soup kitchens, like the "Jeffersonville Community Kitchen" in my hometown, some included food and clothing pantries, while others were able to shelter the homeless. There were a couple halfway houses as well.

The homeless and otherwise destitute are the forgotten people all around the world. Invisible human beings made up of the mentally ill, addicted, down on their luck, or escapees from abuse. The reasons and histories are varied.

They are everywhere. I, like many, don't know how to help, so we don't. It is much easier to look the other way or throw them a dollar now and then. There are some people that play the system. The players and some perpetrators of violence or theft adds a level of distrust that some have trouble getting past. See a homeless person on the street corner, we tend to now ask, are they faking, looking for means to buy drugs and alcohol, or do they intend harm?

After talking to some of the front liners, I am finding it is a hole difficult to climb out of. Harder to get employment with a stigma and no address. There isn't a simple website all homeless and destitute people have easy access to with a complete instruction manual. "Homeless And How to Survive for Dummies". May as well dial 1-800-EATDIRT.

After more research and some lengthy discussions, we located a spot that could use some help and had room for expansion. My wife and I purchased the adjoining building for a song and dance. Currently it was a busy soup kitchen, so the traffic was there, but Susan and I wanted to add more services.

We coordinated with the operators of the soup kitchen, our church, the city, and a group of my friends that wished to lend a hand. I was tickled by the response. Initially we gave the current insides a facelift, replaced one of the stoves, added another, along with a large new refrigerator.

My handy friends and I then proceeded to knock out and move walls to help combine the two spaces, allowing us to initially add more seating. It was our hope to allow more space for them to enjoy their meals in comfort. The worn tables and chairs were replaced with something not only to improve the comfort, but to raise the quality of their dining experience. Their lives are sad enough without having to eat in an equally morose space.

We added spaces for a food and clothing pantry, laundry room with two front loader washers and dryers, a small section for receiving and sorting mail for the homeless, and the final addition, a multi stalled shower room for men and women. When applying for jobs you need to be marketable, complete with an address and means for the employer to contact the applicant. First impressions are critical, so clean clothing is a plus.

With the help of several people, their website was upgraded. We wanted to make sure all could easily access and navigate the site. The other locations are referenced as well, reporting services, dates, and times. Once the facility was properly staffed and stocked, business cards were handed out to the homeless population in the area.

It was bumpy at first, staff needed tweaking, and rules revised, but in the end, it was a success. My wife and I helped serve meals on a part time basis. We are also looking into investing in a portable shower, washer, and dryer, which could be driven around to other facilities.

Chapter 23

The ability to turn a phrase with a smattering of humor is a gift from God that I was determined to use in my maturing years. The wealth of material of late was screaming to be told. Who am I to ignore the history of such a fine gentleman as Jonathan Boynes, or Tad Lincoln?

My first book, "The USS Insurgent", was published six months after our trip to Alabama. I sent free copies to all my friends. It was very well received.

My second book, Tad's Journey, was a journey for me as well. One of research into the past, love, loss, gain, forgiveness, and victory. This venture was extra special and took me a year to write.

Before presenting it to publish, I made a special trip to Mobile. My nervousness was palpable, for I made a promise to give the family, that being Missy, the chance for a final review. It was important and I was seeking their blessing.

My wife stayed behind to help supervise and volunteer at the facility, and care for her flowers. She was loving retirement.

I've heard from many fellow retirees, "I don't know how I got anything done while working? I am keeping busy." As I've said before, I saw my father-in-law go downhill by taking retirement to mean rest and relax as the number one priority. Both of our retirements have taken things up a notch. My version of retirement is a new species all together. The supernatural gift of youthful vigor I have been blessed with so far is allowing me to function at a higher level, good or bad. At some pushing from me, I've been weaned from my medication. I feel great, especially on a golf course. Twice per week is my goal, including while I am in Alabama.

Rose and Paul Thompson insisted on my staying there during my visit. Before I left home, Rose made sure to remind me about bringing my swimsuit and fishing gear. Naturally, I couldn't leave home without my golf clubs.

Rose, Missy, and I sat and talked for well over an hour the first night. Missy is still as sharp as ever. Rose expressed some concern for her health to me. She was now 98 after all. I brought four copies of my manuscript because I didn't know how many wanted to read it. Both the young ladies started on it the next day while I went back north to visit my other friends.

The Frederickson's were disappointed I didn't stay there, but they understood. I was invited to dinner, which I gladly accepted. Mary was a fantastic cook. Before dinner I took a drive into Pickensville, and even stopped by the library to say hi to our favorite librarian. I presented her with a signed copy of my first book and thanked her again for her help. She would receive a gifted copy of my second as well, as soon as it was published.

I hadn't heard from Billy for a bit, so I was anxious to look him up. His number I had programmed into my phone, but the best I could do was leave a message. "Billy Boy," I started, "I'll be down your way the first of next week. Please save me a copy of your paper. Looking forward to seeing you again."

I parked my car across the street. A 2015 red Camaro. It wasn't a midlife crisis red Corvette, but I couldn't help myself. I was now a world-famous author, I tried to convince myself, when signing the papers two weeks prior. Even though we could afford it, we decided some time back in our marriage to never buy new. My thoughts were to let someone else take the kick in the butt on value when driving a new car off the lot. With age does occasionally come wisdom. We also frowned on the installation of a golden throne in the bathroom. My wife laughed about it when I brought it up. During our first visit with the Thompsons my mouth was watering from the thought of seeing us in their house on a golf course. We've resisted so far. Our house is comfortable and not showy.

The newspaper stand was there, but it was manned by another gentleman. Mature, but not quite the age of Billy, and stockier. The man stuck out. I mean literally, with a beer belly covered by a bright Hawaiian shirt. Couldn't miss him. "Good afternoon, sir," I greeted the man, as I handed him the dollar for the paper. It was always good to stay informed. "Are you giving Billy a break today?" I asked, hoping the answer would be yes.

He gave me a questioning look, like he was thinking, "who the hell are you asking personal questions?" "No sir," he finally responded after giving me the once over. "He had been sick, so I took over his stand."

"What do you mean by had been sick?" I asked, feeling concerned.

"Were you a friend?" He asked.

"Yes," I responded, taking note he asked about being a friend in past tense. "Is Billy better?" I followed, afraid of the answer I may be given.

"Is your name Bob by any chance?"

"Yes sir," I responded with a sour look on my face. I was worried and annoyed. Annoyed over the thousand questions.

"He had talked fondly of you. Billy said you changed his life."

A lump started to form in my throat. "Please tell me. Has Billy passed?" I was done dancing around the question.

"Sorry to tell you, but yes. It happened a week and a half ago. His heart gave out."

"Dammit," I said. Strangely feeling annoyance toward the man for being the bearer of sad news. "Did you go to his funeral?"

"Yes sir. He had a decent turnout. No family, but many friends."

My heart was warmed. At least he had some attendants.

"Where was he buried?" I asked, assuming he wasn't cremated.

"He was buried at the old Upper Cemetery out on Old Columbus Road."

We said our goodbyes before asking my GPS to take me to the cemetery. Even said thank you to a bodyless voice. Who does that anyway? Someone detached from reality I would think.

Parking next to several acres of God's green earth, which is the Upper Cemetery, I got out and absorbed what for some can be depressing. "Earth to earth, ashes to ashes, dust to dust" from the Book of Common Prayer came to mind as I perused all the various tombstones, while leaning against the wrought iron fencing, lightly protecting the dead from the living. The markers were arranged in straight rows, with the occasional tree scattered about.

There was no building code here, or any sign of cookie cutter patterns. Variety was the standard, which I prefer personally.

Is a tombstone simply a large, flat inscribed stone standing or laid over a grave, like what is described in the dictionary? I prefer the word monument myself. It means so much more than a flat stone and add to that the fact a monument is meant as a memorial to the person. A fitting example is a cherub of purest white, standing guard over someone's sweet child that left this earthly plane well before what humanity judges as a proper time. Adorning the stone are poems, sayings, names, dates, and words of comfort, revealing what they meant to others and may be of historical significance as well. I don't simply see death in the entombed empty shells marked by stone, but the life prior and the hope of eternity. My view, using my elevated imagination, consists of love and family, service to humanity, inventions, links to fantastic events or people throughout our history. A loving mama that held three jobs supporting her family after the father died young. A young man being the first in his family to be a college graduate who then became a doctor. A human is so much more than dust.

Walking through the open gate, sided by a metal sign saying, "Closed From 8 PM to 8 AM", I began my search. A fresh grave was what I was looking for. How many could there be at any point in time? Fortunately, I was able to locate my friend's earthly resting place after two misses. I was disappointed, not only by the fact I was unable to say my goodbyes but seeing at the head of his gravesite was a tiny stone cap, stating simply, "Billy Peters Oct 12, 1941 – Dec 15, 2019." "Billy oh Billy," I said flatly while shaking my head. "This will not do." I knew he was rich in friends, and his knowing God was finer than gold or silver, but this tiny piece of rock was sticking in my craw.

After saying a short prayer for my departed friend, I took a few snapshots, and walked to the gate, where I took another because there was a phone number listed.

Once getting into my car, I called the number and informed them of what I wished to do. Using my cell phone, I searched Google and found the Jewell Monument Co. here in Pickens County. My intention was to pick out something more worthy of my friend Billy and have them replace the paperweight. My choice was one made of polished black granite. Even though I picked it for its beauty, the symbolism wasn't wasted, for his family learned that black was beautiful too. A plain square one was not what I wanted, so I chose something I quickly fell in love with. It was a shame he wasn't here to help me choose. On one end of the monument was a magnolia tree carved in white, with its branches, leaves, and gorgeous blossoms reaching over the top to provide shade. Carved expertly across the front, in a contrasting light grey, will be the inscription, "BILLY E PETERS; BORN OCT 12, 1941 – WENT HOME TO HIS LORD DEC 15, 2019; BELOVED SON AND FRIEND".

The bill was paid, and I thanked them for their prompt service, giving me just enough time to make it for dinner at the Frederickson's.

Later that evening, when I arrived back at the Thompson's, I told them the sad news of Billy's passing. Passing was a part of life, but it is still sad for friends and family left behind.

Rose was halfway through my manuscript, while Missy, not so much. She was excited by the story so far, but at her age, naps were frequent.

I went straight to bed after calling my wife, telling her of Billy, saying my goodnights and performing kissy face over the phone. We were still kids trapped by maturity.

My stay lasted three more days. I made sure I made it to dinner each night at the Thompson's, followed by enjoyable conversation, some competitive board and card games, and swimming. I started doing some laps, which I enjoyed, and one game of water basketball in honor of Billy Peters. I told my wife that I may want to switch to the YMCA, so I could add some water exercise to my routines. Life was good.

To my relief, Rose and Missy loved the manuscript, but Missy did ask that I add some details she had forgotten. I wouldn't take long and was not about to disappoint. I would proof the manuscript once more after the addition before turning it in. Even with the fact I wrote it, and read it many times, I still get emotional.

Managed to fit in a little fishing and one round of golf. It was a Saturday morning when I said my farewells. My wish was to make it home in time for church on Sunday. Like most goodbyes they were bitter-sweet. I gave Missy a huge hug and a kiss on her forehead like she was a little sister, which in a way she was.

Chapter 24

While waiting on my publisher to clear my second book for publication, I started my third. This one would be a work in progress. Since my life after retirement was stranger than fiction, I thought why not, so I changed names, dates, places, and started writing a book of fiction.

The publisher eventually got back with me. They were pleased. He must love it as much as I do, but my view of the manuscript is more personal than he could ever understand. The book was published on January 20, 2020. For the next six months I spent a lot of time in book signings throughout the eastern part of the United States and helped to hawk my works at various national and local retail establishments. My books were taking off as a result of leg work, but the biggest spark was when Oprah Winfrey received a copy of Tad's Journey and recommended it. For the year 2020 I made it to the New York Times best sellers list. I was flabbergasted, and God is good.

The year 2020 was a very strange year. The Pandemic hit all over the world, which sparked a whirlwind of controversy. It was called Covid19 because it started in 2019, or as some like to call it, the Wuhan Virus. After years it was eventually determined it did come out of a Wuhan lab, but as most politicized subjects go, it will always be debated. Was this pandemic accidental or planned? It turned out to be as much of a political pandemic as a medical one. To be honest, the years after Trump became president were interesting to say the least. It was as if a hornet's nest was shaken, and the devil flew out. Political attacks were many and furious. Wokeness, freedom of speech, 2nd Amendment, anti-partisan, protests, impeachment, border crisis, defund the police, and voter fraud became frequent and vicious subjects. Politics was a hot button topic for many, which split friendships and families. My wife and I became nearly numb listening to the arguments. Susan and I agreed, God is in control, and we need to leave it there. Frank, my Democrat friend around the corner was beginning to ask what has become of his party. He hasn't quite decided to switch to red yet, but I can still hope.

My publisher tried to push for more books, but I wasn't going to be pressured. This was for pleasure, and I considered it my art. The money was never an issue. Love for the subject and writing was going to be what drove me and not money.

It be the year 2021, mate, as my sailor friend may put it. Working on my fourth book, which came to me in a dream, luckily not that kind of dream. I am now 66 years old and on Medicare, and my wife is 62. Happy to be alive and going strong. Finally able to convince my wife to start golfing again, and go with me to the gym, but she was slowing, and her knees were starting to bother her. Convinced my doctor that I only needed a yearly inspection. "Check under the hood and change the oil." I would tell him. After my 50,000-mile inspection he would simply shake his head and tell me, "See you next year." I was tickled and he was confused. "Join the club my friend, but as the old saying goes, don't look a gift horse in the mouth."

"Perhaps I can get a dose of youngster in one of my dreams," my wife once said.

"As soon as I finish this chapter, I will dial the dream of the month club," I told her. I wished I could pass some of what I had to her through a mind meld or transfusion perhaps. My wife was slowing, and I was holding strong.

Jeremiah and Missy both passed in 2021. Susan and I went to their funerals, and Jeremiah's son asked that I write and present a eulogy on his behalf. I wasn't much for speaking, but I was getting used to it. Missy's wake, as I called it, was a different animal. Missy's funeral was a true celebration of life. I was sad and happy all wrapped into one package. I would miss her personally, but I smiled as I looked around the room at the wonderful men and women she helped raise. Logan, or Lurch as Billy fondly called him, was now in pre-med. We keep in touch, and my wife began sending Christmas cards.

When stuck on my writing I would take a walk and stop by Frank Friedlander's house for a spell and rock hours away on his front porch. He lost his wife in 2021, which was another funeral for that year. He enjoyed my company, and he mellowed some, so politics was back on our plates for discussion topics. My feeling, even though he won't quite admit it, was he disliked the Biden administration as much as I did.

Spring, a time of renewal, is a wonderful time for golf and walking the neighborhood. In the spring of 2023, I not only published my seventh book, but I also shot my age in golf, from the tips to boot. I was 68 but felt like I was still in my forties. My wife stopped playing, she just didn't feel up to it. She felt bad she could no longer keep up with me physically. It wasn't her fault. Age, like scouring water rushing over stone, is relentless. Only, "if I could save time in a bottle" as Jim Croce aptly put it. My beautiful wife of 44 years. She volunteered less and was tending more to her flowers and reading. I was saddened, but I wasn't about to show it to her, but I am sure she knew. She is a smart lady.

My next pass by Frank's house after my lowest score ever, I decided to knock, for he wasn't on the porch. Felt like bragging on my score of 68. There was no answer, which didn't surprise me, for Frank enjoyed listening to the classics with headphones on. My initial thought was to head home and leave him alone with the classics. Something was telling me to check for sure. I checked the back yard and around the house. Finally spotted him through his bedroom window with his headphones on as expected. I banged on the window and waved, then called him on my cell, which didn't wake the man up. He must have fallen asleep. I was now determined. I was not going to leave before I made sure Frank was okay. A next-door neighbor came over and started asking what was up. Luckily, I met the man before, so he didn't call the police on me.

"I've called Frank," I told the neighbor. "Knocked on both doors and have been knocking on his bedroom window since I saw him in bed with headphones on. I hope he's just asleep. Maybe I'm too far away, but I can't see his chest moving."

I moved over to the back door, which had four glass panels in it. "Sorry Frank, I'll pay for the repair," I said as I picked up a rock and broke one of the panes of glass out. After using the rock to clear out all remaining glass, I reached in, unlocked the door, and went straight for the bedroom, followed by the neighbor. Frank was propped up on his pillows with his cover pulled up to his waist. I put my hand on his shoulder and gently shook. His chest was moving, but his breathing was extremely shallow. After gently removing his headphones, still hoping he was okay, I almost expected him to jump up and smack the crap out of his uninvited intruders. Frank partially opened his eyes and tried to talk but his words were slurred. Suspecting a stroke, I quickly dialed 911. We sat on his bed and reassured him that help was on the way. There was a noticeable slackening of his muscles on one side of his face, which convinced me that a stroke was the most likely culprit.

"Bobbb, howss t gme?" Frank managed to ask me with great difficulty.

I gave him a big double thumbs up, swallowing the lump forming in my throat. My friend was in trouble, and there was little I could do that I already hadn't. Just being there sometimes was enough.

Frank managed a crooked smile, while a siren was rising in the distance. The neighbor left the room and was sweeping up the glass before he taped a piece of cardboard over the opening. I grabbed his keys that were on his nightstand, for I planned to work on the broken window and lock his house up as soon as possible. I then went to the front door and showed the young EMTs to his room after they arrived. While trying my best to stay positive, when the EMT's were checking Frank over, my mind wandered to the funerals of my other friends. Couldn't help it, death is inevitable for all of us.

The neighbor picked up Frank's cell phone and handed it to me. "Frank will need us to call his family."

After taking it from the man, I tried to get in, but was unable because it was password protected. "Password?" I asked Frank. The man was awake. He mouthed something quietly as best he could. It required I lean much closer to him.

After putting my ear near his mouth, he said "1972" slowly, struggling with each syllable.

We take something as simple as talking for granted. I didn't know the significance of the number, while punching it in. "Eureka!" I hollered with glee. Frank smiled as he was being wheeled to the ambulance. "Which hospital?" I questioned the EMTs.

"Clark Memorial," they quickly responded as they were packing their precious cargo away. The ambulance pulled away with sirens blaring.

After searching Frank's phone, I found his son's number and quickly called to inform him of the situation. He said he would call the others which put me at ease. I didn't tell him about the window, for it will be good as new within maybe an hour. Frank would need his family now, and they needn't worry about his house.

I found a tape measure at Frank's house. After measuring the opening, I went home to grab my window fixit supplies and drove to the glass store. Within an hour, as expected, the back door was fixed, and I was able to secure the house. This accountant had become one hell of a handyman.

Susan and I both went to the hospital. As feared, he had a stroke, and not a small one. He was placed in ICU under guarded condition. After talking to the family, offering up our prayers and our help, we finally went home. Before we made dinner, we said prayers again for Frank and his family.

We got the call three days later. Frank the family man, official member of the shit shooter club and a wonderful friend, never awoke after saying goodnight to his eldest child the night before. Still wondering to this day if he was collected in a dream, like what happened to me, or if he moved straight on and reunited with his wife. His cantankerous self would have the good luck of being picked up by a young staunch Republican female. I sure wouldn't wish that on her, but it would make one hell of a set of jokes.

Chapter 25

The year 2028, much water had passed under the bridge of my 73 years of life. More than just the eleven years since my first supernatural encounter. Our wonderful country placed the first man on Mars. My eyes and ears were glued to this event. It was fascinating. No little green men were there to greet us, offering us a baked cake, or a mug of Martian beer. Another trip was planned later that year, and a woman would be on board, to the glee of my wife Susan. The plan was to build a shelter and perform various tests to determine the possibility of living there. It would be a research station, like what we have in Antarctica. "Honey," I said to my wife one evening. "We could invest and become the first McDonalds franchisee on Mars."

"Absolutely not, Honey," she responded, after looking up from her latest love story. "I prefer Burger King."

"Okay then," I laughed. "Burger King it is. I will call our financial planner first thing in the morning." My wife's focus was back on the book, but she did shrug, as if she was okay with it. "Holstein or Angus?" I asked with a smile.

"What?" Susan asked while looking up from her book.

"What species of cow should we raise on Mars, Holstein or Angus? Maybe something wilder like Bison."

My wife shook her head and smiled, before going back to her book. She wasn't going to play along.

"Maybe with the thinner air and lower gravity, their horns may start working and we can toss the bells."

Susan buried her face in the book, with a detectable smile. This woman was determined. Gotcha, I thought. "Now chickens are another problem," I added. I looked at her, watching for a crack in her hard-fought stoicism. Smiling, I went for the jugular. "But with no roads, the chicken won't have anything to cross, soooo we won't know why Martian chickens cross the road."

"Holy crap, Bob, will you stop it? I'm at a good part." Susan blinked after pulling the book away from her face.

Do you think I am truly done? You don't know me very well. "Do you suppose the cows will give green milk, Honey?"

The book quickly went flying, directly at my head. I ducked and missed much of the force. Couldn't help but start laughing. "What? Inquiring minds want to know?"

"You're an absolute mess, Honey. I suppose that's one of the reasons I love you so much."

"Want to go to bed early, Honey?" I inquired with a wink and sly smile.

"Will you just fetch my book, you horn-dog."

Couldn't help myself. I got down on the floor, picked up her book with my mouth, and took it to her with my tail wagging.

Giving up the thought of a roll in the hay, I grabbed my computer and worked on the next chapter of book number eight. This would be my first true fantasy style of novel. It would be of a young man, who one day, while on his first solo camping trip, was spirited away to another dimension where there were real elves, giants, and fairies. Don't have a name for it yet.

My Susan finally put down her book and went to bed. It wouldn't be long before I joined her. After backing up the manuscript, I put the computer aside and decided to lay back for a moment on my recliner to wind down after my battle with this huge river snake. With my hands folded in front of me, I closed my eyes.

Chapter 26

My partner, Rick Turner and I, Joseph Alvarez, two wily detectives, drove up to the scene in our dark gray sedan. It was early Wednesday morning, May 03, 2025. This was our second murder scene of the week. Two cruisers were parked on each end of the side street to block traffic from the scene still being taped off in downtown Atlanta by our men in blue. The Big Peach or New York of The South are two of many nicknames for the city ranked 20th in murder rate. It isn't St. Louis or Baltimore, but we have our share of fun as Rick describes it. I don't share in his view of what is fun, but he is still a good cop.

We have been partners for five years now, from nearly the start of my current career of six years. We began as beat cops, shaking people down on the streets, or writing the occasional traffic ticket. We complement each other well, like a married couple. Rick was a fine young man of twenty-eight, 6' 2", 210 lb., blond, athletic ex basketball and football player. He was fast, which comes in handy on the streets. I can hold my own, but not near as fleet on my feet as this blond gazelle.

"How's the city's bulldog?" Sergeant Romero asked as my partner raised the tape for me to pass. "Age before beauty," I said. Bulldog was my nickname. I absolutely hate to lose, and when I am on a trail, I don't give up. The nickname was a compliment to my unwavering pursuit for the truth.

Like Sergeant Romero, my dark hair, kept high and tight, and darker skin tone, paid tribute to my Spanish heritage. My father was from Brazil, while mother, of German and Irish descent, was born and raised in Kentucky. As a member of a Southern Baptist church, mother volunteered for a mission trip to Brazil in her senior year of high school. It was love at first sight, according to Mother. "He was one sexy hunk of a man," my mother still says to this day. My dad called her "anjo um cabelo castanho claro," in his native Portuguese, or angel in the light brown hair. Her parents, my grandparents, were genuinely concerned about this situation. They prayed it wasn't a ploy for citizenship. My parents are still married to this very day, and have four children, two boys and two girls, with me being the eldest.

Currently, at the mature age of 44, 5' 9" tall and 180 pounds, I still feel like I could take on the world, especially any crooks that may cross my path. Athletics was never my thing in school, even though I worked out and could be considered athletic. I was an academic, with a proclivity toward languages, which confused the hell out of my family when I chose to go into the service as a grunt. They thought for sure I would have gone to college or at least military school and would strive to become Colonel or Major Alvarez.

Before moving any further, Rick and I slipped disposable booties over our shoes to protect from contaminating the scene or our shoes. The body was in a narrow, clutter free alley between two businesses. The alley was only six feet wide and would be in complete darkness if not for the added lighting. As I approached the body, which was currently covered, we could see where blood had pooled under the head and splattered on the concrete blocks of the small bakery.

Even before my time as a policeman, I was no stranger to blood and death, for I had retired after twenty years with the Army as Master Sergeant of the Green Berets. As a sniper in this elite group, I had spent much time in some of the harshest environments on earth. Currently I am fluent in five languages, English, Portuguese, Spanish, Dari, and Arabic, which comes in handy in some situations. Keeping extremely calm while hitting a target was second nature to me. My idea of relaxation was sleeping under a bush while my spotter kept watch. My specialties were firearms and hand to hand. I was sent on many missions off the books, which can keep me up at night. I am only human.

After retirement, running a desk or being a car salesman was not my cup of tea, which is why I became a cop. My current job has its own level of physical demands, so I frequent the gym and try to run five miles per day. With my service experience and ambition to always be the best at anything I put my mind to, my movement from beat cop to detective second class was rather quick. My current ambition is to catch the bad guys and make the streets of Atlanta safer.

Unfortunately, except for a couple close calls, I never married. My career choices and unbridled ambition wasn't a great back drop for a wife, children, and the white picket fence. Do I regret it? Yes. There would be nothing like coming home to a warm hug and unconditional love, but my hours made it more than difficult. Rick was married however, ten years now. Right out of high school. Lucky stiff. His kind wife had me over for dinner many times. She is a good woman, much better than this slob deserved, I would remind him many times.

"What do we have Sergeant?" I asked, as we carefully approached the victim. The crime scene hasn't been processed, so we needed to be especially careful to not contaminate any evidence that may be here.

"Hispanic male in his twenties," he responded. "Shot twice. Once in the chest and once in the forehead. He had been back here, covered up like a derelict sleeping one off."

"Who found the body?" Rick asked, after moving beside me.

"One of our own," the Sergeant responded. "Someone was going through the man's pockets as one of our cruisers happened by. He got spooked and ran."

"So, you think this person was a male?" I asked.

The Sergeant, looking at his notes said, "our man could tell he was probably male by the way he moved and his height. Near six foot he estimated. His feeling was he was a younger man as well."

"Male huh? I don't take anything for granted," I added, while squatting down next to the victim, to get a better look. "Not to appear sexist, but females aren't generally out at night alone, rooting around in dark alleys."

"Any ID on the victim?" I then asked, concerned the person may have taken off with his wallet.

"Not a stitch Joe. I suspect the little thief cleaned him out."

A bit of commotion started behind my partner and me. I looked over my shoulder and saw the forensic crew had just arrived in their new white van and were unloading their equipment. This part I had learned was extremely critical to any complete investigation, and being the bulldog, I was known to be, they knew I expected their best effort. They may not work for me, but I know how to push.

I turned back to the sergeant. We had to wrap this up so the forensic crew could take over. "Did anyone get a look at the kid? He could possibly be a witness."

"Ah, he is probably just some punk out for some easy pickins," Rick chimed in.

"Not much," the Sergeant responded. "It was dark."

After pulling back the cover, I was startled, and "shit," was the first word that came from my mouth, after revealing the young Hispanic's face. The smell of death and drying blood was already filling my sinuses, while recognition flashed across my mind. The eyes were dead and grey, staring into the unknown. A round hole was expertly shot into this man's skull, dead center. Some blood and brain matter had drained from the wound, but not much. The first shot to the chest was a heart shot which caused near instant death I was certain. This was an execution, was my initial thought. "The young man is Jose Moreno," I informed all who were present.

"Our snitch?" Rick asked in an almost insulted tone.

"One and the same," I responded, while giving the young man's body and surroundings a cursory glance. "What did you see young man before your light was extinguished?" I asked young Jose, hoping somehow, he would answer me. "Who did you see?" I asked finally, as I carefully replaced the covering. Respect for the dead and giving it my all to them was what I was about. Victims were someone's son, daughter, sibling, father, or mother. Can't afford to get too close, but they deserve all the respect we can give them.

"Dammit to hell!" I hollered, while standing and crossing myself as any good Catholic would, even though I was Baptist. "Sorry Lord," I quickly apologized, as anger and crossing myself may have been a bit inappropriate, but I try to cover my bases. "He called me yesterday. I was going to meet him today at our usual spot. Jose said he had some juicy information on the sex trafficking ring our department had been looking into. What a waste. This young man was starting to come around." I see young people wasting their lives every day through drug use, gangs, and violence. In many ways this city was typical of many large cities. It has its underbelly.

"I want a complete description of the kid," I requested of the Sergeant. "He may have some information that could help."

Turning to my partner, I asked, "after the stores open, I want you and a couple of the guys to take Jose's picture around and ask if they saw anything yesterday. Ask about the mystery pick pocket as well. I'm going to see if there are any eyes in the area." By eyes I meant cameras. They seem to be everywhere these days.

We left the forensic crew to do their thing and went for some early morning breakfast at a local diner. Not much we could do until business hours. Some simple bacon and grits for me. Rick had a huge breakfast. He was still a growing boy.

After breakfast we went back to the precinct to catch up on mail and messages. "No rest for the wicked, or those that fight the darkness," I said to my partner, who was at the next desk reading through some of his own mail.

"What are you thinking partner?" Rick asked after looking up from his desk. Rick leaned back in his chair and put his feet up.

Looking up, after documenting some of what I had in front of me, I saw my partner relaxed in his chair, staring at me. "Did you say something Rick?" He must have. I think he did, but I was focused on what was in front of me.

"Yes, I did Mr. Joseph Alvarez," he responded with a smile. "What do you think of the Braves this year?"

He didn't ask me that, I thought to myself. He's a football fan. "Rick, you never ask me about sports. So, what did you really ask?"

The man smiled strangely, as if he were crunching numbers in his head while trying to tell a joke. "What are your thoughts on the Jose Moreno murder?" He finally inquired.

"Plain and simple? It was a hit. That's my take on this until evidence proves otherwise. The same day he calls me on this sex trafficking ring he appears to have been assassinated. The shots were too perfect for some thug or a drive-by."

"You know what happens when you assume something? You've got to keep an open mind," Rick insisted.

"Oh, believe me, I am fully aware of not working a case with blinders on." A feeling of annoyance went through me. Young whipper snapper I wanted to call my partner. "Theories also help me to dig a little deeper or go down a not so obvious path."

"Kind of like a bulldog digging up his master's flower bed huh?"

"Exactly. Especially if the bones are buried there."

"Good point," Rick agreed with a tinge of defeat in his voice. Rick dropped his feet to the floor and leaned on his desk with his elbows. "Okay, Boss. I'll round up a couple guys and canvas the area, while you dig up the neighbor's garden."

"Funny, Rick," I said, while getting up from my desk. "Rather than using my shovel, smart ass, I'm going to see if there are any cameras in the area. Later I'll give you a call and we'll check out Jose's digs."

After gathering our things, we left the precinct together. While Rick's group was talking to possible witnesses in the area, I was on camera search, traffic, and business. Hopefully, something may show up.

We knew the approximate time of death, around 9:00 PM, and when the kid was spotted going through the deceased's pockets. That information narrows down the time of interest for any camera footage I may be able to recover. Everything is in digital format these days, either in the cloud, the camera, or some other portable device.

Detective work is tedious enough, without having to look through film, or stacks of pictures. Digital is more convenient and workable. Even with technological advancements, it isn't the glamour you see in the movies. Stakeouts are my least favorite, even though as an ex-sniper one would think I was used to it.

Rick and I met at Jose's place late in the afternoon. We found nothing. I was hoping for a big yellow post-it-note with details of what he was going to tell me today. If life was only that easy. Nothing is what Rick found as well, after talking to people in the area. It would have been dark around the time of death, so I wasn't expecting, only hoping for a witness.

We were heading back to the office to finish up some of our documentation when my cell rang. We both knew it was going to be another late night. Paperwork, late dinner on the run, and straight to bed. This happened some nights. The glamourous life of a detective. There are some days when car salesman may have been better after all.

"Detective Alvarez," I answered, while pulling into our precinct parking lot. There were a few marked and unmarked units in the lot. Captain William Hanks' car was there as well. He was a dedicated man. Staying late wasn't unusual.

"Detective," the disconnected voice said, "this is Miguel. Miguel Moreno," he said quietly.

The name struck me immediately. I knew of Miguel. That was Jose's older brother. A bit of nerves racked through my body. I don't know if his brother had been informed yet. This part of my job was stressful. Having to tell the families of the deceased was tough. My partner and I do this many times, but because we were already buried neck deep, the captain assigned the task to another.

"Yes Miguel. How can I help you?" I asked.

"Why? Why did they have to kill my brother?" He was now crying. "He had his troubles, but he was a good kid. This is going to destroy mom." Their father died several years back.

A lump was growing in my own throat. This was always difficult. "I am so sorry Miguel. I agree, he was a good kid. We will do everything we can to bring the killer to justice." There was about ten seconds of silence, but I could still hear him breathing and sniffling.

"There were two of them sons-a-bitches," Miguel said with quiet anger.

"Two? Two killers?"

My partner was as still as a mouse. He was holding on to every word.

"I told him not to go, but I followed him. His big bad brother followed him with a 9MM in his pocket. I froze and hid like a little bitch." The young man started to cry again. This was hard to hear, but I kept my composure because this was evidence about his brother's murder.

"Can we meet you at the station, Miguel?" I asked. An official statement was best.

"It happened so fast," he blubbered, ignoring my question. "One of his friends Andre texted and said he had more goods on the sex ring. He wanted to be a cop like you Detective Alvarez. It excited him to help you out on this. He looked up to you. He even kept notes like a detective, which he left here."

"Miguel, can you come in?" I repeated.

"Someone pulled my brother into the alley. They were supposed to meet in front of the store. It wasn't Andre though. It was a big guy. He didn't see it coming. It happened so fast," Miguel repeated. He was talking fast, and I could feel the anger and pain in every word.

"Take a breath Miguel," I interrupted. "Try to calm yourself. I really need for you to come to the station." I insisted.

"I saw the flash," Miguel continued. "Two of them from across the street. Didn't hear a thing, just saw the flash and a shadow of a second man at the other end of the alley."

Pieces and parts, I thought to myself. Pieces and parts to a puzzle coming to life. "Are you at home Miguel?" I continued, attempting to wrangle in the distraught young man, but he was like a balloon with a hole in it. It was all going to come out no matter what I did.

"I'm scared. What if they come after me next? Should have shot them right then and there. I might be dead, but at least I wouldn't be a coward." He pulled the phone away from his face, as the sound of his voice dropped. "I'm so sorry Jose," he said, which came across like a distant echo.

"Miguel!" I hollered into the phone. "I need for you to listen," I followed sternly.

"Okay," he finally acknowledged, breathing hard.

"Meet me at the station Miguel. You'll be safe there."

"No way. I can't trust anyone. These are some rough dudes. They can't know I was there."

"Miguel, you're an eyewitness. I need for you to help me by giving a statement."

"I am not coming in. Someone will see me there and I'll be next."

"We can protect you Miguel," which was a little stretch, for nothing was full proof.

"I can't. I've got to worry about my own ass."

"Can we meet you somewhere?" I asked the young man. He was scared to death. It was an obvious tone to his voice.

The young man was quiet for several moments. "Meet me in the large field behind my house. There's a large oak tree in the center. Jose and I used to play fort and cowboys and Indians out there. I'll bring a copy of the notes."

"When?" I asked.

"Tonight, after dark. No flashlights, okay? There should be enough moonlight for you to find your way."

"This is irregular," I said, but I finally agreed. "My partner and I will be there."

Miguel simply hung up. "I guess that is that" I said to my partner. "We have an appointment with Jose's older brother Miguel."

"He actually saw the murderers?" Rick asked, being able to piece quite a bit together from the one-sided conversation.

"Yes, he did," I answered excitedly. "What a break, and better yet, Jose took notes and Miguel is handing them over. Maybe we'll catch the murderers and crack open the sex ring. If only we could be that lucky." I was cautiously optimistic.

"Where and when partner?" Rick inquired.

"A field behind Miguel's house. There's a large oak in the middle. No flashlights. Miguel is scared enough, don't want to spook him."

"I don't like this, Joe. We're going to stumble around in the dark, in a field?"

"It's a half moon and supposed to be clear. I would prefer some more backup, but the kid will just bolt." I've been in worse situations than this.

It took some convincing for the captain to let us go alone, but he finally agreed to our little rendezvous.

After getting a bite to eat, we took a little rest at the station before it was time to leave. Didn't want to leave on an empty stomach. At the captain's insistence, we put on some body armor, left the station, and drove to the area a little early.

We drove over in my car because it was less conspicuous. A large dark sedan almost screams G-Men. My car is a compact, ten-year-old green car, with a few patches of primer for good measure. My choice is to drive a car until it falls apart. My baby still has plenty of umph left in her.

"Are you ever going to trade up Joe?" Rick inquired as he wiped some dust off the dash and picked up a used wrapper from the floor.

"No need to waste money my man," I responded, or closer to repeated. We have had this conversation before. "There's only me to worry about. If I keep up the maintenance, I don't see an issue. My goal is to make it to 300,000 miles. A man should always have goals," I followed with a laugh. "What of your dull blue grocery-getter my young man? It's nothing special."

"I have a family Joe, so size does matter. My wife and I have been saving up for a Hummer for quite some time."

"Hummer? Are you kidding me? You might as well drive a tank, and with gas being over $4.00 per gallon, you may have to sell one of your kids."

"You're just jealous," Rick fired back. "This tank will keep my family safer."

How in the hell can he afford a Hummer, I wondered? "Enough said," I insisted. After several passes through the neighborhood, we parked in the back of the local school, approximately a half mile away. We will skirt the football field and make our way into the field from the north end. The field was partially wooded, so it is a tossup as to whether it could be considered a woods or field. Personally, the more cover the better.

My partner and I waited until dark, gathered our things and set off around the football field. It was slow going. Don't need a broken ankle. The oak tree was just as Miguel described it. Even in the growing dark, we could see some ropes hanging off it.

"Miguel," I said quietly when we were near the tree. "Miguel, it's Detective Alvarez," I said a little louder this time.

"Is that you?" A voice came out of the dark.

"Where are you? I can't see a damned thing in the trees."

"I'm on the other side of the oak," Miguel answered. It felt like we were in a game of Marco Polo.

After a few moments I located the young man hiding in the bushes by the tree. Rick was right behind me. "Keep lookout, will you Rick?" I asked.

Got him trained well, I thought to myself. Rick moved off about twenty yards, near another, yet smaller tree.

After approaching the young man, he finally left his hiding place, but not by much. I could tell by his heavy breathing that he wasn't comfortable with all this cloak and dagger shit.

Once standing in front of him, I shook the man's hand, for I knew how much this took for him to come forward.

"Your brother would be proud," I said, just as a flash and loud crack instantly followed from a distance, disturbing the silence and darkness. The blood spattered my face, as I felt the young man's grip tighten slightly. My instincts kicked in, as I threw the young man to the ground, with me right beside him.

"Sniper!" I yelled, as I pulled his lifeless body behind the tree. I would recognize the sound of a sniper rifle in my sleep, but this was no dream. Another shot then rang out, hitting a tree behind me. Dammit, he's shooting at my partner. I already realized he had to have an infrared scope.

"You okay, Rick?" I asked with extreme concern. This was now like a war zone.

"Fine," he responded, as I reached inside my pouch, and extracted my own personal pair of night goggles. Always be prepared my dad would say, and wear clean underwear, would be more like my mom's comment.

"Stay put, stay down, and call it in," I insisted of my partner. This was my kind of environment.

After putting on the goggles, which I spent a pretty penny on, the darkness around me came alive. Staying behind the tree, I looked around and could only see my partner, nearly laying on the ground. "Move a few feet to your left," I requested. Better protection behind one of the trees. I instinctively knew the approximate direction of the shot, but he could have already moved.

I put my hand on Miguel's neck, but there was no sign of life. Didn't have time to get pissed. My composure was critical under the current circumstances. Laying a few feet from the body, I noticed what looked like a notebook. After stuffing it into my vest, I slowly scanned the area around us, looking for movement or any out of place heat source.

From a tree about 100 yards off, I could see a man lowering himself to the ground. You're not getting away that easy, I said to myself, but a hundred yards was a little far for my sidearm. Keeping him in sight, I quickly moved in a crouched position from tree to tree. Some movement was then coming from my left, seemingly moving parallel with me. Was it Rick, I wondered? This is a sticky situation. Rather than risk hitting Rick, I dropped low to the ground and decided to wait for the cavalry. I've got the notes and there was no sense anyone else getting shot tonight.

With my head barely above the mound I managed to get behind, I watched in defeat as the sniper moved away from us.

"Joe?" I then heard in a whisper, from my left as expected.

"I told you to stay put," I said quietly, but with noticeable disappointment. It was with reasonable certainty I could have caught up with the man, but not tonight.

"Where did you put the notes?" Rick asked me flatly, as sirens could be heard in the distance.

"How could you know that?" I asked. It became clear rather quickly that this was a trap. My partner of five years, whom I shared meals and jokes with, and cried with, was standing there with his own night goggles placed upon his face and a 22-caliber pistol leveled at my forehead.

"Sorry, Joe. Just business," he said while pulling the trigger, with a coldness of heart, nearly freezing the air around him. I could feel myself rising from the ground, being pulled into the unknown with my anger intact, hearing voices around me, but not here, from somewhere else. A distant echo.

Rick tossed his gun, gloves and night goggles to his partner waiting close by, who then took off to join the other one waiting a couple blocks away. Rick fired a few shots with his police sidearm for good measure. He then instantly searched his partner for the notes. Miguel was clean, his other partner made sure of it. Rick didn't have much time, but after a quick search with the flashlight they were nowhere to be seen.

Chapter 27

My legs were shaking as a shiver ran through my body like an ice-cold creek, and a sharp pain streaked through my skull. A memory of being shot was foremost on my mind. Cold rain was pouring down my face. I found myself in my backyard, standing in a pouring rain, lightning streaking across the sky, with a death grip on my new privacy fence. The fog was lifting from my mind as I was able to start to focus on my surroundings. A powerful anger was rising within me as the pain lessened. Get ahold of yourself Bob, I had to tell myself. Concentrating on just my hands, for they were starting to hurt, I tried to pull them loose. Rather than just releasing the poor fence to live another day, I let out a guttural cry, ripped one of the boards off the cross members, and tossed it across the yard.

The tension began to lessen, and I was able to release my left hand without too much damage besides a few splinters. "Congratulation Detective Alvarez, you succeeded in killing my fence."

With my head to the sky, I let the rain wash across my face, if for no other reason than to calm him the hell down. Another ominous streak of lighting bolted from the sky. "Oh shit!" I shouted, as I hobbled back into the house. It might have been May, but I was downright cold, and my legs were shaking.

My wife was asleep, so I quietly went into the bathroom after grabbing some dry underwear and my robe. My head was splitting. "Tylenol," I mumbled to myself, while rummaging through the medicine cabinet, and praying the bullet didn't come with the dream. Found the pills and downed three of them, chased by tap water. Went to sleep in my day clothes, which now weighed an additional ten pounds. Once my soaked shirt was off and thrown into the hamper, I noticed there was something down my left pant leg, and in my left pocket. I dug the detective's badge out of my pocket, and then after ripping off my belt and dropping my drawers, there was the notebook nearly wrapped around my leg. After setting the notebook and badge aside I hung up my belt and threw my pants into the same hamper. I stayed calm but was annoyed at this point.

After I dried off, and covered up, I stared into the mirror. "Are you there, Joe?" I asked quietly. "Nothing," I said after a few moments. "Shy, huh?"

"So, Lord," I started to mumble, while beginning to pace the bathroom floor. "You thought I was getting bored with my other activities, so you thought you would give me another adventure?" I sat down on the toilet, to finish my one-way conversation, but rather than pacing, I almost looked like I was using sign language. "Why can't I retire peacefully with my wife? Could you pass this to someone else?" Jonah from the book of Jonah, flashed across my memory. Maybe this isn't a total one-way conversation after all, I thought. "Oh great. If I don't obey, I will spend a few days in the belly of a great beast? What of free will?" I asked regretfully, just before another great streak of lightning lit up the sky through the windows of the bathroom, followed by a rumble that shook our very foundation. I quickly lowered my head into my now shaking hands. "Sorry Lord, I'll shut up now," I said, but I had to lighten the mood. "Hey Lord, I know you've heard the joke, but why do cows wear bells?" On the next street over, early in the morning, a car's warning horn pierced the dark of the night. I instantly got it. "That was perfect timing Lord. Now that was funny," I said, as I stood up from the toilet, placed my foot on a wet spot, slipped, and fell flat on my ass. I pointed to the ceiling, wagged my finger, and laughed. "So, I guess the yokes on me."

With a song in my heart, after being humbled by God, the greatest comedian of all time, I decided to make breakfast for my sleeping beauty. "Two ham and cheese omelets coming right up," I said, before starting to hum the tune "Joy to The World", by Three Dog Night, one of my favs.

After taking a few minutes to set the table, I whipped the hell out of the eggs. They never had a chance. I sang quietly, while adding a little milk to the mix. Two pieces of bread in the toaster, while waiting on the pan to heat. The song referenced drinking wine which sounds like a clever idea about now, I thought, as I poured the eggs, cheese, and ham into the skillet. It didn't take long. The mixture was bubbling, and smells were permeating every corner of the kitchen. The toaster popped, but the eggs were too close to being done to butter them yet. I sang out louder, as I gently folded the eggs, and slid them onto our plates, after cutting the large omelet in half. After smoothing out a slice of butter on each piece of wheat toast, I went into the chorus about the deep blue sea, loud and clear.

I saw her at the door, out of the corner of my eye. "You awake now, Honey," I said sheepishly, smiling as I placed the plates on the table.

She stood there for a moment, rubbing her eyes. "You're a mess, Honey," she said, as she moved slowly to the table and sat down in her usual seat. She wasn't quite awake yet. Her hair was everywhere. She must wear a CPAP mask now. Every night, it does a job on her hair and face.

"Darth, what would you like to drink, juice, milk, or something else?" I asked, as I put down a glass of orange juice for myself. I've gotten into a habit of calling her Darth, especially when she tries to talk to me through the mask.

"Milk is fine," Susan said, just before a large yawn broke across her face. It was super huge, I thought. Any further and she'll dislocate her jaw.

"Milk it is," I responded as I brought her a glass, along with the milk and juice, in case we wanted more.

I sit at the end of the table and my wife usually sits to my left. We will face each other in a restaurant, but at our longer table, she sits closer to me.

After we sat down, she looked at me strangely. "So, Bob, what is up with you this morning? You seem awfully chipper."

"Let's say grace first," I insisted, "and I'll tell you." After grace, we started eating. A bite of omelet, followed by a sip of juice. "I think congratulations are in order," I chimed in. "You'll be happy to know I just gave birth to triplets."

I know she heard me, but she kept eating, while glancing up at me occasionally.

"No really, Honey," I said with a smile.

"Is one of them an elephant?" she asked, straight faced. She thought I was telling one of my jokes, so she was trying to get ahead of me.

I grabbed Susan's hand and looked her in the eyes. "Honey, I am serious. Their names are Jonathan, Tad, and Joseph. Actually, it is officially Detective Joseph Alvarez, retired Army Green Beret."

My wife was now staring at me. She had already put down her fork. "Not a bad omelet if I say so myself," I added with a smile and a shrug.

"Are you saying what I think you are saying?" Susan asked, with a furrowed brow and the cutest twist to her lips.

"Yes," I answered simply. "Isn't it great," I added with a half-hearted laugh. "I had a third dream, or whatever we should call them." I rubbed my forehead where the pain was. "I've been drowned, baked and suffocated, and now, shot right between the eyes." I started to laugh, after I grabbed both of my wife's hands. "I'm started to feel like a Timex. "Takes and licking and keeps on ticking.""

"I'm so sorry, Honey, that you have to keep going through this." My wife was with me 100%. Through thick and thin.

We started eating again, while I recounted the story of Detective Joseph Alvarez.

"One good thing, Susan," I mentioned as we were clearing the table. "I have picked up some very interesting skills. I can hit the center of a quarter at 500 yards and gained some cool self-defense skills. Do you remember the movie "John Wick", Honey?"

"Vaguely," she responded, as she took the last swig of her milk.

In my best Russian accent, I could muster. "I can also kill four people in a bar with just a pencil." Susan looked at me strangely. "Only if the need ever arises, of course."

She then put her left hand on her hip and pointed her finger at me. "Now, Robert Franklin Johnson," she said with a stern look on her face. Am I in trouble? I had to ask myself. "If you go into a bar, let alone start killing people with a pencil, I'm coming at you with my broom, and it's a whole lot bigger than a measly pencil. Now, if you don't want it right up the caboose, you had better put down that pencil." She finished with a smile on her face. I love her smile, but she can swing a mean broom too.

We had a good laugh. Besides, what else are we to do? Welcome Joe, to the Johnson residence is what, unless I want to be swallowed by the Kraken. With God's sense of humor, I won't be vomited out after learning the error of my ways, I'll slide out the other end. The coast guard will be extracting this big pile of shit named Bob from the ocean. I'll be the one singing "Joy to the world", while bobbing on the ocean waves.

After cleaning up, we went about our day. I had some notes to absorb. Haven't looked at the first page.

Chapter 28

The notebook was awaiting my attention, but despite the push from inside, I was determined to patch my fence first. "You did it, so you can wait," I said to Joe as if he were a child. It didn't take long. Four new screws, a little patching, and except for the needed future application of sealant it looked as good as new.

I assumed Joe knew how long he had been gone, for he knows what I know, right? Even after eleven years of this, it is still disturbing. They probably know more about my past than my wife does. No hidden skeletons with these guys. At least there isn't a girl involved here.

After getting a grip on my open past, I went inside, grabbed a large glass of tea, sat at the kitchen table, and pulled the tattered notebook in front of me. I was praying nothing was damaged from the rain. I rifled through the pages and discovered some photos in an inner sleeve of the front cover. There were ten photos and twenty pages of notes. All seemed undamaged. This young man had great penmanship, and the photos were high definition, date stamped even, and well done. While handling the notebook, I noticed a small lump deep down inside the sleeve where the photos were held. It was exceedingly small, nearly imperceptible, and almost missed. I couldn't remove it with just my fingers. With a flashlight, I could tell it was neatly taped into the corner. Could have ripped off the sleeve to get at it but chose instead to operate. To avoid damaging whatever it was, I grabbed one of my wife's tweezers, and spent nearly ten minutes pulling the tape loose. This was like a treasure hunt. Turned out to be a mini data storage chip. "Very James Bondish," I said with a smile. "This will require an adapter," I said while turning it over in my hands. "Can't plug it in like a thumb drive." It was in a small plastic case no more than a quarter inch square.

"Great job young man," I said with some sadness. "Now let's see what we have here."

My wife had invested in some high-end computer hardware and software for some of her own artistic endeavors. Each page, including the photographs, were scanned and a folder called "Dream Weavers" created to hold them. No particular reason I chose that, other than this all came to me in a dream. It was important there were at least two copies of this folder that three people died for. In the back of my mind, I was thinking about a fail-safe. If something happens to me, it will be sent to ten different people, and maybe the president. Maybe that high up wasn't necessary, but someone considered large and in charge.

After gathering a blank notebook, magnifying glass, a pen, and Jose's book, I retired to my favorite space. My La-Z-Boy recliner. Do you know when a certain point arrives in a story or movie that is magical or angelic in its power, when out of nowhere a choir of angels belt out "Ahhhhhhhhh!", which is just short of "Hallelujah!". That's my La-Z-Boy. Mine has a massage feature. It's like stretching out on a cloud, except this cloud has a few more doo dads. My wife and I don't spend excessively, but certain comforts are important, I convinced myself before hopping out of the La-Z-Boy store on one leg. It required that I sign over my left leg to them.

Got up a few times, but all-in-all I spent four hours in the chair and didn't even take a nap. Absorbed and memorized every word and with a magnifying glass went just as deep on the photos. One page was a detailed diagram of the businesses and owners connected to four properties. This kid had to be computer savvy to get the information he did. Took four pages of my own notes of key points, adding some from my own memory, or Joe's, or whoever's. Doesn't really matter. We are now joined at the hip or lobe you could say.

Somehow, this young man had located three, not one, but three of the sites where women and some young men were held until they were called up for service. It had been three years, but I could only hope all the sites weren't changed. The photos showed some exceedingly clear pictures of the three sites and some of the player's comings and goings. One of them I instantly recognized as one of the higher ups in the ring. One Franco Domenico. Suspected involvements in sex and drug trafficking. Incredibly good looking and squeaky clean on the surface, but black as pitch underneath his façade.

A few of the pictures appeared to be of Franco's home in the hills, out of the way, and very secure. "Now how did he get these pictures?" I wondered. "You were an amazing up and comer, but you probably went one step too far and got yourself killed." One picture was even a selfie with the home in the background. "You got some balls kid." Jose was even able to name a few of the faces. Couldn't help but smile at the thoroughness of the work. "You would have made one hell of a detective."

After yawning and rubbing my eyes a few times, I stopped. Four hours was long enough. I was getting tired and wanted to do something else. The grass needed mowing and I could use the nap. I created a file folder to hold all of this, and being a little paranoid, I named it "Furnace Maintenance". We have good security, but extra steps wouldn't hurt. That is overkill of course, because unless these guys can trace dreams into the future, they won't see this coming. Until I make any moves, if I do, they will remain clueless.

Susan and I were planning to go out for pizza later, so I had time to mow, shower and get a short rest. After putting all notes into the new file, the pictures were next. While gathering them up however, something caught my attention in the selfie Jose took. There was someone in one of the side windows of Franco's extravagant home. "How did I miss this?" I berated myself. This person appears to be looking straight at Jose. Could he have been spotted? Is this what got this young man on their radar? I quickly grabbed my magnifying glass still on my side table. I couldn't help but curse as I examined the photo. "Gotcha, Gotcha, Gotcha!" I then shouted out while standing and pointing my finger at the stranger in the window, except he wasn't a stranger at all. This was a clear picture of Detective Richard Turner. I started dancing and fist pumping like I just made a fifty-foot putt for eagle. "What a gift this is!" Now I would have to figure out how best to gift wrap everything.

When we went for dinner, I told her little of what I was working on. This is some dangerous information. It was nothing like what I discovered with Jonathan and Tad. This was a hot potato, and I wasn't planning on tossing this scorcher to my Susan. "If I tell you," I said, "I will have to kill you, with a pencil," trying my best to keep things light, because the last thing I need is to worry my wife.

The following morning, while Susan was resting in her recliner, I made a trip to an electronics store, and purchased what I needed to download the data off Jose's device. "Jackpot," I said, as the treasure trove of data loaded onto our computer. The disc included digitized copies of the pictures, videos, financials for Mr. Domenico and some money trails the young man had discovered. This was exciting and very damaging for several people. This boy was a cyber genius even though some of what he did was very illegal.

The remainder of day two I spent going over the added information and examining the pictures closely on the computer screen to verify I didn't miss something important. One particularly important thing I was able to magnify well on the computer was Detective Turner's favorite tattoo of a hoot owl on his left forearm. Nothing like additional identifiers to put an extra nail in his coffin.

Couldn't help but smile as I moved on to the videos, which had great sound. Must have used a sound amplification devise. Wasn't a lot there, except some voices to go with the players, and a smattering of damaging comments spread throughout the masterpiece of videography. There were a few name droppers too. How sweet. My notes went quickly from four pages to twenty and counting.

My time and energy were focused so deeply on the project in front of me, I hardly noticed the comings and goings of my wife. I felt bad about this later in the day. "Joseph," I said. "This is important stuff to you. I realize this, but I've got my life too and my wife is extremely important to me." I filed everything away. "Going to spend a few days with my wife away from the house," was my last word as I sat down next to my wife in the living room. She was watching some cartoonish movie.

I snuggled up to my honey, which doesn't happen as much these days. After looking over at my wife and smiling, as we held hands, a little sadness creeped over me. When we were dating and early in our marriage, our bodies were nearly glued together. Couldn't get enough of the touch of her skin, warmth of her body and love was flowing like honey. I missed that, but I understood life is what happens to you and surviving at times is all that can be hoped for. Our love for each other is as strong as ever, but the body gets worn around the edges, taking some things for granted does happen, and body parts don't quite work as well as they used to. The aging rules have been different for me however since 2017. My doctor, who recently retired, continued to give me A+ ratings, and no medications required. He wanted some of what I had. My physical shape is better than it ever had been, and my strength is notable. People tell me often that I haven't aged a bit, and they mean it. My aging has slowed to a crawl.

I gave my honey a soft kiss, and we settled in watching whatever it is she was watching. It didn't matter because I could feel her heartbeat syncing with mine. Love is a grand thing. My last thoughts, prior to sleep, were of concern for our lives together if things continue as they are. It should be a joyous thing to be given a wonderful physical gift like I have been endowed with, but it is mixed with sadness, thinking my wife will leave me behind.

Chapter 29

The name of this book will probably be "Justice is Mine", I am thinking, as I worked feverishly toward the unwritten and unlived ending. Another true account of a fictional story, or more accurately, a fictional account of a true story? As the scriptures may teach us, vengeance is mine says the Lord, it doesn't say we may not be of any assistance.

It had been six months since Detective Joseph Alvarez became a part of me. In that time, my wife got the best of me. She broke me down and bribed me to bring her in on the story. Her beautiful eyes and pouting lips slay me. I was weak, and besides I hated to keep things from her.

No longer attempting to hide anything, my dining room table is now covered with notes, various documents, or copies thereof, pictures, and our computer. The contraption sure has been put through its paces. My wife now reminds me that I was neater when I was being secretive, but she does enjoy helping with my research.

We have both researched all relevant news for the Atlanta area for May 03, 2025, until today, November 21, 2028. Richard Turner, Joseph's ex-partner, had been promoted to Detective Third Class. According to the news, the racket that was part of the dark underbelly of Atlanta is still alive and well today. I was praying Franco Domenico, and his partners, including good old Richard Turner, would have been busted by now. Jail was to matter of fact for this man. Guillotine would be more appropriate for a man of his stature.

Susan startled me as she put her hand on my shoulder. "Dearest," she started out. Oh no, I thought. Many times, which is how she begins her I need a favor speech. "Dearest detective, author, dreamer, and keeper of my heart," she continued. That's a little thick don't you think? "It's nearly Thanksgiving, and all the kids will be here for once. Can you please give this a rest through the holidays? I would love to spend the time relaxing with our kids and each other. We need this. I especially need this."

The tone of her voice concerned me. "Sure, Honey," I quickly responded. "Are you feeling okay?" I then asked. She had been sleeping in more. But then again, who doesn't like to sleep in.

"Peachy, Honey. Just a little tired is all."

"Are you taking your vitamins?" was my next go to question. She had been almost religious about taking her gummy vitamins. I was the one to be fussed at for that transgression.

"Yes, Honey. I take my vitamins."

"You need more fresh air," I added to my list of cures. "You stopped going with me when I golfed. Even though you no longer golf, I still enjoy your company."

"Yes Dr. Kildare. I'll try to get out more. I'm thinking about joining you at the gym, if for nothing else than a little walking and hip exercise."

"Dr. Kildare? Now that's a blast from the past." I gave her a grin and a wink. "You know, Honey? I'll be happy to give you some home-grown hip exercises."

"You clean this up, and put it away," we'll see what evolves.

"Is that a bribe?" I asked sheepishly, for which I received no direct answer, just a smile from Susan while leaving the room.

We had an early dinner, and early to bed as well. My anticipation meter was up in the red zone, but it was not to be. We cuddled and she quickly went to sleep on my chest. "Well crap," I said quietly to myself, as I ran my hands through her now white hair. Just as soft as ever. "Love of my life, sleep tight," my voice would fall softly on her ears, hoping selfishly she would awake, and she would giggle under the sheets while I did some exploring once more.

As I was nearly asleep, with Susan breathing quietly on my chest, I heard what sounded like the quiet mewing sounds of a cat. Unless it was coming from outside, it couldn't be. We said our last sad goodbyes to our final pet six years ago. She was a calico, very affectionate, but very fat. She loved being brushed, which was a necessity, or her presence would be seen all over the house. She would require an occasional bathing as well. This girl was so fat she couldn't clean her own backside, and there were times when she would be caught with her head halfway in the water bowl. What a lazy thing she was, but we loved her regardless. My wife insisted we get no more pets after she died.

After a short search for the source of this sound, I found it was the scraping of the crepe myrtle bush lightly against our bedroom window. The bush started as a twig, a gift from my wife's mother. Wasn't sure it would survive, but it flourished. So much so, I find myself trimming it each winter. At night, when the wind blows, a few of the pods would gently scrape against the glass, creating the mystery sound.

After crawling quietly back into bed, mystery solved, before falling to sleep, I could almost hear the giggling that used to come out of our room, especially when the kids were younger. Our daughters would get embarrassed, knowing the difference in their mother's giggles when their parents were enjoying themselves, or the impish grin on our faces afterwards. It was our unconscious signal that all was well in the bedroom, or now that our children have moved out, any damned place we pleased. There were times when we gave them a look on purpose, to simply get a rise out of our children and now even the grandchildren. "Yuck Mom," they might say.

"Well, how do you think you got here in the first place," one or both of us would reply. "We don't prescribe to the stork or pumpkin patch method of childbirth."

"Yea, but double yuck," they may say. "We don't need to know all of this."

Now, mom being who she was, would love to mess with them. It was a sight to behold. Without being overly vulgar, she may expound on our little love encounters, just to see what kind of rise she could get. There were times when the receiver of the news had to leave the room, or if over the phone was forced to say goodbye sooner than they had planned. My memories are sharp, especially when it comes to the fun times.

There was one time. I laugh each time I think of it. We were both in our recliners, enjoying a movie together. Our youngest daughter called her mom, so I paused the movie. Can't remember now what the conversation was over. Doesn't matter, for it wasn't the funny part. The conversation went on for some time. Longer than Susan liked, for she saw I had closed my eyes and was almost asleep she thought. Rather than be rude, and cut the conversation off, she switched to a bit of a crude method of reclaiming our time. "Thanks again honey for the new comforter," Susan said to her, changing the subject. They were on face time, and I wished she could have recorded it.

"You're welcome mom," she responded.

"It was so soft," Susan added, as she flashed her patented grin. "Your father and I couldn't help but break it in this morning."

"Mom!" she said, but she knew her and didn't need an explanation. It was more of a stop, Mom. Please stop, Mom.

There was a literary pause, I guess you could say, before she rammed home the punchline. "I didn't know I could bend that far. It was an immediate up periscope for your dad. It was great," she finished with a giggle.

All I could hear, before they hung up, was a long drawn out, "yuckkkkkk Mom."

I nearly rolled out of the recliner, I started laughing so hard. My wife is a pip. Rather than immediately resume the movie, we decided to try whatever rad position Susan had on her mind, and she was correct, she couldn't bend that far.

It was difficult, because I was so close to wrapping up my research and my book, but as agreed, I put it all away for safe keeping. The holidays were fantastic. We were able to spend a lot of time with the family. Weather held up well enough to where I was able to get in four more rounds of golf by year end. My wife went with me for three of those. In the middle of December, we took a short trip to stay at our favorite bed and breakfast and visit our friends in the area. Some of them were appearing especially worn around the edges. Time and life can be unforgiving, but so far, it has been especially good to me.

Chapter 30

The year 2029 came in smoothly but rose to a bang. Something we rarely do is attend parties, especially New Year's Eve. Partier and the Johnsons don't come up in the same sentence. Rose Thompson, still living in Mobile, invited the two of us to a New Year's Eve bash that her family was hosting at their home. We were there only two weeks prior, but we couldn't turn them down, for they were technically or cosmologically family. New Year's resolutions were something we also never cottoned to. If you plan to do something, just do it. I was resolute in finishing this project I embarked on. For obvious reasons, this one worried me the most.

Since I don't consider New Year's Eve as part of a family holiday, I took time to tie together all details of my research and complete my book prior to leaving for the New Year's Eve party. "Justice Is Mine," was now in the hands of my publisher and my safety in the hands of my God.

The party was fantastic. My wife drank a few wine coolers, which loosened her up fabulously. We participated in a couple of line dances. Some white people just can't dance, and I was one of them, but I did my best. We kissed at the stroke of midnight. Our night was complete when we made love in one of the guest rooms at the Thompson's. It was a great party.

Three months had passed. A box of my books had just arrived, and I was as ready as I was ever going to be. A couple of months earlier I just received my license for conceal and carry. A pretty 9MM Glock I had become amazingly comfortable with. Because I do travel, I learned the laws of the various states.

I packed my things, gave my wife a very warm kiss and was now off to Atlanta. Driving was always my preference. This gave me time to reminisce over my very unusual past and consider my future.

Susan had been a great sport through it all, but we did have a heated discussion before I left. She wanted me to just drop my package and run. I informed her that is an option, but I don't think I can do that. The feeling I had was that an additional incentive to accept the information was necessary. I told her she needed to trust me and leave all in God's hands.

On the way down I was praying this was the end, but God's plans don't necessarily coincide with ours. Above all things, God's will be done. Praying for a safe conclusion to this project, and that justice is served, is especially important to me and Joe.

Going up and down hills, especially in Tennessee, reminds me of life itself. It has its ups and downs also. Births and deaths, health and illness, happiness and anger, good and evil, all part of life and the many obstacles we must overcome before the glorious finish line. My memories of dating my wife are varied, heartwarming and exciting. We tell our girls how perfect angels we were. Kept our proper distance, respected our parents' wishes, and saved ourselves till marriage. They were wiser than that. Our girls wouldn't pay a dime for the load of crap we were selling. Were there regrets? Well yes. Would we have done things different, knowing what we know now. Perhaps. I, however, wouldn't change what we have now for the world, even if it required making the same mistakes twice.

Less than 100 miles to go till the outskirts of Atlanta. My nerves were growing with the butterflies in my stomach. "You can do this," I said to myself. Turned on some country music to drown out the silence around me, helped. I was desperately needing some distraction.

While in the area, so it's not all business, my plan was to visit Stone Mountain, get in some hiking and golfing. Not a bad goal for a 74-year-old. It even crossed my mind, while on a hike, to just bury everything I've brought with me, and simply go home to forget all about this. There is a lot more at stake here than mere justice for Detective Alvarez and the two young men. God is more than capable of taking care of that issue on his own timetable.

Using my GPS, I arrived at the Marriott in downtown Atlanta by 1:00 PM. Made it in one piece. A great start for my James Bond adventure. Since there was time before check-in, I grabbed lunch and dropped a few packages off at the local post office. Time in the hotel gym and a few laps in the pool sounded like a great idea. Anything to burn off some of my nervous energy, but my first major task was to check out one of the local parks. I love to sightsee.

After being satisfied I was on the right track and doing the right thing, I grabbed a light dinner and went to my room. It was pleasant enough but missing one thing. My wife. Before turning in, feeling very lonely, I hit the gym hard and followed it up with a few laps in the pool to finish winding down. After a shower, long talk with my wife, to assure her all will be okay, and my nightly discussion with God, I turned in. Spent the first two hours staring at the flickers of light on the ceiling, the mystery shadow in the corner, and the little lights on the electronic equipment attached to the flat screen TV. My eyes finally became extremely heavy and off I went into the shadows of sleep.

My preference would be to dream for the next twenty hours or so, but morning arrived in a flash. We are in control of truly little in our lives, naturally when the morning arrives is one of them. There is no magic watch that stalls time, which would be one neat contraption, or a button that would fast forward through the unpleasantness like in the movie "Click". Time is God's construct, and we simply move through it like an imperceptible glimmer. What we do with our time is within the debatable subject of free will.

All I could swallow was half a bagel and juice. My butterflies had turned into bats. After taking quite some time to prepare for my day, I finally left the hotel looking like a new man.

Under my own free will, and not Detective Alvarez, I drove to a busy service station, but parked around the corner, and asked to use their phone. They were reluctant at first, but I assured them it was local, and who could turn down a feeble and kind ninety-year-old man in a cleanly pressed brown suit and matching brown walrus hat. Coming from underneath the walrus hat, was a beautiful mane of white hair, falling upon my shoulders. Looked something like a hippy professor from the 70s. After pulling a folded piece of paper from my pocket, I nervously keyed in the number for the Midtown Precinct.

"Midtown Precinct, Officer Brown speaking, how may I help you?" Very professional, I thought as I was nearly at the point of no return.

"Yes, young man," I answered in a very weak tone, and followed with a slight cough. Remember, you are ninety and weak. Play the part. It was funny in a way, because it felt like all four of me were wrapped up in this. My resolve was strengthening, along with my backbone. I can do this. "Could I speak with a Detective Turner please? If it's not too much trouble sir." Smooth it on.

"He is on another call sir. May I ask who's calling?"

"Yes, Officer Brown. My name is Jonathan Boynes. That's French you know," I followed with a smile to my voice, and a cough. "Pardon me."

"That's okay. I will tell him you are on hold."

"That is mighty kind young man. May I ask you a question, Officer Brown?" I quickly inquired. My alter ego knew an Officer Brown, and the voice rang a bell.

"Are you Dewey Brown by any chance?" I was hoping so. He was a genuinely nice man, and Joe even met his wife a couple times at some gatherings.

"Why yes, it is Jonathan."

He is warming up to me. Time for some impromptu story weaving. "Your wife. Her name wouldn't be Bernice, would it?" His wife was a beautiful lady and a nurse at one of the bigger hospitals. Floor nurse at the Emery University hospital if Joe's memory is accurate.

"Yes again. Do we know you?"

"I don't think I've met you, but wasn't she a floor nurse at the Emory a few years back?"

"She still is. She's been in ICU for four years now."

"My mind is a little foggy these days. Not surprising for a ninety-two-year-old." Plausible deniability. Any mistakes, blame it on memory loss. "She is a beautiful young lady."

"Thank you," he quickly responded. "I think so."

"I hope you don't get to upset with me, but I think I may have proposed to her. A little doped up you know. Just had heart surgery." I laughed and then coughed for good measure. My story sounds so real, I might even believe it.

"Oh, believe me Mr. Boynes, you aren't the only one. She gets proposals fairly often, but not all are proper."

I could hear phones ringing, so it was time to cut him off before I had to make up more big ones. "Sorry Officer, I don't mean to babble, it's just a small world you know. Go ahead and put me on hold before I start talking about my sons. Got two of them."

"Okay Mr. Boynes. It was nice talking to you. He will be with you soon." After putting me on hold I let out a good cleansing breath.

"Detective Turner," he finally answered after enduring ten minutes of bad background music. The sound of his voice sent shivers up my spine.

"Good morning, Detective Turner," I said with as much pleasure in my voice as I could muster. "My name is Jonathan Boynes."

"Yes Mr. Boynes. How may I help you?" What a proper young man. Makes me want to puke.

"Actually, Detective Turner, I have something for you. "Ask and it will be given to you; seek and you will find; knock and the door will be opened to you." Matthew 7:7," I quoted. He may think I am a bit looney, which is great. Keep the bum guessing.

"Mr. Boynes, I am a busy man." He said with a sigh of annoyance.

"Jonathan. Please call me Jonathan."

"Jonathan then," he said flatly. "What do you have for me?"

"Great question." I paused. "I realize you're a busy man, with all the criminals to catch, but if you give me a little of your time, it will definitely be an interesting conversation." Just enough elusiveness to keep him on the hook.

"Jonathan, can you come down to the precinct? We can talk here."

"Says the spider to the fly," I said quietly with some good tone to it. "No sir, I would prefer to meet somewhere private."

"I think I am going to hang up now," Richard said to me.

“Detective Alvarez wouldn’t hang up on me,” I put out there, which resulted in dead silence, so I continued. “You see, Detective, I know you use snitches now and then, and about four years ago young Jose had a package for Detective Alverez. I now have it,” I added, which now makes me a target. I couldn’t help it. I started looking over my shoulder with a little shiver.

“Who are you?” I could tell his tone had changed. His interest was piqued. That package is deadly.

“Just an interested citizen. I wish to see justice served and don’t mind helping out a fellow officer to achieve that goal.”

“Were you a police officer?” Richard inquired. Fishing the man is.

“In another life son. In another life.” Which is a true statement. “Before that, feels like 200 years ago or so, I was an officer in the U.S. Navy.” I wanted to laugh, because in a way that was true as well.

“Okay Mr. Boynes, where would you like to meet and when?”

“Very good, Detective. Very good. Three hours at the Piedmont Park. Do you know of it?” Naturally, he does. He took his kids to the picnic area and playground.

“Yes sir. I know it well. It’s a big park, so where do you wish to meet, and how will I know you?”

“Great,” I responded with enthusiasm. “Picnic area, and I’ll find you.” After dropping the phone onto the receiver, cutting the man off, I was thinking about how rude that was as I was laughing while driving away.

Surely Richard wouldn’t be this predictable, I was thinking, while parking my car a distance from the actual park, but this wasn’t a chance I was about to take. More proof was required to put the man away for murder. Joseph Alvarez was exerting much influence on this situation, and besides, I was feeling like Bond, James Bond. “Pride commeth before the fall,” I whispered to myself.

Getting to the park early, with a small, but powerful binoculars I had purchased, I watched the obvious spots where a lone gunman could wait in relative secrecy. “Nobody gets the drop on James Bond,” I said to myself, trying to keep the nerves down.

It was nearly one hour and fifteen minutes after I ended the phone call, that I spotted a man of curiosity. He was carrying a bag over his shoulder, and carefully observing his surroundings as he approached one of the target areas. "You little bastard," I cursed, while partially hidden behind a tree about two hundred yards off. I was relatively certain the man shimmied up a nearby tree and was waiting there. "Predictable you are young man."

After putting my glare free, high-resolution sunglasses back on, I carefully made my way to his assumed position. It took over half an hour to worm my way around bushes and trees, making sure I wasn't observed by anyone else in the area. I almost missed him, but fortunate for me, he was in the exact tree I thought he was in. He was rather good, I observed. He made himself a well camouflaged nest on a thick tree limb about ten feet off the ground. There was a small opening facing the picnic area as expected. Fortunate for me, his back and sides were covered. This would give me the needed cover if I could climb the other side of the tree without alerting him.

My newfound athleticism gave me confidence. My age was not a factor. There is the Glock in my holster, but I was certain he had more than the one gun. I was hoping I would never need it.

After I pulled off my hat and glasses, I checked my surroundings once more before deciding to make my move. Time for the rubber to meet the road, I thought to myself, as I very slowly raised myself onto the lower limb on the other side of the tree. Probably the one he used. It was fortunate the tree was mature, or it may have swayed with my weight. Every move must be calculated to lessen the chance for noise or movement. The Green Beret in me helped with the control of my breathing and quiet movements. It was all part of their training.

My next decision was whether to climb above him or swing around the tree and simply jump on board and knock the shit out of the young man. Climbing above I feel would be safer, but harder. The decision became simpler when several kids ran through the woods, awfully close, and carrying with them a grand selection of distracting noises, including some blood curdling screams. Thanking God was what came to mind, as I quickly raised myself up another level and swung around the tree in one quick movement. I was now perched just above the man, who was none the wiser. Tag you're it I wanted to say so bad. I was scared, and excited. Once the coast was clear, I was able to lower myself quietly, drop onto the shocked young man's back and knock him out with one well-placed blow.

After relieving the young man of his sidearm, I lowered him and his rifle to the ground, hog tied him, and tethered him to the tree. He would be going nowhere. After giving him a little sedative, which was Joe's idea, I removed all ammo, and took note of his position before leaving for my meeting. To help assure this man wouldn't be found too soon and cut short my up-coming meeting, I covered him up with a couple branches.

"Not bad," I said to myself, while checking the time. An hour to go. With my extra time, I wandered through the park to make sure no other surprises awaited me.

Back outside the park, walking casually down the sidewalk, I spotted my mark. "Early," I noted. Even though three years older, he was just as handsome as ever. "Nice coincidence," I said to myself. He chose the same picnic table where I had the wonderful fried chicken with his family. The worse part of all of this is what it would do to his family, but I couldn't let him walk on this one. The entire racket must take a bath on this.

An old man, bent from the ravages of arthritis and hard living, leaning heavily on a foldable cane, was seen shuffling slowly along the sidewalk. "Heard a train a comin'," he was singing softly while placing each foot carefully. A break in the sidewalk could be disastrous for a feeble man. "Round that old bend." One foot in front of the other. You can do this. "Something, something sunshine since when," his voice kept scratching out the melody imperfectly. "I'm stuck in this ole prison." Could this be my old friend I see a waiting on little old me? I couldn't think of a better song for the occasion than Johnny Cash's song about Folsom Prison. He was now standing over his ex-partner, with hate burning underneath, but well hidden under the ruse of a smile.

"Detective?" I inquired, already knowing who the hell this was.

"Mr. Boynes," he said politely, before standing and shaking my hand with the same strong grip I recalled from before.

My weak and shaky grip I returned was no match for his, I thought laughingly. Richard waved his left hand to a seat across from him, asking me to sit. Clumsy me. I tripped over my own foot, and nearly fell, moving around the picnic table. Richard tried to grab ahold of me and help, but I quickly waved him off. "Thank you kindly, but I'm okay." Didn't want to run the risk of him discovering my Glock, even though it was strapped tightly to my body.

After resting my ancient ass on the hard bench, I let out a huge sigh, and looked around. "Nice place to picnic with the kids," I commented, while thinking it was also a clear spot for a hit. I assumed there was some type of signal arranged after I handed over the package. Smart young man. You learned well.

"You have a package for me?" He quickly put out there. No time for small talk huh? Just hit and run?

"Patience my dear man. Young people these days. Always in a rush." I was in a hurry to get this over quick, but haste makes waste, my mother always taught me.

"Okay sir, it's your show," Richard said, as he leaned forward and put his head in his hands, propped on the table.

"Actually, Richard," I said flatly, "I disagree, this is all God's show don't you think?"

"Whatever you say sir," he responded. Richard sat there like a lump, obviously perusing me with his detective senses. I was hoping they were as dull as I think he is.

"Jose was one hell of a detective in his own right. Thorough and precise, but a little careless I would say." He was good at poker at least. No break in his countenance. "His brief trip into the world of detective got him killed, didn't it?"

"You may be correct, Mr. Boynes," the detective stated, before sitting more upright, and wiping a bead of sweat off his forehead. "He must have gotten himself into something that was over his head."

A small crack, but it's a start. "The poor child got a shot right smack in the middle of his forehead for trying to do what is right. Damned shame," I said, while lowering my head for effect. "You want to know what I think son?" I asked after raising my head and staring deep into the man's eyes.

“Sure, what are your thoughts on the subject?” He was trying to be cool, but this subject has a lot of tentacles to it.

“Plain and simple? It was a hit,” I said with certainty in my voice. Richard’s eyes raised perceptibly. “The day he called Detective Alvarez on this sex trafficking ring he appears to have been assassinated. The shots were too perfect for some thug or a drive by.”

Ding, Ding, Ding. I think I may have drawn a little blood with that. Sound a little familiar, does it dear Richard? Joseph said almost exactly that on the day he was murdered. The extra glint in his eyes or the way his face twisted, told me it hit something. “Are you okay, Detective?” I asked, but not really caring. “You look a bit peaked,” I added with a glimmer of joy in my heart.

“I’m fine,” he insisted. “I’m fine,” he then repeated, which told me he was lying.

“Never wanted to be a policeman myself, because there is no rest for the wicked or those that fight the darkness.” Strike two, I thought. Another familiar phrase huh?

“How much do you want for the package?” Richard asked. He was done with the banter and our trip down memory lane. He was a little spooked, but I’m not done.

“Why, Detective, I’m surprised. You don’t even know what’s in the package, or if I even have it. I could be feeding you a line of bullshit after all.”

“Look, let’s get on with this. Let me know what you want and show me the goods, or I walk.”

“So, it’s money talks and bullshit walks huh?”

“Exactly!” He said angrily and leaning to the nervous side.

“How about a little taste then?” I asked, while pulling out one of the pictures, I brought with me. “You know, Detective Third Class, your partner had the same bullet wound in the middle of his forehead too. Guy must have been good, don’t you think?”

"Maybe. I don't know," the man sputtered. "Just show me what you got."

The man is on the line. Time to set the hook. "You're pretty good with the old pistola yourself aren't you detective?"

"What the hell are you getting at old man?"

"Testy much?" I asked, while spreading out the picture in front of him. It was the selfie. "That would be our poor Jose," I said, pointing to his picture in the foreground, "trying to fight evil in this world. He just got a little careless and got spotted by the man in the window," I said with a smile, moving the man's attention to a photo of himself three years earlier.

Richard leaned in to get a closer look, and then looked up at me. "That's not me," he now insisted. "Where was this taken?"

"Well Richard, if that's not you, why does the location matter?" Good question I thought.

"Just curious," he responded. Very weak response, I think. Watching him squirm was a joy.

"Why that's your old friend Franco Domenico's place, and that is definitely you, young man," saying flatly, almost breaking character, while spreading out the enlargement of the window space showing a clear picture of him and his tattoo.

The man's face was now red. A cornered animal was a dangerous one, so I became more alert to his movements and the position of my weapon. It was time. "I have to apologize Detective," I said as I pulled a burner phone out of my pocket. "My daughter is supposed to pick me up. I forgot to give her the time. Pardon me," I said as I walked a short distance away and put the phone to my ear and pressed quick dial. The man sat there staring at the photos, not sure what to do next.

"Hi, Honey," I said reasonably loud, while the phone was still ringing on the other end.

"911, what's your emergency?" the very friendly voice inquired. A wonderful service, I thought to myself.

"We have an issue at the Piedmont Park sir," speaking clearly with my hand over my mouth and head slightly turned, keeping one eye on the detective. "Don't know what this world is coming to, but I found a young man in a tree with a rifle. Was sure he was up to no good, so I took the law into my own hands and had to tie him to the tree. His guns should still be there, but I took all his bullets. Don't think he'll be goin anywhere soon, but you better hurry." I gave them the GPS coordinates before I hung up, and before turning all the way around, pulled the battery. Saw it on a movie once.

As I settled back onto my seat, he quickly asked, "how much? I'll want all the copies as well."

"Detective Turner, I never said it was for sale." And the pressure rises.

"Don't mess with me old man," he said quietly after leaning over the table and merely a few inches from my face.

"Or what? I'm 92 years old," I said after leaning back in my chair and away from his bad breath. I am even shocking myself at how cool I was.

"Or you will find a bullet in the middle of your forehead, and then I'll come after your daughter."

"Sounds like a threat," I said.

"Not a threat. A promise, "Rick assured me. "Bring me everything and I might just forget all about this."

Several police cars arrived within the park, men got out and suited up. I was hoping they would be a little stealthier about it. None yet close by. They were closing in on the area I gave them. Luckily, Richard hadn't seen them yet. He was too angry with me. Poor guy, angry makes one a little blind, don't it?

Guns drawn, working their way through the wooded area, like in a movie, they found the young man where he was left. He was just coming around from the sedative. Very strongly tied knots were holding this pig tightly to the tree, thanks to the First Mate of the USS Insurgent.

The police relaxed, and some even giggled, observing the predicament this man was in. Never saw a criminal tied up in a bow before, and with a note attached, which read.

***

To whom it may concern:

Thank you so much for your service and kind assistance giving this young man the justice he has coming to him. This man was sent here at the behest of your very own Detective Third Class Richard Samuel Turner. This sniper was sent in relation to a very volatile package that may already be in the hands of your Captain William Hanks. Dirt comes in all colors and careers, please don't sweep this one under the rug. Oh, and by the way, he may be good for the murder of Miguel Moreno. Might want to test his weapon, and don't forget, Richard was at the scene where Detective Joseph Alvarez was murdered. Coincidence? I think not.

Yours Truly Jonathan Boynes

***

"Remember the night your partner and friend died? That was such a tragedy don't you think? Three men died because of the poison package."

His hackles were up. He started to rise from the bench. He may even be thinking of giving the signal and taking his chances.

"Sit down friend," I demanded. "I am not done." You are such a beast, I thought to myself.

He sat back down, but I had to wrap this up. "Poor Miguel, Jose's brother, was shot down like a dog by another friend of yours, the sniper. Clean and neat." I then pointed to the other side of the park, where I could still see a few uniformed officers with guns drawn. Richard saw them now.

“Your friend should be on the way to jail soon,” I said, while grinning, but watching his every move.

Richard was now sweating profusely. Wasn’t sure at this point if the man was going to bolt or pull his gun. He quickly tried to stand, but I was quicker. I grabbed both hands, and with a powerful tug, slammed his face into the wooden table, probably breaking his nose. In one smooth move, I pinned his head to the table with my right hand, thumb buried deep behind the right ear, pulled his right arm behind him, and effortlessly hopped onto the table and buried my left knee into his wrist. “Painful, isn’t it?” I said while dropping his dead partner’s badge in front of his very pained face. Leaning over and looking deep into his eyes, seeing the recognition, I continued. “Did you feel nothing that night behind your goggles when you pulled the trigger and murdered your partner and friend? Well partner, this isn’t just business, this is pure pleasure,” were my last words before jumping off the man, picking him up like a rag doll, and planting a sharp blow to his jaw. He dropped like a sack of potatoes.

This only took a matter of seconds, too short of time to raise too many eyebrows, but it was kind of violent. “It wasn’t me,” I wanted to tell everyone. I quickly walked away, no cane this time, and no evidence. I wore gloves and looked nothing like good old Bob. As I was passing a police officer, none the wiser, I handed him a tape of my little conversation with the detective. “Can you please see this gets to Captain Hanks. He might find it remarkably interesting.” I kept walking, turned back into the park and another secluded area I had chosen earlier for a quick change.

The old man Jonathan Boynes was gone forever. Just good old accountant Bob Johnson now, climbing into his car singing, “Joy to the world.” I got a new room near Stone Mountain and called my wife before I crashed for the night. Tomorrow I had already scheduled a round of golf and an afternoon hike. There was a great need to unwind before going home to the wife. This was quite the adventure, that no one was going to know about, except Bob the accountant. The memory of the hero’s return to Hobbiton, in “Lord of the Rings”, came to mind.

Arrived home without incident, caught my wife up on my boring vacation, leaving out a ton of details. Sorry, Honey, but you don’t need to know everything, even though I performed superbly, even if I say so myself.

There was no shortage of news to read for the next several days. Atlanta was lit up. "One of Atlanta's own arrested for murder"; "Kingpin, Franco Domenico, brought in on RICO charges."; "Locations raided for sex trafficking and drugs"; "Unknown assailant attacks detective prior to his arrest for murder"; "A break on three-year-old murders".

A month later, a package arrived on the doorstep of Maria Moreno, mother of Jose and Miguel. She took the package to her small dining room table and unwrapped it. Inside was a signed copy of "Justice Is Mine." The word got out somehow this book was based upon what was currently happening in Atlanta. A terrific book of intrigue, murder, sex trafficking, and drugs. As a result, the book caught fire. It may be my best seller yet.

Inside the box, with the book, were legal documents and a letter. Maria sat and read the letter, which warmed her heart and the tears fell. read.

***

Dear Maria Moreno:

You should be immensely proud of your sons Jose and Miguel. Because of their hard work and sacrifice, many criminal endeavors have been shaken, two legged monsters locked up, and dozens of innocents freed from the sex trafficking world. Jose's fine detective skills and grit, and Miguel's bravery to carry on for his fallen brother, is a fine example of what is right in the world. Your son's killers have now been brought to justice and many parents are able to hug their children once more. It is my honor to have known such young men in my life.

You may have already noticed the legal documents in the package sent to you. One is for you and one for the Agape Youth & Family Center. It came to my attention that both of your sons made use of this facility and it appears to be a great benefit to the city. Please contact the facility and make an appointment for the two of you to meet with a lawyer. I have made arrangements for all royalties from the book "Justice Is Mine" to be split evenly between yourself and the Agape Youth & Family Center. It is the least I can do, since the book is based on what has occurred and your sons gave their all for justice. I also insist the contribution to the center be made in remembrance of your two sons.

God Bless

Yours Truly

Robert Franklin Johnson and Joseph Alvarez

***

It took nearly a month of settling loose ends, catch up loving of my wife, getting a third tattoo on my upper right arm of a Green Beret cap and detective shield, representing Joseph Alvarez, and finally many trips to the gym before I could settle into my La-Z-Boy without my mind running crazy. Life was great and peaceful once more, not saying my little side trips weren't exciting and spine tingling at times. But as the saying goes, "there is a time and season for everything under heaven."

Chapter 31

What is time? Could it be a dark creature represented in a riddle game spouted from Gollum in the "Lord of the Rings"?

This thing all things devours.

Birds, beasts, trees, flowers.

Gnaws iron, bites steel.

Grinds hard stones to meal.

Slays king, ruins town,

And beats mountain down.

My opinion? It is a construct of God, and as such cannot be considered bad. It just is. A fact put into place by God. Gollum was a creature from the dark and describes time from his point of view. Time can be about renewal, healing, growth and yes, love. Love and faith are two of God's greatest gifts to men, but without time, where would we be?

Time, a very deep subject for a simple man with multiple personalities, but not from a Freudian perspective, is something more on my mind these days. After twenty-five years, with extra house guests, aging is different for me. I don't seem to be aging. Time is separating me from my honey, my wife, my soul mate. Even though I am older than my wife, who just turned 84, I have several times been mistaken for her son. My doctor is baffled. Still playing from the blues, frequenting the gym, and volunteering as much as I can, but I am starting to stay home more to help around the house. My wife just can't do as much as she used to. The inner guests are quiet these days, and I am focusing on my wife. She needs me and I don't plan to disappoint.

One day, I must bring this up because it was a hoot, my wife and I were shopping for groceries. Her legs were giving her some issues this day, so she rode in one of those motorized carts. I was pulling some baked beans from the other side of the aisle, while my wife was stretching for something on an upper shelf. I would have helped her, but her and I both agreed, she needs to keep active for her own health. A young lady, probably in her thirties, came to Susan's rescue. She insisted, and was pulling down what Susan needed, as I was placing the cans of baked beans in our cart.

"You shouldn't make your mother reach so high," the young girl chastised. "She could hurt herself." Everyone's got an opinion, I thought to myself, and this girl couldn't wait to give me hers.

"Young lady, I assure you, this little minx is very healthy, and she is not my mother." I stated it very kindly. Don't like being mean, and besides I was flattered.

She was a little taken aback by the minx comment I suppose. "I'm sorry," she responded. "Just assumed."

"That's quite alright," politely putting her at ease. "It happens often." My wife was seated again, quietly observing the conversation. "I'm flattered. This is actually my wife," I added with a smile.

The lady was glancing between the two of us, the gears naturally turning, while noting our apparent age differences. My gears were turning too. Let's run with this, I thought. It's been a boring day. "Cougar," I leaned over and whispered in her ear.

She smiled, and turned a little red, after backing away some.

I looked around as if I were trying to keep others from overhearing. "Her family thought I was marrying her for her money, but oh how wrong they were honey," I stated with a smattering of excitement to the voice.

You could now tell she was uncomfortable with the conversation.

"I can't keep up with this woman," I said with all the certainty I could bake into it. "She's a beast in bed," I added quietly, with some fake embarrassment of my own.

The woman was trying to be polite and not simply run for the hills. This old man is nuts she was probably thinking. She raised her hand and shakily waved as she started walking away.

"I keep a whole supply of them blue pills in my nightstand," I said, as I started to laugh, while she was turning the corner. Couldn't wait to get away, I am sure.

Before I turned back to my probably annoyed wife, I felt a sharp smack against my leg, and spaghetti noodles went a flying halfway down the aisle. "Spill on aisle four!" I shouted as I was quick to pick them up while having to chase some under the shelving. "Does the fifteen second rule apply?" I ask my wife sheepishly. She stared at me with absolutely nothing to say. No sense of humor, I thought to myself, while grabbing a second box and holding on to the first.

While in the check-out, the poor lady was only three aisles down trying her best to ignore us. Tried my best to hold it in, but an occasional snicker tried to work its way out. My Susan simply kept her head down and stayed in her chair. I couldn't control myself. "Nice meeting you!" I shouted and waved to the young lady as she was passing us on the way out the door. "Life is good," I said to my wife as we were leaving the line. She said nothing, noticeably embarrassed by her out of control husband.

Over the years, events came and went, global warming is still a thing, a small colony is now on Mars, politicians are still politicians. I think most are on the take and wouldn't know truth if it hit them in the side of the head. Wars and rumors of wars, earthquakes, and hurricanes still ravage the earth now and then. When will Jesus come again and give this place a good sweeping? It is well overdue. Newfangled things get more fanglier if that is a word. What man needs a mistress or lady a lover anymore when you can just order a robot version from a store. This world is going to hell fast.

My wife, bless her heart, had passed the average life expectancy for women in the U.S. of eighty-eight. Men is only eighty-three. What happened to the big political stink raised for years on equality? Doesn't sound very equal to me. Businesses can even be fined now for not maintaining the correct percentages of races and gender. How many genders are there now? I lose track, and I don't actually give a damn. Equality is almost a racket now.

My lovely wife of 67 years, barely able to blow out the two candles, a purple nine and zero, was still beautiful to me. Her skin, though paper thin, was as soft as ever. Our children didn't stay long, for my honey needed her rest. She did however, before they left, repeat the story of our encounter with the young lady at the store. She would not have admitted it then, but like an aging wine, the story grew fondly in her mind as one of many hilarities of our 70 years together.

After the children left, and we were dressed for bed, we shared a spot of hot tea at the table, like we did many nights before bedtime. "Remember that day when I chased you with a broom, and we ended up in bed?" She inquired giddily. I watched the smile on her face and the sparkle in her eyes as she recalled that very day. Memories are strange in a way. Sometimes you can feel the time has long passed, and then there are times when you feel as if the incident just happened. Like the first kiss, soft on your lips, still lingers there like it was only seconds before. Memories can be fantastic.

"Yes, Honey, I remember it very well. The Chinese food got cold, but you were hot as a firecracker." We laughed at the memory and reminisced as we took sips of our tea.

"What happened to them?" She asked, before draining her cup, and spilling some on the table. "Do you think they've gone to heaven now?"

"Who are you referring to, Susan?" I'm sure I knew, but her question came without a prequel.

"Your uninvited guests," she stated, as she pointed to her own head. "You know, your triplets," she added with a laugh.

"Don't know the answer to that. Sometimes I feel them, or perhaps just a little influence, and other times they are quiet as a church mouse for weeks on end. All I can do is have faith and live my own life with you."

She smiled and lightly nodded. "What do you think heaven will be like?" She asked quietly.

"It will be the grandest thing ever. He promised us," I added while gathering our cups and washing them in the sink. We don't dirty a lot of dishes, and I keep them washed up. A dishwasher is a waste for just two of us. I wiped the drops of tea from the table, and a little from the corner of her mouth. She was still smiling and reminiscing I suppose. Men do that too, but there seems to be more empty space in a man's brain. They have that nothing box they can hide in. It's harder for me to find. There are times when I swear one of my guests are squatting there and I needed to shoo them off.

"Would you like something else, Honey?" I asked, after I made sure all was neat. Susan is still very observant and will let me know if I missed something. Reminds me a bit of my mother.

She was still in her trance of remembrance, which is not a bad place to be. I spun the chair next to her around and sat facing her, waving my hand in front of her face. "Earth to, Susan," I said. "Earth to, Susan."

She blinked and then focused on me. The sparkle was back. "Sorry, Honey, I was just remembering when we brought our second little girl home. It was pouring down rain, but it was still a fantastic day."

"Remember it well. I had to make three trips to the car with my large golf umbrella. Couldn't let either of you melt." I leaned in and gave her a soft kiss on her lips. "You are one hell of a mother and grandmother," I added with a smile.

"Did you remember to pick up the Oral gel, Honey?" she asked. "I think our eldest is teething."

All I could do is smile, a sad little smile. The question, though odd, wasn't a surprise. She had been showing signs of dementia for several months now. We had been to the doctors several times over the past year. The COPD she has had for five years, congestive heart failure for six months, and now this. The light of my life is slipping away from me. After some tender reminders that our children are grown, her mind appeared to turn back. "Sorry, Bob. Don't know what I was thinking…I am so proud of our girls. We did good, didn't we?" She asked.

"Yes, we did good, Honey. You are the best. The best wife a man could ever hope for. You stood by me through all this crazy stuff, and for that I am eternally grateful," I said, while watching the smile in her eyes. Her eyes always saw into me, the real me. That I realize is being taken from her as well. The dimming of reality was slow but painful. "I love you, Honey," I said with truth and sadness. Tears began to fall from my eyes. "I love you," I repeated, while rubbing my eyes with my shoulders slumped.

Her knowing smile grew. "I love you too my hero," she said as she placed her hands on the sides of my face and wiped a tear with her thumb. "It will be okay. All will work out." She leaned in and kissed my forehead, like she was comforting a child.

A shaky smile was forced onto my lips, trying desperately not to lose what control I had. "God is good right? All the time?" I managed through near sobs.

"And all the time, God is good," she responded as she always did. True to form, my dearest rock.

Nothing more was said. That said it all. We embraced in the quiet of our home, where the walls held tight to the story of our life. Laughter could almost be heard bleeding through the years of paint, lightening the heart. "God is good," I softly repeated, as I carried my now sleeping wife to the comfort of our bed. She weighs little now, but even then, I would carry her to the ends of the earth.

After tucking Susan in, I realized I wasn't tired yet. There was too much going through my mind. Something I did often, whether to read, write, or simply commune with nature, I laid back in my favorite lawn chair on our back patio and simply stared at the sky. It was dark, and the sky was full of glimmering stars and the occasional white cloud. A cool breeze gently touched my face, accompanied by the peaceful sounds of nature. Accompanying God's symphony are the stars, like ballet dancers of assorted sizes flittering around, on the black canvas, in their sparkling outfits and white dancing shoes. This was God's interpretation of Swan Lake painted across the sky. Virgo as seen by most as a vision of an angel, I can see as a dancer jumping across the stage. The little dipper and the north star, a young ballerina with a sparkle in her eyes, arching her back while passionately waiting for the touch of her lover. A touch I fondly remember.

"God, where are you taking me?" I quietly questioned, letting my voice rise into the tapestry that is the sky. "I'm not aging, and my family is slipping away. How am I to bear this?" Didn't expect a direct answer from the stars, or in the soft whisper on the wind. God's time is not mine. Just have the faith of a child, I continue to remind myself. Doubts and concerns constantly plague my mind, and I keep pushing them away, like Tad pushing his majestic ship, hoping it floats away safely and begins its trip to Mobile. Go and unload, and bring me something good on your return trip, Tad might be saying. Bring me back hope and joy I say. Even while my body is strong, my spirit is weary.

Went to sleep that night, cuddling lightly with my wife, with a prayer still on my lips.

Chapter 32

The fountain of youth, sought after by many for millennia. From the early writings of Herodotus, Prester John from the Crusades, and Ponce De Leon looking for the magic waters in the New World. Current day medical visionaries are still in search of that one magic bullet. What am I getting at? I say, wishing for eternal life in this imperfect world, be careful what you wish for.

Recently, my feet have clacked and squeaked many miles along the sanitized halls of the local hospitals. Nurses and doctors moving about like bees in their hives. Sanitizer and masks available at every juncture. Elderly men and women volunteering and being extremely helpful for those that appear lost. Much older looking than I, but much younger in all actuality. I have mastered the art of inconspicuousness. Feeling like I am in my thirties, looking no more than sixty, counting my years as ninety-five. Inconspicuous is what I strive for. Can't explain what I am, and don't care to even try.

In three weeks, I held the hand of an old friend as he took his last breath. Took my wife to and from the hospital three times when she was in distress. Once when she suffered a minor stroke. At her age, nothing is minor. Many hours in rooms were spent, waiting for the worst, hoping for the best. Hoping things wouldn't get worse, even considering the eventualities, my youngest child was brought in an ambulance one night. She suffered a heart attack, even though not too damaging, we also discovered she had advanced cancer. My daughter isn't young mind you. She is seventy-four, but still our baby. My wife and I are well off, so we could afford the best medical care money can buy, but our bodies have an expiration date. What is mine, I must ask? Is there such a thing as living too long? Starting to feel the answer to that loaded question.

My wife was now at home and comfortable in an especially nice hospital bed. A double, so I could lay beside her. Each other's presence was comforting to us both. This made it much easier to see to her comfort. She hated to see the bed moved out of our bedroom, for it carried fine memories, but I assured her it was simply set up in another room. I would take her to that bed occasionally, so she can enjoy the familiarity of it. One of our great granddaughters is a home health nurse. She would spell me occasionally, so I could get out and run errands, shop, or squeeze in an occasional round of golf. My preference is spending time with my wife. While she sleeps, I work on my next book. When awake in the mornings, I would wheel her to our walk-in shower and help her clean up and dress for the day. Even though she planned to go nowhere, I insisted on her dressing in something comfortable. A flowery dress perhaps, blue slacks and white top with a little frill, comfortable but stylish slip-on shoes. I am sure it makes her feel better. After a light breakfast, I help with her hair, and with some make-up, add a little color to her lips and cheeks. My calling is not hair stylist or makeup, but I have learned a few tricks over the years. With the help of my sailor friend, I can put down some mean braids.

My wife had learned to love poetry, so I would take her out to our patio, grab some rays, and read her a bit of T.S. Elliott, Elizabeth Barrett Browning, and occasionally some of my own. The flow comforts her, and comfort is what I want for her.

Our daughter was home as well, resting from the rounds of chemotherapy. My little girl lost her hair. Went to my barber and had him give me a buzz and a shave, in solidarity with my baby daughter. It gave her some pleasure seeing her dad looking like a cue ball. We took several pictures and showed them to my wife. She doesn't get out much in her weakened state. I want to take her out, but it takes a lot out of her to prepare to a level that would satisfy her.

Spring was now here. The glorious smells of fresh mown grass, wisteria climbing the pergola, sweet alyssum hanging from planters scattered about our property, honey suckle reemerging along our fence line, and my wife's wildflower garden I now tend, to her delight. This year, I sat her in a comfortable patio chair, and under her direction, planted the seeds where she directed. I am more the scatter them type, but Susan enjoys the patterns she helps to sculpt.

Dew was still hanging on the blades of grass. Songbirds were in rare form this very morning, accompanying the spirit of God rustling through the trees. Sights, sounds, and smells were always especially exuberant this time of year.

As a special treat I woke my honey early, so we could watch the sunrise together, and experience the great treat that is nature. Wrapped in a blanket, Susan wove twenty years ago, we sat quietly together on our glider, observing the first rays of dawn flittering amongst the trees like mythical beings, and reflecting off the newly deposited dew. From the patio, she could see the wildflowers beginning their quest for early light and not so subtle invite for the bees and butterflies to feast to their fill and move along the many facets of the wonderous circle of life.

It warmed my heart to see the sun now reflecting off her eyes, bringing joy to her face. Our two daughters were hoping to join us for lunch after the church service. We have been watching on TV. I am seldom able to take her to the services any longer. It's overwhelming. She does like the new preacher. A good-looking man she commented to several of her elder church friends.

"Honey, do you see the white dove perched on the top of our garage?" I pointed the dove out to her, which there were now two. White doves are rare. Couldn't have been better timing. The early morning light almost painted a glow about them. The white dove was one of my wife's favorites, next to the yellow finches and hummingbirds. Her eyesight has been dimming of late, as well as her memory, but she enjoys every speck of beauty she can take in.

"Aren't they the most beautiful creatures?" Susan commented quietly, almost seeming to be talking to herself.

"They don't hold a candle to you my dear," I said in a playful sort of tone.

"Such a flatterer you are my prince," she said with a giggle as she laid her head on my shoulder.

We cuddled there for nearly half an hour. It was a glorious morning.

"Take care of my flowers, Honey," she said in a whisper.

"You know I will, Susan," I assured her as a sadness was building within me. Her breathing was shallow and labored.

"Get you a dog," she requested almost imperceptibly. "You need a dog," she added.

Her hand clenched my arm as a final pain moved through her body, and "I love you," was breathed softly on my neck. Her last breath was used on those lovely words, which will be etched in stone in my memory.

She relaxed fully into my arms. No more sorrow, no more pain, I thought, as I held her tight to my bosom, while watching the flight of the two doves climbing into God's sky. Tears flowed and tightness gripped my chest as I imagined her spirit joining the two rising doves. "Now you can rest, Honey. You deserve it," I whispered to her, before I started sobbing, and running my fingers through her hair. This always relaxed her. "Fly my dove, into the blue sky that awaits you, and into the arms of Jesus my dear love."

Life is full of peaks and valleys. This was my lowest of the low. Strength had nearly left me, but I had enough to carry my wife to our bed. She was light, but the sorrow was heavy. My memory went back to carrying my blushing bride across the threshold of our first home together. My eyes were burning. I tucked her into bed as I had every night, but this time, into our old bed. She would prefer that, I am sure. She needn't be alone, so I laid beside her, with my arm across her chest, waiting for our daughters to arrive.

Chapter 33

Many Springs have come and gone since I lost my Susan. No new visitors after all this time. There are days when I think God had forgotten me. Do I have to wait 400 years like the Israelites to be free from this burden?

"Susan, I brought you flowers from your garden," I said, while placing them gingerly across the base of our granite headstone. It always gives me the willies when I see my name chiseled next to my wife's. "New neighbors moved in Monday," I said, after sitting on the ground facing the stone. I am always careful to sit off to the side, however. Sitting on her grave would be extremely rude, was my thinking. I try to visit Susan every few months, to catch my honey up on the latest news. "The neighbors look like they're twelve years old, with a one-year-old. Our old neighbors, the Greens, you know, the tanned ones," I giggled. "He passed away and I hear she moved in with her daughter, Latisha." I thought about it for a second. "Damn, Susan, they were what, twenty or so when they moved in. It was my recollection that we had a cookout to welcome them to the neighborhood. I don't see much of my neighbors anymore. I have become an oddity. They don't like my jokes either. What has the world come to?"

"That reminds me, want to hear a new joke?" I asked. Oddly, but maybe not so much, a gust of wind blew past and nearly blew the flowers away I had just placed. "Okay. I get it, you don't like my jokes either." I gathered the flowers, feeling a little insulted, and placed them in the stone vase I had just purchased, so they could withstand the next breeze that happened along. I kissed two of my fingers and placed them over my wife's name, as I had done many times. Her kiss is what I seem to miss the most. As I stood, I glanced at my name briefly, and the year I was born. The year of our lord 1955. "What is it 2083?" I asked myself, while walking away to visit several more sites. "Damn I'm old," I quipped. "Older than most of these trees I suspect," looking around the large cemetery with its mature trees. Visiting family here could easily be an afternoon event. Sadly, this was my family reunion I play out every few months or so.

Only three years after my wife passed, our youngest passed. It was hard, but I realized there were many more to come. Between illness, accidents, and the standard, they died of natural causes, I was the only one standing for three generations down. There wasn't anyone left who shared any of my experiences. How to use a dial telephone, party lines, wringer washing machines, and all the many antique notions. I was a relic, like what would be dug up by an archeologist, who would then research old dusty files to determine of what use it was. What use am I anyway? I am a lonely old writer of 128 who hasn't written a word in three years. Tending our garden, staying out of people's way and their endless probing and curiosity. Many times, I had been tempted to pull stakes and build a cabin in the mountains, but my wife's garden still was of importance and gives me some solace. Besides, I keep my promises.

The world isn't getting any nicer. The same story, different day is all. Even though I haven't written anything for some time, I still love to read. Read the "Old Man and the Sea", written by Hemingway, the other day. Even with the millions of books out there, newer ones, I still occasionally enjoy the classics. Could be the older souls within me may have something to do with my choices of reading material. I am certain Jonathan was especially enthralled by the struggle between the man and the sea, and the man and the largest catch of his life. I must admit, I got much enjoyment out of it as well. Never give up is one of my takes on the story. Don't see it as defeatist. There are days when I must remind myself of that very thing.

To help with my somber moods, there is nothing like reading the news. Need a lift, read about another riot in Portland, or an earthquake in Mexico. Nothing seems to change. Politicians in front of a mic spinning tales like Aesop's Fables. Good news seems to be outnumbered 10:1. Good overall truth in news is a relic like me. "Another girl reported missing in Louisville", a local headline reported that caught my attention. My brief interaction with the sex trafficking world, even though many years ago, still plays upon my mind.

A rash of disappearances of young ladies 15-29 years old has been occurring in our three-state area along the Ohio River valley over the last two months. "The count has risen to fifteen," the article read. Sounds like a local sex trafficking ring to me. There was a map available that plotted the fifteen disappearances. There was no visible pattern, except they were no more than five miles north or south of the river and ranged from Louisville to Cincinnati. Carrollton or Madison seemed to be the center. Surely it wasn't that simple. "Well Mr. Detective," I asked of my internal guest. "Do you think maybe they are keeping the girls in a wing of the Madison State Hospital?" I closed the computer, for I've read enough about evil in the world for one day.

After a comforting dream that night, of the day I assisted in the take down of Detective Richard Turner and some of the mess he was involved in, I woke early the next day, still feeling like I needed a few more hours. My third dog was snuggled under my covers at the foot of my bed. Chewey, a Pomeranian, was a great, great, of my second dog. She was a wonderful companion. I could not have stood a totally empty house. My body screamed for it, but I couldn't go back to sleep. Early tee time. Could have canceled, but I decided against it and jumped into the shower after letting Chewey out to do her business. A nap later would be on this day's menu for sure.

A young man, probably in his thirties, challenged me to a friendly match the other day. The loser buys lunch, we agreed. I was warming up on the putting green, when he drove up in the golf cart, a bit on the cocky side I thought. Since he was so much younger, I let him get the cart and load our clubs. If he only knew. This is a subject I avoid like the plague.

"I like my steak rare," the youngster quipped.

"If I win, you may be eating crow," I fired back jokingly. "Don't count your steak before it's put on the grill bucko."

After a bit of light-hearted banter, the young stud fired from the blues and me from the whites. He insisted, and I wasn't going to argue with him.

It was a wonderful day for golf, and I enjoyed myself, playing the young man from Colorado. He was actually a great sportsman and nice young man. Through twelve he was up by one. The gauntlet was laid, and we were battling with our weapons of steel and graphite.

Lucky thirteen, a par three, I stuck my tee shot to within five feet. My opponent was just on the collar. He was sweating it, but he hit a great chip to within inches of the hole. I sunk mine, which squared us up. "I'm a hearin your crow calling in the distance," I quipped. "Time for dinner," I followed with a laugh.

We both were laughing while riding to the fourteenth hole. The group in front of us hadn't teed off yet, so we parked the cart and I got out to stretch a little while my friend went to the john.

I heard the group in front of us daring one of the young men to hit the "Happy Gilmore". It was shocking to me that this was still a thing. That was over eighty years ago. The men were downing some beers, so they were a happy bunch.

I wasn't driving the cart. My friend parked us just off to the side, where I could easily see their antics. As I was coming up from a long stretch, where I touch my toes, the port-a-pot door slammed loudly, catching my attention. Couldn't' help but turn my head toward the racket. At that very instant, the crack of a golf ball connecting with the oversized driver head could be clearly heard. Unfortunate for both me and the idiot who thought it would be fun to bow to the challenge, the clubhead was anything but squared when he ran up and connected with the little round missile. The damned thing traveled nearly ninety degrees away from the intended target, cracking hard against the side of my head. I remember a scream, which could have been me, and then lights out.

Chapter 34

My body felt heavy, like after an extremely deep dream where the body hadn't moved in hours. Consciously wanted to wake, but eyes and spirit wouldn't cooperate. My lack of effort could again lead to floating on the sea of dreams, good or bad. Take two, I thought to myself, as sleep was renewing its grip.

Golfing and pain made a brief appearance in the dark place but was quickly replaced by my drive home after a stressful day at the hospital. In a Prius of all things. Do they still make those? I wouldn't be caught dead in it.

Hospital dreams are some of the worse. Hospitals can be of hope and healing, or death and pain. I had lost many there. This dream was different. Very real has happened before, but different, nonetheless. An ordinary dream, within which I may be aware of it being a dream, but less of a spectator. I glanced in the rear-view mirror and see, not my face, but that of a female, brunette with light makeup. We both were startled, like in Tad's fateful day. A nurse, a female nurse, in a Prius yet, you have given over to my dream. Of all the things, a female exploring my deepest thoughts. Lord you are such a card.

The parking lot was normally dark with no activity at the times I get home from a long shift. I am very careful. Carry pepper spray in my purse and a few defense classes under my belt. One never knows. Being cognizant of my surroundings was one of the first things they taught us, then, if the attacker is male, go for the jewels. Before opening my door, I always check around and have the spray in my hand. I will be apologizing profusely to any friend who has the bad judgement to come up behind me at this time of night. They will get a not so pleasant surprise.

Did everything right. At least that was my thinking, before an unknown figure grabbed me from behind. Felt a sting in my arm and a hand over my mouth before realizing I was in trouble. He was too strong. Darkness took me in seconds, and my body went limp in the arms of the attacker.

The shadowy figure effortlessly tossed Julia Blair back into her own car and drove off into the night. She was a passenger heading to an unknown location and future. Julia Blair, 30-year-old nurse at Baptist Health in Louisville, Kentucky, was her parent's pride and joy. Her little sister, who just graduated from high school, looked up to her. Julia's hard work and ambitions were not wasted on her sibling. She is a great role model. She would not be missed for several days, and the pain of a missing child and sister would be delayed. The abductor knew what he was doing and planned well. This was the last day of her work week. She had been watched for over a week to get a feel for her schedule and he planned accordingly.

The driver was noting the nice form in the seat next to him. A 5′ 6″, delicious 125-pound brunette beauty. A nurse. This would be their first nurse. "She will make a nice addition to our menagerie of beauties," he commented, while pulling down a gravel road toward a prearranged meeting place.

Waiting for them in a secluded area, one of many chosen in advance, was one of the partners waiting with a recently painted van. They used several, with stolen tags, to keep the law guessing. The car pulled next to the van, with the lights already extinguished. No prying eyes expected, but carelessness can increase risks.

"Any problems?" the second man asked, while he pulled the van's side door open. The inside was dimly lit. Nothing in the back except a stolen gurney could be seen awaiting its next guest. Only a modicum of light is allowed during the exchange.

"None at all," he responded. "She was very willing prey," he added, with a sickly laugh.

One grabbed the shoulders and the other the knees. Transferred the unconscious victim from the car to the van, strapping her down for the drive, then checked on her condition. Damaged goods are not tolerated. Body snatchers, under the cover of night they appeared to be, carrying their ghoulish prize to an end of which no one dared venture a guess.

They drove away with lights out until reaching the main roads. After a short drive, Julia's car was dumped, and the first man jumped into the passenger seat. "Let's take route #3 this time," the passenger demanded, after snapping his seatbelt.

Their destination was a secluded and secure place. The group used four routes to travel there. Get complacent and get caught was one of the sayings spouted by their leader often. They don't need the GPS for this, the routes were memorized, as well as alternative plans if they feel they had been spotted. It was an organized group.

The roots of this dark business were carefully grown over two years. Money, power, and sexual deviance was the fertilizer. The tentacles reached deep into the local society. Businessmen, politicians, and law enforcement were in its clutches. To some it was just business, offering a service to the elites with enough money to satisfy their twisted needs.

The drive was silent. With the newest addition to their stock in the back, even though unconscious, they still never discuss details amongst themselves. Loose lips sink ships they often say.

The drug induced fog was lifting from my mind as I was moving toward consciousness. My mouth was dry as dust. After blinking a few times, my vision started to clear. "Where am I?" I asked raspingly. Above me was the ceiling of a van, as best as I can tell, and I was tightly strapped to a gurney. Fear quickly gripped me as I desperately tugged at my restraints.

"You had best be still, Julia," the driver spoke up," and behave, or we'll give you some more happy juice and duct tape your mouth."

"Where are you taking me?" I cried, before straining against the straps once more. My arms were burning with the strain, and the taste of fear rising from my gut. "Let me go," I insisted, knowing it was probably a waist of my breath, which was coming fast and hard as I felt the beginnings of hyperventilation.

"Juice the bitch," the driver said flatly as if asking his partner to simply throw me a treat. The passenger reached down for a small satchel and pulled out a syringe kit.

I started to panic, but a voice inside me was trying to calm me down. "Pick your battles Julia", it said unexpectedly. I instantly stopped straining and calmed myself. "Now tell them what they want to hear. Cooperate," the voice added.

Unsure where this was coming from, but anxious to go along, because it made perfect sense. "Sorry," I quickly said. "You win. I'll behave," I then added with defeat in my voice, followed by a cleansing breath to help calm me.

Giggles of sickly glee came from the front seat as the man put the supplies back in the satchel. "That's a good girl," he finally said. "You be nice, and we'll be nice," he added before settling back into his seat with a shitty smile on his face. Couldn't get a good look at his face. Only saw the side of it, and it was covered partially with a beard. Probably made up to hide his true appearance.

Good girl, I thought. Be nice you say? If I ever get out of this, I plan to do more than simply neuter your ass.

A clear image of the carnage Julia was wishing upon her hosts made an unexpected shock go through her, or perhaps a good old male cringe is a better description of it. Julia closed her eyes hard and forced a grimace across her face as a near pain flowed through her. After only seconds, she opened her eyes, and with much effort kept her mouth shut. What the hell was that? she wondered.

Lying apparently unconscious in a hospital bed, after the golfing incident, Bob's mind was trying desperately to grasp what was happening.

Is this another past event going through my mind? I was dreaming right? Hit by a golf ball and was now having a hum dinger of a nightmare? This was very real, and I, or we, are experiencing this lady's abduction.

How is this possible? Julia asked silently. We were travelers sharing the same coach.

Bob, wake the hell up! I tried to scream. This is too much input.

The doctor was at a loss, while reviewing Bob's EEG and imaging results, and equally baffled by Bob's age as reported by his records. The imaging did show Bob had received a concussion. Some bruising was present on the brain, but nothing some good medical attention and rest can't heal. The EEG readout was something he never seen before. He even consulted with his fellow doctors, redone the connections and used a second machine. All the same results.

In the consult room was Timothy, Bob's current next of kin and emergency contact. He was Bob's great grandson. The doctor came in, shut the door behind him, took a chair across the table from Timothy, and opened Bob's file in front of him. The room was essentially bare, with a small table and a few chairs, and a computer screen on the wall. The screen allowed physicians to bring up needed images to assist with information they saw fit to pass to the family.

With a handheld device, the physician typed in a few codes and a high-resolution picture of Bob's skull appeared on the screen. "Timothy?" he questioned, after glancing at the papers in the file.

"Yes, doctor," Timothy responded.

Since it was a touch screen, the doctor was able to circle the part of the brain he had concerns about with his finger. "If you can see the shadow," the doctor stated, while pointing more precisely to a spot with his finger. "Bob did get a nasty bump on the side of his head, near the left temple, which resulted in a concussion," he said with a complete air of professionalism. "A golf ball I hear."

"Yes. A golf ball took him down," Tim responded with a smile. "Grandpa loves the game," he added. Tim, being in the position he was in, had heard all the stories of tough Grandpa Bob. Never seems to get sick or injured, seriously anyhow. He was the family secret.

"The shadow here is some bruising on the brain. He should be fine," the doctor assured Tim. "We started him on some fine medication, and he appears to be as strong as an ox."

"How long will he have to be in here. He hates hospitals."

"Not really sure Timothy. That's another thing I wanted to discuss with you." He could see the concern rise in Timothy's face.

"Before going on, I would like to clean up a mistake on our records." The doctor glanced at his records again and back to Timothy.

Timothy smiled, for he knew what was coming. The family has had to deal with this one for years now. "His age?" Timothy calmly inquired, trying to shorten the conversation.

"Why yes," the doctor answered, glancing to the records again, making sure he saw the number correctly.

"My great-great-grandfather will be 129 years young on his soon to be birthday." Timothy smiled again, waiting for the pushback.

"That's impossible," he said with as much assurance as he could muster. "How old are you?"

Timothy continued to smile. "I am sixty years old and have all my faculties I assure you."

"But, Timothy," the doctor sputtered some, showing a crack in his smooth veneer. "He doesn't look older than you. Maybe even younger."

"It is what it is," Timothy stated. "My grandmother, God rest her soul, Bob's youngest daughter, was born in 1982, and Bob in 1955."

"I would really love to run some tests." A doctor's fame comes about from dedication and medical discoveries. He saw an opportunity.

"Absolutely not," Timothy said, holding up his hand. "Treat the concussion. He's been through tests over the years. No more."

"But he's a medical miracle," the doctor insisted, as if the grandson wasn't already aware.

"Oh, don't we know it. As Grandpa would tell you, as I just did, "it is what it is," now please leave it."

Obviously disappointed, the doctor folded his hands in front of him, as if his hands were tied.

"So, doctor, how is he doing?" Timothy asked, wanting to move this along, ignoring the redundant question of Bob's age.

"He seems fine physically, but he hasn't woken yet. That and his very unusual EEG results have us baffled."

"He is a baffling man," Timothy responded without much emotion. "Please explain," Tim requested.

"Bob appears to be unconscious, but his EEG is throwing very active Beta waves as if he were awake." The doctor sat back in his seat and folded his arms. "Something very strange going on in that noggin of his."

"Stay calm Julia. Listen and observe," came her inner voice loud and clear. "Gather what you can," I added. "Maybe we can figure out where you are."

"How many are you?" Julia felt foolish asking, but not loud enough for the two in front to hear. She was terrified and confused. What the hell was happening to her? Was this help being offered, or was she losing her mind?

"There are four of us. Bob, retired accountant, Detective Joseph Alvarez, our young man Tad Lincoln, and First Mate Jonathan Boynes. We are all at your service."

I am losing my mind, Julia thought.

"You are not," I assured her.

"Secret government experiment?" Julia asked.

"Nothing like that," I responded. "This is God's doing, so please do as we ask and observe. We can see and hear what you can."

For the remainder of the trip to an unknown destination, Julia was silent and perplexed, and simply watched and listened. They didn't blindfold her, so she was relatively certain they disguised themselves and naturally had no intentions of letting her go, regardless. The thought made the acid rise in her stomach.

The travel became erratic after a while, no longer in a straight line and flat as before, indicating twists and turns, rise and falls. Julia could see shadows of hills through the windshield. Mostly darkness and a rare headlight seemed to reflect through the window.

After a long curve was taken, felt through her shift in weight, they slowed and stopped for what sounded like a railroad crossing bell. Watching intently through the front windshield, she saw the red flashing of the standard crossing, and finally a glimpse of the lowering of the crossing gates. "That's useful information," she thought to herself.

"The best," I added. "Do you know what time it is?" I then asked.

"No. Sorry", she responded without speaking. "I have a watch, but it's under the straps they have me in."

Bob wanted to open his eyes so desperately to find out the time, in case this was live TV, but he dared not. Stay focused on Julia, or the connection could be broken.

The gates came up exactly 62 seconds later, and the van pulled ahead carefully. Julia counted the passage of time in her head. She was onboard.

"Great work," I said. The more details the better.

"You dying to get in there buddy?" The driver asked of the other, who didn't respond. Ten minutes then passed, the van slowed and pulled onto what felt and sounded like a gravel road. The van continued straight for a truly brief period of time before the crunch of gravel ceased as if the gravel changed over to dirt or grass perhaps.

They followed a steep incline for a time, leveled out, pulled around in a semicircle and stopped. The driver killed the engine, opened his door and stepped out, followed by his partner. I could hear them walk away, so I tested my straps once more, but there was no chance of me loosening them.

I laid perfectly still after only seconds of trying my luck, nearly holding my breath, waiting for the next shoe to fall. Could hear them talking but didn't understand all of what they were saying. Nothing helpful. They were some distance away. One thing was certain, there were now three of them. There was a distinct difference in the voice of the third man. Deep and polished with an accent. Australian, I think.

They are coming back now. My fear was palpable, but calm I managed to stay.

"Either of you fellas have a durry?" the third man asked.

"A what?" the driver fired back.

"Sorry mate," the man apologized with polish. "A cigarette."

After several moments, probably time enough for the Australian to light up, the door slid open. The smell of a lit durry, as he called it, drifted in with the fine gentlemen, going about their business as if simply delivering a new washer.

"Why isn't she blindfolded?" the man asked, a bit perturbed.

"Sorry boss," they responded as they tied a blindfold over my eyes and released me from my binds to the gurney. Before helping me out of the van, they bound my hands behind me as well. I was still unsteady on my feet, and required a little assistance to gain my balance, which is much harder when blind.

"Welcome to your new home Julia," the Aussie stated, very properly, and I guess welcoming tone, excusing the circumstances. "You will be well treated here, assuming you cause no troubles and go with the program."

"And what program may that be?" I asked shakingly. My mind was spinning from the possibilities. My family was not rich, so a ransom was out of the question. The other possibilities were making me nauseous. It was good that I hadn't eaten yet, for I felt I was about to lose it.

"We'll get into that later," he quickly stated.

I so wanted to argue, scream, fight, or simply throw up. The strange presence inside was fighting me on this. Striving to calm me down. "Pick your battles," the voice repeated. "Calm, cooperative and observant. Remember?" I said nothing more.

My two abductors were now at either elbow, leading me down a path it appeared, while the Aussie, with lumbering steps, was leading the way. I am considering he must be a larger man than the other two. I only walked perhaps fifty feet, leaves and twigs crunching under my feet. There was a strong smell of plant life, including the unmistaken aroma of honey suckle.

When we stopped, from the sound of things, I could almost picture the larger man, puffing on his cigarette, while moving bushes or something aside, before opening a large, what sounded like, metal door, or gate. A large bolt was moved out of its slot and the entrance was cleared. I was thinking of oil being needed as the creaks, squeaks, and clangs began, which are unmistakably sounds of metal.

Before moving again, I felt something against my hands, which were tied behind my back. It felt like rubber, like in rubber gloves. It was dark, which is good, for I couldn't help but smile. Back pockets are generally a bad place to put things, due to the possibility of damaging it or losing it. Lucky for me, I don't always pay attention. I've found things in my washer and dryer before that I forgot to clear from my pockets. "My bad," I laughingly thought to myself, as I was able to stealthily pull a used glove from my back pocket and drop to the ground. If these voices in my head can somehow track me, I just left a bread crumb.

Once I entered, only one guy was left holding one elbow, while the other remained behind I assumed. The lead man went in first. We immediately descended on what sounded like concrete or stone steps. There were no creaks or any other noise for that matter that sounded like wooden steps. It reminded me of going into a damp cellar. The sounds and musty smells were unmistakable. What was odd is the fact I don't recall ever being in a cellar.

Within feet, we stopped briefly at another door. Heavy but nearly soundless when opened and closed behind us. Heavy bolts and locks were engaged, locking the Aussie and me in. The other man had left and went back up the steps. Based upon sound alone, it was apparent they locked the door above and replaced the covering. Whether they stayed or not, I had no way of knowing.

The boss, I now assume, led me down what appeared to be a long hallway before turning left and down another. He stopped abruptly and turned me away from him. With his hands on my shoulders, he leaned close to my neck and whispered into my ear, "this will be your new home for a while honey." His closeness, foul smoker's breath, and the fact he called me honey, sickened me. The man then grabbed me about the neck and pulled my body into his. My bound hands were trapped between us, being pulled into his gelatinous stomach. The man was fat, as I imagined him to be. A head taller I estimated, as he sniffed at my hair like a dog, then reached around and grasped my breast. "My clients will love you," he said with a sickening tone. The worse of nightmares was coming true. The services offered to the clients had finally become crystal clear. Tears were dampening the cloth covering my eyes and sobs were building from deep within me.

"Please don't," I cried through now deepening sobs.

Along with her fear and disgust, anger was rising from the four gentlemen witnessing this foulness being forced upon Julia. They were deeply connected through a force they couldn't understand. Her feelings were now a part of them as was their anger and abilities a part of her. Quiet observation was no longer an option. Some not so quiet intervention was now on the plate.

Shifting his grip, he pushed me into a door with his hand firmly gripping the back of my neck. He pushed me through the now open door and onto a bed. The door was closed and locked, but the monster was still in here with me. His labored breathing was as obvious as his intentions. "God help me," I said quietly.

"Let me get a good look at your eyes honey," he said as he pulled off the blindfold.

My eyes were already burning from my tears and the bright light was an unwelcomed intruder. I blinked several times before my host came into focus. A balding man as tall and fat as I figured. He was by no means a good-looking man. Sweat was pouring down his face which featured a sickly smile, exposing his almost too perfect teeth. Double chin, brown hair quickly being chased away by male patterned baldness. A yellow polo shirt, not quite covering all his ample belly, brown slacks, and black tennis shoes. With his hands on his hips, he was eagerly examining the goods. He made my skin crawl.

"What do you think honey? Nice room. You should be comfortable here," he added with fake kindness dripping from his lips, like acid.

I was sitting on a full-size bed in a decent sized bedroom. There was a closed louver door, which I assume was a closet. He walked over to the door and opened it, and it was full of clothing. "They should fit you," he said. He opened a second door, which revealed a bathroom with a walk-in shower. Like some agent showing a house, he passed around the room showing the various amenities. A mirrored triple dresser full of clothing as well, all the way down to lacy panties. Two pair of house slippers placed in front of the nightstand holding a touch light, and a small set of books. "For your reading pleasure and downtime," waving over the books and seemingly pleased with himself, "which you will have occasionally."

Do I give a shit? I asked myself angrily. Waiting patiently, oddly thinking to myself, "get on with it, low life." That's not me but go with the flow I say.

After the tour of my future prison, he finally stopped talking about the accommodations, and returned his focus to me. "I'm sure you'll want a shower after such a harrowing day."

"Are you kidding me?" I had to ask.

"No, not kidding," he responded with a slight break in his smile. "After your shower, someone will bring you something to eat if you wish. There are towels and a robe hanging in the bathroom." His smile was gone, and he was being more matter of fact in his speech.

"Not hungry," I said with as much feeling as a rock.

"Okay, suit yourself," he said before a smile returned to his face. "If you stand up, I will help you with your clothes."

"Oh, I'm sure you will," I responded scathingly. "Free my hands and I will take care of myself. I am a big girl after all."

"You are to cooperate miss Julia. That is rule number one. Rule number two is following the other rules." The man took a step forward. "I will release you after I sample the goods," he then said, reestablishing his intentions. "You see young lady," he felt he needed to add, "you are like an expensive wine our customers are expected to pay well for, and I am a connoisseur of fine wines, which I sample now and then." He pretended to hold a wine glass, place it to his nose, taking in a deep breath, as if taking in the aroma. "Understand?" he finally asked with a smile, before taking another step forward.

"Perfectly," speaking in a deep guttural tone. I was wound as tight as an engaged spring. My eyes narrowed and dove deep into his as my spring unwound into something that was a blur to me.

I laid back on the bed, bringing up both knees simultaneously. With one quick thrust, like a piston exploding upward in a muscle car, I kicked with everything I had into the chest of Mr. Nice, vaulting him into the wall, leaving a nice impression where his backside landed. He fell to the floor with a sickening thud, and the air knocked out of him, possibly a busted rib for his smugness. His eyes were closed and moaned as he moved to his side, holding his obviously bruised chest and libido. I quickly brought my knees back up completely to my chest and was able to slide my bound hands under my feet. As I was coming off the bed, the man had gotten to his knees, which is a position I could not very well pass on. With a pro kicker's eye, I launched his balls through the uprights. "And the crowd goes wild!" I shouted with my hands raised.

He was now on his face not moving. "Too much?" I asked amusingly. My anger was not abated yet as I was looking at my bound hands. He was too big to hide and didn't have time to tie him up, and with what, I had to ask. The Green Beret in me climbed on his back and pulled my bindings around his neck, and with my knee in his back, pulled hard to either snap his neck or choke the life out of the bastard.

Time or something stopped me. I hesitated before the door came crashing in. The racket brought backup. There were three. "Not enough," I oddly said to myself. "Remember the Alamo!" I shouted as I rolled from the unconscious man and began kicking some major ass.

During the scuffle, I however felt the all too familiar sting in my arm that knocked me out before. I quickly slowed and was wrapped up tighter than a drum, but not before major damage was done. "My apologies to the hotel staff," I said giggling as the serum was doing its job. Sure, they will send me to a more appropriate room, I thought as my breathing slowed. The room was a disaster. "I am not paying for this," I mumbled into the carpet my face was buried in, right before the lights were turned out.

Chapter 35

Like a Jack-In-The-Box, without the catchy tune, I bolted straight up in the hospital bed. My actions must have extracted a year from the nurse's life. My back was as straight as a board and my head turned to witness the poor lady jump back and almost trip over the chair. Though she was much too young, it was probably reminiscent of Linda Blair in "The Exorcist", when her head twisted to an unnatural position. She was holding her chest, keeping her heart from jumping out. "Sweet Jesus, Mary and Joseph, you scared the life clean out of me," she said with a scant brogue to her voice, still holding her chest and breathing hard through her pursed lips.

"Aye begorra," I stated with me best Irish imitation, smiling hugely. Couldn't help but enjoy the scene. "I know I scared ye my young lass, but no sense in insulting our Lord," I added kindly.

"Ye be like a corpse bolting from a casket," she said, now smiling, and gathering her wits about her.

"I am so sorry Brey," I apologized, glancing at her name tag. "Beautiful name," I added. "One with power and force I think it means."

"You are correct," she agreed with a slight furrow of her brow.

"I read a lot and have a few years under my belt to do so," I added, in case she was wondering.

She smiled and replaced the chair she pushed part of the way across the room during her near spill. I swung around on the bed and asked, "can you please remove everything?" referring to the IVs and the contraption stuck to my head. "I have some very pressing business." Time was of the essence. Julia and who knew how many were being held captive.

"I cannot, before talking to the doctor." She started to turn to leave the room.

"Please make it quick, or I'll remove them myself." I didn't mince words or leave any room for doubt that I meant what I said. Brey nodded and quickly left the room to find the doctor.

Several minutes had passed and I was getting anxious. Julia was still part of me, and she appeared to be unconscious and currently not in any danger. I stood up, looking for gauze and tape, so I could start working on the I.V., when the doctor and nurse came in.

"Doctor, so glad to see you," I said in good humor, to help convince good old doc that I was ready to jump off this train.

"Nurse Brey says you are ready to leave," he stated while pulling out his light and shining it in my eyes, then asking me to go through the motions. Left, right, up, down, he directed me. "Any dizziness Bob?" the doctor asked.

"No sir," I responded. "Feel as right as rain and am anxious for Brey to release the ties that bind me." Always the writer and poet.

"Bob, you just woke up. I don't think----"

"Sorry, Doc, but I have to insist. I'll sign the papers." I held my arm out to Brey, indicating how badly I need the stuff to come off.

The doctor nodded toward the nurse, she shrugged and began working to get me ready to leave. "Thank you doctor," I said as he left the room.

In a surprisingly brief period of time, I signed the paper, dressed, walked out of the hospital, and was driven home by my great grandson. By then, Julia was awake, but tied to a bed in one of the rooms, waiting for a decision on what is to be done with her. Were they prepared to deal with such a hellcat?

It was great to be back home. My head was a little sore, but nothing a little aspirin can't handle. After a quick shower, meal, and donning proper clothing for the task ahead, I was in front of my computer trying to pinpoint Julia's approximate location based on information she managed to collect.

Between mine and Detective Alvarez's connections and knowhow, and some computer research, we were able to gather substantial information on the current case of the missing girls. After gathering detailed street and topographical maps of the areas between Louisville and Cincinnati, I plotted each girl's point of disappearance. That also confirmed for me that she was a new abduction. Naturally, I was making a big assumption that this was related. Gives me somewhere to start. As expected, based on scouring the local news, Julia hasn't been reported as missing yet. I then placed a red stickpin in Julia's home address. All the others were pinned with white pins.

As I assumed before, now confirmed, besides knowing the overall area of the abductions, there was no pattern determined by the authorities in either location or abductees.

Based upon when I was in and out of the hospital, the approximate time of Julia's abduction, and what we could gather from the dream, I had a rough timeline, but would it be enough.

I was in a room identical to the one the Aussie pushed me into earlier. No idea how long I had been out. Strapped tightly to a bed, movement was difficult, and was especially sore in my upper body. "I really kicked some royal bootie, didn't I? Never knew I had it in me," I said, smiling at the ceiling. While wondering if my cohorts were still floating around in my head, or if it was my imagination, I could hear some muffled conversation coming from close by. Best thing now is stay quiet, so they'll think I am still out. Women's voices, at least more than two, I was able to detect, mixed in with some crying. Now I knew I wasn't alone in this nightmare.

My door rattled and was opening slowly. Probably checking on me. Playing unconscious is what I did, and it worked for now, because they finally closed and relatched the door. Must have figured I wasn't going to cause any more trouble. Okay guys, please find me, and soon. I reclosed my eyes and said a prayer for all of us here, trapped in this horrible place.

The train crossing was turning out to be the silver bullet of this search. After pinpointing all railroad crossings with gates, train movements, times, and the description of a long curve coming up to the crossing, there was only one that hit the mark. "Bingo!" I shouted at the top of my lungs, bringing a yelp out of my dog, who was deep in a dream of her own no doubt.

Ten minutes I had written down. Julia said ten minutes more on what appeared to be a smooth and slightly twisty road. They must have stayed on the road that crossed the tracks. It fit the bill. That appeared to be Highway 36, which turns into Easter Day Road. "It goes past a cemetery," I said, smiling, remembering a comment from the dream. "You dying to get in there buddy?" The driver asked. "Well, well, loose lips do sometime sink ships."

I was quickly stumped, however. "The road stops at a light on a major highway." I scratched my head, confused but determined. Chewey was now at my feet, considering my dilemma no doubt. I reached down and scratched behind her ear. One of her favorite things, next to food that is. "The other side is the General Butler State Park." There was never an indication of a turn that early. It would take only a few minutes to get from the track to the park. The map shows no road there. I rechecked my notes and looked closely at the map once more. "Chewey, this has to be it," I tried to convince my dog, who was now waiting for a treat. I kept a small jar of her treats on the table, like a K9 candy dish. Least I could do after interrupting her dream, was to toss one to her, and she immediately sauntered off to the mat in front of the kitchen door.

"Well fellas," talking to all of us, including Chewey, who came back for seconds, "my feeling is that they are in the park, so it's time to resurrect Grandpa Jones and take us on a little back packing trip." I left a message for my great grandson, asking him to watch the place and take care of my dog. One last thing I made mention of in the message. If anything were to happen to me, he would find a package in my nightstand detailing my theories and possible whereabouts of the girls. I asked him to give this to the authorities, but he was to wait two days. "I'm trusting you son, not to mess this up." He was my backup.

After being satisfied with my getup, I packed some camping gear into my huge backpack first, for I wasn't sure how long I may be. My newest goal, since my writing had dried up, was to tackle the Appalachian Trail. It would surely give me new material to twist into an exciting story. A Pomeranian and an ancient accountant on a trail many have tried but failed to tackle and a few even disappeared. My trusty watch dog will surely take care of me.

Packing for the trip I may have been, but I was also literally packing. My new 9MM with silencer, spare magazines, an extremely lightweight set of body armor, and other gadgets no responsible secret agent would leave home without. After grabbing a bite, I couldn't help but hum and sing an ancient ditty that popped into my head. Appropriate I thought. "Secret Agent Man, Secret Agent Man, they've given you a number and oh, they've taken way your name," I sang while packing my vehicle. "Agent 128 is coming to get you my darling," I said while pulling away for yet another adventure. My life had been getting a bit stale lately, so I was looking forward to this in a strange way.

It was getting late when I spotted exit 44 to Carrollton off I71. Late was good I thought. Better cover. Highway 227 would take me directly to that dead end, according to my maps, which I had printed and were on my passenger seat. Got my hands on a topographical map of the park as well. It was near 8:00 PM, which is too late to enter the park through the normal passage, but I had no intention of going in the front door, no more than the criminals would have. I could barely see it in the near darkness, but I found what I had hoped. A small access road was cutting into the park, across from the light, blocked by a gate with a no trespassing sign.

After finding a safe place to park, I slid into the park unseen, and headed toward the entrance.

On this round, three men entered my room, at my request. I had to use the lady's room and urgently. Unless they wanted a mess on their nice clean sheets. I had been shouting for several minutes. Once they entered, I could tell they weren't very happy with me. A girl has to do what a girl has to do I was thinking as they circled my bed. One of them happened to be the fat Aussie, and his look was not only pained, as expected, but extremely angry. I was also able to catch a glimpse of a fourth gentleman outside my door. "All for me?" I couldn't help but ask. "You really didn't have to go to all this trouble."

"You are in no position to be such a smart ass," the Aussie stated harshly.

"No pleasantries then?" I didn't think so. Nature calls, however. "Since there is already a laxity of decorum, I have to say, I've got to pee guys!"

The Aussie smiled at my predicament. He was counting on lots of payback, but my thoughts explored the possibility of scoring another field goal. Should have killed you when I had the chance, I couldn't help but think.

"Help the young lady out of her bindings," the Aussie instructed the other two, while pulling a pistol out of his jacket, with a grimace, which gave me some gratification. I was in a world of hurt here, but any pain they have, is nothing compared to what I am wishing to fall upon their heads. Normally a good girl, but this pisses me off. My demure, frightened little girl is tucked away for a later day. Agent 128 and I are on the job, and I am picking my battles.

"Now," the man added after I was free, which left them all noticeably on edge. Good, I thought. "Take your smart ass into the bathroom, do your business, take a shower and get into your robe."

Being the good girl I was, I went into the bathroom and shut the door, which had no lock, which was no surprise. Sweat was pouring down my face, for I felt I was going to bust.

Fortunately, one of my packed goodies was a pair of military grade night goggles. A flashlight was packed but not yet necessary, and easily spotted if used. Even though moving slowly and as quietly as possible, it didn't take long to locate the start of the small road I spotted. The road was paved, which I thought a little odd for a simple access road, but it further fit into Julia's descriptions. Who did they buy off to allow them to put any type of structure in the park? If I had time to research I would.

Carefully making my way up the road, estimating the distance I had walked, I was able to find the gravel turn off. "I think I am getting close Julia," I whispered quietly. I then felt something brush against my ankle as I turned onto the gravel road. It was a wire stretched across the road, and I realized too late that I had probably signaled them that someone was out here. Of course, a deer could easily have tripped the wire. A little old fashioned I thought. Lasers would have been better, but then again, I would have spotted it with my night goggles.

Thinking fast, not knowing what sort of security equipment could be set up, I stumbled to the ground and stuffed the goggles into my jacket. If it was a camera, set off by the trip wire, an old man with goggles would appear suspicious.

Assuming that I might have been caught on camera, it was time for my acting lessons to pay off. After rising slowly, allowing my eyes time to adjust, and the switch from goggles to flashlight, I stumbled my way up the gravel road using my shaky beam of light. I was now old man Jonathan Boynes once again. Drunk old man Boynes. A little whiskey from a sampler bottle I brought along would do the trick. Take a swig. “Oh, that stuff is rank,” I said as I nearly gagged. Sprinkle the rest on my clothing and toss the empty bottle into my bag. “How old are you now Jonathan?” I asked into thin air. “You don’t look a day over 300,” I giggled as I stumbled again for appearances. “Don’t hurt yourself dumbass,” one of my inner voices chimed in.

I then saw some lights up ahead heading my way, confirming my assumption that they knew I was coming. Flashlights they appeared to be. Three of them. Fifty yards perhaps. This be your favorite I think dear Jonathan, I thought as I started to sing and walk like a drunken sailor, which I had some ancient memory of. “Like a petrel she'll skim the blast. While the spray sweeps her deck with snow. As the waves, in their race, foam past.” I stumbled to the ground once more. “You dumb old man,” severely chastising myself, as the men approached me, obviously amused. “Can’t you even walk straight?” I asked myself as I rose clumsily, pushing up with my left hand and placing my right near my 9MM. “Oh, hi there,” I greeted them with glee. “I once was lost, but now I am found,” I added, thinking I shouldn’t be quoting the bible with what I am about to do. Don’t be hasty, I thought to myself. Shooting good guys might be frowned upon.

“What are you doing out here old man?” the lead man said harshly. Strike one, I thought.

"Went on a hike and got lost," I said, while observing that they all had rifles. Strike two.

"Old man," he called me again. "Turn yourself around and head right back down the road if you know what's good for you."

"Can't I just camp here and sleep it off? You see, I've had a little too much libation this night," I added, while inching closer. Their last strike was when I recognized two of them, even in this light, from Julia's altercation earlier.

"On your way! I am saying for the last time," the lead man said.

"I guess I know where I'm not wanted," I said dejectedly, as I was now within arm's length. They weren't concerned with an old drunken bum lost in the woods. Not too good guys, I thought, as I pulled the lead man in front of me for extra protection, holding him like a vice with my left arm, and in the same instant put two quick bullets into each of the other two.

After separating the third man from his guns, I performed some quick interrogation using very painful tactics. After obtaining an entry key and a little useful information, I had no choice but to allow him to join the other two. There were five more on the inside, if I could believe the man, which I don't. Once I dragged their bodies and weapons into the woods about fifty yards, I placed a small locator with the bodies, so they could be found later.

After putting the goggles back on, I walked toward where I estimated the entrance would be. Be quick and stealthy I had to remind myself. I was still shaking from earlier. A killer I am not, regardless of the need. After a brief period, they would surely be missed. The aroma of a fresh growth of honeysuckle was in the air, as described by Julia. The gravel had ceased some time back. "It should be close by. I can almost feel Julia in my bones." In the strange light, as seen through my goggles, a couple promising paths could be seen. Went down one and then the other until I found what I was looking for. A single inconspicuous latex medical glove tossed to the ground like rubbish. "You should be ashamed of yourself Julia, littering in a national park," I quietly laughed at my luck, as I reached down and picked it up. "Sorry to ask Julia, but I need you to create a diversion. I found the entrance you described, and excellent job by the way. In three minutes, I plan to come in without knocking." I sat quietly on the ground and waited. "This could get ugly." I noted the location and sent out messages to several authorities to hopefully bring in the cavalry, but I wasn't planning on waiting. A lot can happen in the time it would take for them to get here, if they believed my story at all.

Almost done with my shower. It was glorious, except for the fact several dirt bags were hanging outside my door, with who knows what on their mind. "He's here," I then said, startled. I could feel and hear him. Diversion? I asked myself. Women can be great at diversions. I quickly dried and threw on my robe. A plan was formulating, embarrassing as it may be, but my life may and probably will depend on what happens in the next few minutes. Do I still have my mojo? I'll be finding out.

"Gentlemen," and I use the term loosely, "I'm coming out," I stated alluringly, while opening the bathroom door slowly. Work it Julia, I said to myself. You can do this.

I stood in the doorway with nothing on but a robe. The desired impression was extracted and could be seen in their eyes. These guys are like salivating dogs. My nerves were on fire. Wasn't sure if this was simple nervousness or something else. Feeling like I did earlier, and I like it. I really like it. After moving a couple steps into the room, the Aussie raised his hands, instructing me to stop. Without yet saying a word, he motioned the second man to stand on the other side of me. This might be a little more difficult, I thought as I continued to size them up and the distances.

"Let's see what you got young lady," the Aussie demanded, waving his hand as if a gesturing king.

"I was planning on saving myself for my future husband," I said sarcastically, while thinking I had less than one minute.

He was not amused, I could tell, but he managed a smile, for he figured he had me surrounded, and he had a gun.

The steel in me was surprising, for all I could think of was kicking another field goal with the guys' nuts, so I smiled back.

"Now," he said flatly, raising his gun.

"Now!" I repeated to myself, as I let my robe fall, flashing these underserving slobs all my goods. The Aussie lowered his gun. I grabbed the guy to my right, while their eyes were glued to my wares, quickly pushing him into the Aussie, and with a quick move had them on the floor, and his gun in my hand.

Gunshots, shouts, and screams echoed down the halls, creating one hell of a diversion.

The racket, though loud from their perspective, was nearly imperceptible through the two doors. My entry was seamless.

Except for the guy in the room just past the door, a guard position, everyone else's attention must have been on the racket coming from the other end of the facility. Fantastic job Julia, I thought. The guard must have assumed it was his three guys returning when I entered the code and opened the door slowly. "Hey guys we have a problem," he said, walking into the hall without any concern on his face until he discovered how wrong he was.

"Yes, you do," I said, as he appeared in his doorway, and I planted the butt of my gun square between the eyes of the shocked young man. Time was of the essence, so I was forced to dispatch him as quietly as I could, and stuffed him under his desk, away from prying eyes.

"I'm coming Julia," I said, with gun out and edging my way down the first hall.

"Throw the gun out Julia," one guy hollered through the now locked door of the bedroom. There was no doorknob on her side of the door, so she couldn't block it with the one chair she had available.

The two men were dead, and the Aussie was flat on his stomach, whimpering like a child. Like many, so called macho types, they were only macho when they had some control. Julia had propped the mattress and springs against the wall for extra protection from bullets. Julia's knee was firmly in the man's back, hand full of his hair, tugging at his roots, and the gun barrel pressing against the back of his neck. The man was not in control.

"Your sissy Aussie is still alive, and you better back off if you want to keep it that way." I was terrified but had some control at the moment, even in my current state of undress.

"Don't do anything you'll regret," he said in response.

"I guess we'll find out how indispensable you are," Julia whispered into the Aussie's ear. "Regret? Are you serious asshole!" Julia shouted through the door. "I would rather shoot your fat buddy here, and myself before I became one of your play toys. Naturally, if I accidently shoot a couple more of you, all the better," she added for effect.

"What do we do now boss?" asked one of the other four standing guard outside Julia's room.

"Wait her out he said," unconcerned. "She isn't going anywhere." The man then turned to one of the men behind him. "Bring me my hunting rifle. I think I might have a little fun."

As I slipped down the first hall, making my way to Julia, I could hear some girls whispering through the walls and some crying. I said nothing and made no noise, even though my heart went out to them. Nobody could know I was here.

Made my way to the edge of an alcove, part of the way down the first hall. Keeping low with gun ready, I peeked around the corner. The alcove was only four feet deep with a single door at the end. It was different than the other doors, behind which the girls were apparently being held. This one was metal with HVAC painted on it. I had to make a snap decision, go past, or check it out. I was hoping the electrical circuits were in there. Darkness could be my friend. They were waiting Julia out and I wanted to lessen the chances someone would get behind me. Had to check it out.

Opened the door slowly, and noticed a man next to the furnace, replacing filters it appeared. He was not having a fun time of it. Curse words were flying freely, and the filters were winning. The man was wiggling and jerking on the old one. It refused to give up the ghost. Under different circumstances I would have been amused. Must be the maintenance guy, I thought with relief. Knowing gunfire would alert the rest, I put my gun in its holster and pulled out my knife. The saying, never judge a book by its cover, I quickly learned the meaning of.

He saw me coming. Tried to sneak in, but the light from the hallway filtering into the room gave me away. After I closed the door, he was already standing. "Who the hell are you!" He shouted, prior to seeing the knife in my hand. He quickly picked up a two-foot-long pipe wrench. He must be every bit of 6' 5" and 250 pounds. His veins popped out on his neck, and the muscles on his arms were like those of an old fashion blacksmith. Down his right arm was a tattoo of an anchor and trident.

"Navy Seal?" I asked, after seeing the tattoo. Unsure of what to do next, a memory flashed across my brain of Indiana Jones facing the Arabic swordsman. Should I simply pull out my gun and shoot him?

He smiled eagerly as he came at me with the wrench, swinging it with deadly force at my head. I was able to roll under it and take a swipe at his side with my blade, but he was too quick. We circled each other like two warriors on a battlefield.

"You're a disgrace to the flag," I shouted before he took another swing. This time I ducked under it and pinned him and his weapon against the wall. Unfortunately, it was like trying to wrestle with a bear. He was quickly able to immobilize my right arm with his left and fling me like a rag doll into a stack of crates. Nearly knocked the breath out of me, and it hurt like hell. My knife and gun clanked and skidded across the concrete floor. The man leaned over and picked up the wrench he dropped and was heading in for the kill. After jumping up quickly, for I had no choice, I blocked the blow of the wrench, and was able to plant a straight punch into the point of his jaw. That stunned him, so I quickly planted a front kick into his chest, sending him onto his ass. He wasn't stunned long enough, for he got back up, sweating, red in the face and ready for another round.

We traded punches and tosses for nearly a minute. I had no idea how someone else hadn't heard the extreme racket we must have been making. I thought I was doing well. Located my gun and was going for it, when he blocked me and planted an elbow into my shoulder, sending a sharp pain through it. I fell to the ground, grasping my left arm, realizing the man had dislocated my shoulder. My left arm was now useless and badly bruised from blocking his blows. Desperately I pushed myself across the floor with my feet and one good arm, attempting to reach my gun. The Seal had grabbed a metal pole and attempted to turn me into a human shish kabob. I was able to avoid the first two jabs, sending sparks and concrete shards into the air as metal struck concrete. The third one missed as well, and I was able to grab ahold of it and snap my right foot out, squarely into the man's kneecap, bending it backward to an unnatural position. He dropped the pole next to me and was stumbling backward, apparently with a broken knee. His anger got the best of him. He tried to rush me and stumbled with his bad knee, sending the mountain of a man forward. By instinct alone, I raised and anchored the pole, which the man-mountain impaled himself upon. To finish the job, I grabbed him by the collar and pulled down with all I had, sending it through the man's back.

"Sam, you okay in there," I heard from outside the door.

I lost sight of my gun and knife. Already made it to my feet, as the door slowly opened, bringing more light into the room. If he had a gun, I was a goner. Necessity is the mother of invention, so I put one foot on the dead man's chest, extracted the pole with my good arm, and threw the pike at the shadowy figure in the doorway. Like a javelin, it cut through the air and found its mark. No time to celebrate, so I closed and blocked the door as best I could, and drug the two men behind the fallen crates.

Found my gun and knife, but I was stuck in here, half functional, and in severe pain. I didn't hear anything else outside the door, so I assume I was safe for a short period of time. Julia was blockaded in her room and me in here. Her anxiousness was heightened over our situation. "Some white knight I turned out to be," I said, standing there holding my arm against my body. Every move I made sent sharp pains through me. "What was I thinking?" Chastising myself. "Trying to do this alone." I was thinking the authorities would take forever and wouldn't believe me anyway, I was thinking, trying to convince myself I made the correct move. “What now smart man?”

My left arm is useless as is, so let’s fix it. “How hard could it be?” I asked myself jokingly. My mind was full of information, some of it useless, but some comes in handy. With a clear picture in my mind, I sat on the cold concrete, bent my left knee, and grasped it with my fingers. After a couple minutes of bending my back and stretching away from the shoulder, it finally popped back into place. The process was painful, but I felt instant relief after the clear pop. Wasn’t nowhere good as new, but I will have some use of it.

Glancing at two of the many dead bodies I was responsible for, which burned into my heart, I had to decide if it was best to shelter in place, waiting for support, or continue with my original plan.

Chapter 36

It was about an hour into the standoff, when the man finally shouted from the hall, "Julia, times up!" His patience had run thin.

"I'm doing my nails. Can you come back later?" She spoke. Julia had already tied up the Aussie and was lying on her back behind him, with the gun on her chest, and dressed in a flowing black dress, split up the side. Julia decided she might as well look good during the tragic conditions. She could feel the predicament Bob found himself in, so was very worried, but refused to give the bums outside the room any satisfaction. "Bob, I'm scared," she whispered, before starting to cry.

The man said nothing else. He felt they waited long enough. He fired his high-powered hunting rifle into the wall, approximately six feet up from the floor. The sound was deafening while the projectile slammed through the wall, mattress, and imbedded into the concrete wall behind her. Julia jumped and gripped the pistol even tighter. "Bob!" She shouted as her newfound bravery was slipping away from her.

The Aussie was nothing to him, but he hated to lose such a feisty prize like Julia. It would be his pleasure to break her spirit, he was thinking. They have their methods. The second and third shots were lower, and they echoed down the hall, as did her pleadings for rescue.

"Julia honey, please throw out the gun and give up. Nobody can hear your pitiful cries." The man's words were like poison to her ears. The sound of fingernails scratching on a chalkboard had more feeling in it than this evil man's words.

"I'll die before I let you touch me," was her response, before another round imbedded itself into the wall. She was now crying bitterly. All connection to Bob was lost, and her fierceness of spirit with it. She felt now that Bob didn't make it and all was lost. Julia was now empty and felt totally alone. This nightmare must end. The last straw had nearly fallen, while with shaky hands she raised the pistol to her temple.

"Please don't," she heard distinctly echo across her mind, as she was nearly to the point of no return. A smile broke through her sorrow, as did a renewed hope, at the same instance power was cut and the place was buried in darkness.

Cursing and scuffling could be heard outside her door. "Jake, Mark, go check the breakers," the leader commanded. "Damned cheap shit!" he cursed. "Everything's made in China!"

"Bob?" she whispered with a smile nearly bright enough to break through the pitch. The Aussie was mumbling incoherently next to her in the dark. "Shut the hell up," she shouted, smacking him on the back of his head.

Gunshots echoed from down the hall, as the two sent Bob's way were taken out. There was no doubt about it now. Somehow, their well-hidden secret was no longer that. The perimeter had been breached. "Code red!" He shouted with desperation into the communicator clipped to his collar. They were in a maze of hallways, in the darkness of a cave, with an unknown factor running about.

"Cover your ears," Julia could hear silently echo through her mind, but with urgency. Just as she did as she was told, a huge bang shook the walls, while a light, so fierce, penetrated through the edges of the secure door and nearly lit up her entire room.

A stun grenade had exploded only feet from the three remaining men outside of Julia's room, sending them into shock and near blindness. In the renewed darkness, Bob narrowed the distance between them quickly, with his night goggles back in place, he dispatched the three with impunity.

"Julia, it's me, Bob," I said, while knocking on the door. "Don't shoot," I quickly added, not taking any chances. Unclipping the keys off the dead man's belt, I then tried several before finding the one that fit the door. "Coming in," I said quietly and assuredly. "Don't shoot," I repeated, as I carefully opened the door.

I wasn't met with a bullet, but rather Julia crashed into me with a stranglehold of a hug. How she found me in the dark, I don't know. She was sobbing, while pain was shooting through my shoulder. "Please let go," I pleaded. "My shoulder," I then grunted. Fortunate for me, before my shoulder popped back out of place, she released the pressure, even though normally welcomed by a hugger. She stood back in the dark, sobbing deeply, as I removed the goggles and switched on my flashlight.

We hugged again, but much more carefully this time. Her head was on my shoulder, wetting it with her tears. Such a relief could be felt, but I knew we weren't out of the woods yet. My fears were realized, when the lights came back on, and I could hear more of them moving not too far off. I should have pulled the breakers, was my thought, a bit late. "Five my ass," I first said, remembering the count the fella gave me earlier. Without hesitation, I grabbed a couple of their weapons and tossed them into the room. "Lock yourself in," I instructed while throwing her the keys.

I peeked out of the door and was ready to run, when I heard the man on the floor start to whimper. "I said shut up," she said, but not too loudly, right before planting a foot low on his backside. She caught him exactly right. Brought a scream out of him and a grimace out of me. "Damn," was all I could say as I ran out of the room, and the door was closed and locked behind me.

Quickly I moved to the next turn, revealing many more hallways moving off in varying directions. Nearly fifty feet ahead there was a large room with a glass window, and a double door, where I caught a glimpse of tables and chairs. "How big is this place anyway?" It made me wonder if there was a lot more to this place than simply holding cells for young girls and man's evil pleasures. Was also aware there could be someone moving about from the direction I came. Someone switched the power back on.

Moving quietly, with ears open and my head on a swivel, I made my way to the next intersection, passing the large room, staying low and peeking in to verify it was empty. It turned out to be a dining room with a kitchen on one end, like you may see in any small school, but this place is no school, except perhaps for terrorists.

Peering around the next corner, once I was certain there was no gang lying in wait in the dining room, I saw no one. Just more rooms like the others, apart from the door at the end. My curiosity pulled at me. My goal at this point was simply survive and perhaps create some distraction until help arrived.

Just before I started around that very corner, heavily armed men, three of them, came out of one of the side doors no further than 100 feet away. To my chagrin, the door I was curious about started to open as well. This is a real predicament. I had nowhere else to go, I thought, except back. A quick decision was going to have to be made. With guns up, they started shouting, “throw down your gun!”

Certain they wouldn’t let me go, following their command would be foolish. I put up my left hand, and slowly put my gun in its holster, which is not at all what they wanted.

“Toss your gun smart ass!” they shouted, raising their guns, prepared to shoot. After presenting a middle finger flag of honor, I turned and ran, zig zagging down the hall like a jack rabbit on the run, as bullets started to fly. My last zag involved a full body crash into the dining room window. This glass was nothing like the sugar glass in the movies, breaking away easy for the cameras. It was a painful move, especially where some shards pierced or otherwise cut through my clothing and skin. It was the only out I could see. There was no time to be concerned with the pain. Bullets were cutting through the air while men were fast approaching.

Immediately after rolling back to my feet, trying to ignore the shards sticking out of my flesh, I emptied one clip through the broken window and down the hallway, to make them think twice about rushing me. “Bite me,” I shouted, while loading another clip into my 9mm. Might have been an old phrase, but I liked it.

One of the men dropped to the floor and continued to fire, while a second busted in a door on the opposite side and was taking cover in the doorway. I couldn’t see him, but my wild shooting must have at least clipped the third, for he retreated back down the hallway.

Julia heard a couple of men moving down the hall, adjacent to her room, whispering about their plans to slowly move against the wall and catch him by surprise. Bob will be pinned in, she thought in a panic. Outflanked. She couldn’t simply hide in the room with all this firepower. She considered the high-powered hunting rifle, for she was a champion sharpshooter in high school. Quietly, she squeezed out of her door once they passed down the hall and took up position just at the corner. They must have felt they had Bob surrounded, but they were now sitting ducks.

After pulling a shard from my arm and leg, I glanced about the room, considering my predicament. I was certain I couldn't shelter here for long. Another shot rang out, but with a different sound and from the opposite direction. It startled me, as a man dropped to the floor just to the side of the busted window. Julia, I thought. There were two men coming from the other direction, but I wasn't aware until she dropped the second. He tried to retreat into the room next to me, but he didn't make it. "You go girl!" I shouted with pride and relief, while grasping my poor left arm. Wasn't feeling that great at the moment. Pure adrenaline kept me going, however.

That instant, the remaining two directed their fire toward Julia. She was now their biggest threat. With their attention diverted, if only for a second, I exposed myself slightly while emptying an entire clip into the area of the door jamb where one was positioned. I could see just enough of him to present me with a narrow target, which was enough. He dropped into the doorway like a pile of wet laundry. My clothing was damp with sweat and blood. Was starting to feel like a pile of wet laundry myself.

"I am too old for this shit," I said, while loading a new clip, unfortunately my last. Leaning and moving against the wall, keeping an eye on the hallway, I was doing my best to keep upright. Exhaustion and adrenalin were battling for the upper hand. My blood was smearing the wall. Couldn't tell if I was stabbed, shot, or both. "This is going to stain," I said, trying to lighten my spirit, as an item in my jacket pocket reminded me again how stupid I was. Still had one more flashbang, which had slipped my mind. Raising my eyes to the ceiling, I was thankful for the reminder. I quickly pulled it out, extracted the pin, and slung it through the window and down the hall. Timed it perfectly. By the time I turned and covered, it went off in a glorious flash. Leaving caution to the wind, I rolled into the hall and put three bullets into a dead body. Turned out the explosion was so close to the man that it gutted him and seared the wound in one surgical step.

Julia ran into the hallway, with gun raised, cheering like some schoolgirl. "Stop!" I shouted while limping toward her and waving for her to head back. A shot whistled past me and caught Julia in her left shoulder, sending her to the ground. Obviously didn't come from the dead man. The third man, assumingly the one wounded earlier, had made his way back toward the ruckus and was positioned at a doorway well down the hall. "Dammit!" I screamed, firing in his direction, while rushing toward Julia. A couple more shots were fired before I reached her and pulled her back around the corner. One shot was wide, but the other I think may have caught me in the backside. I peeked back around the corner to make sure the shooter had stayed put. I got that answer quickly as a bullet clipped the corner of the wall and through the wall behind us. "Keep low girls!" I screamed, as I saw to Julia's condition.

Julia was alert, though in pain. Fortunate the bullet hit high on the shoulder and went clean through. Fair amount of blood, but I didn't feel it was serious. Without a thought, for there wasn't much to choose from and no time, I tore a long strip off the bottom of her dress to serve as a bandage. She watched with interest as I pulled her strap off the shoulder and commenced wrapping the shoulder to staunch the bleeding. "I usually get dinner first," Julia said with a pained smile.

A flush rose to my face. I returned the smile, while tying knots in the bandage, sending a grimace to this very lovely young lady's face. Even though there are shirts in my closet older than her, I couldn't help but appreciate her beauty.

After making sure the man hadn't advanced, getting shot at again for my trouble, I grabbed the rifle and helped Julia to her feet. "We can't stay here. Too open," I assured her. We needed to lean on each other, as we made our way back to the bedroom. I was limping and holding onto Julia. The pain was increasing, and blood was leaking down my leg. "The bastard shot me in the ass," I stated, which normally may have seemed a bit humorous, but the pain and the fact I was losing blood is nothing to laugh at.

We made it to the room without any further surprises. Grabbed all the ammunition we could find and barricaded ourselves in the room the best we could. The Aussie was still on the floor, tied up and conscious, but had since soiled himself. The odor was unmistakable.

Julia had to lay out the weapons, after she helped me to the floor in the bathroom. My head was spinning, and I felt a flush move across my skin. Passing out wasn't far around the corner.

"Bob, you need to strip, so I can check your wounds. You don't look so well." She was concerned I may be going into shock.

"Can we kiss first?" I asked quietly. "We haven't even had our first date." A slight fog was starting across my vision.

Ignoring my attempt at humor, she quickly pulled off my jacket and then my shirt. The most blood seemed to be on my pants, so they came off next.

"Be gentle," I said to the young nurse checking over my nearly naked body with her experienced hands, turning me over to inspect every square inch. "Wow," was all I could manage, while starting to close my eyes.

"You're a disaster," Julia stated flatly. "What I'm more concerned with is the bullet that entered your gluteus maximus."

"Ass," I quickly corrected her, as I started to laugh and then cough. "Just let me rest here awhile and I will be just peachy."

"I don't see an exit wound from your ass," she said with some light humor to her voice. "The bullet could be anywhere. You need a hospital, and I mean stat."

Oddly, I was starting to feel a little giddy. "Just call up the front desk silly and have them bring an ambulance to our room."

"Yea I'll do just that," Julia responded, while using my knife to cut one of the towels into strips. "All I can do now is stop the external bleeding."

She then ripped off my underwear, for they were in the way. "Hey. Heyyyy." I weakly tried to object, while she applied pressure to the wound and then wrapped the towel strips tightly around my leg and gluteus maximus. It didn't arouse me, thank goodness, but I thought it funny as hell. Couldn't help but expel some weak laughter, followed by some gas. "Ever date a 128-year-old man before?" I asked seriously. "Got to dust me off first though," I added before snorting from amusement as I passed out.

Unknown time had passed, while darkness and light moved together within my mind. Sounds and words were floating about unrecognizable to me. My body was being moved and attended to, but was it dream or reality? Wanted to open my eyes, but they were heavy and uncooperative. My body lifted as if filled with helium, lighter than air, floating toward the ceiling I surely was. Held down by tethers, binding me to this earth. Glimpses of my past were fighting their way through the haze of this dream, unable to break the barrier before them. "Let me go," was what I felt and mumbled under my breath at this moment, a wish that had developed within me for some time.

"Be careful with him," Julia ordered the emergency personnel, as they were strapping Bob to the gurney, prior to moving him out of this den of horrors. They had been through much together in such a brief period of time. "I'm riding with him," she insisted, when the gurney was finally above ground and being moved to the waiting ambulance.

"Ma'am, we need a statement before you leave," a young, still wet behind the ears, officer insisted, trying to block her way. A definite glare was passed from Julia.

"Look, Junior!" She snapped at the officer. "I am hurt," she stated while pulling down her dress strap revealing the bandage and blood stains. "It hurts like hell, and these kind gentlemen," gesturing toward the two EMTs, "feels I should take a ride to the hospital to be tended to. You can come visit me there. Bring flowers."

The EMTs had already loaded the gurney, and with a simple wave invited Julia to ride along. The officer backed up. The EMTs enjoyed the exchange tremendously. Julia jumped into the back with one, who closed the door in the face of the officer, while the other got in the driver's seat, put her in gear, and drove away. The young EMT in the back couldn't help but smile at the extra passenger. She was a looker with plenty of spunk in her torn black evening dress.

After a brief period, once leaving the park, the driver switched on the siren and made his way carefully but expediently down the winding roads.

The siren pulled me, at least temporarily, out of my darkness and back to some modicum of reality. Blinking my eyes, struggling to focus, I realized now I was in an ambulance. To my right I could see the technician, monitoring my vitals. With a slight move of my head, I spotted a vision in black, holding fast to my hand. My wits hadn't quite caught up with me, but the warmth of her hand was welcomed. Took only a moment to be aware her hand was shaking. A powerful ordeal I now remembered going through recently with this young lady.

"Julia," I then attempted to say through the mask that was strapped to my face, while giving her hand a slight squeeze. My strength had left me. I felt helpless.

She leaned over my face and smiled. "How are you feeling?" She asked, while placing her hand on the side of my face.

"Like I went three rounds with Hulk Hogan," I responded, knowing she had no idea who he was. "What happened?" I asked, as a pain wrenched through my body, and I closed my eyes for a second till it passed.

"It won't be long," she assured me, recognizing the throes of pain. "We're on the way to my hospital. We have great people there."

"So, what happened?" I asked again after reopening my eyes. "The last thing I remember is this good-looking nurse stripping me and taking advantage of this old man." I smiled, and the EMT couldn't help but giggle.

"The police arrived soon after you passed out, old man. It was apparent you couldn't handle this nurse." She obviously could give as good as she takes. The EMT was enjoying the conversation immensely, for it kept a smile on his face.

"Did they find all the girls?" I asked, after another stab of pain shot through me.

"You should save your energy sir," the tech requested.

"I agree," she added. "Keep your trap shut, and I'll tell you."

Felt a great appreciation for her bedside manner. I like this woman, I was thinking while closing my eyes, and conserving my energy as instructed.

"All the girls were there and safe they are. You're our hero, Bob," she said with emotion.

It brought a smile to my face, and some tears to my eyes, knowing they were all safe. The word hero had a nice ring to it too, but I had lots of help.

"We did leave a lot of carnage behind, Bob," she added. "The Aussie won't be able to sit for a week. I'm considering trying out as a kicker for the

NFL." She laughed, which raised my spirits. I felt warmth toward Julia, which I haven't felt since my Susan.

"Never did get my kiss," I reminded her of my earlier bantering, which I am not sure why I did. My eyes were still closed, and I seemed to be slipping back to dream land.

Julia leaned over, with fresh tears on her face, pulled my mask aside temporarily and planted a tender salty kiss on my lips. It warmed my heart before I went under once more.

Chapter 37

Awakened again, if only for a moment, while they were working on me in the emergency room. "What's your name sir," the attendant asked me, while flashing a light into my eyes.

"Jonathan Boynes," was my first response. "Sorry. Sorry," I threw in there quickly. "Bob Johnson," I corrected myself. Thought I was still undercover. Too weak to laugh, or I would have.

"What day is it, young man?" was the second question.

"Have no idea. Trash day?" Being honest was the best policy I always thought. Days run together for me anyhow. "How's Julia?" was my question for them.

"I'm fine," she responded from the next bay. "They're dressing my wound."

It made me relax some, knowing she was okay at least. My condition was up in the air, however. Easy to tell, based on how frantic they seemed to be. After much prodding and poking, IV set into place, and cleaning up the other wounds, "we've got one for surgery," the young intern announced. "Internal bleeding," he added. "Call Dr. Steward and get him up there and prepped as soon as possible."

Too weak to open my eyes again. If Jesus was to offer me a hand up, I had been resigned for some time to eagerly slip into the next level of my life. I was at complete peace, ready for whatever was to happen next.

"Bob," I heard Julia say from the next bay, as they were wheeling my bed out. She knew she couldn't go along, even if she wanted to. "Damned rules," I heard her state with feeling. "I'll be praying for you," she added as I was rolling down the hall. "You owe me dinner!" she shouted after me.

Her words tugged at my heart. My life was in the balance. So many reasons to go, but then again.... I love my grandchildren, even though great they may be, they are spreading out and not near as close as my two girls and grandchildren were. Try to visit now and then, but not quite the same. My experiences are my own, very few shared by others. Some only found in the dead-sea-scrolls. There are times when I feel extremely alone.

Bright lights were shining through my closed eyes. Doctors, nurses, and techs, rattled about, checking everything twice, like an orchestra tuning up, shuffling music, and moving chairs in preparation for the grand event. They occasionally said things to me, but I simply nodded while doing my best to relax, which didn't take much. As they were putting the oxygen mask on my face, preparing to introduce the juice that would put me out, I said my prayers. "I am in your hands," was the last thing I managed to whisper as I slipped off.

At first the nothing of darkness enveloped me, followed by something else. Flowers, the splendid smell of them filled my senses. Peace was washing through me as the light of love was cutting through the dark. My pain was left behind. I found myself sitting under the most glorious of trees, on the softness of the greenest of grass, looking upon a gently rolling valley and majestic mountains, with all the smells and beauty even nature would be hard pressed to provide. Wildflowers, my wife's beautiful wildflowers, gently flowing through the valley as far as I could see. The very heart within my chest fluttered at the very sight, of which words would fall desperately short of describing. Warmth of love was hugging me like a soft billowing cloud from above. Overwhelmingly lost in the beauty of the moment I was.

After checking on the progress of the surgery, Julia was ordered to the waiting room. She understood the overzealous family from a nurse's point of view, but it was different from this side of things. "Hope he's doing okay," she mumbled to herself, as she stood again to do some pacing. She felt something for the man, more than normal infatuation with a rescuer. They were connected through the terror of it all, as well as something deeper. He was a bit older than her, but she couldn't help what was brewing inside her heart. He did at least owe her a dinner, she reminded herself.

She was alone in the cold waiting room at first. A gentleman eventually came into the room to join the vigil for loved ones under the surgeon's knife. He took a seat in the corner and sat quietly, reading a book, paying Julia little mind. She had managed to rummage up a spare nurse's scrubs and shoes. The dress was ruined beyond repair, and Julia wanted nothing to do with anything that group had bought for her. It had found its way into the nearest dumpster by now.

After pacing past the man for the third or fourth time, he finally looked up from his book and sighed. "I am so sorry," Julia said to the man, feeling she was becoming a bother. "I'm just nervous, or maybe a little anxious." She sat across from the man, trying her best to calm herself and not be such an annoyance. "You here for someone?" she asked, striking up a conversation, looking at the man as she quickly realized what a stupid question that was. "Of course, you are," she said with a flush rising to her face. "Patient waiting room," she added with a wave of her hand and a nervous giggle.

"Great Grandfather," the man said flatly, with the emotion of a fish. "Gunshot wound. He's in surgery now." If the man were any flatter, he could be a placemat, Julia was thinking.

Interesting, she thought. "I rode in with a man who was shot as well." Strangely she had to convince herself that it can't be the same guy. "You heard about the abducted girls?" Julia asked. "I was one of them. This man risked his life and saved us all. He's my hero for sure."

The man looked up and smiled this time, with a hint of pride and concern showing in his face. Oh my, he is alive, Julia thought. "I am so sorry young lady. Are you okay?" he then asked kindly.

"Fine thank you," Julia responded. "Except a little gunshot wound," she added with a shrug and a giggle. Julia pulled her shoulder strap aside slightly to reveal the bandages.

"Oh wow," the man responded. "How are you feeling?"

"Good," Julia responded with a nod and a nervous smile. "I'm just concerned for Bob?"

"That would be my grandpa," the man then said with pride, for he was told about the incident as well.

Julia stared at the man for several moments, while recalling Bob's strange comment of being 128. "What?" She questioned, with a noticeable rise in her voice. "You're really brothers, right?"

"Noooppe," he responded with a smile. "Great grandson, and nope, I am not kidding." The man added and then he quickly buried his face back in the book, still smiling. He didn't want to continue the discussion of this subject.

She stared for a moment at the now uncommunicative man, then got up and started pacing again. "That's totally insane," she mumbled. "Not possible. Not possible," she was trying to convince herself, but she knew it was true. Somehow, she just knew.

The grandson glanced at the clearly disturbed woman, following her erratic moves, smiling knowingly at her dilemma. "Grandpa is what you call an enigma, a hoot, and a very nice man," he threw out there before turning the page and going back to his reading, hoping to not be asked for further explanations.

"A hoot he is for sure," she commented in passing, as she left the room to go outside. "Need some fresh air," she said.

I saw him naked, she thought, and old he was not. A flush entered her face as she finally got outside. Julia leaned against the wall and stared at the sky, trying to sort out her feelings for the enigma, hoot, and genuinely nice man.

"Is this heaven?" I had to ask, for I thought there were no tears in heaven. Tears were flowing freely. The beauty of all I sensed was overwhelming. A pain went through me strangely but was replaced by the other grand feelings washing over me like a flood.

Children's laughter, I could now hear. If this was heaven, laughter of innocence would have to be part of it. Two children were running through the wildflowers, with no cares to hold them back. The joyous sound reverberated across the valley, causing the very flowers to wave in recognition of the beautiful sight and sound. They were running this way. Pure emotion rose from deep within, when I realized it was Tad leading the way, holding tight to his little wooden boat. "I found my boat Bob," Tad chattered with extreme happiness. The other child? I would recognize that smile anywhere. It was dearest Missy. It so warmed my heart that they were together once more. "We're going to float her down Hickory Switch," Tad said, before letting loose an infectious laugh. "Me and my sister," Tad informed me as he waved her forward. "You want to come?" Missy asked, while reaching out a welcoming hand.

Wanted to go. Wanted to grasp her hand desperately, but something was holding me back. The understanding of it all could be seen in Tad and Missy's twinkling eyes. Their knowledge was beyond my own. Jumping into my arms, their warmth flowed through me as we hugged. "You come along when you can," Tad said, as he pulled away. Missy held on for a moment longer. Much passed between us. "You have done well, my dear boy," Missy said in a more mature tone. "You will always have a place in my heart," Missy added as she stepped back with a huge smile on her face. It was sad and joyous at the same time for me, as they skipped away toward their destination.

"Mate. The dearest of children don't you agree?" Jonathan asked, now sitting next to me. Like mist along the ground, the man formed out of nothing. A great trick, I thought.

"Very fond of them I am," I responded, while I laid my left arm on the shoulder of my first spirit from Christmas past.

"We had some great adventures together," Jonathan stated with a sigh. "But I suspect I have many more ahead of me my bucko."

"That we did mate," I agreed wholeheartedly. We both sat, as true mates would, and observed the beauty together.

With nothing more to say, especially since Jonathan seemed to be a man of few words, we simply started singing. "Like a petrel she'll skim the blast. While the spray sweeps her deck with snow, as the waves, in their race, foam past." Upon the third verse, the man smiled at me and vanished into the mist. "See you on the open seas," a near whisper could be heard as he floated away on the wind.

"I agree with you man, that was some trick," Detective Joseph Alvarez chimed in, just as Jonathan was gone from my life, like smoke on the wind. Jonathan and Tad were so part of my life for many years. Now they are gone, and I didn't know how to feel about it. Now it appears Joseph was saying his goodbyes as well. If where they are going is anything even close to this, I am extremely happy for them, but will miss them dearly.

"Joseph Michael Alvarez," I said, incredibly happy to finally meet face to face. "Detective and Green Beret Joseph Alvarez I might add."

The man scooped me up into a bear hug. "We kicked some butt and took names did we not my friend. You would have made a grand soldier," he added, before he put me down. Surprisingly, I was able to remain standing, and not pulled back to the ground. Not complaining so much, for this is a grand place to relax and spend some time. Reflection would be easy in such a place as this. "You deserve a medal my man, and if within my power I would pin it on you right here." The man was as blustery as I knew he would be. He placed his hand over my heart and turned to the valley before us. "For distinguished service, above and beyond, I present this medal to none other than Robert Franklin Johnson!" He shouted at the top of his lungs, which echoed across the valley.

"Suppose your leaving too," I said, with fresh tears trying to surface.

The man smiled at me. "Bob," he said, while placing his strong hands on my shoulders in a show of brotherly love. "All will be fine my man. Your reservation is set in blood, as is mine." He looked over his shoulder as if he heard or saw something I could not. Turning back to me he said, "I have places to go and people to see my man." This man then kissed my forehead. A very strange but loving thing to do. "You have more adventures ahead my dear Bob." He then laughed, turned, and ran into the open field with hands reaching to the sky, only to dissipate as did Jonathan.

"What did he mean by that?" I wondered. Now alone, standing amongst the beauty, I felt a slight breeze tickling my skin. I closed my eyes, welcoming the breeze and peace that surrounded me. The breeze freshened, and I opened my eyes in time to notice a shimmer of colors moving across the valley of flowers, but separate. It was as if fairies were moving amongst the blooms, dancing thus to add their own magic, tickling my imagination. Soon realized it wasn't fairies, for as the phenomenon moved closer it was forming into a shape. The shape became three. Three beautiful girls in the whitest of white, skipping across the field. The white was almost blinding to me. They stopped skipping and then seemingly glided through the sea of flowers, like a swan on a glimmering lake. I instantly fell to my knees and tears flowed as I realized it was my Susie and two daughters Mandy and Christine. The white suited them, for I always thought of them as my angels. "The lights of my life," I said to them as they stopped at the edge of the field of flowers.

Greeting me with shining smiles, all three. "Honey" and "Daddy" they called out to me. No sweeter the sound of these words heard after all these years. It filled my heart even fuller, if that was even possible. They were ageless and in the image of God, I was thinking. Their voices were pure. I stood and approached them, for a grand hug is what I needed now, like I received from Tad and Missy. My lovelies nestled in my arms once more, is what I wanted to feel. At the edge of the grass, where grass met the sea of flowers, was where I was forced to stop. An invisible force was holding me back. Only feet separated us, yet ages apart it seemed we were.

"Sorry, my brave man," Susie said in the sweetest of voices, like the purest of music it was. Sadness tried to take me, but the purity of it all kept me from falling. "It is not your time, Dearest," my honey told me, which brought confusion to my mind, for my years on this earth should be enough.

"Have I not done enough?" I asked, already having the answer. Through the knowing my girls smiled. They understood as I did, that it is not in the doing, but rather faith in the deliverance by the sacrifice of him on the cross.

I raised my hands to the barrier of life between us, as they did theirs. It felt as if we were nearly touching, and love passed between us. "I love you Daddy," my daughters said in unison, as love and pride in what they were and are shown on my face, and tears continued to wet my cheeks. "You will always be my hero and my love my dear husband," Susan added, while we were nearly touching foreheads, as we had in our past when sharing some of our deepest feelings. "Man is never meant to be alone, and you are the most wonderful of men," Susan told me after pulling back and staring into my eyes. "It is okay to find another. Love is from God, and truly has no limit."

My beauties backed away, whispering I love you through the growing mist. "No," I cried out. I didn't want them to leave but leave they did.

Vanishing into the beauty that surrounded me, my heart was torn, as a second pain shot through my body. "My child, with you I am well pleased," a whisper echoed through the very air around me, as my eyes closed, and I seemed to float away. Darkness overtook me once more.

In the surgery waiting room, the two grew to twelve at that point. The news traveled fast of the seriousness of Bob's condition, and that he was being rushed into surgery. His part in the release of the abducted girls had leaked as well. Two reporters were hanging about, dredging up a story for the next edition. The nurses had asked them to leave twice, and they promised to call security next. He had many friends, none extremely close, but they loved him, for he was a good and generous man. Family, though far removed, were represented well. Julia sat next to Timothy, the first family member she met earlier. He had become much more cordial after a while. The vigil had been hard on all of them.

The surgeon, after a hard-fought battle, came into the waiting room, sparking everyone's interest. The surgery had lasted for nearly two hours. "Family of Bob Johnson," the surgeon announced while looking about the room. Nearly everyone stood up. There were others there, and the room was rather crowded. "All of you?" he asked in surprise. The surgeon went to one corner, where most of the family seemed to be gathered. "The surgery was successful," he assured them, which brought smiles and sighs of relief to many, "but we did lose him twice. It was touch and go but he managed to come through. He is a fighter and is extremely healthy, which boded well for him. It will be quite some time before he can see visitors." Several shook the surgeon's hand and thanked him personally before he left.

As soon as the surgeon left, Julia started crying. "I'm so sorry," she said. "Don't know why I'm crying."

Timothy handed her a handkerchief and consoled her by placing his arm around her. "You like him," Timothy said. "He's easy to like."

"He saved my life." She felt was response enough. She wiped her eyes, and after a few more sniffles, got her composure back. "I probably look a fright." Julia rubbed her face and ran her fingers through her hair.

A lady came over and knelt in front of her, feeling concern, placed her hands on Julia's knees after handing her a hairbrush and compact mirror. "Thank you," Julia said with a smile, while running the brush through her hair and blotting her eyes with the handkerchief. Julia was so grateful for the warmth showed her by Timothy and the lady in front of her. It was helping her to relax. Julia smiled at the woman. Reminding Julia of her own mom, she placed her hands on top of hers. "Great granddaughter?" Julia asked her quietly, which brought a smiling confirmation. "Naturally," Julia said simply, followed by a sigh. Is this a conspiracy? She began to wonder, but somehow, she knew they were telling the truth.

After a moment, Julia was introduced to the family and friends sitting and milling around the waiting room. There were no others remaining there, except the family and friends of Bob Johnson. They were a very warm and friendly bunch of people, once the ice was broken. They were protective of the man that was their grandfather and friend. Enigma he may be, but he deserved his privacy. The stories and laughter began. Julia felt the comradery of it all and felt special to be included.

Substantial time had passed. It takes the patience of Job to wait out the possible long hours in Surgery Waiting. Many left after learning he was doing well. They felt they could visit another day, and besides, they knew where he lived. Several had already made plans to tend to his garden, check on Chewey, and otherwise see to the place as he was recovering.

Only three sentinels were left, including Julia, who had recently fallen asleep in her chair. A genuinely nice hospital volunteer came into the waiting room with clipboard in hand. "Family of Bob Johnson," he announced to the sparsely filled room. It woke Julia up. She doesn't know why she waited; she just couldn't leave. Timothy simply raised his hand as if in elementary school. "Bob is settled in his room, alert and ready for visitors," the man said with a welcoming smile. "Is one of you Julia?" the man asked.

"Yes. That's me," Julia responded, while wiping the remnants of sleep from her eyes.

"He asked if he could see you first," he said with a smile. "And alone," he quickly added.

With surprise on her face, but tickled he thought of her, she looked at the other two to make sure there were no objections. There didn't seem to be, but she wasn't sure she cared that much. She was extremely anxious to check in on the man literally in her dreams that saved her life.

The volunteer took Julia to the room Bob was currently calling home. After leaving her at the door, Julia knocked lightly, and poked her head in. It was a double occupancy, but the first bed was empty. Bob was by the window, so he could look out at the sky. A lump of emotion climbed into her throat when she saw the man whom she shared so much with in such a brief period. She saw Bob was staring at the ceiling, seemingly alert, tears still in his eyes, with various tubes and lines connected to the man.

Bob was still struggling with the visions he saw while under the knife. Though the experience was joyous, and his mind understood, his heart was struggling. The sight of his family was still burnt into his mind, which he never wanted to let go of. The fleeting time was special and should be filed away like treasure much grander than gold or silver. The filing away would be difficult, for he wanted to hold it, feel it, smell it. Letting go would be more than difficult.

Julia was standing beside the man's bed before his attention was diverted. "Julia," Bob said with a warm smile in his voice. He wiped the tears from his face and attempted to square away his emotions. Julia smiled at his feeble attempt to cover, while holding on to her own.

With years of experience, she noted his color looked extremely good for someone coming out of life and death surgery. She was wearing scrubs rather than the black dress, he was, in a man's way of thinking, very fond of. "Are you working?" Bob asked, with a bit of anger to his tone. He could see the bandage on a fresh wound peeking from under her collar. "Surely, they aren't that short staffed," he added.

"Oh no," she expressed with meaning, glancing down at her clothing, understanding instantly his angst. "Just couldn't stand being in their getup one moment longer. One of the nurses loaned a spare set to me."

"You would look good in anything," Bob commented, after shifting slightly to get a better perspective.

Is this man flirting with me? Julia wondered. She couldn't help but be flattered. "You look pretty good yourself," she responded lightly. "Pretty healthy, I mean. Medically speaking of course." She quickly added, stumbling over her words, as a noticeable color rose to her cheeks.

Bob scooted up in the bed, perusing his current state of dress. "What, you don't like my wonderful wardrobe?" he asked with a funning sort of smile, masking his other emotions temporarily. "I was thinking it was chic. It took effort to find a split back gown that would match my eyes and these sexy slippers," he pointed to on the floor next to his bed. Bob then held up his hand, seeming to admire the tubes hanging from it, and the expert taping job. "And this bling is to die for. The price sucked but I was hoping at least you would like it."

Julia pulled up a chair and stared at Bob for a few seconds, sizing the man up. This wonderful, beautiful man, she thought. "I spent quite a lot of time with some of your family and friends, which are wonderful by the way, and they told me some very interesting stories."

"Don't believe everything you hear," Bob quickly interjected, knowing some of them were probably embarrassing.

"They insist you are somewhat of a jokester, and I hate to repeat gossip, but can be a smart ass." Julia raised her eyes somewhat and waited to see if she got an honest answer. She figured she would save a discussion on the more fantastic stories for another day.

Bob raised his free hand to his chin, rubbing his growing stubble. "Ummm," he sounded through closed lips, thinking over the question very seriously. "I plead the fifth," was all he could say, followed by a laugh.

Julia was much amused by the man's quick wit, but she hadn't intended on exchanging fashion tips, nor talk about his family's stories. She came to this room to not only check on his progress but to thank him properly. In the operating room, she almost lost the chance. "Seriously now," Julia said. "I came here to thank you for the risk you took for us." She placed her hand on his, helping to express her gratitude, which sent an unexpected warmth through them both. "You didn't have to do this, and you nearly died for it." A lump came up in her throat as the ordeal was again touching a nerve.

With the ordeal fresh on his mind, he almost preferred to talk about anything else. The weather, recipes, fashion, or golf. Golf would be great. He didn't want the praise. He didn't do this alone. "No, I didn't have to Julia," he agreed. "And dying is just part of living," he added philosophically. "Though, the thought of being in the belly of a fish did help me to decide," he added with a smile on his face.

"What?" she asked. What is he going on about? A fish? This is a modest and confusing man, she was thinking. "You and I…well all of us, went through a lot at the hands of these horrible people. I almost died and so did you. Please don't diminish your part in this. What you did took great courage." The tightening of her lips, new tears and a hint of anger changed the mood in the room, and Bob was taken aback. The last thing he wanted was to hurt this woman.

Bob quickly grabbed her hand. "I am so very sorry Julia," Bob apologized while rubbing her fingers lightly. She tried to pull away, but Bob was having none of it. She was angry with him, and that is something he had to quickly fix. "I don't do well with praise. It simply embarrasses me. I just did the right thing is all, and a simple thank you is sufficient for me." Bob noticed her hand had relaxed, the extreme displeasure on her face had lessened, and she seemed to be considering his words. "Besides," he started to say in a lower voice, almost a whisper, "I'm nervous." There I said it. Truth be known. This woman makes me nervous. It must be the connection we had. That must be it. Could it be something else? A growing feeling for the girl?

A confused look replaced the one of annoyance, which Bob was happy to see. "Nervous? Of what?" Julia asked, seemingly accepting his apology. This is the strongest man she ever met. What makes him nervous? She however instinctively knew, for she felt it herself.

"You," Bob responded quietly, like a frightened mouse. Bob was shocked that this could happen to him at his age. He had emerging feelings for this nurse and wasn't sure what to do.

"Oh," she said simply, pulling her hand away slowly. They were a sight. Like two middle schoolers, testing the waters of emerging love. Clumsy could be a good word to describe the atmosphere. Quickly changing the subject, she had to ask the question. "Bob, what does a fish have to do with anything?"

It was Bob's turn to be confused. His mind had gone well past the earlier conversation, and on to his feelings for Julia. "What are you…. Oh, the fish," he said, as his earlier comment was coming back to him. "Do you know the story of Jonah and the great fish or whale?"

"Vaguely," Julia responded. "But what does it have to do with you?"

He was happy she at least had some Christian upbringing. That was important to him. Bob proceeded to school her on the complete story of Jonah, as much as he could remember. In his years as an avid reader, he had read through the Word many times. "So, you see Julia," he added, "these supernatural connections I have been given over the years, including the very unexpected one with you, is a God thing, and I believe this with my whole heart." He couldn't help himself, but Bob laid his hand back on hers. "It wasn't like he talked to me from a burning bush, or perhaps not as clearly stated as he must have been with Jonah, but my involvements, I feel, were quietly spoken suggestions by God." Bob interrupted his story, being distracted by her eyes. "Your eyes are green," he commented with fascination. "That's kind of rare, isn't it?"

"Yes, they're green, and I don't know," she responded. "Focus Bob, your fish just got away," she added with a smile. "So, Bob, you're saying," figuring to finish the story for him, "before you took a detour into my eyes, that your fear of becoming a fish snack is what guided you to save us.?" I'm not sure how to take that, Julia was thinking.

"Your eyes are beautiful, I must say." Like an emerald, Bob was thinking. Being mushy like this is not the normal me, but she draws me in. I'm bewitched, I'm sure of it.

"Thank you. I'm flattered." He surprises me. Men generally aren't that observant. "Bob? The fish?"

"Oh yes, the fish." Bob smiled at Julia, a little embarrassed by his ramblings. "My feelings on these visitations, as I consider them, are complicated. What I did or didn't do, was entirely my decision, but not getting eaten by a fish was a perk."

“A perk huh. Interesting analogy,” she said. “The connections you mentioned. I thought I was losing my ever-loving mind.” She started to whisper, because she worked here, and didn’t want the word to get out she was cuckoo. “At first I thought the voices were from stress and drugs. You tell the staff here that you hear voices and it’s an instant ticket to the psych ward.” Julia circled her finger around her temple, giving the international sign for nut case, crackers, or insane, followed by goofing up her face.

This very much amused Bob to where he started laughing, which Julia soon joined in. There was more to discuss, but she didn’t want to corner the market on his time, besides she was exhausted and would love a long hot shower. The thought of taking it with him, briefly flashed across her mind unexpectedly, which brought a bit of warmth to her. “Bob, I should go,” she said. “There are at least two visitors still waiting to see you. I’ll tell them on the way out. I need to eat something and go to bed.”

“Till we meet again,” Bob said after grabbing and kissing her hand, a nearly dead practice, which wasn’t wasted on her. The lady giggled like a schoolgirl on the way out the door and wiped her forehead as the latest exchange and her thoughts made her a little flush.

Bob collapsed back onto the bed, nearly exhausted by the visit with this woman. “What am I to do?” Bob asked himself, staring into the blue of the sky outside the hospital window. “What am I to do?”

Chapter 38

Days turned fast, while I rested and contemplated life in my small room. I got many visitors, which warmed my heart, but not the same warmness as my nurse brought me. My physical healing was a near marvel to my doctors. My heart, which is much more delicate and complicated, seemed to heal and renew like a spring morning, which was the larger marvel to me since what I witnessed that day. The spirits of my inner guests were gone. My Susan and two daughters, though gone from me physically, were still present in my heart, and the knowing they were in great hands brings me immense joy.

As promised, Julia and I had our dinner, where we discussed much. Our pasts, and goals. My goals weren't set, and I have learned nothing is concrete in our lives. I haven't talked this much to another in many years. It was refreshing. As expected, my complicated past and that of my guests, was not a short or one time discussion. Fortunately for me I am a writer of novels, which detailed some of our greatest adventures. On our second date, a dinner and movie, before I kissed her goodnight, I gave her some reading material, which I told her may help fill in some of the blanks.

For the first time in decades, I was looking forward to what came next, besides just my end. Before Julia and our near-death adventure in the park, I was stuck, waiting for the days to pass until my eternal rest. Now I am looking forward to more than bedtime and another day to tick away. My mind has opened again to the possibility of more in this life.

Months passed. Julia and I took things slowly. My heart is longing for her. My body is aching for her complete embrace. She is unsure, and I am not pushing for more until I know she is ready. It is refreshing in these times of quick satisfaction that she is holding back. That makes her more of a jewel to me. As many say, I am an enigma with varied experiences. Julia had many questions while absorbing my books. Some of which revolved around how Susan dealt. Julia is such a sweetheart, but scared of a commitment with one such as I.

"You are so different from the other men I have dated," she recently told me. "They were all hands and angered I wouldn't give myself away like some cheap merchandise."

"To be honest," I responded. "My hands are definitely itching, but your feelings are more important than what my hands think." She laughed before we kissed at her door. "Be a gentleman," I reminded myself many times after dropping her off. There was a touch of barbarian in me that wanted to pounce but would have to remain chained.

Her parents, I finally met the other day. They invited us to dinner. We were as nervous as two cats visiting a dog pound. Didn't know what to expect. Guess who's coming to dinner, I was thinking while being introduced.

"Mom. Dad. This is Robert Johnson, the man I told you about," she said with a touch of nervousness to her voice. "Bob, this is my mom and dad, Julian and Dorothy." We shook hands in a formal sort of way. The looks on their faces said it all. Might just as well introduced me as Methuselah. After thanking me profusely for their daughter's safe return, they invited us to sit in the living room, for the roast wasn't quite done. After sitting, they were cordial, but cold began settling into that house like a winter fog.

Family is important to her, and we were feeling uncomfortable. I felt as if I just grew a set of horns. Not much was said at first. The timer went off and Dorothy was happy to leave the room and finish preparing the meal and setting the table, with her daughter's help. I could hear conversation coming from the other room, but I couldn't make out what was said. I was extremely interested, but I had father to contend with.

That left Julian and I alone in the living room for a few minutes. He was as uncomfortable as I was. The inspector and inspected sizing each other up. "So, our daughter tells us you're an author?" Julian finally broke the ice, which felt a foot thick to me.

"Yes sir. An author," is all I could offer up. I was at a loss for words, which doesn't happen often. A joke would have been in order, but my mind went blank, during this momentous occasion. My hands were even starting to sweat.

"You do well?" He then asked, watching me wipe my sweaty hands on my pants.

"Very well sir," I simply answered. Is it hot in here? I wanted to ask. Not comfortable. Not comfortable at all.

We sat and exchanged meaningless words for what felt like an eternity to me. My eyes were betraying me, for I felt for sure our foreheads were thickening and hair was starting to grow on our faces. We appeared as two Neanderthals exchanging nonsensical grunts about the weather. It brought a smile to my face, for I could see the humor in it. Cave mom finally relieved us of our discomfort, by announcing dinner was ready.

When I first came into the dining room, I could see the tension in their faces. The conversation with mom must not have been all peaches and cream. Julia could see the silly grin on my face, carried over from our cave man talk, which thankfully brought a smile to her face. I was visualizing a large leg of roasted mastodon steaming in the middle of the table. Couldn't help but snicker as I pulled the chair out for Julia. "What?" She asked with a smile, while looking over her shoulder at me.

"Later," was all I could say, as I sat down. The meal looked and smelled delicious.

The father offered up grace, which I was pleased with. Good Christian home, I was thinking. The look of discomfort on her parents faces returned, but fortunately they chose to talk about general subjects of the day. Vanilla versus cookies and cream or fudge swirl. I didn't learn until later that her parents always insisted that uncomfortable subjects had no place at their dinner table. The storm came later.

While the mom was clearing the table, Julian asked Julia out onto the back porch. This is where the rubber meets the road I was thinking, as they moved through the back door. I offered to help Mrs. Blair, but she insisted, a little coldly, that I have a seat in the living room.

"How old is this man you are dating Julia?" her father asked, being quick and to the point. They stood against the porch railing, looking out into the night. The night was warm, but she felt it was about to get warmer.

"It's not important, Dad," she said. She absolutely hated keeping secrets from her parents. And being a liar just wasn't part of her makeup. Her refusal to tell my age was difficult for her, and a red flag to him.

"Not important?" Julian disagreed. "I try to keep an open mind on things, but you are my daughter." The man shifted his position to face Julia. "He is substantially older than you, and I know he saved your life, but this relationship makes your mother and I uncomfortable."

"It's okay, Dad," she responded after grasping her father's hands to help reassure. "He is a fine and gentle man. A Christian man," she added, knowing that would be important to her parents.

"A Christian is great, but he's too old for you honey. What are you going to do when he can't take care of himself? You'll be stuck taking care of an old man."

"Dad," she exclaimed. "We are simply dating and nothing more." She wanted much more, but let's leave it there for now, she thought.

The man simply sighed. "My opinion," he then said, "is that you need to cut this off before it gets too far."

Julia pulled her hands back, for even though he said it was his opinion, the tone made it sound more like a command. "This is not your decision to make," she stated with rising anger. Her Irish side was starting to show. "How this evolves is our concern and not yours or mom's."

"Of course, it's our concern. It concerns us deeply." His voice was now raised. "You need to stop this nonsense and look to someone more your age. Not so much hero worship."

That pushed her buttons. "Stay out of this, Dad. This is my decision." There was now fire in her green eyes. "Bob is a hero in every sense of the word, but I am not groveling at his feet like some star struck child. I love the man for who he is."

The "L" word, though sweet, was not something her father wanted to hear. "Love? Dammit," he then let loose. "You can't be serious."

"Very!" she fired back, while leaving to come back into the house.

"Honey," he said, while following her in.

"Stay out of it, Dad!" she shouted.

I heard the last couple of exchanges, as concern rose quickly through me. She came stomping into the living room, with her hackles obviously raised.

"Sweetheart," her mom quickly added, giving her father a not so pleased look. "We're just worried about you."

"You too, Mom?" Julia grabbed her purse and my hand, ready to rock and roll. "We should have had this conversation alone, and not in front of Bob. He probably feels like he was ambushed." I started to raise my hand and speak, to assure them I am fine and would survive, but I squashed the need and kept my mouth shut. But, when the tension got to be too much, and her father gave me the look of damnation, we felt as if we had to leave. I was the villain in their mind and Julia was their little girl. My newly renewed heart was torn.

We didn't see each other for three days. Julia had a couple double shifts to make it through. Even though I could have met her for a quick meal in the hospital cafeteria, I chose not to. A little space was needed for both of us. A fracture in her family was unacceptable to me. Maybe I would have been better off dating someone in the nursing home, I thought. "Lord, why did you open my heart just to fill it with coal?" I had a need to know. "What now?"

On the fourth day, while considering an ice breaking phone call, there was a knock on my door. It was my hope that it was Julia, but my heart jumped when it turned out to be Mr. Blair, Julia's father. His back was up, and he was here to square away my intentions on his little girl. Admittedly an adult 30-year-old woman, but still his little girl. I invited the man in, which he accepted. The temptation was to pat the man down for weapons.

Waved him to the couch and I sat in my recliner, facing each other for what I am sure will be a heated debate. "May I get you something to drink?" I asked out of courtesy.

"No thanks," he answered quickly. He was nervous, as I expect I would be in his position. My respect for the man wasn't any less for this visit. It was more, for he was willing to do what he thought was necessary to protect his family.

"You saved my daughter's life," he started, "for which I am eternally grateful." Here comes the but, I was thinking. "However, don't you think her feelings may stem from just that? You're a hero to her."

"That did cross my mind, so that is one of the reasons I want to take things slow."

The man leaned back in his seat, continuing to size me up. "I just want what's best for my little girl. Then there is the age difference. You look my age, and that concerns me." Add about eighty years, I thought, but wasn't about to correct the man. "Can't you date someone your own age?"

That would be a trick, I thought. "Mr. Blair? I assure you that your daughter's welfare is my foremost consideration. I care for her deeply." Actually, I'm in love with your daughter, which I haven't even professed to her, but I think she knows. The tension in him seemed to grow. He would prefer that I went away. Of this I am certain.

"Her mother and I are having a tough time with this." He started rubbing his face, getting more uncomfortable, and then let loose with what was probably fermenting all along in his mind. "Have you bedded my girl?" There it was, out there floating in the air like a stench to my nostrils.

It was instant red that I was now seeing. Rather than act a fool over his rather crude question, I rose from my seat and opened the front door, waving the man out of my house. "Our conversation is over Mr. Blair." Stoic I stood in the doorway, as a statue, with my mouth shut tightly, holding in other words I would enjoy spewing at the father of the woman I loved.

He rose and walked slowly through my entryway, red rising in his face, assuming he knew the answer to his own question. As he crossed in front of me, the man turned to face me with a rather nasty look in his eyes. The man was taller and bigger than I was, but I was not intimidated. He then grabbed my collar and pushed me hard against the door. "If you hurt my daughter, I will be back to pay you another visit my man," he said with poison in his voice.

My back was up now, but I didn't want it to go any further. She had her father's green eyes, and the spunk must be an Irish trait. "That will never happen, Mr. Blair," I stated with complete calm in my demeaner. "Now, if you will kindly remove your hands and leave my property," I added, in a tone I thought was very nonconfrontational.

"Or what," he then said with a touch of insolence.

That was enough for me. The man was challenging me. I grabbed both his thumbs, and with a painful twist, brought the bigger man to his knees. Moving him with little effort, outside of my front door, I went into my house and closed the door in his face. He left quickly, a little less sure of himself. "This is not a great situation," I said to myself as I went back to my chair to calm myself and think through what was to be done.

The following day, knowing it was Julia's day off, I paid her an unannounced visit. It was near noon. It was a gorgeous day except for the little cloud of gloom hanging over my head. Didn't want to go too early and mess up her sleep as well as her day. After knocking, she came to the door quickly, which was a relief. At least I didn't wake her.

"Bob," she said, a bit surprised. She was barefoot, dressed in shorts and a white tee stating that "Nurses Rock". "Come in," she said, after opening the door fully and standing aside. Before I made it all the way through, she grabbed my arm and planted a quick kiss on my lips, then waved me over to the couch, inviting me to sit.

The kiss and her fun outfit weren't going to make this any easier. I settled on the couch, and she sat next to me. Her closeness and warmth were stirring me, but I was going to stick to my guns, even if I shoot myself.

"What's wrong?" she quickly asked, noticing the pain in my face. "It's my parents, isn't it?" Julia put her hand on my knee. "They will come around Bob," she assured me.

I placed my hand on hers. Her hand is so soft. My heart was already breaking, but now I would have to break hers. What I was about to do was for the best. I was awake all through the night, struggling with this, using an accountants' logic to solve the issue, which now that I think back, was dumb as owl shit. This wasn't an account that needed balancing, and numbers rarely work on issues of the heart. I was definitely out of practice. "Family is extremely important to me Julia, and I assume the same applies to you."

"Yes, it does very much," she agreed, crinkling up her nose in anticipation of a troublesome follow-up.

I took a deep breath, to help me get out what I needed to say. "Julia, I can't be the cause of a fracture in your family," I threw out there painfully.

"What are you trying to say?" she immediately asked, while pulling her hand back, with her voice raised slightly. A storm was brewing behind those eyes.

"Julia. My hope was that our relationship would continue to grow. You are incredibly special to me."

"I feel the same. I like what we have together," she added with a pleading tone. Worry was moving into her face.

This is killing me. I would rather jump into a pit of snakes. "I'm old fashion. Respect for parents, their wishes, and tradition is important. Strong families are rare these days, and you have a good one. Breaking you apart is not what I want to see, and I feel that would eventually scar our relationship as well."

Tears were now welling up in her eyes. "Are you breaking up with me?" She asked, staring at me with those sad green eyes.

I should have just shot myself; it would have been less painless. My own tears were fighting to surface, but being a man, means to hold back. Right? "I think it best. You don't need to be with an old coot like me." I thought that sounded a little martyrish as soon as I said it.

Tears were now flowing down her face. "You are far from an old coot. You are strong and the nicest man I've ever known." I could now see her hands were shaking some, as well as her voice.

"This is so hard," I then said aloud, which wasn't the smoothest comment.

"Hard?" She asked with a hint of disdain, or maybe a little more than a hint. "You want harder? How about the fact I've fallen in love with you? Hopefully, that makes this easier for you." She got up and walked to her front door and opened it. Boy this looks familiar, I was thinking. "The fact you saw fit to not discuss this with me first, really pisses me off. So, before I say something I am sure I will regret, I need to ask you to leave."

Feeling like a punished puppy with my tail between my legs, I approached the front door. There was now a knot in my throat the size of an orange. I've hurt the woman I loved and now wished I could take it all back, but still felt it may be best. I stopped inches from her, wanted so much to kiss her one last time. My tears were now leaking down my face. "I'm so sorry Julia."

"So am I," she said, with a sniffle. I leaned forward, to at least give her a kiss on the forehead. "Don't," she said. "Please don't."

I left quietly, with my head slumped. After she closed the door, I heard her start to cry. At that point I felt like the biggest cur of all times. "Did I make the biggest mistake of my life?" I'm sure I did, but I couldn't get myself to turn around. Driving home that night felt about like I was slowly sinking in quicksand.

Chapter 39

A week had passed since the break. Julia and Bob were both miserable, having trouble concentrating on anything else except the licking of their wounds, hoping they would heal. Julia's mom hadn't heard from her daughter for a little over a week, which was unusual, because they generally talk weekly at least. She called her twice, but Julia wasn't answering nor returning the calls, so they decided to pay her a visit.

There was a knock on her door. She was hoping it was Bob, but when she looked out and saw her parents, she just sighed. She didn't want company, and especially not them. They were the instigators of this pain she felt in her heart after all.

Julia opened the door and welcomed her folks with as much warmth as she could manage. "Mom. Dad. Good afternoon," she greeted them. "What brings you out on such a gloomy day," she added. Her father looked over his shoulder at the sky, which was as clear as a bell. He just shrugged off her comment, while he followed his wife into her living room.

"Want something to drink?" Julia asked. Always the great hostess.

"No thanks, Honey," her mom responded. "We wanted to come over to see how you were doing," she said as the two of them sat down. Her father appeared a bit down cast to Julia, which didn't concern her so much, because she was still angry with him. "We hadn't heard from you in over a week and thought maybe you were avoiding us."

"Now why would I do something so horrid?" Julia asked with noticeable sarcasm.

"You have every right to be angry sweetheart," her mom said in her motherly tone. "We were out of line," she added, turning then to her husband. "Right Julian?"

The man cleared his throat, and sat up straighter, preparing to grovel a little. Something her father wasn't used to. "Your mom is right. You aren't fifteen anymore, and I had no right treating you or your friend that way."

Julian looked at his daughter, who was sitting quietly, hanging on his every word. "Julia, I owe you and Bob an apology."

Julia sat quietly for a moment, staring at her parents with a blank look. "You don't have to worry about us anymore," Julia said with resolution. "There is no us."

"What happened, Honey?" her mom asked.

"He's a lovely, gallant, old fashioned fool! That's what happened," she said with growing anger and tears in her eyes. She couldn't quite place the anger. Was it on the parents, Bob, or herself for not fighting harder? "You see Mom and Dad, his respect for you and our family bond is stronger than what he wants. He would cut off his left hand before harming this family." Julia turned to just her father, who was feeling worse by the minute. "You would have liked him, Dad. He loves to read, garden and golf, your favorite hobby. He may kick your butt, but it would have been fun, and he wanted to get me involved too."

Julian started to squirm in his seat. "I am extremely sorry," he said.

"You shouldn't have gone over there, Honey," her mom said, assuming Julia knew about her father's visit.

Julia sat up straighter in her seat, wondering if she heard her mom correctly. "What!" she shouted. "You went over to Bob's? Did you spout some more of your bullshit?" she screamed in anger.

Julian was surprised Bob didn't tell his daughter about the little discussion they had. That sort of man is rare these days, he was thinking, even considering himself in that same group. "Julia, I said I was sorry, and going over there was a mistake, I agree."

"You think," she commented. "Dad, please tell me you didn't do something stupid." Her dad was known to get out of control in his past, and he did box some in college.

Julian shifted in his seat. The look in his face spoke volumes. "Well," he said in a high pitch tone, combined with a telling scrunch to his face.

"Dad, you could have been hurt," Julia said. "Bob broke into a secure compound, alone, and had to kill ten men to save us. And trust me on this, he didn't do it with a calculator and a chicken sandwich."

The color went out of his face some, for he wasn't aware of all the details. It wasn't common knowledge, and that wasn't something Bob wished to brag about. "Nothing happened sweetheart," he tried to assure his daughter, while looking down at his still slightly sore thumbs.

"We've got to fix this," Julian insisted. "I've got to fix this," he added.

Julian took his wife home, made a phone call, and headed straight for Bob's place, counting on him being home. His hope was he didn't get clocked at the front door.

He knocked several times, but there was no answer. "Should I leave him a note?" Julian wondered. He thought he would check his back yard first. When he approached the back fence gate, he spotted the man squatting in his vegetable garden, pulling weeds. The back yard was well maintained and colorful with all the flowers here and there. Julian entered the yard unannounced, when a killer Pomeranian burst out from behind a large tomato plant and charged the man like a true watchdog but stopped short and proceeded to bark Julian to death.

"What the hell Chewey!" I shouted. "Chasing a squirrel again?" I asked. But I was startled when I saw Julian standing in my backyard, the man that threatened me a week ago, cornered by killer, shouldering his golf bag, with an unexpected smile on his face.

"Did you come to take me out with your pitching wedge," I asked the father of the girl I love, amused by the sight.

"No. I hear you're a fair golfer. You up for a challenge?"

This is very strange, but I'm game. "What's the stakes?" I asked, still a bit wary of his visit.

"Five dollars a hole," Julian offered up.

I removed my gardening gloves and approached the man. "Down, Killer," I ordered Chewey, who immediately backed off.

"Well trained." Julian stated, while putting down his golf bag.

"Thanks," I said, offering him my hand. He took my hand and shook it vigorously. It invigorated me, the thought of a change in heart from the man that recently threatened me. "Where and when?" I asked, looking over his nice set of clubs.

"Hidden Creek Country Club, and we tee off in one hour."

"So soon? I don't know. Really need a shower and change of clothing."

"Take a quick rinse and throw something on. I'll take it easy on you." Julian smiled.

He didn't go there, did he? I may be old, but I still enjoy a challenge. "Give me a few minutes. You're on," I said, running to the house. This is a strange man, I was thinking. Rather than holding out an olive branch he holds out his driver.

We drove our own cars and got there with ten minutes to spare. The match of the century was on, and wounds were healed along the way. At the 19th hole we shared a quick beer, which I wasn't that keen on, but to achieve detente I would drink swill. The man apologized for his actions and reluctantly gave permission to date his daughter, which is still odd considering she was thirty years old.

On the way home, I was thinking, shower, nicer clothing, and a bouquet of flowers to present to Julia as a peace offering for my haste.

Julian went home, carrying his clubs into the house. He preferred not to leave them in the car. Unexpected, Julia's car was parked out front. "Hello girls I'm home," he hollered when entering.

Dorothy and Julia were in the kitchen. A wonderful aroma and his wife met him immediately upon entering. "You went golfing?" Dorothy asked. "I was beginning to wonder." Julia remained in the kitchen doorway.

"Yes, I went golfing. Bob and I actually went golfing, and even had a beer afterward." That got Julia's attention, which brought her into the room.

"You and Bob?" Julia asked excitedly.

"Yes, your father and your Bob went golfing."

Julia was smiles ear to ear. "But Bob hates beer," Julia added.

"Didn't know that," Julian said. "He could have drunk something else. I wouldn't have been insulted." Julian thought back and remembered that Bob took the glass gladly and drank without a word. "He is a bit old fashioned, isn't he?" Julian added, remembering back to his daughter's comments.

"Well, how did it go?" Julia was dying to know.

"It went fantastic," Julian said, before looking over at his wife who had taken a seat on the couch. "Except, Honey, I may have to borrow some cash," he added with a funny smirk. "Bob kicked my ass!" Julian exclaimed, followed by a huge grin.

Julia threw herself into her father's arms, while Dorothy simply shook her head. "Men," Dorothy stated with humor. "Men and their sticks."

I put away my clubs and laid out clothes alongside the bouquet of white carnations I purchased on the way home. Floating on the air was the spicey floral smell of the flowers mixed with funk. A quick rinse only, followed by a sweaty golf match, was demanding a hot soapy shower. I wanted to put my best foot forward, like it was our first date.

After stripping and placing my dirty clothing into their appropriate spots, I couldn't help but think of Susan and how memories of her still holds fast, even the small things like laundry etiquette. With a smile, I turned on the water and stepped into the already steaming shower stall. There was once a day when quick showers were my thing, but I have learned after many years to enjoy each moment of life. Long showers can be relaxing and invigorating.

While soaping up, I couldn't help but sing Jonathan's favorite song of a sailor. Parts of him are still with me, but his true spirit was not. I miss him and the others. They had become a solid part of me, in some ways like my Susan, but memories remain and are great to keep close to my heart.

I don't have a great voice, but not bad. The acoustics of my shower did improve on the effect somewhat. With a head full of suds, my song echoed through the house. It was my anticipation to hear Chewey join in with her own melody. I was happy and a little nervous, thinking about what I would say to Julia.

My voice was raised, while my fingers were massaging every square inch of my scalp. Cleanliness is next to Godliness, my mother always said. My focus and raised voice must have been the reason I didn't hear the shower door slowly open. Taken completely off guard I was. Generally, don't lock my doors during the day when home. I'd always wondered if an enemy I made during one of my adventures would be waiting to take me out one day. Rather than a villain named Boris with his silencer and evil grin upon his face being the last thing I see in this life, it was Julia, naked as the day she was born. I must be dead or dreaming, I thought.

Out of reflex I covered myself. Her smile simply got bigger, and I could swear her green eyes got greener, diving straight into my heart. The sight of her standing there with steam starting to glimmer off her smooth and perfect skin, sent a shock through my body I haven't felt in many years. The young lady that started in my dreams, moved into the shower with me and closed the door. "Julia," I started to say, before she put her finger up to my mouth. She grasped my hair and brought my mouth down to hers. Her wet lips were softly brushing against mine, followed by her exploring tongue, then her need rose, as her kiss went deeper and harder. Her tongue explored my eager mouth, gently moving along my tongue as lovers may embrace. A moan came from deep within me, signaling Julia she was touching all the right buttons.

My arms were now wrapped around my love, squeezing our wet and heated bodies together. I could feel her need rising as her wet body moved against mine and I firmly squeezed her ample breast with my now shaking hand. "Ummmm," she nearly sang through her exploring lips. "Now," she insisted breathlessly, after pulling her lips from mine. "Now. Please," she now pleaded, while reaching down and grasping me strongly in her hand. After turning her and pressing her body to the wall under the shower, I lifted her, and we made love under the falling water. I imagined we were under a waterfall in Hawaii. Julia's whole body vibrated against mine and a guttural groan rose from deep within her when her body released with pleasure, followed by my own. "Again," she gasped through the last twinges. We couldn't stop. I couldn't stop until our bodies seized a second time. It felt like we died, as we slid down the wall, exhausted, the now chilly water splashing upon us. But we didn't care. "I love you," she whispered into my ear. "I lubbe yuth," I slobbered through my nearly numb lips, half emerged in the cold water.

The gloom left me fully after that day. Her parents invited us to a second dinner, which went much better than the first. Except for her time with her career, which she loved, and an occasional golf outing with her father, we were inseparable. She was taking golf lessons herself. She was a natural. I felt young again. Life was good.

Summer turned to fall, my garden was turned down for the coming winter, and the trees turned the most glorious of colors. On October 31, 2083, Julia agreed to become my wife. A month later, with a few books in hand, the same process I followed with Julia, her parents were brought in on my secret, and then sworn to secrecy. The following spring, March 25, 2084, the date we technically met, we were married in front of family and friends in a small local church. Julian gave his daughter away and her mother cried. They knew Julia was happy, so they were as well.

Chapter 40

During our many conversations, I learned Julia liked to camp, which made me happy, for I did as well in my youth. After our honeymoon in Acapulco, we made my home our home. On May 12, the sky was supposed to be extremely clear, and a meteor shower was expected. As a surprise, while Julia was at work, I set up a tent in our backyard, so we could spend the night under the stars cuddled under a blanket. She loved the idea. After dinner, we retired to the tent, and as dusk came upon us, we indoctrinated the tent. We've already made love in every room of the house, and the garage. The tent was a no brainer.

We spent hours cuddled in the dark, watching the meteor shower and naming as many constellations as we could. It was nearing midnight, and Julia was asleep on my shoulder, with the blanket pulled up to her neck. Rather than naming the stars, I made believe I was attaching memories to each one, like post-it-notes. That way my memories would flash across the sky each night. Bob's constellations I could call them.

My first day in school, excited to start kindergarten. I laid awake that night for a bit, while sharing a room with my two little sisters. Earliest strong memory. My mother making my favorite dish. Making snow ice cream when the snow was clean. Collecting fireflies. Fighting with my sisters. I had a great family growing up. They are long gone, but not in my mind.

Graduations, family trips and my marriage to my lovely Susan. I had to look at Julia's face shimmering in the firelight. With God, I have enough love for each of you. The birth and growth of our children, and the grandchildren you can spoil and hand back to the parents. The first time I held our first child was especially wonderful. My heart is full of love for each and every one of these precious memories and people that go with them.

The big one reminds me of Tad and his grand hopes and ambitions. He is so happy now with his little sister. Maybe they're up there now, skipping rocks across the dark pools between the stars. The thought of it is exhilarating.

Memories are like the stars and planets, varied and numerous. "Frank," I said quietly so not to wake up Julia. "Your oak tree is looking great. I checked it the other day. Jonathan? I still have your father's scrimshaw. I'll probably keep it until I die."

I sighed and pasted many more memories into the sky, thinking carefully on each one, to write them down correctly. The stars were moving slowly across the sky like a slow train, carrying my memories off to the west. Slow train going home, clanking on the tracks, blowing its whistle in that haunting tone, echoing across the sky and valleys, waiting on its mate to return its call. I'll come again tomorrow it seems to moan through the dark of the night, hoping to find you well so you can join it on this lonely trip. Tears well up in my eyes, as my memories move across God's sky. See you tomorrow, so I can add new, but not to replace but to enrich, I was thinking as I watched my newest love sleeping with the face of an angel.

Careful not to wake her, I carried Julia into our tent and tucked her in like she was the most precious of jewels. "Goodnight my love" I said, followed by a light kiss on her forehead. "May God's hands hold you lightly through the night, protecting and loving only as he can."

I slid in next to her, and ever so slowly placed my arm across her chest, to feel close to her through the night.

"Z, did you know about this?" Jerry Sanders asked of his friend of thirty years, Dr. Zelick Abram, as he continued to pace in front of his desk. Z had been Jerry's nickname for his friend for years. Jerry had just finished explaining his discoveries and troubling theories, just before slapping the file on his desk. He had his doubts his friend was involved, but he had to know. The doctor's office was in the basement of one of many buildings on the prestigious Harvard University campus. Dr. Abram had been with the college going on forty-five years now. He is a tenured professor, research scientist, and current head of the Harvard Innovation lab. The man was well respected and had published some of his research in many scientific journals over the years.

"Please calm down, Jerry," Dr. Zelick quickly responded, feeling insulted by the insinuation. "What you just told me is outlandish. You listen to too many conspiracy theories, Jerry. Are the Illuminati paying for this?" Zelick asked sarcastically.

"Dammit Z, please don't treat me like a child," Jerry was quick to push back. "May seem outlandish, but so far everything points to this being a distinct possibility, and sometimes conspiracies have threads of truth."

"Sorry Jerry," Zelick apologized. "But I would never be involved in such a plan," Zelick assured his friend, "and besides, your theory is only that, a theory."

"Dammit Z! The results from your research being possibly used to create this abomination doesn't concern you?" Jerry's hands were now on the desk, leaning in, staring down his long-time friend, while questioning the man's morals.

"You may have what you think is proof, but you can't know for sure," Zelick responded. "That was forty years ago, and after results were verified, the samples were destroyed."

"Cloning a human is an abomination Z," Jerry insisted, as if Dr. Abram wasn't as convinced. "There is no other way to look at it. There is the fear that entire bodies will be cloned for nothing more than organ donors. Humans will be grown like cattle for dissection. Or better yet, let's grow people to infiltrate society, or secretly replace someone in position of power. Like what I suspect in this case."

"Our goal was to duplicate human organs and tissue to advance medical science and nothing more. We were never going to duplicate a complete being. That I never would have agreed to."

Jerry finally sat down, leaned back, and crossed his arms. "Did you supervise the specimen collection or disposal process?" Jerry asked with newly found calmness. He feels he knows his friend and was hoping this would not have happened with his approval.

"Actually, no. My assistant did," Zelick responded with eyes lowered. He chose not to lie to Jerry, but he knew this would just keep his fishing trip active.

"So, the possibility does exist," Jerry added, while running his fingers through his hair, as he checked off yet another box in his search for the truth. "Do you watch the news Z? This abomination could be our future president," Jerry added with a look of disgust. "The election is this November," he stated while tapping his finger loudly on his wooden desk to help express urgency.

Jerry then pulled the two pictures back out of his file and pushed them in front of his friend. The first was of the presidential candidate. A very good-looking young man of forty, average height and weight, with auburn colored hair. The second picture was a very old picture of a man, that would chill the blood of any Jewish person with a reasonable knowledge of their history.

"But Jerry, the cells used were from volunteers. This can't be." Zelick insisted with a sigh, for he didn't even want to think of such a possibility. "Jerry, even though I admit the similarities, history is full of lookalikes, or doppelgangers if you will."

"I pray you are correct, but it still appears you may have been an unwitting participant in something very sinister."

"I still can't and won't believe something so far-fetched, and besides, what am I supposed to do about it? My research has and will do mankind a lot of good."

My friend is so naïve and blind, Jerry was thinking. "Z," Jerry said after standing. "Only God can put a spirit into the body of men. What evil do you think is walking around in that shell? The new world order may be coming sooner than we think and hiding your head in the sand isn't going to change it."

"I've got a paper due," Zelick then brought up, wanting to desperately change the subject. "And some tests to grade, so I've given you all the time I can spare." This is too way out there, Dr. Abram was thinking. The doctor then put the pictures back in Jerry's folder and handed it back to him. "If you have any concrete proof, call me," the doctor finally said dismissively, after sitting back in his chair and moving his own work back in front of him, indicating he was done with the subject.

Jerry was so disappointed in his friend. He figured his best friend of all people would be on his side, but he now is feeling the grants and his science were more important. "If this is what I think it is, your people will be right in the middle of what is coming." Jerry opened the office door and was prepared to step out before he added, "your own ancestors died at the hand of evil like this over one hundred years ago now, while many of the Jewish people and others simply hid their heads in the sand. I was hoping you would be different. I'm not giving up," was Jerry's final say as he slammed the door behind him.

After Jerry left, Dr. Abram put his head in his hands and shuddered at the thought of what this could mean, if true. His great grandparents Josiah and Rebecca Epstein both died in a filthy Nazi camp, and he knew of the man in the picture, who was one of many dark figures at that time, Dr. Josef Mengele.

My eyes shot open, and I growled due to my distaste for the dream I just had. It was still dark out and quiet. I looked up at the roof of the tent and sighed. All I could hear was the deep breathing of my sleeping wife and a gentle breeze rustling through the trees. Julia's head was on my chest and her arm across my stomach. The dream was sharp in my mind, but I wasn't about to disturb my lovely wife to discuss this dream. It can wait till morning. There is a possibility it was only a dream, but I had my doubts.

I said a quiet prayer, asking for peace and a quiet remainder of our night. I closed my eyes, and after counting some sheep, was able to get back to sleep

Just before dawn, while dew settled on the sleeping grass, Julia was awakened by my voice calling out bitterly from somewhere deep within my dream. "Mein Gott! Mein Gott!" I was hollering to anyone who could help, but there was no help.

My wife, child and I, Josiah Epstein, lived in Hamburg, Germany during tumultuous times. We were proud owners of a small flower shop until the terrible night of the Kristallnacht, or "night of broken glass", on November 9-10, 1938. Many Jewish shops and homes were ransacked on that night, and many of our men were taken. My family and I were spared at that time, but our livelihood was destroyed. Of those remaining, some managed to escape Germany, but my family was not so fortunate. The remaining were eventually rounded up like sheep or cattle. Unlike the feisty, and focused, sheep dog, or the dusty cowboy riding his Mustang, our people were rounded up by soldiers with guns. Like cattle, we were branded, but unlike the mark from a hot brand on our skin, we were forced to wear the yellow star. Disobedience was met with violence, and sometimes a bullet. By this time, we were stripped of much of our dignity and abilities to defend ourselves. Our homes and shops were emptied as if we were vermin under their feet.

We were packed into box cars, with little light and irregular ventilation. My little boy kept looking to me for comfort, but I had little to give. My wife's head was on my shoulder, holding her own sorrow in check for the sake of our son. We had lost everything and now we're being relocated we were told. A small glimmer of hope these words may have held for some. There were nearly one hundred of us packed between the wooden walls of our prison that still held the stale smell of its previous residents. Our car was fitted with a bucket latrine with no privacy offered. What little dignity we had left was slowly scoured away on this slow train to the unknown.

Hours turned to days on this train of sorrow. There were several times we stopped, raising our hopes that we were finally going to be released to breathe fresh air once more, only to have our hopes dashed, when we realized we were being held back for another train of soldiers and equipment. Their cargo was much more valuable to them.

Sleep was near impossible until exhaustion and weakness creeped into our very beings. Many slept sitting up because space was limited. There was frequent shuffling to make way for visitors to the latrine. My wife and I took turns holding our precious child, hoping to give him some comfort. Time moved slowly, and the stench grew while the space between the walls seemed to shrink. Prayers were offered to the God of Abraham, Isaac, and Jacob, but their fate seemed to be set.

There was no water, and the air about us seemed to thicken. For some, weakness led to sickness, as coughing and moaning could be heard moving about the closing space. I was once a strong man in the eyes of my wife and child, but this trip was taking its toll on my very body and mind. Cries could be heard in the darkness as some of our group died on this very trip. Adding to the stench, was the smell of slowly rotting flesh. If it were not for my wife and child, I too may wish to sleep and join Adonai in the place of glory.

Upon our fifth stop, and nearly four days into this hell, the doors were opened, and fresh air was almost painfully sucked into our lungs. Was the trial over, and hope taking its place, or is there merely more to come? Knowing we did not. Only fear, and a very slight glimmer of hope was all we were left with. Some had to be carried off and thrown into a waiting wagon, as if this was standard operating procedure. The smell of death was floating in the air.

My throat was dry, body weak from sickness, sorrow was dripping from the train like blood from a slaughterhouse, and fear for my family was unbearable. We were separated like cattle when leaving the train. The trip was long and harsh. Perhaps the people that died along the way are the lucky ones.

"Bose Nazi(Evil Nazi)," I heard one foolish young man shout out before he was shot on the spot and drug to the side to be thrown away later like trash. My wife and child, my very life, were torn from my grip, and I was knocked to the ground. Some of the men were singled out from my group. The stronger of the group were pushed along, while the weaker were left behind, unsure of their fate. I was one of them. Part of my hand was lost two years ago in an accident, and I didn't do well on the overcrowded train.

Fear was like a floating stench in the air. We were marched under armed guard to a large warehouse with black smoke billowing from a stack close by. The smoke flowed across the sorrowful land like a blast from the devil's nostrils. Like dirty snow, some of it lightly covered the ground we were walking upon, and now it was sticking to our skin and clothes. We were told we were to be given showers to disinfect our filthy Jewish bodies. We could do nothing. We were ushered into one room where we were ordered to remove everything. Our clothing, shoes, and jewelry. We were then moved to a large chamber that looked like it could be showers, but it wasn't. We were packed in like sardines and the doors closed. It wasn't long before I was gasping for breath. I was suffocating from something invisible in the air. My last thought was of my wife and child before blackness overtook me. The Jews, like a plague to the Nazis, were being exterminated.

I quickly rolled to my knees on the floor of the tent, coughing, and crying. Julia was trying her best to comfort me and convince me it was just a dream, but it wasn't an ordinary dream. I knew this instantly, and Susan would have known what I was going through, but Julia would now be my companion in the next chapter of my life. Sorrow and loss were buried deep in my chest, with seemingly nowhere to go. My wife and child were probably gone, floating on the breeze of crushing evil. "Ich bin Jude", I cried out in the fading darkness. "I am Jewish" I repeated in English. "My God, my God, please save my family from this evil!" I finally shouted before collapsing into my wife's arms.

It wasn't until after dawn when I finally came out of my nightmare fully. This one seemed to linger longer than the others, but it was just as real and painful. Julia had already run into the house and gotten a cool cloth to soothe my warm forehead. Initially she was afraid I had a fever, but the thermometer told a different story. My temperature was low, like the cooling of a dead body. However, when I came around, physically I seemed fine, temperature back to normal and I was able to smile up at my wife and assure her I was okay. "You need to go to the hospital," Julia said. Boy did that sound familiar, I thought.

I convinced her after a few minutes that what occurred wasn't something medical science could deal with. Reaching under my leg I pulled out a folded piece of dirty yellow material. I carefully unfolded the 140-year-old piece of dark memorabilia from an atrocity like few others. It was the six-pointed star the Jews were forced to wear as a badge of shame by the Nazi's under Adolf Hitler. The word Jude was printed clearly in the center of this badge. I rubbed the word softly with my fingers and begin to cry again as my wife held me tight to her bosom.

My wife held me for nearly an hour before I could completely calm down. This was different somehow. Deeper and more painful physically. The bright light of morning was now flowing into our tent, and I was able to sit up and breathe deeply, the morning air.

After kissing me softly on my lips, my Julia pulled back. "Bob", she said, while looking at me strangely.

"What?" I asked, while observing her wide eyed perusal of my appearance. Was my fly open or did I grow a new appendage?

"Honey," Julia said, while pausing to give me another once over. "Your, ah, ... gray hair is gone," she added, while running her hands over my face and down my chest. "You look younger," she said with amazement written on her face.

She seemed pleased with the look, but shocked, nevertheless. "Bob, this never happened before, has it?" She then asked.

"No Julia, this is something new." I put my hands on hers, not knowing what else to say, so I shrugged and leaned in to kiss her. Just another mystery in my life. Couldn't wait to visit with the bathroom mirror though.

During our kiss with strong love for one another, a message seemed to form within my mind.

I knew you before birth and loved you dearly.

With you I am well pleased.

Tightly held to faith, love, and devotion did you.

Even through trials and temptations you held fast.

For those that have been trusted with much.

Much more will be asked.

I pulled back from Julia and looked deeply into her eyes. Smiling, while understanding the message, I put my forehead against hers. "I hope you like roller coasters," I said to my wife, which is rather cryptic, but I had nothing else. I also still had to consider the earlier dream and discuss with my new wife. They are definitely connected, but I must figure things out. I am not in control, after all. I am your soldier to lead, but where do I go from here Lord? My wife and I sat together, watching the growing morning. “Looks as if it will be a great day,” I said, while watching the clouds go by.

Author's Note

The human condition is always one of imperfection as is the world around us. This story explores the question of how one would feel to outlive all close family and friends and continue on in a fallen world. As we all stumble through life, please hold on to what is important, keeping God, faith and love at the top of the list. If you enjoyed this read or have any questions, please feel free to contact me at djspeth79@gmail.com.

Dedication

I dedicate this book to all of my family and my Lord, with which many memories were built, and fondly held to this day. A final shout out and thank you to my wife Liz for reviewing my work.

Description

Have you ever questioned the reality of a dream? After his very first day of retirement, Robert Franklin Johnson's dreams took a dive into the supernatural, which led him to not only question reality, but his own sanity. For many, declining years some call it, retirement provides more time to relax, explore hobbies and spend time with family, but God had additional plans for Bob that no human could have envisioned. These strange dreams, paired with unexpected physical gifts, will test this man's inner strength, moral fiber and faith. It is said that you will be provided with what you need to accomplish good works through faith in God.

Author's Bio

I was born into a Christian family, and as a typical teenager I strayed from the faith until I met my wife. Through my relationship with my wife and her family, I recommitted my life to the Christian faith, even though imperfectly. I graduated from Indiana University Southeast in 1983 and worked in an exciting career as a corporate accountant until my retirement in 2018. My wife and I, still happily married, currently have two beautiful girls, four grandchildren and one great grandchild. What a great blessing. Part of my bucket list was to delve into more artistic endeavors, including writing. The trip has been enjoyable and exciting.

www.ingramcontent.com/pod-product-compliance
Lightning Source LLC
LaVergne TN
LVHW010541160826
845677LV00013B/2951

9798362770587